# A FAST WOMAN

LARALYN DORAN

For information contact Laralyn Doran at:
P. O. Box 234
Monrovia, MD 21770-0234
www.LaralynDoran.com

Book and Cover design by Deranged Doctor Designs
Edited by Holly Ingraham
Copyedits by Elaine York, Allusion Publishing

ISBN: 978-1-7353474-0-0 (eBook)
ISBN: 978-1-7353474-1-7 (Trade Paperback)
First Edition: September- 2020

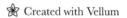 Created with Vellum

*For my family*

## CJ

Adrenaline and love—both were God-given, naturally occurring and highly addictive drugs—the temptation, the euphoric rush, the path to destruction.

Love was too toxic, and its sudden loss was devastating.

But adrenaline—ah, adrenaline was my drug of choice. It was exclusive to the junkie and, unlike love, it wasn't expected to be shared or reciprocated.

And nothing—absolutely nothing—pumped adrenaline through my body more than flying at one-hundred-ninety mph around a twenty-four-degree banked turn, strapped inside a metal cage on four wheels.

Gus's voice broke through the headset in my helmet. "Alright, CJ, darlin' how's the old girl feel this morning?"

That's me. CJ, short for Charlotte Jean—Charlotte Jean Lomax. The "Sweetheart of Stock Car" or "Token Woman Driver," depending on who was talking about me.

It's true, I'm a woman race car driver, but no one considered me much of a sweetheart.

At only five four, not many people considered me much of a threat either—until I was behind the wheel of a thirty-three-hundred-pound machine. On a racetrack, strapped into a stock car, it didn't matter if I had a cock or not, I still ran them into the ground.

"First, G, after fifteen years of friendship, you know what happens to boys who call me

darlin'. Second, you aren't my crew chief yet, and she is a bit testy today, so she doesn't need you calling her old." My enthusiastic, but teasing tone laced through the deafening growl of the engine, increasing the energy pumping through me.

The weight of the G-forces against my chest, the odor of rubber and oil that choked the air, and the vibrations tore across every nerve—it brought me down to Earth, but the familiarity kept me smiling.

This was as close to flying as I could get without leaving the ground. I was a mortal projectile launched into the stratosphere as life rushed at me like a 4D IMAX movie.

I rocked out to the deafening roar of the eight-hundred-horse-power stock car engine under my feet. The sound at odds with the serene Carolina sky as I flew around Charlotte Raceway during my practice runs.

With the custom-made seat and specialized HANS head restraint, movement was practically impossible. The fire-retardant suit and shoes were meant to withstand a burning vehicle—because that was an actual possibility.

It was part of the risk, and why only a handful of people in the world were capable of doing this job.

I was one of them.

Tommy had been another. He'd been my adrenaline partner. My love addiction. Until he was no longer around to be either.

*Focus.*

I flew through another turn.

"Hell, yeah." I forced the words out of my mouth as I smiled and pledged aloud, "G, adrenaline and a race car are all the love I need."

"So, you keep telling me, darlin'," Gus deadpanned.

"The boss man is in the box with some VIPs, probably sponsors." Wild Bill's gravelly voice permeated the noise of the engine. Bill was the chief of the car, but more importantly he'd been a mentor to me for years. "Hon, show them why you're one of Energy Blasts's top drivers. They should be begging us to put their logo on your car."

I gripped the steering wheel tighter, as if someone was going to try to pry my hands from it. "Don't jinx me, Bill. No one has tapped me to replace Trent, yet. All I was asked to do is take this car out for a practice run."

*Focus. Grit. Unapologetic determination.* That was my mantra.

A shiver ran down my back as a memory whispered, *you've got this.*

I shook off the intrusion and was grateful to latch on to Bill's voice as he said, "Formalities. Just put on a good show."

"I don't have to put on a show…" I opened up the engine, slingshotted out of the turn and, with a confidence I didn't have outside the car, I purred, "I'm always good."

# 2

*Grady*

"Who's the driver?" I strode into the press box, nodded in the direction of the track, going for casual but clenching my jaw to prevent "Who the fuck's driving my car?" from spilling out.

I passed Everett Merrick and his son, Everett "Junior" Merrick, as I headed for the wall of glass overlooking the mammoth racetrack. I didn't need to turn around to know my buddy, and acting manager, Cooper Sullivan, followed me. His shaggy, auburn hair, and hazel eyes shifted, taking in our surroundings. His lumbering gait was in cadence with mine as he saddled up next to me.

My hands were in the pockets of my custom-made, steel gray slacks, and I relaxed my shoulders as I still strived to remain unfazed. But that was the number thirty-six car—my car.

"CJ Lomax," Merrick answered.

Cooper's phone rang, distracting me. He pressed a button, sending it to voicemail.

"Excuse me?" I turned my attention back to Merrick.

The thunder of the car's engine reverberated through my chest, even inside the confines of the press box, beckoning to me.

"The driver. It's CJ Lomax." Merrick's eyes narrowed, examining me.

"Just one of our Energy Blast drivers." Junior gave the track a dismissive wave as he maneuvered himself between me and the observation glass. Junior, with his custom-made suit and perfectly styled hair, attempted to pull off a Northern-bred vibe rather than show his Southern roots.

Merrick's expression shifted to his son, falling between chastising an employee and holding the disappointment of a parent.

"She's one of our champion Energy Blast drivers." Merrick's pride was evident as he referred to the lower circuit of racing.

The car was a white blur that held a green sheen as I grew jealous of whoever was driving while I was up here with these suits.

Until Merrick added, "And the one who will be splitting the season with you."

Red flashed across my vision and my head whipped around.

*Excuse me? What?* It was one of the few times I was at a loss for words.

Merrick stared me straight in the eye. I glanced to Junior for an explanation, but he was studying the generic carpeting with extreme interest.

A unicorn could've flown out of Junior's ass and it wouldn't have surprised me more.

"Excuse me, what?" I parroted my thoughts aloud and stepped up to the two

Merricks.

Cooper's phone rang again. He fumbled with it before sending it to voicemail and stepped beside me. Cooper's eyes dodged back and forth between Merrick and Junior. "That wasn't what Junior told us. We didn't come down here for Grady to share a season with anyone."

Awkward silence descended on the press box and accentuated the presence of the car—my car—roaring down the back stretch again. The two Merricks glanced at each other with raised eyebrows as if to say, *"You want to explain this?"*

I'd heard of her, CJ Lomax, The Sweetheart of Stock Car. I'd also heard that nickname was given in mockery. Never met her. Not sure I even recalled what she looked like outside of her having dark hair and being small. Just heard she wasn't exactly a sweetheart, no matter how hard PR tried to make her out to be one.

The silence was heavy as I glared at the car again and then over to Merrick, my mood darkening by the second.

Was this a joke?

I was an Indy champion, for Christ's sake.

I shouldn't have to audition—especially against someone who hadn't raced at this level before.

It was insulting.

My mind raced faster than the car on the track.

This was drama I didn't need—I didn't want to be caught up in some inner-team conflict. I wanted a fresh start in a new industry.

I gritted my teeth and tried to control my frustration.

Cooper stepped in. "This wasn't what we talked about. I thought we were down here to discuss Grady replacing Trent?"

"We're discussing it," Merrick said, walking toward me, staring me down.

"Perhaps, we should discuss this in the boardroom I have set up," Junior said, trying to usher us toward the door.

"No, let's discuss it here," Merrick ordered, walking up to the stadium seats that were usually filled by journalists and broadcasters. He motioned for me to sit next to him.

Instead, I stepped down, putting me eye to eye with the man.

Merrick leaned back in his chair, his sports jacket fell open revealing his large silver belt buckle, his hands clasped across his lap. "I'm going to level with you, Grady, because that's just the type of guy I am. We were ready to pull CJ up from Energy Blast and put her in Trent's seat. Junior reminded me you were free and interested in crossing over."

He held up a hand. "Now, I know you have your reasons for leaving your successful career with McBane. That's your business.

You may be an open-wheel champion, but you're a stock car rookie. With the season already starting, I thought this would be the best solution. Both you and CJ would get experience and exposure."

Intense anger boiled to the surface at the mere mention of my family name, and I imagined the steam billowing out of my nose like a raging bull. I had to remind myself it wasn't Merrick's fault I was in this position and that he wasn't purposely waving a red cape.

I grew up in the shadow of my family's empire, and after a series of dumbass choices, it turned out family loyalty only extended so far. I was pushed out of the industry by my own brother—and that's on him.

Junior circled us like a fly. "With Trent leaving, the sponsors were skittish about sticking around. Neither one of you have the same marketability Trent had. However, a side competition between two drivers on the same team has never been done before and would probably drum up more exposure. With your good looks and reputation, and CJ…well, with CJ being CJ…it would draw a lot of attention, which would lead to more publicity. Sponsors pay for publicity. It's why they want their name on our car."

"There's also that…" Merrick flicked his hand in acknowledgment of his son's point. "We are both admirers of yours. Drivers have made the leap from Indy to stock car very successfully, but some have had difficulty with the change."

Cooper's phone rang again. He rolled his eyes and looked down at the display. His back straightened, eyebrows drew together, and his eyes cut to me. He was going to answer it, and that could only mean one thing. I knew who it was.

*Damnit.*

I didn't need this now. I'd been avoiding her call and she didn't like being ignored.

Still, I could wring Cooper's neck for answering it.

"Hello, Mrs. McBane…Yes, ma'am, I apologize—yes, ma'am, I know…he's, um, we're in a meeting—" Cooper walked out, likely in search of privacy so no one witnessed him having his balls handed to him over a cellphone.

I dragged my hand through my hair and rubbed both over my

face. I tried to concentrate on the two Merricks, praying to God that, for once, Cooper could handle my mom.

Cooper walked back in the room within fifteen seconds with the cell to his ear. He charged at me, the cell shifted to his outstretched hand like a bayonet.

Who was I kidding—no one handled Meredith McBane.

I gave it one more try and held up my hand in a silent *no* as Cooper invaded my space.

He put his hand over the phone, shook it at me, leaned in and whispered loud enough to convey his determination, "She's *your* mother. You know as well as I do, she'll just keep calling both of us until she reaches you, or she'll send someone down here who will physically shove the phone in your hand."

He had a point.

I dropped my shoulders and caved, not very graciously, grabbing the phone from Cooper who tried to bluster through his guilt.

As if they were center court at Wimbledon, Merrick and Junior both stood quietly watching the exchange.

I gave them a tight smile, held up the phone and said, "Excuse me a moment, I need to take this."

"Go. Don't keep your Mama waiting." Merrick motioned to the door.

I nodded and refused to meet the man's eyes as I stepped outside the press box, into the concrete halls of the stadium where the sound reverberated and even a whisper carried.

"Yes?" I attempted to suppress all annoyance and put on the hat of the dutiful child.

"Grady Patrick McBane, is that anyway to greet your mother?" said a voice that could peel off twenty years of my maturity. "Especially one who has been trying to reach you for days. I didn't raise you to treat me this way."

"Hello, Mom. I've been busy." I closed my eyes, attempting to hold onto my dignity and straightened. "Is everything ok?"

"Everything is fine—"

"Mom, I'm in a very important meeting. Can I call you back?"

"Are you meeting with those Merrick people?"

"Mom, please, can we not do this right now? I love you, but I need to get back to this meeting."

She let out a big sigh of retreat.

I held the phone away from my ear and stared at it. Meredith McBane didn't retreat. Ever.

I put the phone back at my ear.

"Fine." Defeat laced my mom's voice.

"Wait, what?" What was I missing? I surveyed the halls of the causeway as if she were going to jump out from behind a column.

"I respect what you are trying to do, but we aren't done discussing this." The weariness in my mother's voice cut at my resolve. Her voice dropped to almost a whisper, "I could strangle your father for letting this happen."

The weariness hinted at the toll our family feud was taking on my formidable mother. I was an ass to be avoiding her.

I closed my eyes and rubbed my forehead as the weight of more guilt settled on my shoulders.

Shit. Where the hell was my brother?

"Mom, as soon as things settle here, I'll fly home, okay?"

"Alright, honey. That sounds good." Her voice held a tone of hope. "Call me later. I still want to hear what the hell is going on with you." She tried to go for firm, but it fell short. She rallied and ended with a heartfelt, "I love you."

"I love you, too. I'll call later." I waited for her to hang up and gripped the phone, probably a bit too tightly before remembering it wasn't mine to break.

"I apologize." I strode back in the room, trying to save face and ignoring the fact that my mother still had the power to reduce me and Cooper to eight-year-old boys. "She's been trying to get ahold of me and there are things going on…"

Merrick shook his head, now standing at the observation windows before turning to face me. "No explanation needed." He nodded. "I respect that your family means a lot to you—which is why I question why you left Chicago?"

I ignored the leading question, and instead parried with my

own, "So, where were we? You were saying how I had to compete with CJ Lomax to race your car?"

"Yes, I know Indy drivers have made successful jumps from Indy to stock car—"

"Yes. And I was counting on being one of them. What I wasn't counting on was becoming a sideshow." I stalked farther into the room and handed Cooper his phone.

"I'm not sure I follow you." Merrick tilted his head.

"Because my father won't admit CJ isn't the right driver for the team and needs to be convinced the industry won't accept her as a full-time Cup driver." Junior struggled to shake his Carolina accent, but it snuck in when he was agitated.

Merrick glared at his son. "There are a few reasons for doing it this way, Grady. CJ is a talented driver who can bring home wins. Her best tracks are ones an Indy driver would find more challenging. Having you handle the road courses, while she handles the more aggressive short and restrictor plate tracks, will let you get your feet wet and we can see how she handles this level of competition."

It was my turn to shoot a glare at Junior. But I addressed both Merricks, disliking this situation more by the minute. "If she is so capable, why not just give it to her?"

Merrick walked the length of the windows. "Full disclosure. CJ is like family to me—"

"She's not family." Junior jumped in, a hint of juvenile anger and resentment lacing the statement.

Merrick's lips pursed, and pity swept over his face.

Junior glanced away as though he was ashamed at his outburst.

Merrick straightened, tilted his head and changed positions. "As you can imagine, being a woman isn't easy around here…but CJ has other hurdles, let's say." He glanced at his son. "That being said, being close to me hasn't done her any favors. People think I've given her too many opportunities because of who she is."

"Because she's a girl." Junior's eyes narrowed ever so slightly as his tone dipped just enough to hint at bitterness.

"Because she's like family." Merrick's voice was firm, indicating he caught the tone.

I threw my hands out. "So, I'm here to help you prove CJ is deserving? I'm not going to waste my season propping up another driver's reputation. I have my own to worry about."

"No! No, that isn't what this about." Junior rushed to my side as if he were going to grab my hand.

"From what I've heard so far, the only reason you aren't giving CJ the number thirty-six is that she's a *woman*—which is so absurd I'm not even going to acknowledge it—and she's too close to some of your family. So why am I here?"

"Because this is a business, Grady," Junior said, straightened and gave a nod of his head. "And when it comes down to it, I think you're a better business decision than CJ."

"What about you, Mr. Merrick?" I crossed my arms over my chest and turned to the older Merrick. "Are you willing to break ties with CJ when I prove to be the better driver?"

He stood legs spread, battle ready and his arms on his hips, studying me. "The competition will benefit CJ, as well. Trust me, son, she won't be easy. But yes, you both will come into the competition with a blank slate. I want the competition. I think it would be good for you, good for CJ and good for the Merrick team. Honestly, you could both learn something from each other."

I began to pace up and down the row of windows, with the race car taunting me from the track. "I just don't want to be the outsider who is branded the bad guy when I outperform her," I interjected. "I plan on making this my home, and I don't want to start off on the wrong foot."

Merrick's eyes shot up to his hair line. "Well, son, your arrogance precedes you. This will be your first season, and we're putting you straight into a Cup car, so you're a risk, too. You're talented, by any standard, but it was your name and the publicity from the break-up with your family that got you straight into that seat."

Ouch.

It was to the point and probably the last thing my pride needed to hear. My family was what got me into this position and now I was going to be a dog and pony show.

*Fan-fucking-tastic.*

Merrick pointed at the track. "Your name and CJ's name separately aren't enticing enough on their own to keep sponsors around." He turned and waved a hand at me and at the track. "But together…well, that may be the formula we need. So, it's a battle of the sexes—a modern day War of the Roses. You both get a world stage to show the industry what you're made of."

I stared into the older man's eyes. Logically, what Merrick said made sense. When it came down to it, racing was a tight-knit industry and I didn't have many options. I had to make this work, or join a European open-wheel circuit. Turning down this opportunity, alienating or insulting Merrick, was probably akin to burning another bridge.

"What do you say, Grady?" Merrick stood with his hands clasped behind his back waiting with confidence.

I joined Merrick at the wall of glass, as the car thundered by again. The sound teased through to my very soul.

My next target.

"Mr. Merrick, just so we get something straight. It won't matter if she's a man or a woman. If CJ is all that's between me and that car," I pointed at the blur circling the track, "I will show no mercy. There can only be one winner—and I don't intend to lose." I couldn't afford to lose.

Merrick's eyes connected with mine as he held out his hand. "Understood." One side of his mouth quirked as he added, "Don't expect her to show you any mercy either."

"Fine." I nodded, offering my hand. "I'm in."

"Good." Merrick stepped away, walking toward the door. His hands clapping together was the throwing down of a gauntlet. "Junior will set up a time for you to meet the team at the office tomorrow and work out the details. Good to have you aboard, Grady," he said, as he left.

Cooper stepped over and stood beside me. "It's just a minor bump. It won't be a problem. At least we're out of Chicago for now, right?"

"I need a drink," I muttered, more to myself than to Cooper, watching the car continue to taunt me as it raced around the track.

Junior flanked my other side. "Grady, with your looks and charm, sponsorship won't be a problem. I'm sure you will win over the fan base. You won't be the bad guy." His tone hinted to a secret that hadn't been revealed.

"Why do you say that?" I said.

"Once you meet CJ, you'll understand…"

# 3

## CJ

"Just wait until it's *my* birthday." I glared at my best friend, Harper Merrick, while I simultaneously tried to conjure more material out of the slip of a cocktail dress she'd shoved on me. I swear it shrank since I started walking down the street, and I worried I was flashing the couple behind us.

"Why would you want to spend tonight with a bunch of suits, instead of going out to celebrate your birthday? Hell, I'd be willing to do a wine bar or something—why are you doing this to me?" I tugged on the hem and double-checked none of my assets had popped out of the top.

Harper strode down Charlotte's city streets in take-charge stilettos, typing something on her phone, dodging pedestrian traffic, and ignoring my fidgeting. "We have a quick meet and greet. I know an agent who is in town with an executive with Prince Automotive, and they want to meet for a drink. I'll do the talking."

"Fine." I was resigned to my fate and focused on keeping pace with her lengthy strides. "It's your birthday."

"Stop squirming." Well, she wasn't ignoring me completely, I guess.

Harper and I had been best friends since our mothers put us on a blanket together as toddlers and I ran over her baby-doll with her brother's Tonka truck.

"Payback, Harper…I have a few months to plot my revenge."

"All I did was curl your hair, throw on some makeup and…" she slowed her stride to take an appraising gaze over me—pride in her latest project. "I'm sorry but seeing you in that dress and shoes will be worth any retribution."

She refocused on the street ahead of us. "You act like I'm asking you to walk through Dante's nine rings of hell."

I concentrated on the pavement in front of me, making sure I didn't get a closer view of it by tripping in my four-inch platform Louboutin heels—they were also her idea and should come with a liability option. "I'm only at the seventh level. Eight and nine would occur if my crew caught me in this get-up."

"Your crew wouldn't recognize you," she said.

I didn't have time to react before the flash of her phone went off and she was able to capture the moment for posterity—or blackmail.

Harper typed something on her phone as her long, memorable legs strode down the sidewalk. Hinting at the drop-dead smile she easily employed, she said, "You get so caught up in being a woman in a man's world, that I think you forget that you *are* a woman."

She was also the closest thing I had to a sister, and the most beautiful woman I knew. But what made Harper unique was while she knew how to capitalize on her looks, she didn't define herself by them.

Harper and I each had our own individual strengths. This— men, makeup, marketing—this was her arena. Anything to do with machines, metal and motor oil—that was mine.

Dressing me in a short skirt, four-inch heels and telling me to be charming, was like putting Harper in a fire-retardant suit, strapping her in a car going one-hundred-ninety mph with forty-two other drivers and telling her not to wreck.

"If I believed you wanted to be an obscure driver, I'd leave you alone. But I don't. I think since Tommy died, you've hidden behind the wheel of a race car because it was simple, and, for you, it was safe. It's time to come out and show the world you have boobs and curves, and embrace the fact that you are, in fact, a woman."

Harper stopped, opened her purse to put her phone away. "Besides, if you're serious about wanting to be a Cup driver, a full-time Cup driver, you have to get serious about your image."

I closed my eyes and groaned, "Please, don't start with that again." Harper had on her game face and her public-relations-professional-marketing-guru hat.

"You have to use your assets. You're beautiful. I'm sorry, I know you hate hearing this, but it's true. Part of this industry is sponsorship and marketing. Sponsors are the businesses that pay your salary. They're the bread and butter of racing. They pay for the parts, the tires, the best mechanics, everything this industry needs to survive. If you don't have sponsors, you don't race." She straightened and began walking again, signaling for me to follow.

"You're starting to sound more like your father," I grumbled. Her father was my boss, the man holding my future in his hand, Everett Merrick. It was complicated at times, but we made it work.

She ignored me. We rounded the corner and reached our destination, a swanky, upscale bar and restaurant. "Do you honestly think if Gus was a driver, I wouldn't be putting him in board shorts and lathering him with oil on a beach, or in an expensive three-piece suit with a leggy blonde draped over him to sell watches? I would in a heartbeat, and he'd have sponsors throwing money at the team."

Gus's nickname was GQ, because even hungover he looked like he walked off the cover of the magazine. "Hell, I still may do that." She stared off; her eyes gleamed with a thought that didn't bode well for Gus's modesty.

I straightened to protest. "Harper—"

"Alright, fine. One project at a time." Indicating I was the project, she reached for the door and gestured me inside. "Be good."

I played nice.

I smiled, and nodded, and did everything Harper asked of me for sixty-two excruciating minutes.

I dealt with stroking their egos and the name dropping.

I met Chase Dermott, an executive from Prince Automotive, and Jordan Darcy, Harper's friend who introduced us. Both were what I expected business executives at a swanky bar to look like. Prettier and better groomed than I would be—ever.

Dermott's hair was jet black and perfectly combed back with enough product to keep it in place but not look slick. Darcy was slightly taller, with indistinguishable brown, but perfectly tousled, hair and a handsome-enough face. I didn't know much about suits, but they were well-fitted, and they wore them confidently.

Occasionally, Harper glanced at me out of the corner of her eye, as she did an excellent job directing the conversation, feminine yet with an air of authority. She knew I was plotting her death. If there was one thing I didn't tolerate, it was sitting still and being quiet.

Chase Dermott crowded my space, draping a hand over my chair and behind my back.

"CJ, may I call you Charlotte? CJ is such a masculine name for such a beautiful woman."

I opened my mouth to answer, but he didn't bother waiting for my permission. "Charlotte, I have a real good feeling about you. Of course, I need time to consider

things." His other hand moved to just above my knee under the table and he leaned in closer. "But I'd like to continue to talk about the possibility of Prince Automotive being involved in your ascent into the Cup series."

His hand burned like toxic slime up my bare leg.

And I was done.

I'd now put in sixty-four excruciating minutes. I deserved a medal.

"If you don't want to call me CJ, Ms. Lomax would be sufficient." I lasered my eyes at Harper as I firmly grabbed his wrist and lifted his hand high enough so she could see I was removing it from my leg. "Mr. Dermott, if you need more time to consider sponsoring me, that's fine. I can promise backing me would be a sound investment." I made eye contact with him as I stood. "I also promise you won't find anything to sway your decision on my legs or between them."

Dermott's brows furrowed, and his mouth grimaced as his expression flashed from bemused to annoyed.

Harper took my cue and began to stand, but Jordan continued their conversation.

Dermott stood as if to approach and pursue, his gaze still on me.

"Excuse me, it was nice meeting you gentleman. Harper, I'm going to the restroom. I'll meet you outside."

I wanted to pull a Cinderella and escape out the back door, except I didn't want this "Prince" executive to follow.

I darted through low-slung leather chairs, intimately surrounding small tables, that peppered the lounge area and lengthened my strides after I spotted my refuge—the ladies' room. I was cruising to my destination, when my traitorous feet decided they were done with the four-inch stilts I'd forced them into and chose that moment to rebel.

I was about to kiss the floor with my knees and flash the rest of the bar with my assets, when an arm slung around my waist, saving me.

"I got you." A set of arms cocooned me, pulling me back against a firm chest. Long sleeves were rolled up firm, tanned forearms and I grasped onto them like a lap bar on a rollercoaster.

It definitely was not toxic slime touching me.

While trying to get my feet back under me, I peered over my shoulder.

Damn. Four-inch heels weren't easy to stabilize when your world has been rocked.

Disheveled sandy blond hair in need of a trim, framed gray-blue eyes that locked onto mine. His five o'clock shadow was accentuated by the lighting in the most delicious way, tempting me to rub my hands over it.

He shifted me, his hands remaining on my waist, and I gripped dangerous biceps longer than necessary while I tried to lock-in my traitorous knees.

"Where's the fire?" His half smile gave a teasing quality to the cliché, as his eyes roamed over my face and settled on my lips. "Are you okay?"

"Yes." I ran my hands down my dress, discreetly checking for any wardrobe malfunction that would stretch embarrassment into humiliation. "Sorry…thank you."

I stepped away and straightened.

He slipped his hands in his pockets, shoulders relaxed. The quirk of his smile gave him an air of congeniality. But the focus of his eyes, the slight tilt of his head, reminded me not to turn my back on a wolf.

---

The door slammed open and I ran into one of the stalls, not even noticing if anyone else was in the restroom.

*Breathe.*

*Come on, CJ.*

*What the hell?*

I practically faceplanted in front of that man, all because I was walking in a pair of shoes

I had no business walking in. Because I wasn't the person I was pretending to be. This wasn't me. I squeezed my eyes shut harder, trying to will the image of me falling into his arms out of my head.

I washed up, touched up my lipstick, putting it back in the damn sparkly purse, straightened my posture, and put one foot in front of the other until I marched myself out of the restroom.

"What the hell are you doing here, asshole? You can't seriously think you could make the jump to stock car…" Dermott's voice dripped with derision.

I stepped back against the wall separating the restrooms from the rest of the establishment, peering around the wall imitating a secret agent not wanting another run-in with Mr. Toxic-slime-hands.

The man who saved me from falling was slumped in the low-back leather chair, legs splayed, with a lowball glass dangling from his hand. His white dress shirt pulled out, opened at the neck and a soft light spotlighting him in the dark bar caused him to resemble an unpretentious king on his throne—a god in men's clothing.

A mocking smile spread slowly across his mouth as if he just registered who was in front of him. "Well, if it isn't my dear friend Dermott." God-man stared up at Dermott and kept the mocking smile as he brought the low-ball glass to his lips and took a sip of his drink.

"McBane. You got kicked out of Indy and chased out of Chicago and you had to run down here with your tail between your legs and your hat in your hand, huh?" Dermott's face was turning red, his shoulders drawn up. He clearly didn't like the man who saved me earlier.

God-man—McBane's amiable demeanor was unrattled. "Tell me, how's Sasha doing these days? Did you manage to get her off her knees long enough to get her down the aisle?"

Dermott lunged, "You fucking sonofabitch!" McBane shot up as if summoning a thunder bolt, but still smiling at his barb and ready to take on Dermott.

A man with auburn hair appeared at McBane's side and stepped in, easily fending off Dermott until Jordan came up behind Dermott and pulled him back. Dermott pointed a finger, "You won't make it here either, fucker. I'll see to it." Jordan turned Dermott around whispering to him and ushering him out of the front of the establishment.

"Jesus, man. Did you have to go there..." his auburn-haired companion turned and

scolded. "Was rubbing Sasha in Dermott's face really worth ruining your chance of landing a deal with Merrick? That weasel would do anything to see you fail on a spectacular level. Taunting him before you've locked down that ride was a dumbass thing to do."

Wait. What?

Why was God-man talking about Merrick?

The auburn-haired man gestured to him, frustrated. "You need to stay away from him until we have things settled with Merrick. Let's just hope you didn't just screw your chance with that stunt."

"There are plenty of other sponsors out there, Cooper. Dermott isn't the only one. He can go kiss my ass." McBane finished off his drink, put the glass on the low table and sat back down on his throne.

"Yes, but damnit, Grady, there aren't plenty of cars, and you're a driver without one at the moment."

He's a driver. Talking to Merrick. Grady? Grady McBane. Indy driver. Merrick had another team, but as far as I knew, they had no plans on replacing their driver.

*Son of a bi*— What the hell was going on?

"I'm going to go close out the tab. We need to get out of here. You have an early meeting tomorrow at Merrick's office with the new team and that Lomax woman. You need to be sharp." Auburn-hair—Cooper—moved away, leaving Grady running his hands through his hair.

My blood ran cold. He was a driver. He was meeting with Merrick. He was going to replace someone. He was going to replace…

Me. Because that was supposed to be my car.

I needed to find Harper. Now.

I glanced at Grady. He sat forward, his elbow on his knee, his other hand cupped the back of his neck.

I needed to get out of here. I shot out of my foxhole and made it about five strides when a hand gently caught my elbow.

I stumbled and he had to grab my other arm to help me. Again. "Hey there…I never caught your name…"

I stiffened and turned to meet his eyes. "That's because I never gave it to you."

"Well, why don't you give it to me now?" He held out his hand. "I'm Grady. Grady McBane. And you are?"

*Oh, I know who the hell you are...*

"Thank you for saving me from the face-plant, Mr. McBane," I said, stepping back. "I'm afraid I've had enough of these shoes." I distractedly searched for Harper.

His lips held back a smile as he glanced down, letting his gaze roam over my legs. "I will say they look amazing on you...except for the train you seem to be dragging behind you..."

My head flew down to my feet.

*No.*

About six squares of toilet paper were caught on the back of my engine red Louboutin heels like a little bride walking down an aisle.

Marrying me off to permanent humiliation.

I couldn't. I just couldn't.

I kicked off the offending shoe and pulled off the toilet paper, throwing it back at the bathroom as if it would be sucked into a vortex.

In my haste to rid myself of the paper trail, I grasped onto God-man—Grady's—bicep for balance. After replacing my shoe, I straightened, muttering a number of unsavory phrases I learned growing up inside garages full of men.

A low chuckle built up from Grady.

It wasn't possible to become anymore embarrassed. I was as furious with the universe, and Grady was the universe's proxy.

My hip was cocked out, I glared from underneath my heavily mascaraed eyelashes, and I'll admit to a little head bobbing. "Am I funny to you?"

He placed his hand over this mouth, but it couldn't hide the laughter in his eyes. His gorgeous, damnable eyes.

He was laughing at me.

Laughing. At me.

My fists started to clench, and I was tempted to take him down the way Tommy and Gus taught me to take down a man twice my size.

"You're seriously laughing at me. You *are* an asshole," I said. "I should've known."

He gently grabbed my elbow again. "No, no. Darling. I'm not laughing at you. Really."

I swear his eyes glittered and I was questioning whether it was charming or condescending.

Wait. Who the hell cares?

I stared at his hand on my elbow and then landed a glare that had been known to stop lesser men.

"Okay, maybe a little." He pinched his finger and thumb together. "But I've never seen a woman so indignant with a piece of toilet paper before." He softened his tone, "And still manage to look so beautiful."

I'll admit...I may have melted... a bit.

*Wait. He called me beautiful.*

*Not the point.*

I reinforced my defenses. *He's a driver. He's out for your ride.*

"Thanks for the save, again. Nice to meet you," I said, determined to get out of this hell. I added on as an afterthought as I walked away, "Still an asshole."

"Wait, come on...I haven't even met you, yet." He stepped in front of me to cut off my path.

Cooper came back over, wedging himself between Grady and me. "Grady, man. We got to go."

"Not until I get her name," Grady said, not taking his amused smile off me. "In case you need my white-knight-services again..."

"Only my friends, who aren't assholes, get my name." I began walking backwards to an approaching Harper.

"I can be your friend." His eyes drew me in, and his smile was more teasing than arrogant.

"I have enough friends." I turned, determined to get the hell out of there. I didn't want to deal with this right now.

He raised his voice, "So that's it? I think it will break my heart if you leave without telling me your name. What if I never see you again?"

Harper's pace slowed as she recognized Grady and her eyes

widened as she took in my expression. I held up my hand to silence her before turning one last time to Grady McBane, gifting him with what I hoped wasn't the smile of a serial killer. "Don't worry. We'll see each other real soon."

I grabbed Harper and pushed her through the maze of chairs and people. As we walked out the front door and onto the street, she tried to get me to stop, but my blood was pumping and there was no way I was able to stand still. There was a seismic shift in my perfectly laid out road and I never saw him coming.

"Was that Grady McBane? What's he doing in town?"

With his teasing presence gone and the connection between us cut, the realization settled in and fury stampeded through me. "He's here for my job."

# 4

*CJ*

"Let me handle this," Harper said, coming off the elevator at Merrick Motorsports's office building the next morning. We were scheduled to meet with the full staff within the hour, but after the bomb that was Grady McBane landed on us last night, Harper called her father immediately to find out what the hell was going on.

I called my agent, who was clueless. I think he was clueless all around and I told him to be clueless with someone else. Time to get a new agent.

Harper's confident stride past the receptionist and the fury on her face inspired me to act.

I grabbed her hand.

That's what I wanted. Fury and confidence.

Someone who would fight hard for me as if it were their own career at stake. Someone I could trust with my dream.

"CJ, it'll be fine. I'll get to the bottom of it. We'll talk to my father, then I'll make some calls about finding you a new agent. Jordan was ready to sign you—"

"No. I don't want Jordan."

"Come on. I know he was a bit of a slime-ball, but he's a shark."

"No. You. You're a shark. A shark and a tiger all wrapped up in crystalized sugar they never see coming. You're what I need. I want you to be my agent, my manager, whatever…Harper."

I could've told her trucker hats were the hot new spring accessory at New York Fashion Week and she wouldn't have looked more dumbstruck.

Her mouth moved but failed to make noise.

"Come on." I dragged her down the hall. "We don't have much time before the team meeting, and you've a lot of work to do, agent Harper Merrick."

She pulled up short. "CJ…you're serious."

"Dead."

"I don't think…that is…I think now more than ever you need a professional…"

I crossed my arms and glared at her. Not in anger toward her, but at the situation and to get it across to her what we were up against.

"If Grady is being brought in, it's because of the lack of backbone the company has about putting me in the full-time car. You know it, I know it."

She tipped her head down and ran her hand through her perfect, wavy hair, deep in thought.

"We don't have time to find an agent who's going to represent me properly in what will probably be a battle-laced with old-school, chauvinistic views."

"My father isn't a chauvinist."

I had to tread lightly here. I didn't think Merrick was either. If he were, he'd never have funded my career thus far. It was why none of this made sense. Why pay for my cars, for my gear, for my education, and my career, and then cut me off at the knees just as I was reaching my goal?

I nodded my head in agreement. "I know. That's why none of this makes sense. My point is, I need another woman at my back. You're the fiercest, cleverest businesswoman I know—"

"I don't have the experience...I'm not an agent. My expertise is in marketing—"

"You have grown up in this industry. You have the contacts, the knowledge and the instincts. You have the guts, and you believe in me. That's what I need now. I need someone who believes in me to have my back." It was the closest I came to begging. "Listen, I don't have an entourage or anyone, really. I have you. You're all I have."

She grabbed my hand and I squeezed it. I didn't do public displays of affection—even with her. She knew that, which was another reason she got me and squeezed back.

With the confidence, and contained aggressiveness of a female panther, she led me to the back offices, saying over her shoulder, "Let's go find out what the hell has gotten into my father. I'll be all you need."

---

Everett Merrick's office was a throwback and contradiction to the rest of the modern, glass-adorned corporate offices. It had dark wood paneling with a dark wood desk in front of a dark wood bookcase lined with trophies and other accolades. He wasn't arrogant and he wasn't an insecure man—he was straightforward. His life was built on racing. His family was rooted in it and made their fortune off it. So, having the mementos as his backdrop on the wall was as natural as decorating his office with family photos.

He stood from his chair behind the desk, with resignation aging his demeanor, and walked around it to greet us. His eyes landed on me, and the kindness and warmth he always gave me was still there. As he gave his daughter a kiss on the cheek, he shook my hand. This was always our unspoken custom. When I walked into his home as Harper's friend, I got a kiss on the cheek, but at the office, it was a handshake.

Harper had already given him an earful last night. While he refused to divulge his plan over the phone, he called us to his office this morning.

"Would you like some coffee or tea?" Merrick said.

"No, Daddy, we're fine."

"No, thank you, sir."

"Sorry, I was running a bit behind," Harper's brother, Junior, said, walking in the door and closing it behind him.

"No one said we were waiting for you," Harper conveyed my own thoughts. "Actually, no one said you were even invited to this meeting."

Merrick leaned against the front of his desk crossing his arms and legs. "Junior is here because what I have to say concerns him as well, and I want all three of you to hear the same thing."

Harper pursed her lips in frustration, refusing to look at her brother.

"Mr. Merrick, why is Grady McBane in town? Is he taking over the number thirty-six?" I came straight to the point.

"Well, yes and no," he said.

Harper jumped out of her seat, mouth open, words ready to fly.

Without breaking eye contact with me, Merrick threw up his hand to stop his daughter's tirade.

"Grady has been asked to drive for half the races this season. CJ, I'm offering you the other half—"

My heart dropped. I didn't hear anything positive in that response. If anything, I heard pity. He didn't feel confident enough to give me the season, but he felt guilty about taking it completely.

It was worse than being dismissed.

"What the hell?" Harper released the banshee. She turned on her brother. "This was your idea, wasn't it?"

I tuned out whatever went back and forth between the siblings. It was just noise. My stare settled on Merrick's boots because that is about how low I felt. At the bottom of the man's custom-made cowboy boots.

His silence was heavy, and without looking up, I knew he was waiting for my reaction.

I stood.

Harper stopped arguing with Junior.

"Mr. Merrick. I appreciate all you have done for me and my career. Besides your investment, I cannot tell you how much your tutelage and mentoring has meant to me, but I don't need or want your charity. If you don't believe I have what it takes to be a full-time driver, I request you release me so I can become a free agent and find another team willing to take me on full time."

I didn't need to shift my focus to Junior to know he was satisfied with the result of his machination. I also didn't doubt this was his doing. Merrick was a good, intelligent, and supportive man. But he was a father, willing to indulge his children to a fault and wanting Junior to be a better man than he was. Junior's inability to cut it as a driver or in the garage only left the offices for him to leave his mark —Merrick silently still hoped for a protégé to emerge.

"Harper, Junior, give us a minute," Merrick said softly.

"Daddy, I'm representing CJ now, so I must be present—"

"Father, as your Vice President—"

"Out," he said, his fatherly tone leaving no room for debate.

Harper grabbed her purse and squeezed my shoulder before leaving the room with her brother. Their arguing resumed the moment the door clicked shut.

Merrick's eyes closed, begging the universe for the patience any parent of feuding children well knows.

Merrick came over, gesturing for me to sit as he took the seat next to mine.

"CJ," he said. "I was ready to hand the seat to you. The moment Trent mentioned the possibility of retiring, I began thinking about your transition. Of course, I'm aware of Junior's angle in trying to sabotage your advancement. I'm not an idiot, and I'm not blind to his jealousy. I keep hoping he'll grow out of it." He gestured to the door and shook his head with weariness. "But it got me thinking."

I gripped the sides of the chair waiting for the explanation. I waited to hear him say he didn't think I was ready, that I wasn't good enough to drive his car, or to represent his team.

He placed his hands on his knees and gave a resigned sighed before speaking. "We don't often talk about the obstacles you face around here and what barriers women face, in general. I hear the comments, I try to dispel the lack of respect, and many times I think your record and your aptitude speak for themselves. However, there are a lot of idiots out there." He stood and waved his hand to dismiss the entire world.

"And the fact of the matter is, I can't force respect, it must be earned." He stepped toward me. "In your case, you must demand it."

"Then give me a chance to demand it. Put me in the car. I can do it." I hated the pleading that was in my voice. With him standing above me, I was like a child begging for a toy.

God, that pissed me off.

He suddenly leaned forward and closed the distance between us, shaking his clenched fist at me, the tone and volume of his voice emphasizing his sincerity. "You need to grab them by the balls and demand it, CJ."

He pointed at the door. "On a national stage, driving against one of the most respected Indy racers in the country, show the naysayers what you can do in a car. Show them that you don't need male anatomy to out-race the damn lot of them."

I stood abruptly and pushed past him. "I can do that without this stupid competition," I grumbled and left it at that. I respected this man too much to spill the other words that were zinging through my brain. They weren't meant for polite society, let alone a business discussion.

I crossed my arms across my chest so hard, all the muscles in my body were flooded with tension.

"Everyone knows you're a favorite of mine. They know of your relationship with my family. I wouldn't do you any favors by giving you the job straight out."

He turned and walked toward his desk.

"I can't make it appear to be easy. I know it's not fair, and before you say it, you're right. If you were a man, I wouldn't be doing this."

He began shifting papers around his desk as if he were tying up this conversation and moving on to other things on his agenda.

"This will also give you more exposure and will make you into a household name. This competition will be more publicized than if you just replaced Trent—increase marketing, increase in sponsorship. That helps you on the business side and makes you more money."

He put his focus on me to get his point across. "Don't think about leaving or trying to find another team." He paused, took in a deep breath, and his lips thinned with determination.

"You're like a daughter to me, and I won't let you out of your contract. I'm sorry if you think that is unfair. You wouldn't get as close to a full-time Cup car anywhere else as you would with me.

"The animosity Dewey has toward you about his brother's death makes the Duprees an issue. While I'm sure they know how much you loved Tommy, his death still haunts them." Dewey is their only living child, and he gets what he wants. While everyone sympathizes with you, no one will cross them. Except me. I'm your best chance at a top-notch team.

The dull ache, that over the past few years had replaced the stabbing pain at the mere mention of Tommy's name, was joined by anger as I was reminded how much his brother blamed me for him not being here.

"Furthermore, you will be overlooked by the commentators, by the fans, and ultimately by the sponsors. I'm doing what I'm doing for you, Charlotte Jean."

That stung. And he called me by my given name. He never did that.

He braced his hands on his desk. "Don't let your pride tell you otherwise. It's the truth. I've always been straight with you. You've always known this wasn't going to be easy. But I've also done what's best for you and your career. I'm doing it now, too."

I couldn't bring myself to look at him. My eyes burned. Too many emotions, and I refused to let them overwhelm me in the office of a man who was a pseudo-father to me. Was this the tough love of a pseudo-father, or a man I trusted with my career who was stringing me along?

"I'm pitting you up against a handsome, charismatic, womanizing Indy driver. Kick his ass and see what happens." He gestured for me to come to my own conclusion. "You won't just garner more respect; you will become a highly marketable personality *and* you will legitimize women in the industry."

I couldn't answer him and be polite. I needed to get out of here and clear my head before the team meeting we had scheduled later. I couldn't meet the guys so visibly shaken. I had to get out of here. I turned to leave. "I don't want to be the head of some movement, Mr. Merrick. I just want to race."

How dare he cast me into a position I didn't ask for.

His departing words surprised me. "You already are."

# 5

**Grady**

My mood was about as bleak as the Carolina spring morning. It was gray and threatening to storm; so was my temper.

I may have overdone the scotch last night. I probably didn't need the other one I had when we got back to the room, but seeing Dermott was like the cherry on top of a shit-tastic day.

We woke up late, left the hotel with a failed promise of finding a Starbucks, and now we were on our way—uncaffeinated—to the dreaded meeting that was sure to bring even more shit-tastic news.

Cooper drove as I leaned against the passenger side window trying to find comfort in the coolness for my pounding headache. I closed my eyes to empty my mind, find some serenity, and focus on what I wanted to get across today—I was their man.

I was the driver they wanted.

An incredibly loud rumbling started to shake the window my head was leaning against before I even registered the noise pollution it caused my ears. The vibration didn't do any favors for the headache that was creeping into migraine territory.

I peeked out, wishing my eyes contained lasers I could shoot out at the monstrosity roaring next to us.

A steel gray Ducati pulled alongside us. The driver was draped over the machine as if they were an extension of the bike. The unequivocal female form wore a fitted, black leather riding jacket, faded jeans, and a matte-black, shielded helmet. The curvaceous driver knew how to handle the beast of a machine as it came to a purr next to us.

A smile of appreciation crossed my face before I could even register it, which undoubtedly morphed into a goofy grin as I gave a juvenile wave.

The driver revved the engine—loudly—and it didn't help the situation with my head. My hand covered my eyes, instead of my ears, as if that would stave off the pain.

The Ducati howled as it pulled away when the light changed, leaving us in the dust.

Cooper gave a low whistle before following.

"Nice...bike..." Cooper said. Yeah, he wasn't admiring just the bike, either.

It was official, my head was going to explode.

We pulled into a parking lot with a large sign presenting the Merrick Motorsports campus. There were two modern, glass-adorned buildings—one was their visitor center, complete with gift shop, and the other held the garages and offices. A large parking lot off to the side was filled with cars. Fans from all over the country traveled to visit the garages, watch the guys work on the cars from the observation windows, tour the museum, shop the merchandise, or hoped to run into a driver. It was like football's open training camp six days a week most of the year.

I reached in the glove box for some more ibuprofen as Cooper pulled around back to where the owner and other drivers parked. Right next to a familiar steel gray Ducati.

I threw back two pills and finished off my water as we climbed out. Somehow I managed not to scowl when we entered the bright white fluorescent office hallways and approached the receptionist's desk. After Cooper gave our names, she began to show us to the conference room. I excused myself and ducked into the rest room.

Before leaving to find the group, I splashed water over my face and stared in the mirror, giving myself the cheesy bathroom mirror pep talk.

"You got this…get your shit together…"

I needed to convince Merrick that this competition was a bad idea.

I also needed for my head not to explode.

I stepped out and walked into a woman with two hands full of hot coffee. Even with lids, it managed to spill on her hands.

"Sonofa—" She wore a navy V-neck t-shirt, with "Merrick Motorsports" emblazoned over her chest. She had on very little make-up, and her hair was pulled back in a ponytail. But I immediately recognized the sexy-sassy-stilettos-with-no-name beauty from last night.

If I had any doubt that it was her, the expression on her face confirmed she remembered me—and I don't think it was with fondness. Why? What did I do?

"Goddamnit," she growled at me.

The coffee. I knocked it all over her, for starters.

"Oh, shit! I'm sorry…here, can I help?" I said, grabbing tissues off a nearby desk. Her

glare froze me in place before I could approach her with the tissues.

"No—I—it's fine. I got it," she said. She didn't look at me as she put the coffee on a

nearby desk and grabbed some of the tissues to wipe her hands.

"I met you last night." *Great intro, bro.* "I guess this is what you meant by seeing me soon. Did you know I was coming in today? Why didn't you just say you worked for Merrick?"

She continued to ignore me, but mumbled, "Trust me, this was all a surprise to me, too."

"Oh. Well, would you mind showing me to the conference room? I'm supposed to meet with Merrick and his team to discuss coming to work here, actually." Her back straightened more and I quickly added, "I really am sorry about the coffee. Could I carry them for you?"

"No. I said, I got it."

"If you're busy with something else, I can ask the receptionist?" I tried to capture her attention and soften my words.

Still not even glancing at me, her tone belied the verbal eyeroll I was getting. "Of course, I'll show you. I'm sure I can spare the time." She threw the tissues in the trash can with the same vehemence as the offending toilet paper from the night before, and the memory brought a smile to my face. I was smart enough not to bring it up, though. She picked up the coffees and walked by.

I should have paid attention to the hallway and the office space. I could have made eye contact with some of the staff, maybe given a "Hi, how are you?" and been my charming self. Instead, my focus was on the sway of her hips and how her jeans hugged her curves.

I was a dog.

But her indifference, even disdain, toward me had me even more intrigued. I liked her fire—even if it was directed at me. Without her sky-high heels, she maybe came up to my chin, just high enough for me to catch the scent of her hair—a hint of citrus that brought flashbacks to how she felt when she fell against me last night. Everything about her was scaled down in size—her hands, her feet, her waist, even the width of her shoulders—and it called to me in a strange, primal way, as if she needed to be protected.

She sliced a glance at me as we turned a corner leading to a large conference room, and that's where her fire showed. It was the strength of her backbone, the determination in her stride and indifference in her acknowledgement of me.

With her free hand, she mockingly gestured for me to enter. "Here you go."

"Thanks," I said, attempting a charming smile.

"Welcome to Merrick," she said, her tone indicating the charm was lost on her. She turned, walked in the room and over to a Sam Elliot look-alike, handing him one of the coffees.

I'd been dismissed.

The Sam Elliot look-alike listened as she murmured something to him in confidence, then glared at me. His salt-and-pepper mustache covered a hint of a half-smile. Dark eyebrows framed his eyes as he glanced over, quirking one up at me.

I approached him with a friendly smile and an outstretched hand, "Grady McBane."

He slowly met my hand and shook it, "Bill Gibbons, chief of the car."

"Nice to meet you, I suspect we will be getting to know each other soon."

Stepping back, I turned my attention to my beautiful, helpful guide, who clearly had not forgiven me for the spilled coffee. She was adorable, but my head was throbbing. I pressed my finger and thumb over the bridge of my nose and into my eyes, begging for relief before dropping my hand. Her arm brushed mine as she began to walk away, and I touched her hand to get her attention. "Hey, hon, could you get me some of that coffee? I've got a horrible headache and some caffeine would be great."

Silence fell and the air stilled as I slowly made my way to the other side of the conference room where Merrick had been talking with others. I stopped and surveyed the room. Everyone was studying me and watching the door with varying degrees of confusion.

I glanced back at Bill who stared me down with an expression I would have to know him better to discern. Surprise, exasperation, amusement, I have no idea. But it didn't give me the warm feelies.

Cooper called me over to the back of the conference room where he stood with Merrick and his son, Junior, who was grinning as if I just bought him a pony for Christmas.

I walked forward, focused on Mr. Merrick and the task at hand. The man was dressed in a white button-down and jeans with a black belt sporting a large silver buckle. His bushy gray eyebrows were drawn together; his tight gray goatee framing his down-turned mouth. He was…for lack of a better word, I think he was unhappy with me. Like I was an errant child.

Scanning the room for more information, Cooper, and a few others I didn't recognize, stared past me.

Before I could turn to see what caught their attention, Junior, dressed more casual in a company polo and khaki pants, walked up to greet me. "Grady, hey there, so glad you're here." He shook my hand, grabbing my shoulder with his other hand and guiding me over to Merrick.

"Good Morning, Grady," Merrick said, his southern hospitality not disappearing, but his smile didn't meet his eyes. We weren't okay —he and I. I did something wrong. I just didn't know what.

"It's a pleasure to be here," I said.

"Let's all have a seat."

I took a seat to Merrick's right and noticed a black helmet with a visor placed to Merrick's left.

The beauty from last night was standing in the doorway, speaking animatedly but in hushed tones with Bill, again. She was staring daggers at me as he placed a hand on her shoulder and encouraged her to move forward.

Daggers. At. Me.

What the hell was I missing?

Merrick was still standing.

"CJ, are you going to join us?" Merrick said, slowly, in a voice a parent would use with an obstinate child.

The mystery lady—Ms. Sassy Stilettos, Ms. Contemptuous Coffee-lady walked around the side of the conference table as if it were the side of a boxing ring and Bill was her trainer. The *Rocky* theme played in the background of my mind as she took the chair to the other side of Merrick, directly across from mine. Never once breaking eye contact with me.

CJ.

CJ Lomax...pulled the seat out in front of the black motorcycle helmet, sat down, leaned forward on her elbows, gritted her teeth and said, "Get your own damn coffee."

# 6

## *CJ*

Screw him.

I wouldn't say I wanted to run out of the conference room before the meeting was over—because I wouldn't give those assholes the satisfaction—but if I didn't leave soon, things might get ugly.

As angry as I was at the situation, I wouldn't disrespect Mr. Merrick by swearing like a sailor in the middle of a business meeting. So, I sat there plotting the things I'd like to do with that hot cup of coffee he was lucky I never fetched for him.

I'd hoped the ride I took before the meeting would've calmed me, but there he was at the traffic light.

I tried to get a simple cup of coffee and get my thoughts together…there he was…again. Tried to find time to talk with Wild Bill, my mentor and one of the few people whom I listened to, and the asshole asked me to get him coffee.

It pushed me past my limit for the day.

Bill, knowing me and my temper, sat next to me during the

meeting, occasionally stepping on my foot to remind me to stay calm.

*Get him coffee—take my car—who the hell did this guy think he was? Ouch!*

Down would go Bill's boot on my poor sneaker-clad foot. I'd jerk and glare at Bill.

His side-eye held censure. *Focus.*

After my initial outburst about Grady getting his own coffee, I ignored his existence and promised myself it was my strategy for the remainder of the season—just ignore him.

Merrick stood and placed both his hands on the conference table, leaning toward us. "We will have a press conference tomorrow to announce our plans. I expect a lot of questions and coverage over this unorthodox set-up. Both of you will be there." He took turns staring down both Grady and me. "You will be professional and smile. You will be enthusiastic and excited about the coming season. You can tease, and banter, but you will be professional." He had the nerve to stare at me and emphasize "professional." As if I ever gave him reason to believe I'd be anything but professional.

He'd known me since I was a child, and undoubtedly, he saw the petulant eight-year-old in the woman sitting in the chair next to him. With both my parents gone, the Merricks became not only my family, but my road to racing. So, unfortunately for me, my boss was familiar with all my faces. Including, my I'm-pissed-and-plotting-how-to-ruin-the-life-of-the-man-sitting-across-from-me face.

The minute he called the meeting over, I was out of there.

I almost forgot my damn helmet.

And now my hands were shaking.

Damn adrenaline.

I couldn't pin-point what was tipping me over the edge.

Was it Grady's stare and his side-long looks? His disbelief when Merrick cleared up my identity?

Or was it the incredulity—or possibly shame—in mistaking me for a gopher?

Since I was a woman and worked in a garage, I must be a secretary or receptionist? Even if I was a secretary, who'd he think he was, ordering me to fetch him anything?

Was it sexism or just plain blue-blood haughtiness which made him think I was there to serve him?

I needed to get out of here before I did or said anything to give the rumor mill more fodder about me—the cold bitch. The Dixie Cup Princess—that was the oldest of the nicknames the boys gave me. They said I was tiny like a pixie, but the only Cup I'd ever win was a Dixie cup. They used to leave them for me on my cars as a joke. Except the joke was on them when I'd beat them, week after week. Whether it was quarter midgets, bandoleros, legends…whatever they put me in—I beat them. Everyone but Tommy.

I had tunnel vision as I walked through the hall toward the stairway. I didn't bother with the elevator. I couldn't stop the momentum. I had to move.

Then there was the absurd proposal I didn't seem to have a choice but to accept.

Junior tried to sell it as the Open Wheel Champ versus the Sweetheart of Stock Car. But what Junior really hoped was that by putting Grady McBane—the Charismatic Professional Champion— up against me—the Token-Woman-Driver—he'd prove that I had no business in these ranks. It was in the gleam in his eye. Junior had been searching for a legitimate way to get rid of me since the day he realized he'd never beat me behind the wheel.

Grady and I would alternate races, and whoever had the best record at the end of the season would receive the full contract. Winner took all.

I took the steps downstairs at a record pace, holding in the hellfire of fury inside me.

Grady was already starting off with an advantage, though, simply by being Grady—charismatic, handsome and a media golden boy. His hair, his eyes, his body—dammit—even the way he walked. Sponsors would fall over themselves to be in his orbit. How was that even fair?

Screw them.

Screw all of them.

And screw Grady McBane and his golden boy good looks most of all.

"CJ," Harper said, trying to catch my stride.

I didn't stop, and instead tore through reception and past the receptionist, who was undoubtedly giving Harper the low down on what she witnessed. Used to trying to keep up when I was determined to leave, Harper somehow managed in a pencil skirt and heels.

I showed restraint in not kicking the door leading outside, but slammed into it hard enough the sound reverberated as I made a beeline to my bike.

Harper flicked down her aviator sunglasses as I put my helmet on the seat and reached inside the saddle bag to grab my jacket.

"Whoa. You can't leave without telling me what happened," Harper said. "What did Daddy say? What did Grady say when he saw you?"

"Nothing," I said. Clipped. I didn't want to talk. Because if I started, I may not be able to stop. I wanted to get on the bike and go fast. I wanted the wind against my body and the sensation of flying to overtake all other emotions.

Harper knew me better. She stilled me and turned me around, "What happened?"

"Nothing," I said, throwing my arms out before resting them on my hips, "Fine, you want to know? Your father admitted that he can't put me in the car without this asinine contest because I'm a woman and I won't be accepted. Then I had to go into a room full of men who all thought the same thing and sit across from another man who saw me as inferior. Grady didn't say anything to me besides giving me his coffee order and ogled my breasts and ass. There."

"He thought you were—"

"He thought I was there to serve him. He thought I was his gopher with tits and ass in a pair of jeans. Thanks to you, and the way I was dressed last night, that is all he will see me as. Not as an equal, but as a pair of tits behind a wheel."

Harper flinched. "C—"

I held up my hand as I turned in a circle to pace. Harper gave me the moment. I dropped my head—deflated. "I'm sorry. That wasn't…that was mean, and I didn't mean it. It's just…"

Harper approached me slowly and put her arm around my shoulders. "I know. I made you drop your guard, and today you needed it. It will be okay. You're a bad-ass—you know that. They —" she motioned to the building, "—know that, too."

Grady McBane chose that time to make his dramatic exit from the building. I swore the sun broke out of the clouds just for him and it made me both hate him more and, if I admitted it, envy him a bit. To have the sun shine on you like that—how could you not envy it?

His determined stride halted every third or fourth step with enough hesitance to give me some satisfaction that he wasn't completely sure of himself or of my reaction.

"And from the look on that man's face, I think he knows what a bad-ass you are, too," Harper whispered.

About seven feet away he locked eyes on me, waiting for permission to approach, and Harper slipped away.

I leaned my backside against my bike, and going for the complete laid-back composure, crossed my arms and legs. I wanted to reach into my saddle bag to fish out my mirrored sunglasses but figured that would be too obvious.

How did someone his size even fit in a race car?

Even in daylight, with the gold shining in his hair, he reminded me of the thunder god.

Because I was missing my mirrored sunglasses, I resisted the urge to roll my eyes, barely. I refused to determine the urge— whether it was in annoyance at him just being there or at myself after admitting my attraction to him.

Before I was able to glean an answer, he was closer. "I need to apologize," he said.

"For what, exactly?" I tightened my crossed arms around my chest and looked past him.

He shifted his feet.

"For not knowing who I was? For assuming I was there to fetch your coffee? For assuming I wanted you to ogle my breasts. Or for trying to take my job?"

His hand went to rub the back of his neck and he winced—just slightly.

"First, I didn't know who you were—that's true. I'm not as familiar with the drivers in this circuit. I'd heard of you but hadn't ever met you. You didn't look like your press photo when I saw you last night—obviously, you—"

"—looked like a woman."

"A captivating woman I couldn't take my eyes off of."

"A woman whose boobs you couldn't take your eyes off—"

He smiled through lowered lashes. Did he really think now was a time to try to be charming?

"Well, you kind of fell into my arms—twice. They were hard to miss."

My eyes narrowed. I didn't find him reminding me of my double dose of embarrassment endearing. "This isn't helping your apology process."

"As far as this morning, I was out of line. I'm not myself. Junior never mentioned the dual driver idea to me when he asked me to come down here. Merrick sprung it on me yesterday and, well, it isn't sitting all that well. I'm sure you aren't as thrilled about it either."

He sighed and waited for a reply.

I gave him a curt nod.

"I had a headache this morning on top of everything. I'm sorry if I offended you."

I straightened and leaned into him. "Don't get me wrong, I used to run errands and answer phones for these boys. But you should never assume when you see a woman around the garage or office that she's there to serve the men."

"Message received. I promise." His hand went over his chest. "Can we start over?"

I studied him for moment. His eyes were focused on me. The flirtatious smile was gone but his face was warm and sincere. If he'd been trying to charm me, it would've been received differently, but I didn't get that vibe.

Nothing sat right with me, but the guy did make a point to come out and apologize.

It was more than Junior or any of his ilk would've done. It didn't do me any good to start off with him as a contentious enemy this early in the season. I had enough of those. I shifted, braced my hands on my bike behind me, and gave a begrudging nod.

He put his hands in his pockets and tilted his head. "Listen, I know we're lined up to be enemies of sorts, and I'm not saying we need to be friends, but I do respect what you're doing, and this morning I studied your driving record. I'm not big on the drama they're going to try to stir, or the whole reality TV vibe they're going to try to portray. What do you say we just try to keep things professional and civil between us? I really don't want to be part of a shit show."

Well, that was cutting through the crap. I could respect that.

"I think that is the best thing I've heard you say yet."

He smiled, and again the sun shone so bright it even caused him to squint a bit which made his expression warm my insides even more.

I still didn't like him, though.

I stood up abruptly, causing him to take a step back. "We have the press conference tomorrow to announce the team's plan going forward." I reached behind me, found a welcomed comfort as I slipped on my sunglasses, and grabbed my helmet.

He stepped closer. "Yes, Junior mentioned it. I get the feeling you and he don't get along very well?"

"You'd get that right. Point is, if you want to prove we can get along and be civil, tomorrow will be the first test." I straddled my bike, eager for the escape it offered.

"What does that mean? I've done press conferences before—I know they can be chaotic, but why won't it be civil?"

I adjusted the helmet, but delayed putting it on while I searched for a way to word my explanation. I gave him what may have passed for a smile and said, "You'll see." I needed to go. The sunglasses weren't enough to make me comfortable. He was talking to me without condescension. The guy was kind of...not as much of an ass.

I replaced the sunglasses with my helmet, slipping them in my saddlebag. I kicked up the stand and started up my baby. The roar of sound drowned out any possibility of further conversation, and drew my focus off him and back to the monster of power under me.

Revving the engine, I took him in one last time—my stomach in so many knots I wasn't sure I was ever going to untangle them.

I gave him another curt nod before leaning over the bike. He stood there, legs spread, arms crossed, reflective shades concealing his gorgeous eyes, with just enough of a damnable breeze to toss his gorgeous blond waves. It all looked staged as one side of his mouth tilted up just enough for me to question his thoughts. Then, I took off as if the flames of hell were hot on my ass—and not Grady's eyes.

# 7

*Grady*

Cooper and I arrived back at Merrick Motorsports the next afternoon for the scheduled news conference to announce the team's plan for replacing Trent Lawrence. Between my arrival and CJ's long association with Merrick, speculation was already running throughout the garages.

"So, this will be interesting," Cooper said as we walked, gesturing at the building. "Try to be nice, but not too nice." Cooper side-eyed me.

"I think we have an understanding, we're on the same page." I think.

I wasn't quite sure what to think of the woman. At the bar the night before, she definitely caught my interest. At the office the next day, she wanted to knock my teeth out. Not the reaction I was used to, and not exactly the complication I needed to deal with right now.

"Wait, what do you mean, 'Not too nice'?"

"Thank God she's definitely not your type." Cooper gave me

half-cocked smile. "I was afraid once I saw she was the woman from the bar that we might have a problem, but with the disdain she has for you, I know we're good."

I pulled up short. "She doesn't disdain me."

He stopped. "Grady, man. You're trying to take her ride. She isn't going to fall for your normal routine."

"Jesus, Cooper. What the hell?" I walked away from him. "You make it sound like I intentionally lead women on and cast them off."

"No, you're right. The women flock to you. But not her—I think that's the attraction." He tagged my arm. "But it's not worth what we have going on here. This is your comeback opportunity. It's not worth it."

I stepped around him.

He grabbed my arm, "Come on, man. It wasn't like you saw her the night before and thought, 'Hey, there's a woman I'd like to have a meaningful relationship with.' No, you looked at her and thought, there's a woman I'd like to—"

"Screw you." I shoved him, annoyance building in me. He was my friend, but he was also dragging out my conscience, which was what I was trying to forget about. My conscience was constantly reminding me what a fuck up I'd become—especially when a woman was involved. "I don't need this shit, not from you," I mumbled and turned to leave him.

"Grady. Wait." He stepped in front of me. "Alright, I'm sorry. All I meant was she's not your type and I'm glad things won't get more complicated by you trying to sleep with her."

"What? Why?"

"Why, what?"

"Why isn't she my type? Why wouldn't I try to sleep with her?" I stumbled. "I mean, why wouldn't she be my type? I mean, why would that be a problem?"

Cooper stared at me and ran his hand over his face in exasperation. "I...I...You..."

"Okay, fine. I know...but I didn't know I had a type? Why isn't she my type? Why would you dismiss it right out of hand?"

"Do I need to go find a *Cosmo* article so we can analyze this shit or something?" He pointed at me and started ticking off his fingers in my face. "She's not your type because she's not falling all over you. She doesn't like you. You shouldn't like her. You need to win this to save your career, and there are plenty of women out there who are less work and less complicated."

Well, there it was.

Yep. The fact that she seemed completely disinterested was a bit of a challenge, and I think it was the aphrodisiac that was fueling the attraction I already felt toward her. The forbidden fruit. The one who said, "Not interested." Yep, that's what it was.

That, and an unusual dry spell.

And her hair, and her eyes, and her lips and her mouth—and what came out of her mouth. And her body wrapped around that bike. And even her eyes narrowed on me like she wanted to climb me—I wasn't sure if it was to rip out my eyes or suck on my mouth.

I didn't care. Yep. None of that mattered.

What almost did me in was when she straddled that monster of a motorcycle. I swore I was jealous of a machine. I never saw something more erotic, fully clothed. My dreams weren't kind to me last night.

But CJ on that Ducati, my libido competed with the roar of that monster engine.

Nope. I shook my head.

Cooper caught me and began to open his mouth.

"No," I said aloud this time, and held up my hand to him. "You're right." My life is

enough of a clusterfuck. "Let's just get this done and get out of here. Merrick is holding a cookout at his place up at the lake tonight. After that, I think I need to go out."

We walked into a holding room where CJ was leaning back against a wall, head down, studying her phone, appearing bored and unapproachable. I walked past her and stole a look into the pressroom at the wall of windows which overlooked the two-story garage. There was a riser to the left with a long table, set up with three microphones and a podium. I turned back to the hallway outside the pressroom and joined CJ.

Junior proceeded to block the door, while over his shoulder the pressroom filled with reporters as they took their seats. "Let me go introduce you two, Gus, and myself. You all can come in and I will run through the plan and schedule and then open the floor for questions. Anything to do with the cars specifically or the tracks, refer to Gus. Businesses and sponsors I will cover. Answer questions directed to you specifically, and by all means, please keep them short and—" he pointedly looked at CJ "—sweet. Grady, be your charming self. CJ, try not to glower at the camera so much; you may scare small children."

I caught CJ straightening her head enough to roll her eyes at Junior as he left.

CJ was dressed casually, in a nice pair of dark jeans with a team logo quarter-zip pullover, and still managed to look as beautiful as if she were in a little black dress and heels—although I'd love to see that, too. Her hair was down, straight, and behind her ears, her makeup was minimal, but with a girl-next-door look that softened her—though her she gave off a no-nonsense vibe.

She leaned toward the door, peering into the press room.

I came up behind her, tall enough to see over her head, close enough to catch the scent of mint from her hair. "One of these days, I'd love to hear why there is so much love lost between you two."

She straightened and peered out to the press room. "There wasn't really any love between us to begin with. I've known Junior almost all my life. His mother and mine were best friends, and I've been friends with his sister Harper since infancy. It's quite boring and juvenile, and not really worth explaining."

"Well, I'd still like to hear it sometime."

"No—really—" She turned and was face-to-chest with me, my arm outstretched above her, braced on the doorframe. My body involuntarily closed the short distance even farther, and our eyes locked before I took a quick step back, realizing what an intimate position I'd inadvertently put us in.

She cleared her throat and straightened just as Junior said, "Introducing the newest member of the Merrick family, Indy champion Mr. Grady McBane, and the other driver for the thirty-six car this season is CJ Lomax."

*The other driver? What an ass—why doesn't Merrick do something about that?*

I glanced down at CJ, who was already stepping aside, waiting for me to precede her in the order we were announced.

But that wasn't the way I was raised. Driver or not, she was a lady first, also the veteran with this team, and clearly, Junior was being petty, even with the introductions. I held the door, gesturing for CJ to step forward and go first. There was a tilt of her head and a furrow of her brow for a moment before understanding dawned.

"He introduced you first, just go," she said, with a dismissive wave.

I held out my hand to her, waving her forward. "Come on."

"Fine, whatever." She straightened and tilted her head high, a surprising surge of pride in her teased through me.

Junior was an ass.

She was used to his petty swipes.

I placed a protective hand on her lower back as I escorted her through the door, and she stiffened from my touch.

I quickly pulled back my hand. The move had been subconscious, but I realized my mistake. This was uncharted waters and I needed to be more mindful.

She was a desirable woman. I was attracted to her and found her intriguing—but she was also my competition. I was out of my element. Women usually welcomed my advances. CJ, not so much. When we met, she fell into my arms that first time. I saw the softness and the connection. But ever since then, nada.

Plus, I had to be more aware of our public image—how the media was going to read us—individually, together, and our interaction.

Navigating this was going to be dicey.

I waited as she stepped up the riser and took her seat as far as possible from Junior, who stood at a podium. I sat between them—and didn't that seem like a sign of things to come?

I took a sip of the water in front of me, while Junior rattled on about my accomplishments and listed off my bio—which I dreaded. Then they got to the elephant in the room—where had I gone for the last part of the year? Why did I disappear from McBane Racing in the middle of a season and just now resurface?

I focused on a spot at the back of the room and stared intermittently at it as a way of trying to zone out the looks, the questioning glances.

Then Junior got to CJ and the enthusiasm was forced. "CJ Lomax has a long-standing history, both with Merrick Motorsports and the stock car industry. As many of you already know, CJ began her career racing legends, bandoleros, trucks, and stock cars. For the past few years, she's been driving for Merrick in the Energy Blast, racking up three pole positions, fifteen top ten finishes, five wins, and falling just short of the elusive championship last year."

*He didn't just say that? How can anyone listen to this guy?*

CJ sat ramrod straight; her hands were folded in front of her on the table, her face unreadable but with a pleasant demeanor I sensed was practiced.

I needed to look at her history more—it would be wise to know who I was competing against. Study what tracks she excels at, which are her weaker ones.

"So now let's open up for questions," Junior said, before calling on a veteran reporter from a major sports outlet in the front row.

Might as well start off swinging.

"Grady, what made you decide to take the leap into stock car? Was it the fallout with your family?"

Well, that was getting straight to the point.

"I felt it was time to branch out and try something new. When Merrick offered me this opportunity, knowing what a strong, reputable organization they were, I was honored and thought it would be a great new direction."

I moved on and waited for Junior to call on someone else. But this reporter was a veteran and knew what he was doing.

"If Indy ever lifts the suspension on you from racing, would you consider going back, and what does your family, particularly your father, think about this move?"

With a confident, well-rehearsed tone, I replied, "This is what I considered to be the next step in my career. Something I had been looking forward to pursuing."

I'd been expecting this but wished they would've at least let me warm up.

Junior jumped in and moved on—thank God.

"Joe." He called on someone from the other side.

"Grady, what do you think you can bring to Merrick Motorsports that would differ from CJ? As stated, she's been here for a few years and proven to be a skilled driver. What do you offer that would cause them to look outside their organization to you?"

Wow. Should've seen that coming.

If possible, CJ went even more still, her face unreadable as she pretended to glance my way, but seemed unable to look me in the eye. How to answer this—answer it as I would if she were a man—hard and fast and to the quick. Do I give the impression she was found lacking and that was why they went outside the organization? Or do I expose the truth that pettiness and the need for PR drives this ship, and I was more than likely the one who would get the shaft?

Truth—I didn't know.

"I think that's a question only Mr. Merrick could answer, since he was the one to make the decision. I have the utmost respect for CJ and all those at Merrick. As far as what I can bring, my record speaks for itself. I thrive on new challenges, and switching things up was what I was looking for. Mr. Merrick and his team gave me a new opportunity and I'm grateful. I am sure I will learn a lot from all the people here at Merrick, including CJ, and the driver of their other team car...and I look forward to it."

At least I cut Junior out of that answer. No sense in aggrandizing his role in this.

Junior moved on.

He called one of the few women in the room, "Yes. Stacy?"

"CJ, what is it like working alongside one of the most eligible bachelors in sports?" She gushed and glanced at me. "Many women will be flocking to the racetracks now that Grady McBane has resurfaced and is single again."

*Was she serious?*

CJ produced what I now knew was a fake "You-are-trying-my-patience" smile. "I really haven't had an opportunity to spend much time with Mr. McBane. We are both focused on our separate roles in the organization. I'm sure his dating status will be something others can spend time mulling over."

With that, she turned to me and gave me a knowing look I was sure all the reporters caught and would be spread over the Internet within the hour. It would be the photo that summarized our now-declared competition.

Game on.

"Another question for CJ," another reporter shouted out. "CJ, you've been driving for Merrick for years, even as backup driver for Trent Lawrence in the past. What do you think of Merrick bringing a virtual outsider in to compete against you for a position that should be offered, if not to you, then to someone at least from the Energy Blast circuit?"

She took a moment to gather her thoughts, and then leaned forward into the microphone. Tucking her hair behind her ear, she said, "I have great respect for Mr. Merrick and his organization. I'd have gone to another team long ago if I didn't love working here and if I didn't think the world of this group. Likewise, I know he respects me and appreciates what I bring to the table. Otherwise, he wouldn't put me behind the wheel of any of his cars."

Gesturing to me and then to the press, CJ continued, "Grady McBane is like an all-star, Super Bowl-winning quarterback who just became a free-agent. He's a household name. From Stacy's question alone, we can all see what a savvy business decision it is to bring him on. But most of all, he is a talented driver. Am I happy about him being here? No. I want the seat in that car." She pointed at the garage visible by the wall of windows.

"But, talented, winning, good-looking, or popular, it doesn't matter. I will still drive my damnedest to make sure, in the end, I'm the one who deserves to be in that seat."

She stood, looked down at me straight in the eye and I swore my heart skipped a beat. "Sorry, Casanova, you better strap in. You're in for the ride of your life."

She held out her hand. I stood and took it. Nerves in my body came alive at the contact of her touch.

This was it. This was the photo op.

"May the best man win," someone shouted.

"No." She gave me a devastating smile, and then shared it with the room. "May the best driver."

# 8

## *CJ*

I pulled up to the Merrick's lake house in my pickup, parking behind many other pickups and muscle cars lining the circular driveway. I wasn't good at putting up a front on a good day.

Facing Junior, Mr. Merrick, and Grady in the same house, at a picnic, wasn't exactly what I wanted to deal with the evening before hitting the road to Tennessee. However, Harper's mom, Violet, was a Southern woman, which meant welcoming new members into the fold with a dinner. Since the entire team was expected, it meant I was, too. It was times like these, when crossing the line between business and friendship was a complicated situation.

I'd make an appearance and leave. Maybe I'd even try to fake smile.

I'd been practicing.

Harper said I didn't look like a constipated serial killer anymore. Just a bit bitchy, which was a good look for me.

I jumped out of the cab of my truck and turned to grab the pies I made last night. Even though I was more tomboy than Martha

Stewart, when I was stressed, I baked. Since I was also an athlete who had to stay in shape, and couldn't indulge in what I baked, I had to give it away.

Plus, Violet was a surrogate aunt to me and taught me never to show up empty-handed—even if it was a party at a multi-million-dollar lake house that was probably catering the entire thing.

I mistakenly left my hair down and was cursing the error, as I tried to flick it over my shoulder without dropping the pies, when a voice came up behind me.

"Here, let me help you with those…"

"Oh shit!" I said, bobbling the pies while hair flew in my mouth. Grady.

I used my shoulder to nudge the hair out of my face. When it didn't work, a warm hand gently swept it behind my shoulder and tucked it behind my ear, the back of his fingers lightly brushing my cheek.

The evening sun haloed his sandy blond hair. His eyes were a brilliant blue as he smiled at me.

"Damnit, Grady. You almost ended up with a face full of pie."

"I like pie. What kind of pie?"

"Cherry and chocolate." I nudged the door of the truck closed with my hip and readjusted the pies in my hands.

"I love chocolate." He leaned for the chocolate pie.

I handed him the cherry.

I marched past him to the house. "Are you just getting here?"

"No, I've been here. I saw you pulling up and thought I'd come greet you. I didn't get a chance to talk to you after the press conference and just wanted to check in."

"About what?" I glanced back.

He slowed down as we were quickly approaching the door.

Impatience was an emotion I was vastly familiar with, but with Grady it was on a constant loop. With the conciliatory raise of his eyebrows, he was aware of it.

He held the pie with both hands and gestured to me. "You handled yourself well with the press."

"Thanks," I said, hesitantly, not sure where this was going. "I have had press conferences before. The Energy Blast races may not be as big as others, but we still got press coverage."

"You mistake me. I mean, they were trying my patience. While they were a bit invasive and tenacious with me, that's to be expected. But I was surprised at how...well, *condescending* they were with you."

"Ha." That was old news and I started toward the house again. "That's normal. At least this time they didn't ask for my opinion on the color of the car."

"Huh. So, is it always like that?" he called after me.

I started climbing the stairs to the front door. "Basically."

He moved to open the door for me but paused to say, "Well, you handled it well, not to sound patronizing—"

"I get it. Thanks. Let's get moving. Not sure if you've met Ms. Violet, but she'd not take kindly to us standing on her porch chatting where she couldn't hear what we were saying."

Sure enough, Violet opened the door and greeted us both with her trademark smile. "Well, it's about time, CJ. Oh, but you brought your pies, so your tardiness is forgiven. And isn't Grady such the gentleman, going out to meet you."

She leaned in and gave me a kiss on the cheek and a pointed look already inquiring as to why Grady went out to greet me.

I gave her a kiss back and said, "Hi. I was packing for tomorrow. I'm sorry for being late." Not bothering to satisfy her with any sort of explanation as to why Grady was with me, because frankly, I didn't know.

Violet took the pie from me and led us into the house. "Grady, as you know, the guys are out back talking shop. CJ, why don't you and I join Harper in the kitchen?"

Grady gave her a wink, and handed me the other pie, as he strode through the family room and out to the open doors to the deck overlooking the large patio leading to the lakeview out back. I tried not to roll my eyes.

I loved Violet—I did. "Don't roll your eyes at me, I won't keep you long." She knew me well. But why did I always get pulled into the kitchen for the gossip instead of being allowed to attend the "shop talk"? I imagined it was this way in the Old South when men would retire to the library for their cigars and brandy, and women would settle for the parlor for tea and cookies. I could drink brandy. I've had a cigar, damnit.

"Hey, girl, 'bout time you made it," Harper said, handing me a sweet tea.

Violet scurried to the window overlooking the outside and then turned dramatically, fanning herself. "Good Lord Almighty, but that man…"

Harper scoffed.

"Girls, if I were fifteen years younger——" Violet put the pies in the sub-zero fridge.

"And not married to Daddy…" Harper added.

"Well, yes, and that, too."

Harper's Aunt Sadie walked in. "Are we talking about the Adonis who just walked out into the back?" Sadie was Merrick's younger sister and a widow. Her deceased husband's family were the original owners of Charlotte Raceway before it was sold to a large corporation. Upon his passing, Ms. Sadie became a very wealthy woman. Also, a bit eccentric, lovable, sometimes ornery, always outspoken, Southern woman.

I believe Violet may have bitten her lip. "Yes, ma'am. I'm serious, he is so yummy and so nice and gentlemanly."

"He's also trying to take my job," I quietly reminded her and pulled up a stool to the bar-height counter.

"Well, there is that," Violet conceded with a tilt of her head, but a wave of her hand to signify its insignificance. "Not sure what Everett was thinking with that stunt." She put a hand on mine and said, "He won't discuss it with me, darlin', just says he has his reasons. But, honey, I know he loves you and it isn't a reflection on you or what he thinks about your abilities."

"He's listening to your asinine son," Sadie said, once again pulling no punches.

Harper pulled up a stool next to mine, crossing her legs under her short, sky-blue sundress.

Violet gave Sadie the side-eye.

"What? We all know he's jealous of CJ. It ain't a secret." Sadie took another deep drink of whatever was in her tumbler.

"What are you drinking?" Violet asked. "That isn't tea, is it?"

"Sure is… the Long Island kind." Sadie smiled and sat next to Harper. She was dressed in a light linen button shirt, a pair of linen pants, and bare feet. Her hair was perfectly coiffed, as if she'd just come from having it set at the hairdresser.

Harper straightened. "Mama, can you talk with Daddy?"

"Harper…please, don't start," her mother said, and turned and grabbed her own tea. "I'm sure he has his reasons. Your father doesn't let people dictate what he does. Not even your brother."

Violet redirected her attention back to the window. "But back to the eye candy out there. All I'm saying is he seems like a sweet boy. He is a breath of fresh air for you girls, and you both would be fools not to take a second look at him."

"With the reputation that man has, I don't think either one of us needs to do anything else with him but look," Harper said. "Men like him are better to admire than to get involved with. I don't think either one of us needs that kind of trouble."

"I'd take on that kind of trouble…" Sadie muttered, before taking another sip out of her tumbler.

"No one said anything about trouble—what about fun? I'm not saying diving in, but nothing wrong with testing the waters and having a little fun. I'm just saying go splash around a little," Violet said, fanning herself again.

Both Harper and I studied our plain sweet tea. I began eyeing Sadie's glass as she turned it farther from me.

"Come on, girls, you both need to get out there. Get back on the horse. You're both beautiful, strong, successful women…" She brought the tea up to her mouth and said softly, "who aren't exactly getting any younger," before taking a sip.

"Mama, we both have our reasons. We will get there when we're ready."

"Posh, Harper Scarlet." She stood up and almost slammed her tea on the counter. "Your asinine ex doesn't deserve your tears, and it's about time you realize that. Bygones. Goodbye and good riddance," she said with more vehemence than I had ever heard from Violet before.

Harper stood from the stool and took a step back, thrown by the anger in her mother's voice. Violet's eyes widened in surprise at her own outburst. She drew in a breath and turned to me.

Sadie's reaction was just to lift an eyebrow.

Violet's face softened when she turned to me. But clearly, it was my turn and I stood, preparing to flee. "It's time to let him go, CJ. Tommy wouldn't want you isolating yourself so much. You've been working so hard and have had such success, you deserve to have someone to share it with you."

I didn't need this lecture. Not today.

I didn't want to be angry at Violet. But I didn't want to talk or even think about Tommy.

I understood that Tommy was gone. I didn't need anyone reminding me how hollow I was, for Christ's sake.

I felt it every time I stepped up to my car and saw all the other drivers get a hug and kiss from their loved ones before the race, or exuberant congratulatory hugs after the race. I knew the void of not having someone to go home with, someone to celebrate with and share their successes and failures.

The repercussions of youth, the absence of Tommy, was a physical pain that lashed at me each and every time I walked down pit road, knowing he should've been there—knowing he should've been getting into his own car. Both of us strapping in our cars, preparing to race each other. Just the way it used to be when we were kids.

Instead, love interfered with dreams, with focus.

"CJ, honey...I'm sorry..." Violet said, putting an arm around me.

"Mom, she's got enough stress as it is, she doesn't need this right now. Just let her be, okay?" Harper said.

I grabbed my tea so I had something to do with my hands, stepped back and began walking outside. I glanced over, gave them both a half-hearted *I'm okay* smile. "I'm...um...I'm going to go outside and talk with Bill about this weekend."

"CJ?" Violet said, her voice laced with regret and a little frustration in her inability to help me.

I waved and walked out. The window Violet had been looking out was still open and I paused, overhearing the mother-daughter conversation from inside the kitchen.

"You need to stop pushing her, Mama."

"It isn't healthy, Harper, and if you weren't still stewing over that poor excuse of a man, you'd both be out there acting your age and not like two dowager old women burned out on love."

"It isn't that simple, Mama. Aunt Sadie…" Harper was asking for her favorite aunt to intervene and take her side. Sadie was a strong, independent woman. Even though once married she made it clear she never needed a man, they were more of an accessory to her.

"Girl, not to add insult to injury, but I've had more action than the two of you combined over the last year. Time to get back on the horse—both of you. And that stallion was meant to be ridden…"

"Sadie!" Violet's tone was admonishing, but amused. "I wasn't always married to your Daddy, Princess, and he wasn't the only man I ever dated. I know it isn't simple, but it is a choice. It's your choice —you both need to make it and move forward. Right now, you're each other's excuse for standing still."

So, I didn't stand still—I walked away.

---

The barbeque was like every other Merrick function, intimate, classy, and casual. A catered event that mimicked grilling burgers on the back porch for friends, except instead of Mr. Merrick manning the grill, he was holding court down by the dock—a king and his subjects.

Even with the serious nature of the kitchen conversation, and the stress of the upcoming days, right now I sat among friends with a full belly, my mood lightened, and my body relaxed as the sun began to set.

I sat next to Sass—nicknamed Sasquatch—a fuel man who was

the size of a sasquatch but had the heart of a teddy bear. He'd been updating us on his ten-year-old daughter who was home recovering from a broken leg. "I'll come by to see Daisy, or maybe we can have her out to one of the races."

"That would be great, she will be so excited to see you. She's going stir-crazy. She doesn't take kindly to being told to sit still." He glanced over at Grady who'd been talking with Harper. "I haven't had a chance to tell her your news," he whispered the last part. "She's going to be pissed." I gave a small smile. She *was* going to be pissed. Daisy was my biggest fan. It seemed she'd been waiting for me to make it to the Cup Series for as long as I had.

Just as the thought crossed my mind, Grady whispered something to Harper that made her throw back her head and laugh. When Harper laughed, she did it full-on. She loved hard, laughed hard, but she also fell hard. In fact, she was still getting up from the last fall.

Violet's comments were on repeat in my head.

*"Harper Scarlet...it's time you get back out there..."*

Grady was Harper's type—the all-American boy...hopefully, he wasn't also an asshole like the last guy she fell for.

Harper and Grady.

My stomach dropped as it did when I was spun out at one-hundred-eighty mph. What the hell?

I shook my head.

"Is there something wrong, CJ?" Grady was staring at me.

"No. Why would there be?" I said, playing with the flatware in front of me.

"I don't know?" he said, leaning in and dropping his voice. "You were scowling at me."

"She scowls at everyone. It's how you know you've arrived," Gus said, coming over to sit on my other side.

"Don't you have something you need to be greasing, August?" Junior asked, sitting on the other side of his sister with a plate full of food.

Gus glared at him. He hated when people used his given name.

"Don't be an ass," Harper said to her brother.

"Don't bother, Harper," I sighed. "That would be like telling a cockroach not to be a cockroach."

He ignored us and began shoveling food into his mouth.

"CJ, they got you a hotel room reserved for tomorrow night. Get in touch with the office tomorrow morning."

Before I could even respond, Harper loomed over her brother. "Wait, what? Why doesn't she have an RV?"

"Grady gets it." Junior shoveled in another helping of potato salad.

"Grady isn't racing this weekend, she is. She should be at the infield, not at a hotel."

"Wait, wait." Grady leaned past Harper. "I don't need the RV, Harper's right. Give CJ the RV, I don't need it," Grady said. "I have my own I had driven down."

He motioned to Cooper who said, "Yeah, it arrived and is being set up this evening."

"Whatever." Junior got up and left with an undisguised huff.

Junior's attempt to make me feel inferior wasn't completely thwarted. It still left a mark. I hated when others came to my defense. I wasn't a damsel in a castle. But even acknowledging his attempt would give it credence; it's why I ignore him and pick my battles. He's the prodigal son, after all. He held power over my career. This latest move was his way to prove it.

"Okay, so that's settled," Harper said.

"I would've been fine with a five-star hotel, Harper. Room service, hello?" I joked. I got up but couldn't think of a reason to leave, so I just said, "Alright, well, time for pie."

# 9

**Grady**

"What is it with those two?" I asked.

Sass came back to the table with a few pieces of pie for every-one. Sitting next to Gus, he leaned forward and answered, "Junior carries a grudge because CJ has bigger balls than him." he said.

Harper eyed one of the slices Sass placed on the table. "She scares the crap out of him and he's petty."

Sass added, "Amen." He reached for a piece of cherry pie.

"Seriously, what am I missing?" I wanted more information about what I'd walked into.

"CJ and I have been friends since we were in diapers." Harper folded her arms and leaned into them on the table. "While stock car racing is an industry, it was originally a network of families. And just like baseball, racing has a little league that starts young, and kids come up the ranks growing up around the track. While I never really showed any interest in racing, CJ was always a natural." Harper smiled with pride.

"Early on, my brother fancied himself the next Earnhardt or

Petty. All little boys in Charlotte did. Arrogance and the Merrick name gave him the belief that it was owed to him. Quarter midgets, bandoleros, legends, sprint cars, didn't matter. Junior and his buddies always had the best, but never performed as well as she did." Harper nodded toward CJ.

"Well, not as well as she and Tommy," Gus added, softly, not looking up.

"Tommy?" I asked.

"Tommy Dupree. Her boyfriend." Gus looked me right in the eye. Before my confusion could be expressed, he added. "He died when we were young—"

"Those two had a hell of a lot of raw talent," Sass interjected and stood to claim one of the other slices. "But for Junior, he learned having the Merrick last name, a legacy name, and all the best equipment money can buy could only get him so far."

Gus took over the story. "Everyone loved and looked up to Tommy. He was a year or two older than most of us, so it didn't chafe as much, it was just accepted that he was the one to beat. But, when you're a young, arrogant boy and are being shown up by a small, slip of a girl without the pedigree, well—it didn't go over well for some of the legacy boys."

Harper absently reached for Gus's pie with her own fork.

Gus rolled his eyes in acceptance at her stealing his pie, then added, "It got worse once Harper's dad and some others in the industry saw her talent. She caught the eye of people like Wild Bill who began watching and coaching her. You get Wild Bill's attention, you get a lot of people talking."

I had to be missing something.

"What about CJ's parents? Where are they in all this?"

Harper and Gus caught each other's eyes.

"CJ's mom ran off with another man when she was young. Eventually died in a motorcycle accident." Harper ate a piece of pie. "Her dad was a drunk. He was a talented driver when he was younger, but he got blackballed for being an alcoholic and showing up to the track drunk one too many times. Eventually, he died in a bar fight. My family stepped in and she's been with us in all but name."

"But your brother hates her, and your father just overlooked her and hired me," I said, putting it together while thinking aloud. The weight of what was going on with CJ and with the Merricks more apparent. Jesus, why the hell was I here?

Silence.

Harper's head fell slightly and her eyes unfocused as she absently played with her fork. "Yeah. But I'm sure my father had his reasons. He isn't a man who does things without a reason."

"That's still a shitty move for someone she thinks of as family." I knew what it felt like to realize family loyalty only stretched so far.

Gus cut in, "Piece of advice, because I can tell you're trying to be a good guy and you were just dropped in the middle of this. CJ catches wind of any pity from you, and you will be cut off at the knees. Use this piece of information against her, and I will cut you off at the balls."

"So noted." These people respected her, and I would respect that.

CJ returned with a piece of chocolate pie on her plate, she but pulled up short when she noted the solemnity of the table and everyone throwing furtive glances toward her.

"Is there something wrong with my pie?" It was the first time I heard her Southern twang.

I studied her concerned expression before quickly digging my fork into the chocolate pie Andy put in front of me.

I wasn't giving much thought to eating it, just doing it to ease her worry. But when the chocolate sweetness smoothly awakened my taste buds. I fell back in my chair, closed my eyes in bliss and groaned—loudly. "Oh my God...CJ."

When I settled back down to Earth and focused on CJ, she resembled a virgin at a *Magic Mike* show. Her cheeks were crimson and her eyes as wide as saucers. The silence was thick among those at the table as their eyes bounced between us.

Sass tried valiantly to hold it in, but the laugh burst from him.

Harper's followed. Gus covertly studied CJ out of the corner of his eye and then glared at me.

What did I do?

Harper gave me a knowing smile—well, maybe the groan was a bit much.

"What?" I asked. "This pie is amazing!"

CJ seemed to have trouble swallowing.

"You okay over there, CJ?" Harper said. "Gus, you may want to give CJ some breathing room. I think it's been awhile since she's heard a man groan her name."

If it were possible, I think CJ turned even more red. That was until she picked up the plate of pie as if she were going to throw it at Harper. Gus caught her arm and took the plate.

"Easy, killer," Gus whispered. "No need to waste good pie."

CJ—she actually began to smile. First at Harper, then Gus, and then at me. I was trapped. Her smile was everything. It transformed her and mesmerized me. Her face softened, her eyes brightened, her lips…God, her lips…

CJ's body began to shake. She was laughing and it was as if the heavens opened.

It was beautiful.

I did that—even if it was unintentional. I made her laugh. It was the best rush I'd had in…awhile. It was better than when I opened up the engine and slingshotted through the first banked turn.

I wanted to do it again.

Harper and CJ had the entire table laughing. I joined in.

I felt at home with these people. I just met them yesterday, and already I was at home with them.

In all honesty, some of them probably would hate me by the end of the season—including the captivating, complex woman whose laugh I was fixated on.

But tonight, the cool, spring, lake weather in the dimming evening, surrounded by people who genuinely liked each other and who seemed like family—I wanted to be part of it.

Gus's head popped up, he stood and was directed to the house. I turned to see what caught his attention just as he tapped Sass on the shoulder in silent command and began swiftly, with purpose, striding toward the side of the house.

A silence fell over the otherwise boisterous group, broken by an anonymous, "Aw, shit."

I glanced over the table to catch a clue about the shift in the atmosphere, as Harper struggled to stand while grabbing ahold of CJ's hand.

"CJ, don't. Let Gus handle it," she said with a low, firm tone.

Through the tree-lined pathway from the side of the house, a man appeared, followed by

two others.

# 10

## *CJ*

Dewey Dupree and two of his minions walked into Merrick's back-yard as if they were family invited over for the reunion.

"Well, hey, everyone. Sorry to drop by unannounced. I wasn't aware you were having a get-together." Dewey's face was delighted to be crashing this party. The more attention he derived, and more people who gathered around him, the wider his smile grew.

"Sonofabitch—" someone muttered. I stood, pushing back my chair so hard it tipped over. He was here to start shit. This wasn't a casual social call. He wanted to ruffle my feathers before tomor-row...and I wanted to pluck out each one of his. But for now, I would go tell him where he could stick them.

Gus and Sass were already walking his way as Harper grabbed my arm. "Don't give him the satisfaction. That's why he's here. He wants the confrontation with you," she growled. "Don't let him goad you."

"What the hell is going on?" Grady came over to Harper. "Is that Dewey Dupree?"

"Yes, guess he's come to wish me good luck." I sneered, but I snatched my arm out of Harper's grip. I knew she was right, but I didn't have to like it.

Grady stared over to where Gus and Sass joined Bill and some other men to meet Dewey and his crew before they could get farther into the gathering. Junior was practically running out from the house to intercept all of them.

"What are you doing here?" Gus continued walking toward Dewey and didn't seem to slow down the closer he got to him. Dewey took a half step back before realizing his submission and stiffened his stance.

"Was driving by, thought I'd stop…wish everyone luck. Talk a little shop with Junior." He leaned around Gus and spotted Junior, "Hey, Junior, how's it going?" The air of gentility was so ill-fitting on Dewey, it was hard to watch. "Wanted to talk about this new scheme you guys have going." He stepped around Gus and over to Junior.

Merrick and Violet joined them. "Hello, Dewey, what can we do for you?"

"Hey there, Mr. Merrick, Ms. Violet. Beautiful night for a barbeque."

"Yes, it is. What do you want?" Merrick repeated. He didn't invite him to join us, which is what most families would do.

"Oh, well, I will be out of your hair in no time, just need a quick word with your son."

Dewey stuck his hands in the pockets of his shorts, and even though Grady often did the same, on Dewey it didn't produce the same air of confidence.

Junior motioned to the house. "Hey, man. Uh, why don't we go in the house and I'll get us a drink or something?"

"Nah, no need. I can see you're entertaining, and I won't take up that much of your time." He searched the crowd until he found me. His expression changed, and gentility morphed into calculated triumph, as he turned to face the crowd to make sure his voice carried.

Grady and Harper flanked either side of me. I wasn't sure if it was to protect me or to restrain me from charging Dewey. Since

Grady didn't know the situation, I think he was just there to watch the show.

Nevertheless, it was a nice feeling to have both my sides covered.

But I couldn't have others protecting me, and I stepped forward just as Dewey locked his evil scowl on me and sneered. "I just came to congratulate you, Junior, on an ingenious plan to change the direction of Merrick's team."

"Here we go," Harper muttered.

Dewey glanced at Junior, perpetuating the ruse that he was there to speak with only Junior and congratulate him.

Then he looked back at me. "What a perfect way to finally test CJ. No offense, Mr. Merrick, you've always had a soft heart for the girl, but putting her in this position to finally prove herself based strictly on her performance is a very fair proposal."

The mumbled words from those around me coated the air. I crossed my arms, cocked a hip, and pursed my lips. "Don't give him the satisfaction of a response." I glanced to my right to realize it was Grady, not Harper, giving me the advice.

Ha.

Poor Grady didn't know me, yet—I couldn't possibly let this go. I practically burst with the anticipation I had in unleashing myself. "Darling dim-witted Dewey, are you telling me that you drove your ass out here the night before you're supposed to leave for Bristol to interrupt a family barbeque just to impart your wisdom and approval on a team that has always had a better record than you, regardless of the driver? "

Silence reigned, as Dewey's egotistical smile turned sour.

"Dewey, I honestly don't get you." I raised my voice so everyone —even the people in boats on the lake—could hear us. I let my arms fall in confusion. "Let's forget about the fact that you have never, ever beaten me—ever. Put that aside." I motioned as if I physically put that fact in a box and set it aside. "If I'm such a bad driver, why wouldn't you want me leading this team? Then, suppos-edly, you may actually have a chance at beating Merrick."

He practically flew down to get in my face, and Grady was there before Gus and the boys could catch up.

I didn't flinch at his sudden closeness. He blinked.

I just won. He knew it. I knew it.

Harper pulled me back out of his reach. But I leaned forward and pretended to whisper—making sure I was still loud enough for everyone to hear and damage to his ego even more. "Because you see, Dewey, wasting your time the night before you leave for a race, to stir up shit like a high school bully, isn't just juvenile, it really isn't the best strategy." He wrestled, trying to get away from the guys holding him. "And, even if Grady beat me, and I lost this so-called contest, which you claim is a given, there is no way in hell you'd ever beat this guy." I motioned at Grady. I placed one hand on my hip and scratched my head with the other one. "So, I'm really confused as to what your purpose is in being here."

"You worthless, trashy whore!" Dewey was being dragged up the lawn by his two friends, followed by Sass and a few others.

"And now we're back to the name calling. So mature..." I rolled my eyes at his lack of comeback.

"Give me a reason, Dewey..." Gus said, clenching his fists, the way we both did before we let them take over. "If your daddy had a sub driver this weekend, his car may actually finish the race this time."

"Fuck you, Quinn. Did you fuck her yet? Did Tommy know about how you wanted a piece of that—"

Bam. One right hook from Gus, and Dewey went down.

Dewey the demented ass, got up and laughed. "That just cost you your crew chief this weekend," he announced to the crowd through what appeared to be a busted lip. "I'm filing charges for assault. Expect a police officer in the next hour."

"Get him the hell out of here," Merrick growled at the men around him.

# 11

---

*Grady*

Cooper came up next to me and said, "Damn. Well, tonight became more interesting than I anticipated."

I nodded toward the bob of red hair parting the sea of people. "I don't think it's over."

"Dewey Dupree, what hell have you brought down on my brother's house? Do I need to call your mama?" A disembodied voice came from inside the crowd.

Sadie Mae Merrick-Thompson, whom I'd been introduced to briefly as Merrick's sister and Harper's aunt, burst onto the scene like a modern-day Fury from Greek mythology.

She marched up to the boy, because that is what he appeared to be even if she was almost a foot shorter than him. "Ms. Sadie. Ma'am, I wasn't aware you were here."

"Why wouldn't I be here? It's my brother's home. And it's my granddaughter's best friend—a girl I think of as a niece—you're attacking. My question is, why are you here, boy?" She was in his face. Up against his chest, straining her head upward, but prepared to take him down.

He was like a deer in the headlights.

"Is it wrong that I'm having flashbacks to elementary school right now?" Cooper whispered to me.

"Fourth grade, when Robbie Stillman got yelled at by Principal Benton in front of the whole school and was never heard from again? Yeah."

"She scares me a bit," Cooper added softly. And I thought the conversation was quiet enough to be between us—I was wrong.

"Aunt Sadie can be terrifying because she's ruthless. You don't want her disappointed in you—let alone mad. And you definitely don't want her thinking you're threatening her friends or family." Harper leaned between us.

"So noted," I said, not taking my eyes off the scene.

Merrick stepped up behind his sister, putting his hand on her shoulder. I was unsure if it was to protect her or to protect Dewey from her.

"You came here to cause a ruckus, call my CJ names, and when Gus rightfully shut you up, and you act like a pansy ass and want to call the police. Well, let me tell you something…" She pulled out her phone. Pushed a few buttons and started the playback on a recording. "You call the police and this recording is going to the media so they can see what a pansy ass you really are, and how CJ handed you your balls without even laying a hand on you.

"There won't be police or any more of this drama. Dewey Dupree, get home. I swear to Christ, I will call your daddy. You gonna come in here acting like a child, I will treat you like one. Boys, please see him and his friends to their car without any delay."

Dewey glared at Gus, then CJ, giving her a non-verbal "this isn't over." There was buzz from the bystanders, but my attention was on CJ as she walked up to the house with Harper and Sadie.

"You ready to hit the road, man?" Cooper motioned for the front of the house.

"Yeah, let me say thank you to Violet. I'll meet you up there."

CJ was having a heated discussion with the women as Gus joined them.

## 1 2

### CJ

I swear, God and the Fates were conspiring against me, and I would love to know what the hell I did to piss them off. Not only did I have to prove myself a better driver than this golden-god Indy champion, I had to check my temper with dickheads like Dewey Dupree.

While Junior Merrick might be a jealous little prick and dislike me, Dewey Dupree hated me with every narcissistic bone in his body. In his mind, I was the reason his brother died. I was the reason for all his misery and shortcomings. It was a problem that never seemed to go away.

It was the figurative salt in the gaping wound that was my memory of Tommy.

"Forget it. It's over. Let it go." Harper struggled to keep up with my fast pace as I raced to the house. I had had enough for the night. Since I was in my low-rise chucks and she was in her strappy sandals, I finally had an advantage over her long strides.

Sadie, on the other hand, was a lot faster than anyone would think. "Don't you let that little weasel get to you...don't give him that power."

I ignored their ramblings. I didn't want to talk to either of them. My anger and frustration were near the edge, and I just wanted to go be alone and simmer down.

"CJ," another familiar voice called out, and it was the straw that broke the camel's back.

I flew around at Gus as he caught up with me and I growled, "What the hell were you thinking?"

He didn't even bother to look surprised. He was annoyed and put up a hand to me. "Don't."

I had a fighting stance, one hand on my hip and the other one thrust at him. "'Stay cool, CJ'… 'Don't give him the satisfaction, CJ'…'He isn't worth it, CJ…' Always lecturing me on how I shouldn't let Dewey get the best of me, not to give him ammunition. And what do you do? Swing in like I needed my honor defended and punch him. Set yourself up for assault charges the night before a race. He probably came here just to get just that reaction from me or you, jackass."

Gus contritely held his head down. "I know."

"Then why the hell did you do it?"

He opened his mouth, wouldn't make eye contact, and looked up to the darkening sky. "He...Tommy...Tommy wouldn't have wanted him saying those things about you—"

I let it out—the words exploded on Gus. "Oh, give me a break. This isn't about Tommy anymore—for either one of you. It hasn't been for a long time, so stop using him as an excuse. It's about ego and pride. Stop trying to be my savior—I don't need a freaking savior." Tommy knew that. He understood.

I pointed at the front yard and practically screamed. "I need that asshole to leave me the fuck alone. He won't do that if we keep giving him the attention he craves." The purge of frustration over, I stepped back and noticed the remaining people watching, taking in a deep breath.

Grady was the first I locked eyes with—they entranced me for a moment as I tried to read them. But they were unreadable. There wasn't the devil-may-care expression I'd become used to. It held more pity than jovial charm. Damnit. I didn't like it. "What the hell is your problem, McBane?"

He was stunned when I turned my attention to him and quickly held up a hand in defense, "Nothing. Just wanted...um, to make sure you were okay."

That stirred my anger up again. I hated pity. More than disrespect.

"Okay? Why would you want to see if I was okay, McBane?"

Harper whispered, "CJ," as a warning to dial it back and not focus my vitriol on him.

Too late.

His head cocked to the side and his stunned expression morphed to confusion and a twinge of defensiveness. "I was just trying to be nice. Be friendly."

"McBane, we aren't friends, we're competitors. My friends think I need to be saved. You think I will be defeated. You're both wrong. I just need to do my job and get the hell out of here." I stomped off and was frustrated how far I still had to walk to get back to the house, wishing I had a door to slam or something.

I was still within earshot when I heard Harper toss out, "Welcome to the team, boys."

# 13

---

## *Grady*

"Maybe showing up here was a mistake," I said to Cooper, as we walked around the infield at Bristol race track.

"We're contractually obligated to be at each race. Even if you aren't the one in the car." He strode next to me, but his focus was on his phone, responding to a text.

Nonetheless, after the scene at Merrick's, I felt like the unwelcome distant relative at the family reunion—you were expected to show up, but no one really knew what to do with you. CJ's boyfriend had been Dewey Dupree's dead brother. CJ was the pseudo-adopted daughter of the Merrick family. I was there trying to destroy CJ's dream. It was a real-life drama, and it appeared I had been cast as one of the villains and it didn't sit well.

"I feel like I'm crashing a party or something." Two teenagers walked by gawking, unsure with my mirrored aviators and baseball cap if it was really me. It amazed me how much camouflage two items could gain me. Enough to cast doubt when I walked fast enough, I was rarely stopped—at least not in the Bristol infield. If we were at an Indy race or another open-wheel race, it may be another story, but for now, I enjoyed my partial-anonymity.

We were walking to Merrick Motorsports trailers to see who was around after the drivers' meeting. I probably should've gone and observed what was discussed, but I was trying to give CJ her space and not appear to be homing in on her day.

"You're just as much part of that team as she is," Cooper said, without looking up or breaking stride. "A few more weeks of practice, and you will be the one in the gear and she will be the one walking around the infield."

"She'll probably just sit in the pit box and sneer at me when it's my turn." I adjusted my hat and ran my hand through my hair.

"Does it matter?" He finally finished his text and slipped his phone in his pocket.

I shrugged. I guess it didn't. As we approached the team trailers and RVs, Harper walked out of one of them, dressed in light pants and a light blouse, stylish and professional even on a warm spring Tennessee day in the infield of a racetrack. She leaned back into the RV and shouted, "Shake your tailfeathers, girl. We got to go!"

Cooper and I stepped up behind her with our backs to the RV under the awning.

"How's it going, Harper?" Cooper greeted her, and Harper gave us her Scarlett O'Hara smile—the one that always left me wondering how sincere she was toward us.

"Hello, gentlemen! Didn't think we'd see you around here."

"Just getting the lay of the land," I said, putting my hands in my pockets. "Where is the lady of the hour? Powdering her nose?"

Open mouth, insert foot. I was such an ass.

But this woman had me so screwed up. I didn't know what I was doing or saying when it came to CJ Lomax. I wasn't used to women disliking me, and yes, I knew how egotistical it sounded, even in my head.

As soon as the words did a swan dive off my tongue, I knew it.

Harper's Scarlett O'Hara smile morphed into the pity given to a man walking to the gallows, and it was all I needed to prove my suspicion.

CJ was right behind me.

"Nice move…" Cooper whispered. *Yeah, thanks, asshole, for the heads up* was in the glare I shot him.

I hung my head in resignation, studied my shoes, and rubbed the back of my neck.

"How's it going…um…CJ?" It was on my tongue to add honey, or sweetheart, or tiger, or some other type of endearment that in the past helped women warm up to me.

But the manual didn't seem to apply when it came to CJ. I pivoted on my heels to meet my punishment.

CJ was in her race suit, which was unzipped and tied around her waist by the arms, with a plain white T-shirt underneath that had MMS emblazoned on it, repping Merrick Motorsports.

Her hair was in a tight, low ponytail and she had aviators perched on her head. Even with the unimpressed expression she shot me, my body came alive. There was nothing remotely feminine or overtly sexy about what she wore, but she was captivating.

The T-shirt was fitted enough that I could see the swell of her breasts, her hair pulled back so I could see the curve of her neck. Without make-up, I could see the flush on her cheeks—was that from the heat or from me being here? She in her race gear had the same effect as seeing her in her stilettos that first time at the bar.

She studied me as if I were out of place. "McBane." She pulled down her aviators to shield her eyes and began walking. Gone was any chance of studying her further without being more obvious.

"Hi, CJ, what's going on?" *Really, that's what you open up with? What's going on? Brilliant, Grady—asshole.*

Man, I'm so off my game. I don't know if it's this city, or if it's this woman.

"I was just strapping on my balls since there seems to be a rule you need some in order to drive a car." Then she gestured over her shoulder, and a look of pure sincerity flashed over her face. "I have an extra set in the RV, if you'd like to borrow some…they may be a bit small for that ego of yours, but they're probably better than nothing, right?"

Cooper laughed, not bothering to restrain himself.

I didn't hold back my smile—because I deserved it.

"Again, what are you doing here, McBane?" Satisfied with her jab and the reaction it received, CJ took the hat Harper handed her and strode forward.

Her purposeful stride did nothing to rein in my imagination, thinking about the body she had under that suit. She was petite, but her smaller body seemed unable to contain all that was CJ. Her energy, drive, presence—and I would suspect her desire. I'd seen how toned her legs were in the skirt from the first night I met her. I knew the strength and athleticism it took to control a stock car for hours on end, I could use my imagination with the rest.

Man, my imagination was going to keep me up at night, as I wondered if she surrendered all that control, or if she demanded it.

Given how I ran to fall into step beside her, I tried not to see that as an example of how I would be with her in bed. Because, damn— I was chasing the woman. I don't chase.

*Slow your roll, McBane.*

Two of her steps equaled one of mine, so I was able to walk at a casual pace to her determined one. "Just came to see how it's done. You know, watch and learn…" I said.

Even now, she competed to put the smallest bit of distance between us. Yes, I noticed her watching us step for step.

I would have fun with her.

"Where to now?" I asked and grabbed at the hat she carried. Prince Automotive. Prince Automotive meant Chase Dermott—the man who was partially responsible for me being here. The hat burned my hand.

Since CJ had her race suit tied up around her waist, I hadn't seen the sponsor emblem on it. I turned enough to show the hat to Cooper, who walked behind CJ. Cooper grimaced in agreement— this wasn't good news.

This was a deal made with CJ specifically. I wasn't part of this. No way Dermott was going to sponsor me. Dermott was going to sponsor CJ, tease Merrick with his money, and at the end of the season threaten to pull out if they used me full time. Dermott and I were bad blood. Everyone in the open-wheel circuit knew it. It wouldn't take much to find out why. In fact, I'm sure Merrick already knew.

I doubt Dermott told him his fiancée carried on a duplicitous affair with me and that he set out to demolish what was left of my career. In all fairness, I didn't know she was engaged—and she pursued me. When the scandal blew up, it didn't help the fact that the woman was also the daughter of a prominent family in the industry, and they weren't happy with the damage to her reputation, or their family name.

It just further cemented the issues I had with my family. "Grow the fuck up, then we will talk about being treated like an adult." That led to the beginning of the end of my time with McBane Racing. It was downhill from there.

CJ tore the hat out of my hands and I readily let it go. "Last minute photo ops on the way to time trials," she explained.

"So, Prince Automotive, huh?" I commented over my shoulder to Harper, who I knew would be more talkative on the subject.

"Yeah, what about it?" CJ placed the hat on her head, threading her ponytail through the back.

"Guess Dermott made you an offer you couldn't refuse?" I fished.

I didn't have to look close to see the scowl as her answer.

"You could say that," Harper answered for her.

"Grady!" Junior strode over with the excitement of a socialite with a juicy piece of gossip. "I'm glad I caught you. I needed to update you on the latest." He gave his sister and CJ a glance and a smirk, his lack of telling them to go to hell meant he wanted them to hear, and that they would be unhappy with his news.

After an appropriate amount of time to ensure all eyes were on him, he widened his stance, crossed his arms, and announced, "Mingle Singles has agreed to sponsor you full time for the remainder of the season."

"Okay, well, that's good news," I said, glancing at Harper and CJ for a clue as to why this should be earth-shattering.

"Of course, they will sponsor them, idiot." Harper rolled her eyes at her brother. "They've been CJ's sponsors in the Energy Blast circuit for the last two years."

His smile grew to mimic a cat with a mouse in hand. "Yes, but they aren't sponsoring CJ—they're only sponsoring Grady. Effective immediately, they've dropped CJ, and their contract is exclusive to Grady's races only."

Oh. Boy.

"What the hell!" Harper walked up as if to strike her older brother. He wisely took a step back.

CJ's face was stricken. Her gaze flew from Junior's and settled accusingly on me.

My hands went up defensively. "I had nothing to do with this. I don't even know who the Mingle Singles people are," I said.

Her mouth tightened. Her brow drew down. If it were possible for lasers to shoot out of her eyes, I'd be a dead man. "I should've expected this to happen," she whispered to herself.

She straightened her spine, threw back her shoulders, and grabbed Harper by the elbow. "Don't give him the satisfaction, Harper. There are others. Let the weasels have their small victory. Mine will be on the track where it matters. When I get the wins, Mingle Singles and all the other doubters will be back."

"Go crawl back under the rock you came from, *brother*. I wasn't aware we were playing that way. But if the rules are, there are no rules—fine. Just don't go crying to Daddy when I beat you at your own game." Harper turned on her heel, locked arms with CJ, and the Mutt-and-Jeff pair began to walk off.

Not wanting to stick around with Junior, who was appeared less appealing to work with, I followed Harper and CJ like a puppy dog wishing for redemption.

"I really didn't have anything to do with this. I wasn't even aware that we were going after separate sponsors."

"I wasn't either—until now," Harper said, but didn't stop walking. "But now that I know the gloves are off, we have somewhere to be, Grady, so we will catch up with you later."

"You're going to Prince?" I ran in front of them and started to walk backwards, trying to engage them and get them to stop for a moment.

I was forgotten as Harper began walking around me and pulled out a clipboard—yes, she carried a clipboard. I didn't know anyone did that anymore. "So, Dermott has some executives for you to meet, shake hands with, take photos, etc., and then you have to head over for the drivers' meeting with Bill." Harper slipped the clipboard in her oversized shoulder bag and continued, keeping pace with all three of us in her small heels. "Did you say something, Grady?"

"Prince Automotive?" Cooper answered for me as he caught up with us.

"Oh, yeah," she said, directing us over to the large tent with the Prince Automotive logo emblazoned on it. "They were very eager to work with CJ." She gave CJ a conspiratorial smile as she emphasized her name.

"Junior will be responsible for lining up sponsors for your races, I'll be responsible for CJ's. Looks like this contest will be between me and Junior, as well. Sorry about that, Grady." Her smile indicated she wasn't at all sorry.

CJ finally stopped and turned to me without expression. "I have work to do, Grady. Why don't you go see what other sponsors of mine you can steal, while I try to focus on my race." She turned on a dime and strode into the Prince tent.

I held up a hand, stopping Cooper before he walked into Prince's tent. It was like crossing the no-fly zone. No sense in stirring the pot any further.

Harper and CJ caught our abrupt halt.

"You ladies have a good afternoon and, CJ, good luck today. I will watch and learn." I saluted her with a smile and hoped it came off as sincere with just enough mock to tease.

She slipped on the sleeves of her race suit, gearing up for her presentation, but through the aviators, I saw the furrowed brow.

She wasn't sure what to make of me either. Well, good. That made two of us.

# 14

## *CJ*

Grady texted me after our teams favorable qualifying time—favorable enough to put us in one of the top five starting positions. Not sure how he got my cell number, and not sure how I felt about him having it, I gave my phone to Harper for the rest of the day, not wanting to think about it anymore.

Also, wasn't sure how to respond to his comment. So, I didn't.

I worked on focusing and getting my head in the game.

Even after years of attending the pre-race drivers' meetings, a mandatory meeting given by race officials for the drivers and crew, it took a conscious effort not to bow under the scrutiny while walking in the door. On the outside, I railed against the stereotype I openly defied, while on the inside a small part of me still felt I was a little girl trying to prove I belonged with the big dogs.

The sharks in these waters smelled the blood of my doubt. Nonetheless, I searched out each competitor I knew who put a target on my back. It wasn't all forty-two drivers, just a handful I had to make a point of looking square in the eye, so they didn't think they intimidated me.

At least Grady wasn't in here to further ruffle my feathers.

With my other senses coming online, I took in the cacophony of voices and sensed Bill still behind me.

At this level of racing, I was a rookie. I was essentially a substitute driver working with a new crew, not a veteran team. But I was coming in with one of the fastest qualifying times in the field. That was enough to keep my name flying through the air.

My own personal pain-in-the-ass, Dewey, and his crew sat to the right, in a semi-circle like a schoolyard bully.

He snickered when he spotted me.

Seriously, he snickered.

It was as if he'd never been run off the Merrick property with his tail between his legs. He was just going to keep going at it.

Let them stare. Let him glower.

I was fully clothed. I wasn't standing in front of a room full of bullies in nothing but my underwear.

"Don't," Bill whispered to me, his mustache camouflaging his lips from moving. "Don't get into it with him."

"Oh, I'm cool," I said, and dismissed Dewey as an afterthought.

We found our seats.

"He'll be too far behind in the pack for me to have to worry about him anyway," I said, making a point to focus straight ahead. Bill threw a look back over at Dewey.

"Keep your guard up with him. He may be playing the cool cat, but he's madder than a hatter, and that usually spells trouble for you," Bill said, as the officials came in and we found some seats.

I shrugged. "This isn't kids go-karts anymore. He'd be a fool to mess with me on such a large stage. Not with so much at stake. He hasn't been running well. He doesn't have the clout here to mess with me."

"Daddy's pockets run deep. He can get away with almost anything here. Watch your back. Don't need this car messed with because that little shit wants to act like a little shit. Just stay clear of him."

"Yep." I nodded. He had a point. Time to grow up and let Dewey continue to act like a child.

"Hey, CJ!" Brian Hines, Merrick's other team's driver, joined us. Brian was a good guy. Newly married with a young, pregnant wife, he'd always been a gentleman and kind to me. "You've got some tongues wagging." His smile was genuine as he held out his hand for me to shake.

"I hadn't had a chance to talk with you since everything had been announced," Brian said. His handshakes were good, solid, and firm—sincere with respect. None of this weak, limp hand crap that you would give when you shake hands with your dog. I hated that.

He and I walked outside, while Bill held back talking with some other drivers and chiefs. "Right as rain. How's your better half?"

"She's fine," he said, but turned back to me, concern etched on his face. He dropped his voice, "You did great this morning, don't know what Merrick was thinking with this dog and pony show. We all think you should've been given the rest of Trent's season."

Pity.

Great.

That was pity in his eyes.

It was worse than Dewey's contempt.

Contempt I knew what to do with.

Pity—ugh.

Brian meant well and was trying to offer support, but still.

I waved him off. "It's fine. I always do my best when doubted."

That made him smile, "I'm sure you will give them hell. Just let me know what you need from me. I've met Grady, and he seems like a nice-enough guy, but you deserve this break and you definitely belong in that seat." He glared over my shoulder. "No matter what obstacles you face. Don't doubt it."

"Thanks, Brian," I said, knowing whoever was coming up behind me wasn't welcome.

"Brian, my man, how's that lovely wife of yours," Dewey said.

Brian gritted his teeth but managed a polite smile. "She's good, thank you for asking." Brian turned to me. "CJ, want to catch a ride back to the garage with me?"

"That's okay, Brian." He was such a gentleman.

I'd be damned if Dewey ran me off. He obviously came to stir some shit. Let's get it over with. I rolled my eyes. "I'm supposed to meet Harper here, we have another meet and greet before I can suit up."

He studied Dewey with a warning in his eye. "Have a good race, and I'll catch you later." I nodded at him.

"You, too." He nodded back. "Dewey," he said as way of departing, but noticeably not wishing him luck.

"What do you want, Dewey?" I went for polite indifference, but I could never pull it off—I'm sure my annoyance glared through.

"You," he emphasized the word, "don't even deserve to be sitting in that seat."

Normally this barb would wound, but not today. "Well, from how you've been driving, it doesn't appear you deserve to be sitting in that seat either."

He towered over me, grabbing my arm before I jerked it away from him.

A few race fans walked by, noticed us, and made their way over. Dewey loved adoration and plastered on his fake public persona. For my ears only, he gritted out, "You're such a bitch. I don't know why my brother ever wasted his life on you."

"Have a good race, Dewey." I walked away, ignoring his attempt to throw me off my game. He knew where to hit me. And I knew where to hit back—I threw over my shoulder loud enough for the fans to hear, "Try to keep up."

## 15

**Grady**

CJ jumped out of the car, sweaty, her face flushed, clearly drained, but cool and composed. I stepped closer, wanting to congratulate her, and stopped myself.

Harper handed her a sponsor's hat and another sponsor's drink to take a swig of while the cameras and reporters approached her for the post-race interviews. She wasn't the winner, she was just shy of the top five, but it was her first race, and with the attention our side competition had drummed up, she was the notable underdog.

I held back in the crowd with my hat lowered, not wanting to draw attention. With her head held high, back straight, legs braced apart, she spoke with the right amount of pride in her team, giving an analytical breakdown of her performance, and just enough confidence to show she wasn't surprised by the outcome. She thanked the reporters and they moved on.

Harper gave CJ a side hug. "You're such a rock star!" Harper kissed her on the cheek. For a moment, CJ's façade dropped, and her true pride and excitement peeked through.

Harper turned to me, "Isn't she a rock star, Grady?"

CJ leaned around Harper and we locked eyes. There was a hint of the devil in her glance with just the right amount of sass in her smirk.

I nodded once. "She's something."

CJ ignored me and nudged me in the stomach with her elbow as she walked by. I swear she put an extra sway in her hips as if she knew I was watching them—because damnit, I was.

Confidence was hot. Sassiness in a woman was hot. Both thrown at me, subtly or blatantly, had become my new kryptonite. I never saw it coming. Then again, I never could have seen her coming either.

While I was at a loss for words, my brain told me her skill and attitude were bad news for me, and my hormones didn't give a damn, I couldn't take my eyes off her.

---

The following Monday, Gus had arranged for me to get some track time at Charlotte. The more time I had behind the wheel, the better. I'd been in a stock car before, but making the jump from open wheel to stock car was like going from a sleek thoroughbred to a war horse.

The Indy car was a sleek, one-seat, open-wheel vehicle designed for turbo speed on smooth surfaces. The stock car's history came from bootleg running moonshine on back roads. The cars were, by design, heavier and made to take a beating. When you were in a stock car, you were on a battlefield. When you were in an Indy car, you were flying.

While I was getting used to the feel of the war horse, my lack of experience with the other combatants on the track was going to be my weakness. Studying films and talking it over with Gus and the other members of the team wasn't going to prepare me for the experience of being knocked around like a pinball doing around one-hundred-and-fifty to two-hundred mph on the track.

At least my first race with this team would be a familiar course, just in an unfamiliar car. I'd raced at Sonoma in an open-wheel car numerous times, but being in this behemoth, I might as well be a virgin.

Charlotte was a ghost town in the cool, early morning. They opened part of the road course that was intertwined and woven around inside Charlotte's traditional oval course so I could get some practice on it.

Secretly, I was relieved CJ wasn't around that morning with the other team members who were setting up the car. Not that I was feeling self-conscious, but I didn't need the added pressure of having her there reminding me of how well she did in last weekend's race.

I jumped in my gear while they got the car to the track.

Insecurity wasn't something I was familiar with. It sucked, actually. But after watching one of the last week's post-race analysis programs on a sports station, newfound insecurities were gnawing at me.

One commentator commented after CJ's remarkable weekend and my inexperience with this down-and-dirty kind of racing, "I'm not even sure if this is a fair competition."

Ouch.

Of course, then another asshole, washed-up retired driver who was a hack at commentating had to put in his two cents. "CJ Lomax is a gimmick. She's good for sparking life into the promotion of the sport, pulling in more women fans, but she's not experienced enough for this level of competition."

Another bitter guy who never made it far in the Cup series was quick to jump on the dissing the CJ Lomax bandwagon. "Yeah, it's a shame such a tactic takes a seat away from a more deserving driver just so they can pull in new sponsorships. I don't know what's happening to the sport when marketing means more than racing."

I know it should make me feel better, two out of three of them felt that I had a better chance. But that wasn't what they were saying. They were saying that CJ wasn't fit to be driving because she was a woman, and having her drive was a gimmick.

Clearly, by how she finished, it wasn't a gimmick.

And now, even I was defending her.

I had to rethink my concerns. I wasn't going to be the bad guy and I was going to be lumped together with assholes like these guys who sounded like washed-up sexist pigs. I didn't need these guys in my corner.

Clearly, CJ couldn't have gotten to where she was, couldn't have won races in the Energy Blast circuit or done as well as she did last weekend, if she was just a marketing gimmick. How couldn't they see that?

But Jesus, how could I go out there and defend her? If I went out there and shouted all her accomplishments and praises, wouldn't I be shooting myself in the foot—making my lack of experience in this circuit even more obvious?

Speculation as to the reason for Merrick's course of action was starting to grate on me. Add to that the numerous calls I refused to take from my brother and I really, really wanted to take a long walk off a short bridge…my mood was a bit on edge.

"Alright, Grady, let's see what you're made of. Give it a few runs to warm up the tires. Let us know how she's feeling—just like we talked about." Gus's early morning Carolina accent was heavy over the headset.

"You got it." I blocked out everything else and pulled out on the track. I revved the eight-hundred-horsepower engine and let it bring me to life.

---

It was over before I wanted it to be—it always was. I drove the car into the garage reassured and confident in my ability to communicate with Gus how the car was performing. The communication between the spotter, Aaron, the chief, and the driver were paramount to a good team. There was a good rhythm with us. If we could see it through during the heat of a race, we'd be in good shape. It was a great start.

I climbed out of the car, taking in a deep breath of relief that came with a success. Bill walked over and clapped me on the back.

"Great job, Grady. We'll work on the few adjustments we discussed and run it again after lunch."

"Sounds good." I was removing my helmet and thinking about lunch when CJ walked over to the pit area where Bill was sitting. The well-worn, fitted jeans, sneakers, and old baseball hat did nothing to hide her beauty. Her dark mane in a ponytail poking through the back, swinging with her stride, made me want to reach out and wrap it around my wrist and pull her back to me.

*Get a grip, Grady.*

A small smile spread across Bill's face as he watched her approach, his gaze shifting between us, as if waiting for the fireworks to start. CJ wore aviators, but I felt the daggers she threw at me—like I was caught playing with her toy, and even though she was told to share, she was supremely pissed about it.

With her ponytail swinging dramatically, she turned her back to me, making it clear no one—especially me—was invited to whatever discussion they were going to have.

She began whispering to him as I stuck my gloves in my helmet, strode over, and placed both items on the table near Bill.

She stopped talking as soon as I approached. "So, have you taken the training wheels off yet?" she threw over her shoulder as she greeted me.

Nope, not taking the bait.

"Good afternoon, CJ," I said, unzipping my suit to roll down the top portion so I could cool off.

She still wore her sunglasses to shield her eyes from me, but I could tell by the tension around her mouth, and the angle of her head, she was looking at my chest. I had on a T-shirt with a CJ Lomax caricature wearing a crown and "Princess" emblazoned across my chest.

I didn't bother to suppress the smile.

Okay, so maybe I'd hoped she'd stop by today.

"Nice shirt." She turned back to Bill who refused to look up at her, but his shoulders were shaking. "I'll be back tomorrow, and we can work on *my* car."

"Sounds good," Bill said, still not looking up from whatever he found so intriguing.

She began walking away without saying goodbye to me. Then she called out, "Be careful that car doesn't turn into a pumpkin before I come and take over tomorrow, McBane."

───────────

Cooper was leaning against my Tesla when I walked to the back of the infield garage. His arms were crossed, his broad shoulders drooped, and his auburn hair was down across his face so I couldn't see the expression he wore. No need, I wasn't going to like what he had to tell me.

Crap.

"This morning was the first time I was back in a race car in months, Coop, the longest I've gone since I was fourteen, and it felt fucking fantastic." I threw my head back and held my hands up to the sky in predicted aggravation. "I even managed to ruffle CJ's feathers today. Why are you going to go and ruin it for me?"

Cooper took in a deep breath, ran his hand over his face, and pinched his eyes. "Grady, there is no easy way to tell you…"

My stomach dropped, and I straightened. "What. What is it?"

A driver's side door opened on a black Mercedes that was parked on the other side of my Tesla. I didn't immediately see the person who got out, but by the pained expression on Cooper's face, I took a better look. I saw the top of familiar mahogany hair on a head too short to completely clear the top of the roof.

"Grady, your mom is here," Cooper said, just as she appeared from the back of the car.

"Thanks for the timely update, buddy." Sarcasm laced my tone.

My mother was beautiful. I wasn't saying that because she was my mom. Meredith McBane was ageless, and even under the stress of my father's illness, she was still put together—on the outside. However, with the objective lens that time away had lent me, I witnessed the toll everything had taken. She was currently dressed as if she was heading to a business luncheon—designer slacks, silk shirt, and short, sling-back heels with a designer purse she had delicately draped over her arm as if it were an extension of her.

She walked over to me and stood still, taking me in from head to toe—hip cocked, arms crossed, expressionless. My mom was almost a foot shorter than me, and I had to look down at her.

"Mom. What are you doing here?" The tone of my voice cracked like a pubescent boy after being caught doing something wrong.

"Well, son, it's good to see you, too." She raised an eyebrow to me.

I stepped over to her, holding her hand. "That's not what I mean…I meant…you've surprised me. Is everything okay? I mean…does Dad know you're here?"

"Everything is fine. Cal and Vanessa are keeping him occupied while I'm down here. Now come here." My mom's emotional track switched, and she opened her arms, wrapping me up, squeezing me as tight as she did when I was small enough to fit in her lap. "I miss you," she said aloud, with so much warmth, the guilt speared me as I held her.

I kissed the top of her head. "I miss you, too. But why are you here? Do they know you are down here?"

She pulled back and nodded. She was blinking fast, sniffing slightly and trying to hide the fact that her eyes were misty. She waved dismissively at me. "Your father is fine. Fine. Just fine." It was one too many fines. "Just thought I should look in on you."

Cal thought it was a good idea. Of course, he did. And Vanessa, his girlfriend, was such a "godsend"—I may want to puke. I wasn't her biggest fan and honestly, I didn't think Cal was either, which is why I didn't understand how she was even there.

"I just wanted to come down here and see what all the fuss was about." She pointed around her. "What's so important you couldn't come back home?"

Here we go. My mom didn't mince words—she got straight to the point. Still, my mother wasn't acting like herself.

I stepped back a bit farther and looked down my nose at her

with a playful smile, to try to charm her out of the lecture she flew down here to repeat in person.

Time to divert her attention. What would interest her enough to distract her?

"Mom, I forgot how beautiful you are. This Carolina sun becomes you. You're just in time. Cooper and I were going to go look at lakefront houses after my practice was over. Do you want to go with us?"

"Houses? You're buying a house down here? Grady, you don't even have the job yet. Isn't it too soon to think about buying a house? Hell, you have to beat that woman first, and from what I saw last week, it isn't going to be as easy as you said it was—"

Okay, maybe real estate wasn't the right topic.

I girded my backside for the figurative butt smackdown I was about to get, but my mother's attention was drawn to something over my shoulder.

CJ was walking out of the garage and to her bike. She placed her helmet on the seat and was adjusting her ponytail and sunglasses.

"Is that her?" My mother broke through my CJ-induced fog. "Hello…Grady?"

"Yes, that's CJ." I turned back to my mom, but I kept my face away from her so I didn't see when she escaped my periphery and headed over to the woman in question.

Oh, God. No.

It was like watching two worlds colliding.

My feet wouldn't move. But my brain was telling my ass to get in gear because I couldn't let the two most strong-willed, opinionated, no-filter-speaking women in my life meet and not be there.

"CJ Lomax," my mother held out her hand by the time I got my ass in gear and reached them. "I'm Meredith McBane." I stood next to my mom with my hands on my hips, unsure of how to proceed or even what my mother was going to do.

CJ was struck dumb. It was almost worth the unease I was suffering. My mother offered clarification, gesturing to me, "I'm Grady's mom."

I gave CJ a rueful wave, as if she didn't know who I was.

CJ reached for my mom's hand, and a slow smile of recognition spread across her face. Not recognition of who my mother was, but recognition of what an opportunity this was for her.

Damn.

She tilted her head and offered my mother a sincere smile. "Mrs. McBane, it is a pleasure to meet you. I didn't know you were heading down here."

"Yes, well, I'm afraid I surprised Grady. I like to keep him on his toes."

"Well, it's fun to see that." CJ flashed that smile at me. "Did you get to catch any of his practice?"

"No, unfortunately, I just got here." Mom turned to me. "Are you done for the day? I thought you were going to go look at houses?"

"Oh, I'm afraid he needs much more practice," CJ said with solemnity, a bit of authority, and a slight smirk.

Mom caught the tone and cast a glance back and forth between the two of us before her eyebrows flew to her hairline. She turned her back on CJ to catch my expression, and a small smile peeked over her lips.

"Well..." my mom adjusted her purse and turned back to CJ. "I guess I could wait. I wouldn't want to interfere with his practice. From the looks of it, he will need quite a bit to keep up with you."

CJ smiled in thanks at my mom, and then narrowed her eyes, slightly assessing me and my mother's angle. She grabbed her helmet, thinking that was the end of it. "I'm off to get some lunch."

"What a great idea. I know, why don't we all go get some lunch? Cooper said you had time before your next practice, Grady. The five of us can go—CJ, since this is your town, why don't you suggest something?" She walked over to CJ, gently taking her arm, not giving her a chance to backout, and passing her helmet to me.

"Um..." CJ's eyes darted to me for a rescue. "Well, I..."

I couldn't help it, I was amused. My mom was handling CJ.

"Trust me, you don't want that guy hungry. He's a bear if his sugar drops. Of course, you may have discovered that lately.

Normally he is a pretty laid-back guy, but if you don't feed him, he tends to get a bit ornery," my mom whispered, as if this was the secret to understanding me. They walked by and I stood there with CJ's helmet in my hand. I was still in my racing suit and my afternoon had just taken a turn into the unknown.

"Go get changed, Grady. Don't keep us waiting. CJ and I will drive ahead and get to know each other. We will text you where we end up, and you and Cooper can meet us."

My mom smiled at me as she unlocked the Mercedes, opening the door for CJ in case she was confused as to where she expected her to go. CJ looked over her shoulder at me with a dash of fear and uncertainty in her eyes that quickly morphed to fury if I didn't get her out of this.

I chuckled.

"Aren't you going to go change?" Cooper said, taking CJ's helmet from my hands. I instinctively held onto it.

"Huh? Yeah, I'll go change." Not in much of a hurry, though. I enjoyed the death glares CJ was casting at me through my mom's car window. And then a sinister smile snuck up her face as my mom looked up at me.

"You do realize the longer you take to change, the more alone time CJ has with your mother?"

It clicked. And the more time my mother had with CJ.

I threw the helmet at Cooper and ran to change.

# 16

## CJ

Initially, I was a mouse cornered by a cat in Mrs. McBane's car. I couldn't for the life of me get a read on her, and I was desperate for Harper—she would've had this in hand.

Meredith McBane was engaging, at ease, and very welcoming. However, deep down, I knew I was being evaluated and measured. She asked me to call her Meredith, but addressing her with a "Ms." seemed completely unorthodox. I tried it, and she said, "CJ, please don't age me more than I already am. Let's just pretend you don't want my son back in Chicago as badly as I do."

After that it was hard for me not to admire the woman.

I drove her to a nearby café. A frazzled Grady arrived in record time, with Cooper trailing him.

After Meredith greeted them both with hugs and kisses, as if she hadn't seen them already, we all sat and ordered. Grady was extremely impatient with the staff, and his unease amused me.

"How is everything at McBane?" Cooper asked when our drinks arrived.

Meredith's face dropped slightly before she covered it. A tilt of her head gave way at the strain it took to put up the mask. "Good. Everything is going well. Cal's been assuming more responsibility lately." She glanced briefly at Grady, who looked away.

Cooper, maybe realizing his mistake in opening the can of worms, tried to backpedal and struggled for another topic.

Not knowing what to contribute, I glanced at Grady. He was leaning forward with his head down.

Meredith, seeming not to want to go down that path, changed the topic quite abruptly by turning to me.

"So, CJ, tell me. What do I need to do to get Grady back to Chicago?"

'"Mom..." Grady side-eyed her.

"Fine." She rolled her eyes. "CJ, tell me about yourself."

His mother questioned me about my history in racing—my experience, my record, my goals. She seemed to know her way around racing, in general, and asked very poignant questions. She'd assessed his reaction out of the corner of her eye when he wasn't looking. When he was staring at me. I realized the point wasn't to interrogate me, it was to prod and observe him.

Then she started touting his achievements in open-wheel and how well he'd been doing there. He blushed at her boasting as if he were a middle school Little League player.

Finally, she turned to me and laid it out.

"CJ, I'll be honest. I don't get it. I don't get why my son would leave a successful career in an industry he was dominating to go somewhere else and start over." He opened his mouth and she waved her hand away at him, preempting his well-worn argument. "Yes. Yes, I know your reasons. You, your father, and your brother are stubborn, proud men with monster egos, but with the common sense of a flea when it comes to working together. That's why you have women in your life."

She straightened, her expression all business.

"But I want to hear CJ's opinion as a driver in the industry you're trying to break into." She turned back to me. "With your experience and success in stock car, if you could keep an unbiased opinion, do you think this makes sense? Do you think my son can make a successful move to stock car?"

Mrs. McBane's—Meredith's—eyes were large, knowing, and maybe pleading with me, expecting me to prove her point. Grady was rolling his, expecting me to take her side and send him packing. Cooper was trying not to laugh at the byplay. I answered her with a complete straight face. "Well, Mrs. McBane...I think your son's chances of making the move to stock car are very good..."

My smile grew exponentially as Grady's eyebrows shot up. Mrs. McBane's drew down.

"As long as he stays out of my car and out of my way."

# 17

## CJ

The next day, I was out on the Ducati enjoying the beautiful weather on my way to visit Sassy's daughter, Daisy, who was home recovering from a broken leg. I tried to let the ride on the bike elevate my mood before seeing her.

I was flying high after my finish from the past weekend and my amusing lunch with Grady and his mother, yet it wasn't enough. Today was my birthday, and the change in mood was as if someone flipped a switch the moment I woke up.

Today was also the fifth anniversary of Tommy's death. Losing Tommy almost broke me. Usually I spent the day alone, so I didn't have to dodge anyone's attempts to keep my spirits up or those *is she okay* looks. I hated those looks.

A visit with Daisy would be just the distraction and comic relief I needed to make this day go by faster.

I pulled the bike into the driveway of the sweet Cape Cod that Sassy and his wife shared with Daisy and her older brother. I took off my helmet and jacket, stowing it in the saddle bag and taking out the latest video game I bought us to play.

"Hey, there!" Sass came out to greet me.

"Hey, Sass." I smiled at the burly man. "How's it going?"

He reached for me and gave me his Sasquatch hug that he was known for, practically lifting me off the ground. "Better now that you came to visit. Thank God, Daisy won't shut up about it. 'When's she gonna be here?' 'Is she here yet?'" He mimicked a flapping mouth with his hands. "My God, that girl can burn your ears with how much she gabs." He opened the screen door for me, and we walked in.

"Oh, Sass. Just wait, she isn't even in her teens yet."

"Daisy, CJ is here…" he announced to the house. But then to me he said, "Don't remind me."

I whispered, "You love it."

He just gave me a secret smile. Because he did. Sass loved his girl.

"Daddy! Tell her to come here!" Daisy's voice pleaded from the back of the house.

Before I walked down the hallway, Sass tugged me to him and gave me another hug, whispering, "Happy birthday, hon." He pulled back and gave me a small smile. I replied with the same small smile. Sass knew I didn't celebrate.

"Okay, then. I'll just go wait on our other guests." He disappeared out the front door.

Daisy's voice met me as I walked down the hallway. "Introducing the hottest driver on the circuit, watch out, boys, she's coming for you! CJ Lomax…" Daisy made cheering sounds from her bed.

I turned in the doorway and she was bouncing up and down from a seated position, her casted leg propped on a pillow. Her blond hair was in a messy ponytail, she wore a blue T-shirt with my logo across the chest, and a huge smile.

"Hey there, Daisy-girl," I said, and came over to give her a huge hug. "I missed you this weekend."

"Ugh, don't even get me started." She rolled her eyes and waved a hand at me.

"What did you do to yourself? What's all this?" I motioned to the leg.

Outside, a car door slammed and Sass's voice boomed, "Hey, thanks for coming."

Daisy let out a beleaguered sigh. "Boys. Boys happened." She crossed her arms. "Danny Sawyer was picking on my friend Heather at recess. After school, I was riding home on my bike and decided to make it clear that it wasn't cool."

"O-kay, did he break your leg?" Because if he did, Sass would be in jail.

"Oh, no." She shook her head. "I rode up next to him and hit him upside the head." She looked down at her hands and tilted her head slightly.

"Daisy!"

"He was standing in front of a large pothole. It's hard to look tough when you're flying over the handlebars." She crossed her arms over her chest and leaned back on the pillows and sneered the words, "Boys. I'm never going to live this down."

I covered my mouth with my hand.

Sass was in so much trouble. God forbid she puts that much work into defying him when her interest in boys changed.

Unintelligible voices led by Daisy's mom, Kathy, were coming down the hallway. "She's in here with CJ."

Daisy pulled herself up and straightened in her bed. "Did you bring him?" Just like flipping a switch, her interest moved on. "Mom, is he here?"

In walked the last person I expected. The last person I really wanted to see today.

Grady's smile was soft and genuine as he looked between Daisy and me. I noticed a small dimple in his right cheek I hadn't noticed before. He walked to the other side of Daisy's bed and stood before her. "Hello, Ms. Daisy. I've heard you're a big fan of CJ's and have been waiting to meet me." His charm was turned up and radiated through his golden hair and skin as an aura most couldn't resist.

Most except Daisy.

"Cut the crap," Daisy drawled, and rolled her eyes at him.

Her mother, Kathy, standing behind me in the doorway, gasped, "Daisy Marie!"

Sass's laugh burst out before he could hold it back, and Kathy, glared at him.

But Daisy couldn't be swayed by that smile. She didn't remove her glare from Grady.

"Your charm won't work on me, Mr. McBane, I'm only nine and I don't like boys."

Grady was gobsmacked at her bluntness. But nothing I could ever do or say would top what Daisy did to Grady in those few words.

"I must be losing my touch," he whispered to himself, but with a sidelong glance it was also meant for me.

I dropped my head and bit my bottom lip.

Grady shifted on his feet. I don't think he had a lot of experience with kids or with females who didn't fall for his allure.

But…Daisy wasn't done. "I especially don't like boys who takes things from girls. It isn't fair."

Grady took a small step back from my defender's bed and glanced over his shoulder. There he saw a signed poster I gave her for Christmas, next to the photos of her family and her pet dog, and another one of me and her at the track last year.

His eyes danced back and forth between us and he said, "Well, I can see you're firmly entrenched in the CJ camp, and I wouldn't ever be able to turn you. I admire your loyalty." He took a step closer, pulling up the chair on the other side of Daisy's bed.

He put his hands on his knees and leaned forward. "Truthfully, Daisy, I'm not crazy about this situation either. But you know what, I think CJ and I are making the best of it. Competition doesn't have to be a bad thing. You need to be challenged in order to grow. If anything, I think it has brought out the best in us. I'm branching into a new industry and CJ—well, even she has to admit that she's never run better."

Daisy gave me a dubious glance and a raised eyebrow.

I replied with a shoulder shrug.

He leaned closer to her. "And I'll tell you a secret that no one knows—and it's important to keep it quiet, okay?"

She nodded, but her apprehension about letting Grady off the hook was evident.

He leaned onto his elbows and over the bed. He was closer to her. "I think she's a pretty damn good driver, too. And if anyone were going to beat me—it would be her." He pointed at me. "That's what makes me a better driver, and it's what is going to make her one, also."

"You can be CJ's biggest fan...I'll give you that. But I want to be in contention for her second biggest one. Okay?"

Oh. He's good. I'll give him that. He was really schmoozing now. I cocked an eyebrow at him and couldn't help but smirk.

"And when you are back on your feet, we will talk about a fan club or something." Mischief poured off his tongue. "We can have video chats and race day events." His excitement climbed as he added, "I already have ideas for the T-shirts." The jerk winked at me. My smirk turned into a hint of amusement.

For the first time in five years, on the anniversary of the day my world fell apart, there was a glimmer of lightness in my heart.

## 1 8

**Grady**

If I ever wondered what CJ was like in mini form, I just met her. While I didn't have much experience with kids, let alone nine-year-old girls, Daisy had me on my toes and didn't pull punches.

After reminding me numerous times what an interloper I was, I eventually had her talking smack about other drivers, not just me. We bonded over our mutual dislike of Dewey—so that helped.

CJ sat next to Daisy against her headboard and chimed in occasionally, but otherwise was suspiciously quiet. She did smile at our witty banter, though, which only encouraged us.

"Well, we should get going soon, Daisy-girl." CJ stood up and I joined her at the foot of the bed.

"Wait! Mom!" Daisy bellowed. "You can't go yet, CJ. Mom!" Daisy leaned forward as if it would be far enough to see through the door and down the hallway.

Footsteps came from down the hall. "Yes, I know, I will get your surprise, honey."

Daisy beamed. "I couldn't get to the store or anything because of this—" she motioned to

her casted leg. "But Mom propped me up in the kitchen and I was able to make you something."

Sass lumbered in the room, shrugged apologetically. "I'm sorry," he said softly to CJ. "She overheard it was your birthday. I wasn't sure if you'd be up for it, but Daisy is nine, and birthdays still mean everything."

With a homemade chocolate cake and pink and blue candles, I joined in as they sang "Happy Birthday" and found forced appreciation in CJ's expression with a hint of uncomfortableness. It quickly switched as she beamed and leaned into hug Daisy before stepping away with a genuine smile, her eyes glassy with unleashed emotion.

The smile dropped when she looked up at me, vulnerability laid bare across her face. I instinctively reached for her and touched her arm, the contact sealing an unspoken pact between us.

This was sacred. I won't hurt you with this.

Moving to the cake, not breaking eye contact, she paused and then blew out the candles, leaving me wondering—did she wish to beat me? Did she wish to run me out of town? Did she wish for something else from me entirely?

We walked out of the Martin's house, waving goodbye to Sass and his family, promising Daisy a day at a race as soon as she was back on her feet and we could arrange it. It was still to be decided whether it would be one of my races or CJ's.

Once out to my car and CJ's Ducati, thunder rolled in the distance. CJ carried her helmet in one hand, and a bagged present from Daisy in the other.

"So, did I win over Daisy, or do I need to watch my back once she is mobile again?"

"Verdict is still out. She isn't a big fan of your gender these days."

"I've heard. Makes me wonder why I was invited over today."

"She wanted to check you out. Heard a lot about what's been going on and felt left out of the drama. She played the injured-little-girl card to get you there. Wanted to see it for herself."

"Crafty little thing…"

"You have no idea. Sass has his hands full with that one."

"Couldn't help but wonder if she is a mini-version of you at that age?"

She was still for a moment in thought, and then looked up to the distance. "I guess I never thought about it. I think I was more upfront. Not as scheming or as subtle——"

"Daisy is subtle?"

"Compared to me at that age, yeah." The one side of her mouth tilted up. "I grew up in a garage of men and boys of all ages, don't forget. My only female influence was Harper and Violet, but I wasn't around them as much as the guys. There was a lot of tomboy in me."

She fidgeted with her helmet.

"Today is your birthday, huh? Must have some plans…I don't mean to keep you."

She shook her head. "No plans." The wind began to pick up.

"Aren't you doing something with Harper and Gus?" The dark clouds crept up on us and came from the direction I knew CJ would be driving home toward.

"Nope. They know I don't celebrate my birthday." She turned as if to get on her bike.

I left that comment alone, more concerned with the weather. "Wait. Listen. I'm not sure if it's a good idea for you to ride home right now." I pointed at the sky.

She grimaced. "Damnit." She sighed. "I guess I'll go back into Sass's for a bit."

"Nonsense. Come on." I held out my hand and motioned to her. Small drops began to fall. "Let's go get some dinner nearby, and I'll drive you back to your bike after it passes."

She studied me, then studied the sky, and then glanced at Sass's house.

"I won't bite, and I won't tell a soul. I'll even let you pick out the restaurant since I don't know my way around here." The drops started picking up. "But hurry up, because you don't want to see what I turn into if I get wet."

As a sign of her acquiescence, she grabbed her helmet and Daisy's present and we picked up our pace to the Tesla.

---

She gave me directions to a farm-to-table restaurant she liked nearby. I guided the Tesla onto the highway, and we sat in an awkward silence. The rain began to pick up, falling in a staccato rhythm. I motioned to the sound system. "Feel free to turn on some music if you like. I have my playlist programmed in there, but you can switch to a station if you want."

I glanced over and CJ was leaning her elbow against the door, staring at the rain out the window. "I thought it was going to be a beautiful day out today. Figures."

I leaned forward, taking a good look at the darkening sky and the increase in speed of the rain coming down. "We were in the house for a while."

That ended the talk about the weather. Now what?

I went for levity, my fallback. "Your birthday, huh. Do you have anything against getting old?"

I got the side-eye from her that would freeze the balls on the devil.

Okay. That was the wrong path to take.

She took in a deep cleansing breath. "I'm surprised no one told you." She lowered her elbow, dropped her head, and let out a sigh as if she had a tedious task to perform.

I pulled up to a stop light, just as she ripped off the Band-Aid.

"Tommy died on my birthday five years ago. I don't celebrate my birthday because it was also the day that he died."

Silence.

The car behind me honked.

"Grady, go…the light turned green."

Like a novice teenager with his license, I jerked the car forward and started to drive, but was scrambling for words.

"I'm sorry for the comment," I said with a tone I never heard come from my voice. "I'm also sorry for your loss."

"And this—" she motioned to me while looking forward, her hands went over her face and through her hair in frustration. "Was why I don't tell anyone or talk about it. Now comes the pity look and the pity tone and the 'I'm sorry...' Just cut it. I'm fine. I just hate being reminded about it. Today is just a day. I don't celebrate my birthday—big fucking deal. I don't celebrate Tommy dying either. Period. Now, can we drop it and just get some food?"

"Okay. I'm—"

"Don't say it, Grady..." she gritted out her teeth but didn't make eye contact. "Just drop it. You know now."

We parked in the lot around back of the restaurant. She zipped up her hoodie and was going for the door when I put my hand on her thigh. She tightened and her head swiftly turned to me. "What?"

In the enclosed space of the Tesla, the act seemed much more intimate than I meant the comforting gesture to be. I slowly started to move my hand from her thigh but stopped. "I'm assuming you don't have to tell many people about Tommy. In fact, have you ever had to tell anyone about what happened to him?"

She was staring at my hand on her leg. Her hand was an inch away from mine, but she wasn't removing it. She also hadn't broken any of my fingers, so that was a good sign.

"CJ, have you ever had to tell anyone about Tommy? Have you ever talked about him? Not just what happened to him, but who he was? What he was like?"

She shook her head. "Everyone already knew."

"Can you tell me?" I placed my hand slowly over her fingers. I didn't grasp her entire hand, just made a small amount of contact to see if it was welcome. She didn't flinch, so that was another good sign.

We ran inside, her with a hoodie pulled up, and me with a baseball hat I found in the car. The hostess recognized CJ and gave us a booth in the back. We did this with minimum use of words. After ordering, and with nothing else to do but look at each other, I couldn't take it anymore.

I stared at her with what I thought were kind eyes and a warm smile.

She rolled her eyes and leaned back.

So, I started. "Tommy. He must be the antithesis of Dewey because I simply can't see you with anyone close to that douchebag."

She let out a guffaw. "Everyone thinks Dewey was a changeling brought up from the bowels of hell. Tommy and Dewey couldn't have been more different. They were Irish twins. Dewey was older, but Tommy was brighter in every way. He was just…more."

She was quiet as the waitress brought us water.

"Tommy was older than me, and of course, he hung out with Gus and Junior. We came up in the ranks and all grew up together. It's sort of like being in Little League—you may be on different teams, but you spend all your time at the track, and those are the people you see every weekend."

She took a sip of her water.

"Anyway, Harper would hang out at the track and of course, I spent most of my time, when I wasn't at the track, with the Merricks because my own family life was shit."

CJ played with her napkin and I stayed quiet, waiting for her to continue.

"Believe it or not, Junior treated me like his little sister. Which meant he both teased me, but he also let me tag along. Initially, he never saw me as anything except a pipsqueak."

"What happened with you and Junior, then?" This was a question that still bothered me because it was at the root of why I was even here.

She shook her head. "I think you need to ask Junior for that explanation because I'm not entirely sure. Things went downhill with us after Tommy's death, too." Her voice was melancholy, more vulnerable. "I lost more than just Tommy when he died."

Her hands fidgeted and she stared at them aimlessly. I wanted to reach out and hold them, to encourage her, but it would be the wrong move. Patience. I needed to sit still and be patient—it wasn't my strength, but I wanted—needed—to hear her tell me this. I told myself it was because it would explain what I'd gotten myself into—it wasn't the complete truth.

Really, it was because it showed me CJ. It explained her complexity. It revealed who she was. I needed more—I needed to see more. "How long were you two together?"

"Since I was fifteen. He was older, so we weren't 'official'," she gave air quotes, "until I was sixteen, but no one came near me or messed with me because I was known as his before he ever even kissed me." She smiled sadly. "He was my first everything."

"Don't get me wrong, we were all sweet and sugar. We fought like cats and dogs. We were competitive as hell. Most of what I learned, I learned while trying to beat Tommy."

"So he was that good."

She nodded. "He was. I won't bullshit you. He was better than anyone out there." Finally, she was on a topic that was safe. Racing. Her eyes cleared, she sat forward on the table and she talked business. "He was fearless, but not stupid. No one else had reflexes like his or had instincts as sharp as his. And he knew people. He knew drivers, he knew cars."

"I watched, he taught me, and I credit a lot of what I know from him. Wild Bill may be my mentor, but Tommy was my teacher." She sighed with nostalgia.

"You loved him?"

She nodded. "Just not enough."

The comment threw me. She'd been mourning him for five years.

"What does that mean? You've been mourning the man for five years. How is that not enough?"

She put her head in her palm and looked at me and then away, confessing, "Some would say that was guilt, not love."

That was it. I reached out and brushed my fingers over hers. "What happened to Tommy?

Blank faced, she turned to me and said, "He proposed to me and I said, 'No'."

I wasn't going to let it go. "There is more to it than that."

She straightened and let out an annoyed breath. "Fine, on my twentieth birthday, he proposed to me. I didn't see it coming, I almost laughed because I thought we were too young and didn't think he was serious. When I realized he was, it was too late. I told him I didn't want to get married. He was hurt and went out drinking with his brother and their friends. His asshole brother proceeded to get him rip-roaring drunk, all the while talking shit about how I was a flirt. I was in an industry swarming with eligible men, I had him in my pocket, why would I want to be tied down. All the same shit he spews even now."

She moved on, preparing to drop the climax of the story, clinically and without emotion.

"I was staying with Harper, and that night got messages from Tommy breaking up with me, telling me off. Each one he was more drunk, and each message was worse than the one before. I eventually turned off my phone, hoping in the morning when he was sober, we could talk things out."

CJ stared off, narrating the replay of the memory, not reliving it.

"The next morning, Dewey showed up at the Merrick's home yelling for me. That's how I found out Tommy wrapped his car around a tree on his way over to the house at two a.m. to see me. It seemed the messages he left eventually became apologetic once Dewey left and he began to sober up." Now it all made sense. Dewey was a bigger ass than I ever thought was possible. A narcissistic ass.

"But, in Dewey's eyes, it was my fault. If I hadn't insulted his brother by laughing at his proposal, it wouldn't have happened. If I hadn't had him so whipped, been using him to get ahead and manipulating him, his brother would still be alive. All my success is because his brother is dead."

My head was held low, and I knew I was clenching my jaw thinking of all the insults I heard him throw at her already. All the times I held back from decking him and all the comments made around the two of them.

"But, one thing is right, if I hadn't been so freaked out, if I hadn't been so focused on my own career, on myself, and if I had enough courage to say, 'Yes', he'd be alive."

"You don't know that." It was all I had. It was hollow, but it was my immediate response.

She cocked her head at me, her expression conveying my response wasn't original—it was the same one she'd heard before and it was lacking.

I shook my head, annoyed with myself.

The waitress took that moment to arrive with our food. Good grief, I forgot about the food.

Once we quickly assured her we had what we needed, she left, and I wasted no time following up my comment. "Come on, CJ. If Tommy was the guy you all keep telling me he was, he would've been someone I would've liked. He wouldn't have been a guy who would've sat around and listened to that crap or taken that reasoning—"

She was warming up to argue, to tell me I didn't know shit and to put me in my place. I held up a hand to stop her. "Wait, slugger. Before you come out swinging at me and telling me I don't know shit. Just wait. You are right. I didn't know Tommy; I don't know Dewey or you very well, for that matter, and I wasn't around back then. That is why I'm perfectly objective. Now, maybe I'm nothing like Tommy—I'm sure you can find plenty of things that are different about us. However, I don't consider myself anything closely relating to Dewey. I love to race, I love everything about racing, and I can relate to a few other family dynamics. Plus, we both have you in common—granted, in different ways—" Good Lord, I think I'm blushing at the thought of how lucky Tommy was and how much more I'd like to have in common with him—"eh...hmmm, meaning we both admire you...admired your driving. So..."

I shifted in my seat like a fourteen-year-old boy telling a girl he liked her, for Christ's sake. My discomfort wasn't made any better by the large eyes CJ was throwing my way, and the tease of a smile that told me she caught my unease. "My point is, I think I could safely say that Tommy would tell you that this martyrdom you're going for is bullshit. You weren't at fault—he was. You shouldn't be throwing yourself on a fucking sword."

"You didn't say you didn't love the guy, you just said you didn't want to marry him…you weren't even old enough to drink yet." My voice raised at what a ridiculous expectation I thought it was.

"It wasn't ridiculous—" her brow was furrowed, and her lips thinned in defiance.

"You were twenty. My guess is there were other men sniffing around you and he was getting jealous. He wanted his ring on your finger before you started to wander." I shrugged. "That's what I would've done if I were in love with a girl like you at that age. With Dewey as his brother, I'm sure he was whispering doubts in his ear earlier than just that night."

She sat back. It hadn't occurred to her before.

"Honey, Tommy was what twenty-one, twenty-two?"

"He'd just turned twenty-two."

"Twenty-two-year-old guys can still be pretty immature and hot-headed." She stared at me blank-faced. "I was one once." I dipped my head slightly, reached out again and touched her fingertips, softening my voice so she wouldn't hear condescension, but genuine truthfulness. "CJ, honey, he made a deadly mistake. That was all it was. But it was his deadly mistake. Not yours. I would bet he'd say the same."

Her eyes began to glisten slightly before she blinked and then closed them, sitting back and shaking her head. The moment was gone. I didn't want to pressure her to respond, so I also leaned back and simply said, "Alright, then. Thank you for telling me. Now, I know." I glanced up at her while I grabbed my fork to judge if she wanted to say anything. She also grabbed her fork. I took it that that was the end of our moment. "Let's eat."

I changed the subject, making small talk about the restaurant and asking her questions about the surrounding neighborhood. She answered politely, at first, but didn't carry the conversation. When the subject turned back to racing, she relaxed, and we started to laugh at stupid mistakes we both made on and off the track.

I asked for the check, insisting on buying her a birthday dinner. She raised her brows at me and gave me a smirk. She crossed her arms over her chest. "Fine."

"I'm making progress," I murmured and winked.

"Grady," her voice was soft, and she loosened her arms, letting them fall to her lap. She was more relaxed than she'd been all day. Success.

"Thank you." She didn't have to say what for. "I probably will think you're an asshole tomorrow, but this was the best birthday I've had in a while."

I smiled as we stood, placed my hand on her back, instinctively, and led her out of the restaurant. I was tall enough to look over her, and saw she was smiling also. We were halfway out the door when I noticed she hadn't pulled away from my touch, so I let my arm drape over her shoulder casually as I would a friend's, turned my head, smiling into her hair, and said, "Happy Birthday, Charlotte Jean."

# 19

## Grady

My mother insisted since I was only staying in Chicago for one night that I stay at their house. The moment I walked through the doors of my childhood home, she embraced me with the vehemence a mom gave a son who'd been away for years.

"Oh, Grady. I'm so glad you're here." She reached up on her toes to grab me around my neck and pull me down with the grip of a professional wrestler attempting a head lock. Capping off the loving assault with my head clasped between her tiny, strong hands, she kissed me on both cheeks. "It's good to have you here."

She dragged me in as if I may escape. "Come, I have some lunch ready for you."

I surveyed the foyer of my parents' home—the home I spent most of my life in—and it was like seeing it through a set of fresh eyes—the coffered ceilings, the marble floors, the wraparound staircase and elevator discreetly camouflaged into the mahogany walls. This was home to them—this was Chicago.

My mom had lunch laid out in the kitchen, but even that looked like a semi-formal affair. "Your father is in the middle of something, so he will meet up with us later," she said, not making eye contact with me as she went to grab our drinks.

I stopped as I drew out my chair. "Mom, does he know I'm here?"

"Of course." She sat down and focused on placing her napkin in her lap.

"Mom, does he even want me here?"

She took her time looking up at me. "Grady, your father was complicated before all this started. Right now..." She reined in her emotion and swallowed back what appeared to be tears, "Right now, he's not himself. He isn't in the...well, he isn't himself. This disagreement you're having with him and Cal—"

"Mom, its more than a disagreement. They kicked me out."

She pounded her hands on the table hard enough to make the silverware jump. "Grady Patrick, don't act like you're inno-cent in this situation." She pointed at me. "You're a man pushing thirty who acted like a horny teenager without a care in the world. Your father isn't getting any younger. He already handed over the reins of McBane to Cal, he wanted to hand over the automotive component to you—give you the team—and then you act like an ass." She leaned back and threw up her hands. "You destroyed decades of business agreements, partnerships, and respect by acting like a horny teenager on a drunken rampage further—"

"I know what I did, Mom, but how long do I have to pay for it—"

She leaned in toward me with her face red with exasperation, "Until you grow the hell up and admit you're wrong, apologize, mean it, and stop acting like a wounded animal kicked out of the nest."

She fell back in her seat and rubbed her hand over her forehead, closing her eyes. My beautiful mother was weary—not just tired—but soul weary. "Jesus, Grady. What did I do in raising you, that you became so self-absorbed that you never saw what was going on around you?"

Damn, that hurt more than anything else anyone else ever said to me. It tore at me.

"Maybe I should leave?"

"No, you won't run again!" My mother took in a deep breath. She closed her eyes; her face was etched in pain as she got up and moved to my chair. She came up behind me and wrapped her arms around me from behind. "No." She leaned down and whispered in my ear. "I'm sorry, darling. Things are raw right now. I love you." Her voice hitched. "There is just so much going on. With Cal, with you…with your dad. Please. It's more than just you leaving. It isn't just about you and the fallout with McBane."

"Okay, Mom." I held onto her arm and worry washed over me. Yes, my mom could get mad at me, and I rightfully deserved what she was dishing…but this outburst wasn't her.

"Let's just eat and try to enjoy a peaceful lunch before things start up again, okay? This wasn't what I wanted from your visit. Please."

"Okay," I whispered, still reeling from her outburst. What the hell was going on around here? This wasn't my family. We weren't the sitcom-perfect family, but we weren't always so dysfunctional-explosive either. Guilt washed over me as I still considered the timing of this change was the same as my fall from grace.

Later that afternoon, I went looking for my father. He was where I expected him to be, in his den. I knocked.

A deep but muttered, "Yeah" was the response.

I entered a room where the heavy drapes weren't opened enough to really show what a beautiful sunny day it was outside. My father sat in an armchair in a pair of sweatpants and a North-western sweatshirt, wearing a pair of house slippers—far from the put-together man I knew him to be.

He'd aged twenty years since I'd seen him last.

He tilted his head upward with the stiff upper lip…that haughty expression that I was more likely to associate with him when he wanted to be king of the castle.

"The wayward son returns," he muttered.

"Hi, Dad." I stepped in front of him and put my hands in my

pockets, trying anxiously not to feel as if I was called to the carpet for busting out a window, or getting caught drag racing in his new sports car.

He leaned back and steepled his hands over his chest. "So, tell me, to what do we owe the pleasure of this visit?"

I shifted uneasily. "Um…didn't Mom tell you she invited me to come visit?"

"Invited you to come visit…as in, this isn't your home?" He dropped his hands to the armrest of his chair.

I saw my error.

"Well, I'm in the middle of a season, Dad. I have the weekend off, but I still need to fly back for the race—"

"Oh yes, the race. The one for a team you're a rookie, back-up driver for…the one you threw away your career for and abandoned your family for…right?" He stood up and walked behind his large mahogany desk. "I must have forgotten about that," he muttered.

I didn't want to go down that road. He knew what I meant, and I wasn't going to argue about it.

"I wanted to check on you and Mom and see how you were doing."

"I'm still alive. You can return to your life now."

"Dad, that's not what I mean…"

"You drag the family through a major sex scandal, alienate business partners and friends, and get blackballed from an entire industry, for Christ's sake. Then you publicly humiliate us further by leaving and running off to join the circus or some shit as a back-up driver." He waved at the door again in disgust.

Just as quickly, his shoulders slumped and in a defeated tone he said, "Just go visit with your mother and leave," and sank into his chair, exhausted. "—you seem to be good at that."

An arrow shot through my already damaged organ, so I turned and left.

## 2 0

### *CJ*

If it wasn't for the heavy, fire-retardant race suit, walking down the hot asphalt through the clamoring crowd of people, I may have appreciated the beautiful cloudless June sky at track in Pocono, Pennsylvania known for its triangle shape.

I was about to climb into a car for a grueling three-and-a-half-hour race on a two-and-a-half-mile track, covering four-hundred miles. I didn't have time for contemplation. Unfortunately, the only peace I could hope for on race day were the few moments inside the car after being strapped in, and before hitting the ignition switch. I passed other drivers getting in their last photo ops with sponsors—lucky for me, Harper had all my obligations with the sponsors and media fulfilled.

I had a few words with Gus and Bill about last-minute adjustments to the car as I walked down pit row. It was all routine.

My gaze scanned the other drivers all kissing their wives and girlfriends before climbing into their cars. I lamented—not for the first time the empty feeling I had inside me—and then chastised for that weakness. Then I focused on my name above the door of the car and rubbed my hand over it to remind myself why I was here.

Focus.

Grit.

Unapologetic Determination.

That small pang persisting in my heart was unwelcome. No family to come to my races. No someone special to come kiss me good luck. Everyone else I knew traveled with the racing circuit, so I didn't have anyone to see me off before a race.

It had been less than a week since Tommy's anniversary, and it was still lingering in my mind. My talk with Grady helped change my perspective on things and I was thankful to him for it. I still mourned Tommy, of course. But it was also the idea of Tommy.

No one to kiss me or hug me or even wish—

"Hey—"

The word jarred me and broke through the considerable noise on the track. He was behind me—so close that when I turned, we were almost chest to chest. My back against the car, with goose-bumps, even in the heat of the tracksuit, I gripped the open window of the car for stability.

Grady.

Jean-clad, wearing the standard Merrick Motorsports polo and mirrored aviator glasses, his hand moved through his sandy-blond hair that managed to glint in the sun. Even disheveled, he was adorable, as one side of his face broke into a smile. "Almost missed you."

I shielded my eyes, trying to hold back my traitorous smile that warmed me through to my toes. What I wouldn't do for a pair of sunglasses to help hide my pleasure in seeing him. Something to hide the emptiness he was unknowingly beginning to fill—and the turmoil that that caused.

"Well, you pretty much knew where I'd be," I joked and poked his shoulder, wanting to touch him in some way, and chastising myself even as I did it.

It was like the most popular boy in school just showed up to carry my books for me. Outrageous. Who the hell was I?

We had texted a few times while he was gone. The first one came after an interview I gave on Race Day. I couldn't tell if he was amused or annoyed. I simply said, "Grady is making great improvement. I think he's really coming along. This past weekend they were able to take these off." I leaned behind me and grabbed something. "He's doing a fantastic job without them." I held up an old set of training wheels.

The guy interviewing me thought it was funny.

It was hard from a text to hear the tone of his response, but he didn't tell me to "eff the hell off," so I took it as a good sign. His text simply said, "Nice. So, it's going to be that way, huh? Game on, Dixie."

How did he find out about that name?

It had to be Junior.

From there he'd ask me for a phone number of someone in the office or ask me a question about a driver's history he easily could have looked up. Then we'd start a few lines of banter. I didn't know his reason for reaching out, but I got the feeling he needed the distraction. Grady did a me a great kindness the night we went to dinner, but I didn't think it was a holdover from then.

I knew he went back there to visit his family. I could tell from the conversation with his mom that it wasn't going to be an easy visit, so I assumed by his texting that he was looking for distraction, and I was returning the favor.

I lifted my head up and smiled, "How was your trip home?"

His smile slipped briefly. "Uneventful. Just saw Mom…and Dad."

I'd admit we'd become more than competitors, maybe teetering toward friends. However, I hadn't gotten that story from him—yet. I wondered if he'd ever open up to me the way I had with him.

Friends, huh. I had two problems with that. One, I liked it, and two, I didn't know what to do about it. Logically, I knew it was a disaster waiting to blow up on me.

So much for the "focus" portion of my mantra. Sheesh.

But it gave me warm fuzzies.

Me—warm fuzzies. I don't do warm fuzzies. Until now, I wasn't even familiar with the concept.

And then reality descended and reminded me why I needed to keep my fantasy and hormones in check.

"Well, isn't this a great photo op of the cute couple..."

Dewey.

"Hey, Dewey, good to see you." Grady walked over and held out his hand as if he were a long-lost acquaintance.

Dewey was apprehensive but noticed the media approaching and shook Grady's outstretched hand.

Grady jerked Dewey's hand, pulling him off-balance and into him with a smile that was a marketing goldmine and clasped his shoulder. "So, CJ told me about your life-long acquaintance. She told me about everything. I get it, I do. I'm sorry about your brother. I get that you don't like her. I get why. I get that you have issues and displaced anger toward her. But, how about growing up and dealing with that shit without bringing it onto the track, huh?" He pushed Dewey back, still smiling as if he just told him the juiciest secret, well-aware the media was eating it up and snapping photo after photo.

Dewey's mask of civility fell briefly, as he glared at me and then back at Grady. "You'd do best to stay out of things that don't involve you."

The tension in Grady's arm increased, as if he were tightening his grasp. "Oh, they involve me. Because they involve her." He pointed at me. "As much as she may loathe me at times, she's still part of my team—competition or not. Just leave your issues off the track and we got no problems."

Dewey sneered at both of us. "You walk around here like you belong. You belong here about as much as she does—"

"Nice talking with you, Dewey..." He broke off the conversation with him, turned his back on Dewey, and faced me. The media inched closer, smelling blood in the water and wanting the sound bite.

Grady winked at me when he dealt a final blow loud enough for that sound bite. "What kind of name is Dewey anyway? Isn't that a synonym for 'moist'? Don't women hate that word?" Then he turned around, facing the media with a disingenuous startled expression. He leaned over and stage-whispered, "Oh, did I say that too loud?"

Chuckles erupted as Dewey stormed off, half the media following the driver with the worst temper in stock car racing, and the others sticking with us.

"Grady, any last-minute advice to CJ?"

"CJ, what's going on with you and Grady? You were looking kind of cozy there before Dewey showed up."

*Wait, what?*

Grady jumped in, "Nah, we have a few things in common—we both think we deserve this contract, we're both competitive drivers, and we both dislike narcissistic assholes who talk a lot of smack." He made a dramatic glance over to the direction Dewey exited in a huff.

The reporters laughed and he smirked at me. I side-eyed him. But it did its job. It distracted them and gave them something else to fixate on.

Grady found it amusing. I found it concerning. First, someone picked up on our "friendliness," second, he was putting himself on the Dupree's shit list, which obviously, wasn't a good thing.

Grady casually put his hands in his jean pockets, rocking back on his feet, and stood next to me, flashing everyone his devastating full smile. "You shouldn't have said that about Dewey; you don't want to ally yourself too closely with me. I'm a lightning rod when it comes to him."

He shrugged. "He doesn't scare me."

Just look at him. How in his element he was—how sure of himself he was.

Then, there was me. Put me in the monster machine and I was a beast. Confident, strong. But here, on the outside of the machine, standing next to this man with his golden aura and oozing charm? My confidence was as small as my stature suggested. Did they know?

I turned my gaze from the myriad of faces and focused on his.

He looked down at me. And I knew that would be the next photo to go viral. The twinkle in his eye said he knew it, too.

But I wasn't alone.

He turned to face me, and quiet enough so I was the only one who could hear, he said, "Let's get you in *our* car."

Damnit, I wanted to hug him.

*Hug* him. I wasn't a hugger. I wasn't even affectionate.

What the hell?

Maybe it was seeing the other drivers with their families and the thought of Tommy earlier. The thought of being a bit lonely.

Grady put his hand on my shoulder and the contact seared straight through me. It electrified me.

"Good luck, kick ass…run them over…put them in the wall…all that…" He lifted his hand as if to place it on my head before I stopped him.

"If you ruffle my hair, I'll kick your ass right here on national TV." I smiled and sweetly said it through clinched teeth and stepped on his foot to get my point across.

Just like that, he threw his head back and laughed.

I punched his arm and motioned to the stands before climbing into our car—my car. "Get back into the stands where you belong, McBane." A team member came over to help me get in and secured. Gus pushed by Grady with an unreadable, unwelcome expression directed at him before checking in on me.

Grady stepped back to let them work. He put his hands back in his pockets and strode backwards. "I'll wait for you at the winner's circle, Charlotte."

Warmth flooded through me.

Goddamnit.

He called me Charlotte.

Sigh.

Shit.

Focus.

The keys to the last few laps of Pocono were conserving fuel, driver skill, and team strategy. I was coming around turn two, also referred to as the Tunnel Curve, with number sixty-seven, Eric Muñoz, at my back panel, and number twelve, Dan Lucas, a car-length ahead of me. We came out of the short stretch when my spotter came on the comm. "Be careful, CJ, sixty-seven's going to move." I pulled up higher on the track just as the sixty-seven made a move to bump me, the movement gave him a fraction of a jump on me, and we were both nose to nose gunning for number twelve, headed down the front stretch and into turn one going into the last lap.

My adrenaline was electric, even though it had been pumping for over three hours, when the number twelve car fell low on the track and began losing speed.

My spotter came back on, "Looks like Lucas just lost his gas. It's up for grabs—"

I didn't hear anything else. I didn't even look over at the number sixty-seven, I just focused on the road ahead of me.

Gus's voice came on, and in a calmness that was eerie to me said, "CJ, honey—"

"What did I tell you about calling me honey!" I yelled.

"Okay, okay. CJ, this isn't bumper cars now. It's you and the checkered flag. Just do as we talked about. Ignore everyone else. You got this. Aaron will keep an eye on the other cars, you worry about your car and the finish line."

I came out of turn two and couldn't help but look over at Eric in the sixty-seven. I wanted it more than him. He was a three-time Cup champion. I could feel the smile he had on under his helmet. He wasn't going to give it up easy.

Screw him. It was my day, damnit. I narrowed my eyes.

I went low and into turn three gaining a few feet on him, refusing to look anywhere else except dead straight ahead down the front stretch and past the finish line. *Focus. Grit. Unapologetic* goddamn *determination.*

I won.

I won the race.

I won the whole fucking thing!

I won the race at Pocono Raceway.

Moments of passing car after car, dodging cars that had gotten loose and took out groups of competitors in front of me, watching other cars blow tires as I went by, my team kicking ass on pit stops—it all culminated in me clinching the checkered flag.

The yelling in the comm was competing with the pounding of my heart.

"Holy—" I gasped. "G? Bill?" My foot was still on the accelerator and I was on autopilot as my car continued to fly around the track, my mind not registering that we were finished. Then it clicked and I found enough breath to yell, "We *won!*"

"We won, sweetheart. We won," Bill said calmly, as if he expected it all along, but I could hear the smile in his voice. There was a roar of celebration behind him from the team.

"Darlin', get your ass over to Victory Lane before you really do run out of fuel and we have to push the car over there," Gus practically yelled.

"G, what did I say about calling me darlin'?" I laughed, grinning so hard it was almost hard to speak.

But this—this was it. The moment I practiced and envisioned ever since I was four years old and pulling up on the brake of my Big Wheel and sliding into a big skid on the road. While other girls imagined their wedding, or being a princess, or becoming the President—this was my dream.

I wasn't a showman like some of the more popular drivers who did flips or dramatic bows off the side of their cars when they won.

But every driver did burnouts, or donuts as some called them, wearing down what tread remained on their tires, to the point that they sometimes couldn't even drive the car to winner's circle. I held back tears of joy while I tore around the track, laying the remaining rubber of my tires down on the track as a marker to paper.

If I cried, I couldn't get past the helmet to wipe away the tears, and I'd be damned if I was climbing out of this car with a tear-streaked face.

After doing a respectful amount of damage to the tires and track, I drove to the winner's circle to meet my crew who were already celebrating. Gus climbed on top of a riser, yelling and shaking some sort of drink all over the crew below him. When I drove up, he almost pulled a *Dukes of Hazzard* jump over the hood of the car to get to me.

He helped unlatch the screen on the window, taking the detached steering wheel, and practically yanking me out of the car as soon as I had the helmet off. I was laughing and smiling too much to quell his enthusiasm.

"Shit, CJ! Darlin', you did it!" Gus's excitement almost trumped my own. His body vibrated with energy. He spun me around, and I knew he considered throwing me up on his shoulders but restrained himself. I pumped my hand in the air, and more cheers went up.

It was a high I'd never experienced.

My first true Cup victory.

This had to cinch me as a viable contender for a full-time contract.

My gaze took in the mob of people who were there to congratulate me. Out of all the well-wishers, I could've sworn I caught the glimpse of golden blond hair.

Allison Jaffey, the reporter for the network broadcasting the race, stepped in front of me and broke my line of sight. She was trying to get my attention and her post-race interview. I didn't hear a word she said.

"Omph." I was picked up by two of my crew members and summarily handed off and lifted from one set of shoulders to the next. They passed me around like a trophy until I was standing in front of Bill, who put his arm around me. His gruff voice had a small hitch when he pulled me to his side and kissed the top of my head. "Great job. Proud of you."

That's when my eyes started to burn. I glanced up at Bill quickly enough to see his eyes were glassy, too, but looked away before we both broke each other's resolve.

My eyes, my body, my heart couldn't decide whether it wanted to laugh, cry, or just fall over. I bent forward, hands to my knees for a moment of escape, to collect my thoughts.

Allison made it up to the platform, undeterred, and approached me. I straightened and decided to get the interview over with while I still had enough adrenaline keeping me up straight.

"CJ, how does it feel to get the win today?"

I tried to remember the lines I went over with Harper, but frankly I was too excited to remember everything. "Yes, I'm so proud of our team…the Prince Automotive car ran great and our team was excellent…" I wasn't sure what else I said; I was holding back tears. Finally, my true self emerged, and I just about exploded with excitement. "I'm just so fu—"

Harper jumped in, grabbed me, and short of putting her hand over my mouth, added, "CJ is happy…beyond words."

I just nodded my head with her hand over my mouth, holding back the words not meant for public broadcasting. I pushed my way through the crowd, with my head held high, working my way up the stairs to the stage.

Before turning around, I pinched my eyes, begging them to stay strong. Gus moved up behind me and patted me on the back. "Come on, Dixie."

I slugged him in the gut. He did it on purpose, to bring me back online.

It's what he did. It was what all the guys did. They poked, they teased, they didn't do feelings or emotions—they were guys. I shifted gears and slugged him again—it felt good. I smiled at him as a thank you for stopping me from losing it.

When I turned, our entire team was on the platform and they were getting ready to present the trophy. Mr. Merrick was up on the podium giving a few words, then a few other people spoke. I scanned the clamoring bodies below me and wanted to kick myself for searching.

There he was.

Standing by our car.

Leaning against the side door that still had my name listed above it as if he belonged there.

His arms and legs were crossed. He wore a baseball cap low on his head which was tilted to the side, studying me as if I were a piece of art. When our eyes met and he knew he had my attention, that playful half smile came out and it grew. And grew. And grew. He dropped his head and then peered at me from beneath his lashes. I could see the hesitant respect he was offering, as if he were uttering the words, *"Yeah, alright. I'll admit it, you rocked it."*

Amidst the sea of people, we were in a moment that belonged to just us. I felt cocky and I winked at him. I winked. At. Him.

Who was this woman?

Message sent—*"Yeah, about time you admitted it."*

He threw his head back and laughed. At that moment I wanted to run and launch myself into his arms, knowing he'd catch me. That was how I wanted to celebrate, with me in his arms and him wearing that beautiful smile—the smile I put there.

No one could hear it through the noise, but it tickled my heart as if he were right next to me and the vibrations ran through my body.

Gus was trying to talk to me, Bill was pulling at me. I knew I needed to pay attention because they were going to give me my trophy. The moment was broken.

When I looked back to Grady, the swarm of people between us had grown and the barrier seemed symbolic. He still smiled but it was more resigned. He placed a hand over his heart and mouthed, "Congratulations."

Then he dropped his head, his hands going in his pockets, and turned to walk away. Noise began to invade my world, and it became louder as he moved farther out of my line of sight.

It didn't feel as much of a celebration after that.

Him leaving took some of the wind out of my sails.

That pissed me off.

This was mine.

This was what I had worked for.

Why was I letting this man change it for me?

I focused my attention on Bill, who guided me to the officials. I was handed a large trophy with an American eagle holding an American flag. I shook hands, smiled, and played humble-but-excited to the media. I reveled in the joy of my first Cup win.

"CJ, do you think this gives you an edge over Grady in the run to see who gets the number thirty-six car next year?"

I searched the crowd, but knew he was gone.

"I'm focusing on the moment. I'm proud of our number thirty-six Prince Automotive car and the team behind it. Merrick Motorsports has put together an amazing team, and that includes Grady McBane and the rest of our teammates. For now, I'm only concentrating on my races. One race at a time."

The other interviews were the same. It was only a few races into the season for Grady and me, but the media wanted to hype up the competition. The rivalry. They wanted Grady and me to draw blood from each other. They saw my win as a way to ratchet up the level of animosity. Jeez, no wonder Grady left. The questions he must be getting thrown his way had to be grueling. I realized that with my winning, it must make it appear as if he was losing.

---

The team was still riding the high and enjoying the champagne from the celebration when we boarded the Merrick plane that flew them home. The cars, trailers, and RVs would be driven home by a separate crew responsible for transporting the machinery, while the drivers and crew flew home for a few days' rest, before being swept off the next weekend to the next race.

Trying to be subtle, and knowing I failed miserably, I searched the cabin for Grady.

Nothing.

"He took an earlier flight," Harper said. "He wanted me to tell you."

I took the nearest seat and dropped into it.

The adrenaline crash began just as my cell phone dinged.

Grady: Congratulations. Great job tonight.

The sight of his text sent my heart plummeting to the Earth and my hormones surging above the clouds.

CJ: Thanks. Why'd you take off?

Grady:Didn't want to distract from your limelight. Your first Cup win should be yours. Sleep well. Enjoy the spoils.

If I were a girly-girl, a kissy-winky emoji may have accidentally appeared and been sent before I could stop my finger from reacting.

What the hell was wrong with me?

"Grady?" Harper's sing-song-implied tone wasn't a question as much as a point.

"Yeah, just congratulating me," I said.

Gus kneeled in the chair in front of me and said, "Kinda shitty that he didn't stick around to congratulate you in person. Like a sore loser or something."

Gus threw cold water on my buzzing good mood.

"It's not like that. He didn't want to cause a bigger circus by being there." I put my cell back in the pocket of my hoodie. "If anything, he was trying to let me have my win without the complication of him being around."

Gus wasn't buying it. "He didn't want to be shown up. What's with you, CJ? This guy is as much your competition as any of the other forty drivers out on the track. More so. He could send you back to the Energy Blast circuit next year. Do you get that? Are his pretty-boy smiles and attention worth it?"

Harper settled in the seat next to me, her eyes narrowed at Gus. "What's your problem, G? Just because they're competing doesn't mean they can't be friendly. Geez. You're getting as bad as the media."

"Friendly?" Derision dripped off his tongue. "Guys like Grady aren't friendly with girls like CJ."

"What the hell does that mean?" I sat on the edge of my seat, ready to stand up and get in his face.

He leaned in, closing the distance between us. "Come on...you aren't that naïve. Don't you find it suspicious how much he's sweet talking you lately? Maybe it's a tactic? Ever think of that? There's all sorts of speculation around why he separated from McBane—no one really knows. But everyone knows the man has a reputation. Don't get swept up in the hype with him." He stood up and stepped back. "That's all I'm saying. You don't get to be a guy like Grady without earning the reputation he has."

"Shut the hell up, Gus."

"Pot meet kettle," Harper sneered. "Like you're one to talk."

"It isn't like she's got a lot of experience with men like him, Harper. She has to get her head out of her ass and see what he could be doing."

"Cut it out with the territorial big brother bullshit," I said. "Grady doesn't think of me that way. I'm not his type."

"Exactly, so why is he spending so much time sniffing around you?"

That silenced me.

"Fuck off, Gus. Go find you a hook-up for tonight and stop pissing on CJ's parade." Harper stood in front of me to end the conversation.

"Grady sniffing around isn't a good thing. Mark my words, Harper. This also has your brother's strategy written all over it. Besides, aren't CJ and Grady supposed to have some big rivalry they're supposed to play up? How's that going to happen if she's all dreamy-eyed over the guy."

Forcing myself to stay in my seat, I flexed my fists. "Gus, get the hell away from me before I have to get out of my chair." I looked at him out of the corner of my eye, and he stared at my fists.

His lips thinned and he turned to walk back to his seat, as he threw over his shoulder, "Fine. Whatever."

Harper sat back down next to me, but something Gus said about Grady warranted more thought.

"Do you think Grady is only being nice to me to throw me off?" My insecurities screamed at me, and my pride was desperately telling it to shut the hell up. But it was Harper, and she gave it to me straight.

Harper put her phone in her lap and turned to me, a touch of softness settled across her face. "Honey, why does Grady need a reason?"

I fidgeted, twirling my phone around. Wondering if he'd text me again. God, I was literally sitting by the phone waiting for a boy to call. What the hell?

Maybe it was the small amount of champagne I had, but the

moment of introspection seemed misplaced. I just won my first major race and was wondering why a boy was being nice to me.

"Come on, Harper. I'm not exactly Ms. Congeniality—"

"And you have your reasons for it…but it doesn't mean you aren't likeable," Harper said. "Grady is a good guy. Don't let GQ's overprotectiveness mess with your mind or tarnish whatever is going on with you and Grady."

I opened my mouth to respond, but she cut me off.

"Don't argue with me. It's been a long day. The boy is being nice to you. Accept it. Be nice back. It will make everyone's life easier—including mine." She turned to the rest of the cabin. "Hey, CJ needs more champagne!" Then she refocused her attention back to me. "There's a limo meeting us at the airport to drive your ass home, so have more champagne and try to relax. You deserve it." She put her arm around me, kissed the top of my head and squeezed.

"I'm so proud of my Charlotte Jean!" she yelled, and the entire plane raised their glasses and clapped.

## 21

---

### CJ

It was late when I was dropped off at my modest house in an unassuming neighborhood in Charlotte. I had one glass of champagne, but I was coming down off my adrenaline high and starting to fall asleep on the plane before I could drink any more. I unlocked the front door, waved at the Merrick chauffeur, dropped my suitcase and purse, and took a satisfying, deep breath of exhaustion as I scanned my very empty house.

Empty.

No one there to congratulate me.

Harper wanted me to stay with her tonight, but we each wanted our own beds.

Now everything seemed anti-climactic.

Just as melancholy teased my mood, my phone dinged with a message. My heart sped up with hope. How ridiculous.

Grady: Is it too late for a visit?

Heart don't fail me now.

CJ: Where are you?

There was a soft knock at the door. My heart was revving louder than my race car.

I paused, staring at the door.

No.

I approached the door as if it could catch fire and parted the curtains next to it. There he was, too gorgeous to be real, on the doorstep in the early hours of the morning.

My hand shook as I unlocked and opened the door.

He stood, leaning with his arm against the door frame. His hair hung over his bent head and was tousled, as if he'd been running his hand through it. He rubbed his hand over scruff, looking up at me with uncertainty from under his lashes.

"Hey." I held onto the door for support. Why was he here? "What's wrong?"

"Nothing." He stood and threw his head back, looking up at the sky—not at me. "I…" He scanned the area, still not looking at me. He shifted on his feet, taking a turn to stare down at them. "I'm not even sure why I'm here. It's a bad idea, I know, but I had to see you."

He slowly drew his gaze up my body until it met my eyes. "And tell you how proud I am of you. I know that sounds condescending as hell, and I tried to figure out a better way of saying it. I thought about it the entire way home. I tried over and over to text you and kept deleting it because the message never seemed right."

He shifted, bracing both his hands on the door frame, and leaning into me. "I drove my ass over here figuring I would know what to say once I got here."

His eyes were so blue. Even in the darkness, with only my artificial porch light as illumination, I was frozen in place by how blue they were.

It was a moment in time your soul took a snapshot and locked it in the vault of your heart.

"And now?" I barely had the air to get the words out, but I needed to prompt him, I needed to know what he was going to say.

"Now it isn't words I'm thinking of." He stared at my mouth. "It's the elation of your smile on that podium, it's in the confidence of your swagger, and the swing of your hips when you strutted your ass up there to get that well-deserved trophy. It's also the determination and the sexy, snarky bites you take out of me."

His smile turned mischievous. He knew I wanted to hear more. He saw the weakness in my defense and approached, a lion stalking its prey. His wariness disappeared. My submission and arousal evident. I walked backwards into my house and he followed, closing the door behind him. My back hit the wall of my foyer and I braced myself for whatever came next because I knew it was going to turn me into putty.

"It's how since the moment I met you, even when you're insulting me, I wanted to taste your damn mouth. Can we forget about everything for a moment so I can just kiss you?"

I had no words.

He came within inches of my body. Not caging me, but leaving the final distance to be breeched by me. I touched his forearm, the corded muscles tensed. I stared up at him. His lips were thinned, and his jaw clenched. He wasn't going to make the next move. He was waiting for me.

I ran my hand up his forearm and over his bicep and shoulder. I traced his jaw, luxuriating in the feel of his stubble, and over his lips. He closed his eyes, moaned, and his tongue peeked out to lick his bottom lip, chasing my fingertips.

With my other hand, I slowly threaded my fingers through his gorgeous mane of hair, never breaking eye contact, and pulled him down to meet my lips.

His reaction was immediate. His arms locked around me, my body melding to him. He didn't just kiss me; he devoured me. He dove in, licked and tasted. His hands grasped and roamed. He kissed me with his whole body.

We groaned into each other, and his hands traveled down my ass and lifted me. I was up against the wall and he pushed into me, deepening this kiss, consuming me.

I never wanted to be part of someone so badly.

It wasn't about every nerve in my body going electric, and every muscle melting. It was more. It was about wanting to melt into him.

His hands roamed up and down underneath my thighs while he grinded against me in constant motion.

We came up for air, foreheads still touching and breathing hard, staring at each other. "This probably isn't a great idea." I ran a finger down his jawline.

He nodded slowly. "I know."

"Then why are we doing it?"

His kisses turned to licks, and he worked his way over to my ear and down my neck as he whispered, "Because I'm an asshole with very little restraint around you."

My feet fell to the ground as I dragged my hands down the planes of his chest. I wanted that chest naked. But he was doing incredible things to my neck, and his hands were making their way up my sides to my breasts.

"Oh God, Charlotte. What I want to do—"

"Grady—"

Banging erupted on the front door loud enough to rattle the windows.

What the hell?

The doorbell rang multiple times for emphasis.

"What the fuck?" Grady growled, and the way his body covered mine, I couldn't help comparing him to a lion being interrupted during his meal.

More banging, followed by a bellowed, "CJ!" It was Gus.

What the hell?

"Why is Gus here?" Grady was staring at the door, and then at me.

I straightened myself, running my hand down the back of my hair, as if I had been caught by my parent making out. "I have no idea?"

"CJ. Open up!"

I walked to the door, turning briefly to see what Grady was doing. He leaned casually against the wall, his shirt askew, his hair unapologetically disheveled; he wore it like a crown with his arms and legs crossed…a scowl on his face at the interruption.

I opened the door and Gus pushed his way in.

"What the hell is going on in here?" He strode in purposefully with my carry-on bag. Crap, I hadn't even realized it was missing.

Gus pointed at Grady. "Why is he here?"

Grady's brows rose in a mixture of annoyance and boredom. "Why are you here? It's the middle of the night."

"I…" Gus swung the travel bag in the air, "brought her bag to her. She left it on the plane."

"Thank you—" I went to take the bag from Gus, but he held it back waiting for an explanation.

"And that had to be done in the middle of the night? How noble of you," Grady deadpanned, and didn't seem to be buying his reason for the late visit.

"Gus lives a few streets over," I offered.

That didn't help Grady's suspicion. "Well, isn't that cozy."

Gus walked up to Grady, who hadn't flinched. "Why are you here?"

"Because I came by to congratulate Charlotte." Oh, Lord. He called me Charlotte. No one called me Charlotte.

"Charlotte?" Gus said it with derision, as if it left a bad taste in his mouth. "No one calls her that."

"I do." Grady straightened and walked up to Gus, challenging.

I grabbed Gus by the arm and took the bag from him. The men realized I was still there, and their testosterone took on a new focus.

Gus turned me away from Grady. "Why is he here? Do you want me to get rid of him?" His eyes roamed over me. What I could only imagine were my flushed cheeks, swollen lips, disheveled hair, and dazed eyes.

Gus straightened. "What did we just talk about?" Parental disappointment and censure laced his tone.

"This isn't any of your business, Gus." This was getting ridiculous.

He shook his head. "Jesus, you just won your first Cup race. You finally have an edge against this man." He blatantly pointed at Grady. "He shows up at your house in the middle of the night and charms you out of your panties? Seriously? You aren't that stupid?"

Grady obviously had had enough. "I think it's time for you to leave."

Gus straightened. "Not unless you do."

Oh, Lord.

"Gus, I don't need a watch dog." But this dog smelled blood in the air, or maybe it was

pheromones.

"The hell you don't." He stood in front of me as if Grady was going to ravage me right

there in front of him.

I stepped around Gus. My shoulders drooped, and I sighed. I touched Grady's forearm and knew Gus caught the move. "I am exhausted. It's probably a good idea for me to get some shut eye. Thank you for stopping by." I tried to communicate with my eyes how much I wished things were different, but how badly I didn't want Gus to know any more than he already suspected.

Gus walked to the door and opened it, waiting for Grady to walk out before him. Of course, then there was a standoff as to who would walk out first. I physically pushed Gus out the door.

Grady held a small, contemplative smile on his face that warmed me as he leaned over and kissed the top of my head. "Congratulations, Charlotte. It was an amazing night." And I was pretty sure he didn't mean just the race.

## 22

***Grady***

"Ready to go, boss?" Cooper bellowed, as I changed in the trailer at the race track in Sonoma. "Time to go earn your keep."

It was time to do the pre-race routine: sponsor appearances, media interviews and more sponsor appearances, and fan meet and greets. Not my favorite part of the job, but the most necessary.

"Yeah, I'm coming." I walked out of the trailer and Cooper handed me the latest sponsor's hat. I glanced at it briefly, seeing the Mingle Singles logo and feeling a twinge of guilt that disappeared like a flash in the pan when I also thought of Prince Automotive emblazoned across CJ's chest at last weekend's race.

Not that I was looking at her chest—alright, of course I was looking at her chest. The logo was on her chest—you're supposed to look at the logo. I wasn't studying it in detail. I didn't have a reason. I already knew what the logo looked like—just not how it laid across the curves of her breasts.

The breasts I came within inches of exploring until Gus, the "Guardian of her Virtue" interrupted.

I still needed to repay him for that, but I wasn't sure if it was with my fists or with gratitude.

I needed to be smart about my career.

But I wanted her back in my arms. I ran my hand over my face, forcing myself to let go of the image of her eyes hooded, lips parted, as she pulled me down for her kiss.

Why did I get myself into these situations? I shook my head back and forth and paced.

CJ's won her first Cup win in only her second appearance. That was unheard of for any rookie. She was racing with Prince as her main sponsor. Dermott wanted to see me go up in flames and dance around my burning body.

And now I was sabotaging myself further. Could I possibly screw myself over any other way? Well, yes—I could sleep with her. Or worse—I could fall for her.

Damnit.

It turned the screw a few notches on the amount of pressure I was under. It also screwed with my head.

Today was the first day I had to prove myself.

I stepped out into the California sun and donned my sunglasses. Pausing to readjust my thoughts, my focus. I vowed to protect my career, to readjust my priorities.

"Is our princess here? Do you know if she will be in attendance?"

"Don't think you can fool me." Cooper grinned. "We all know she's *your* princess..." His voice took on an airy, teasing tone that only a best friend could get away with. He didn't know about my late-night visit to CJ's. If he knew, he'd skin me alive.

Sometimes having your best friend as your manager had its drawbacks. He noticed my non-response. "Didn't you talk with her?"

Automatically becoming defensive, I picked up my pace, not wanting him to see my expression, "Why would I have talked with her?"

He shrugged. "Thought you two would've had a pre-race meeting with Gus and Bill this week.

"We did a conference call." I wondered if Gus found that odd? CJ and I hadn't spoken since that night. She called in for the meeting claiming to be under the weather. She made some excuse about "woman's issues." I called her out on her bullshit and texted her.

CJ: Didn't think it was a good idea to have the three of us in the same room so soon. Thought it would be better to have you and Gus focus on this week's race without me there throwing kerosene on anything.

I wasn't sure what to write after that. She hadn't said anything else or addressed what happened. Did she think it was a mistake, too?

I shook my head again. Cooper was talking to me, no idea what it was about, but judging by the teasing smile on his face, he was giving me more shit.

I gave him a side-eye glance. "We need to find you a woman, Coop. Then you'd have other things to occupy your time." I took in my friend with his golden-russet hair—a brawnier Ed Sheeran.

"Keeping up with you is all the life I can handle right now," he mumbled and looked down at some papers he was holding. "Let's get moving."

Dressed in the standard, pre-race uniform—royal blue polo with team logo on it and a pair of jeans—my hair was still partially wet. Didn't matter. The hat was on until the helmet replaced it. For the rest of the day I'd be as decorated with sponsorship logos as my car...our car...I meant—*the* car.

My body and the car were like ad space on a billboard. The moment I walked out of the trailer, what I drank, what I wore, even what snack food I carried was all sponsor-related. It was what paid the bills.

Cooper's lips twitched. "As for your princess, she's already been over to the media tent. They've been very interested in her comments about your 'rookie' appearance."

"Shit." If there was one thing CJ was full of—it was opinions.

The raceway was located in the Sonoma Mountains and was one of the few road courses. Instead of three or four banked turns, the track contains twelve flat turns within a two-and-a-half-mile track on hilly terrain that changes one-hundred-sixty feet in elevation. Within the one-hundred-and-ten-lap race, the drivers will have made eleven-hundred turns. It was far from what stock car drivers were used to, and it was the edge I had over the other drivers—including CJ. This was my advantage, and I had to have a good run today.

I didn't want to admit I was looking for CJ. I was totally scouting the area for her. We'd seen each other in passing, and I caught her glancing at me. But neither of us approached the other, and we certainly hadn't addressed me showing up at her house the other night.

I was chickenshit.

But I simply didn't know what the hell to do. I didn't think she did either.

We obviously had a hell of a lot of chemistry.

I couldn't stop thinking about her when I was in the shower, in my bed, and now even

moments before I took my life in my hands by getting behind the wheel—still thinking about her.

Focus. I needed to go see her in front of the media, and racing suits were unforgiving—it wasn't easy to hide a bulge.

I could only imagine what sound bite they were going to use from her today.

I adjusted my hat and quickened my stride.

"We need to go see the execs at Mingle Singles and then over to the media tent."

"Alright. Let's get this over with."

After all the handshaking and photo ops, Cooper pulled me out of the Mingle Singles tent, and we climbed in a cart. "We need to jet back to the trailer before your interview."

I leaned back in the seat, content with how the meet and greet with the execs went. Mingle Singles was an online dating service, and they were talking about the new campaign they were rolling out with me as their new spokesperson. Lots of money being discussed —both for the team and for myself.

"Why the change in schedule? I thought Junior wanted me at the media tent."

Cooper was leaning over the wheel of the golf cart and not looking at me. "Just a quick change, will only take a minute. I already told Junior." He was zipping around groups of people walking, barely slowing down when they got in his way, pulling up to our trailer in record time.

"Go on in, I'll be right there. Might as well get your gear on, so we can save time and head over after your interview." Cooper looked down at his phone, not even bothering to get out of the cart, and again refusing to look up at me.

"Man, what the hell is with you?" I grumbled and went to the trailer, throwing open the door with too much force and taking two steps at a time. I tossed off the hat and began stripping off my shirt.

I stopped mid-step with my head coming out of the shirt.

Fuck.

Fuck me.

Fuck Cooper.

My switch was flipped. Fury.

"Cooper!"

"Don't be a drama queen and come in," my brother said, sitting in my trailer, leaning back behind the Formica collapsible table as if it were his massive desk in his penthouse office.

"What the fuck do you want?" I asked my older brother, who had the audacity to be bored at my appearance in my own trailer.

"To see you. To see how you're doing. To wish you luck." He gestured with his hand with an air of royalty. "This track was always a good track for you. Seems like a good place to start."

"Like you give a shit. You came to see if I'd fail, and to be nearby to bask in my failure if I do."

Cal pursed his lips in slight annoyance, his expression mimicked parental disapproval

as he picked a piece of lint off his impeccably tailored trousers, which he wore with a short-sleeve polo shirt.

Condescending asshole.

149

"I don't want to see you fail. I came to talk to you. To wish you luck and throw up the

white flag. You don't need to race for Merrick."

I held up my hand as I strode to the back of the trailer to grab my gear and began to strip

down. "I don't have the time or head space for this."

I was sitting on the bed in the back room, slipping my legs into the suit when he blocked the doorway. "Grady, I promised Mom I'd talk with you and bring you home—"

I stood, took the arms from the suit, and tied them around my waist. "Am I a child out past curfew—Jesus, Cal. I have a fucking job. I can't come when you and Dad crook your finger anymore. Take your fucking guilt trip and get the fuck out of my trailer," I growled low at the floor as I slipped on my shoes without looking up at him once.

"I didn't set out to run you out of—"

I stopped long enough to glare up at him. "Don't you fucking dare…"

I stood and strode toward him. He backed up and let me pass. "You did a damn fine job all on your own."

I halted. Nope, not going to let him bait me. "Not now—" I glared over my shoulder.

My brother had his hands in his pants pockets—mimicking my own usual casual stance—and I made a note to myself to cut that habit. "It was your own arrogance. Your own pride, and your own stupid mistakes that burned many of those bridges." He didn't need his normal uniform of suit and tie for his pretentiousness to show.

There was a knock, and before I could even answer, Harper walked in studying her phone, wearing a navy company logo shirt and tailored shorts that showed off her long legs. "Grady, have you seen Junior? My pain-in-the-ass brother isn't answering my texts."

She tore her gaze from her phone and noticed Cal. "Oh, I'm sorry. I thought you were alone."

"No, I'm *his* pain-in-the-ass brother who showed up because he wouldn't answer *my* texts…Cal McBane." The motherfucker-charming-cocksucker held out his hand to her, all charm and refinement.

And there went Harper's megawatt Southern-charm smile. "Harper Merrick, pleased to meet you."

"Harper, you're Everett Merrick's daughter. CJ Lomax's agent." Cal had been doing his homework.

"Agent, Girl Friday, and best friend, yes."

"And you're at Grady's trailer." His tone hinted at speculation—he was fishing. "Isn't he competing against CJ?"

Harper was a smart cookie. She was undoubtedly seven steps ahead of Cal. He was like a spider who thought to lure Harper into his web, unaware that Harper was a beautiful bird who would eat him alive.

"Oh, don't you worry about me, Mr. McBane, I'm not here to take advantage of your brother before his race—although many women would be tempted." She exaggerated a wink at me. "I'm merely here to find my wayward brother who is probably as ornery and bullheaded as you are when it comes to working with siblings." She finished it off with a beautiful smile and a tilt of her head that stunned a man into not knowing when he's been slain.

She turned to me. "Have you seen him?"

"No, sorry. But I need to get over to the media tent." I grabbed my sunglasses and hat off the chair on my way out.

Her tone turned mischievous. "Yes, well...you may want to... CJ's been warming up the crowd for you."

*Great.* I groaned.

The trailer door practically came off the hinges when I opened it. Cooper sat in the cart as he said, "Grady—listen..."

I grabbed my best friend by the collar and pulled him out of the cart, throwing him aside, then climbed in the cart and drove off.

I had until I got to the other side of the infield to get my head on straight before getting to the media tent.

To say I was in a foul mood was an understatement. I tried to paste on my normal, jovial smile, but it conflicted with the cyclone of anger inside me, and probably looked a bit psychotic—not something you want in a person who was going to be behind the wheel of a thirty-three-hundred-pound machine in a few hours. Immediately, I was approached by fans who had snuck into the tent, or who were friends and family. I signed autographs and said a few words to each of them—regretting not dragging Cooper as my buffer. But I was more pissed at him than I was at Cal.

"Grady!" Junior rushed me, decked out in his Merrick gear and his all-access pass swinging around his neck. "Come on, you're late. They had to start interviewing CJ to fill in the time." He all but pushed me in front of the interviewer who was in mid-sentence with CJ.

"I'm sure Grady has prepared for the race and will give it his all." She smiled at me, baiting me with her eyes before adding, "I sent over videos of my race from here last year for him to study, and he's been working so hard." Even with the condescension dripping in her tone, she was flirting with her eyes—so unlike with Cal, I forgave the tone. With those eyes, I think I'd forgive anything.

She was back to channeling her inner-sweet Southern girl who was giving backhanded, patronizing insults. Her sidelong gazes, her unassuming flashes of a smile, and the slight blush when she caught me looking at her. It lightened me. Two could play at that game.

"Hey! I'm here now, sorry for the delay." I walked into the camera shot alongside the commentator.

Camden Grant's eyes alight with the prospect of having us both to interview at the same time. "Grady McBane, welcome. We were just discussing your preparation for your debut race."

"I heard. Thank you, CJ, for stepping in while I was delayed," I said with all the graciousness I could summon. "I'm afraid there was a bit of a struggle getting the booster seat out and the blocks off the pedals from when you last used the car." I turned to Camden. "There is obviously a major size difference between us." I pretended to secretly wince and indicated with my hand CJ's short stature. "They need to put in special pedals and a seat so CJ can reach them."

"Smaller frame means less weight for the car to have to drag around the course." CJ smiled at the camera. She did have a pretty smile when she wanted to grace people with it. She turned the smile on me—she was amused.

"Nonetheless, I still am amazed you manage to see over the steering wheel sometimes," I said and winked at the camera, bringing them into my teasing.

"Don't you worry about me; I do just fine watching the other drivers as I fly by them." She tilted her head with sincerity. "Maybe one of these days, if you make it on the track with me, I will be able to wave at you in my rearview mirror, also."

Our banter was lifting my mood. It had the same effect on those around us. Camden was chuckling as he said, "Alright, you two. Obviously, there is a good ol' friendly competition going on here. CJ, you've had a great showing the first two races, but today is about Grady. Any last-minute piece of advice?"

She stepped right up to me, close enough that we were within a hair of touching. Her head tilted almost straight up to make eye contact. Clear as day, she declared, "Don't wreck my car."

And there was the money shot.

She turned on a dime and walked away.

---

After the interview, Cooper joined me. He didn't utter a word, and I didn't speak to him. He just took his place next to me, smart enough to know I wasn't going to talk to him. Involuntarily, my eyes continued to jet around looking for Cal. Now that I knew he was in the area, it was like I expected another sneak attack.

I made my way to pit row, planning on discussing last-minute business with Bill and Gus. My eye was caught on a diminutive figure by one of the trailers, her dark ponytail swung when she shifted her weight from one leg to another. Her back was to me, but her rigid posture and crossed arms made me believe she wasn't comfortable with her company. Given it was Chase Dermott, one of Prince's execs, I could understand why. He graced her with what others may consider a charming smile as he reached to touch her elbow. She shifted, moving her elbow subtly and placing her hand on her hip.

I made my way over to them, dodging attempts by others to gain my attention as I approached the pair from the side to hear what was being discussed. Dermott leaned into CJ to draw them into a more-intimate conversation, seeming to corral her against the trailer. CJ took a determined side-step from the man—her eyes narrowing as she scanned the crowd, a small, forced smile on her face.

"CJ, there you are," I said, placing myself directly between them. "Bill is looking for you."

She jumped slightly at hearing her name, and her shoulders relaxed then straightened. "Mr. Dermott, I appreciate the interest you've taken in the team and in my career. However, as I've stated before, the only thing your money can buy is sponsorship space on my car's panels."

Dermott's smile remained but turned a shade cold.

"CJ, it was a pleasure…we can continue our conversation another time—"

Dermott tried to step around me and lean into CJ as if to kiss her cheek, but I purposely stepped between them. There was no need to block him, however, because she was already gone.

I turned to Dermott, removing all pretense of expression from my face. He was a smarmy bastard. Sure enough, Dermott's gaze was on CJ's ass as she walked away, and he was biting at his bottom lip.

"Whatever you plan on doing, don't," I said with a low, deep voice. Not quite a growl, but quiet enough to be heard just by Dermott.

"Fuck off, Grady," Dermott said. "CJ knows I'm her meal ticket. She'll come around. And you—well, paybacks are a bitch. Getting a piece of that ass—it's a bonus."

There it was. No surprise. Of course, I knew this was probably the case as soon as I heard Prince was her major sponsor. But to have it shoved in my face wasn't something I relished.

"Your arrogance is catching up with you, McBane. Come

September you'll be out of a ride again. I wonder if big brother will swoop in and save you? Tell me, are you going to be ready to beg for your job back? Looks like your pride is writing checks your skill can't cash."

Whatever. I was racing today. He was trying to get me to swing at him. Idiot.

Proud of his strikes, Dermott adjusted himself and said, "Meanwhile, I'm going to better acquaint myself with the soon-to-be newest member of the Prince racing family."

Without thought, I had Dermott, who was about four inches shorter than me, against the trailer. My words failed me, but my fists were ready to express themselves. I held the man with one of my hands on his chest, my other pointed in the man's face, and through clinched teeth said, "Don't."

"Get the fuck off, McBane," Dermott managed to grit out.

"If what you say is true, I have nothing to lose…"

"You ready to burn another bridge here? Come on, let's do it. You're already known as a difficult prima donna, a womanizer, a loser… You won't race again—you're finished after this season—do you hear me?"

"Grady—he's not worth it." Cal. Could this fucking day get any worse? "Let him go and go get ready for your race."

Fuck Cal. I didn't want it to appear I was backing down because Cal said to, but I also wanted to drive today and not draw any more attention.

A small hand was on my back, "Grady, come on…Gus is waiting for you."

CJ.

"Grady, I heard him. I get it. Just—go. Don't let him bait you like this," Cal said.

I risked a glance at Cal and CJ standing together. What the hell?

"I don't have time for this shit." I pushed off Dermott, didn't look at any of them and walked away.

I was dangerously riled up—angry enough that I shouldn't have been getting behind the wheel of a heavy piece of machinery. But I needed to keep to the itinerary.

I found Cooper and checked in with Junior before following Harper to her golf cart outside the tent. CJ was sitting in the driver's seat—and wasn't that becoming symbolic.

"Well, look at that, Grady, you are some kind of super VIP to garner a driver of this caliber," Harper teased, as we climbed in.

CJ rolled her eyes. No other explanation given. We drove to the driver's meeting, Harper droned on about the rest of the day's schedule as if I were her driver to direct. She included the fact that I also had a two-hundred-plus-mile race to run also.

Harper jumped out of the cart, and I stood, adjusted my mirrored sunglasses, and turned to thank CJ for the ride.

CJ was hanging on the steering wheel but turned to face me. "I heard you and Dermott."

"You ran to get my big brother to intervene…gee…thanks."

She sighed, "No, he was walking by. Yes, I grabbed him because the place was swarming with VIPs and media, and Dermott is an asshole. If you did anything to him, you would've been thrown out of the race…or worse."

"Wouldn't that have solved all your problems?"

She bristled. "I don't play that way."

I refused to look at her. What the hell? All day people had been making decisions for me. "I don't know what I ever did to give you the impression that I can't handle myself and make my own damn decisions…" I turned to walk off.

The sprite was quick, though, and was in front of me in a minute.

"I was trying to help. Don't be a jerk."

"I didn't need your help."

"Yeah, well, maybe I didn't need yours? Ever think of that? You started the whole thing by interfering with my conversation with Dermott to begin with."

The heat traveled up my face and my voice raised without warning. "He was coming onto you. He's a leech, CJ. I didn't think you wanted that kind of attention. He practically had you pinned in a corner."

"I had it handled."

"Didn't look like it. What did he say to you? He wasn't asking for your pie recipe…"

People were starting to stare at us. It didn't escape me that I sounded like a jealous boyfriend.

"He wanted to 'further' our acquaintance and said it would benefit me if we became more

familiar with each other. That he could help give me a 'full ride' next year." She used air quotes around the term.

I fisted my hands, wishing I had swung at him before they intervened. Now I was really acting like a jealous boyfriend.

CJ continued, "Guys like Dermott do this all the time. They think women need them to get ahead and that we will prostitute ourselves for an easier path. I'm not one of those girls. I have made it clear to him twice that I'm not one of those girls. If there is a third time, I will make it clear in a way that will leave an impression that won't heal easily."

I stood over her, she needed to understand what was going on. "Dermott has it in for me. He wants to see me ruined. But more than that, he sees…" I shifted.

*He sees that you mean something to me.* Nope. Not going to say that. "He sees that you're my friend—or he thinks you are."

She gave what I said some thought, but instead of asking about the "friend" comment, she asked, "What does Dermott have against you?"

"It's a long story. I don't want to get into it now."

"I've dealt with pricks like Dermott since I was able to fill out a bra, and I don't need a hero, Grady. I can take care of myself. I always have." She stared past me as discomfort appeared. "But," she hesitated, "It was nice to hear someone stick up for me…so, thanks."

That response wasn't what I was expecting. She sighed and relaxed her shoulders.

"I've been told I need to learn to accept when people try to help." She looked at me from below her lashes, and even though she claimed she wasn't good at being coy, she had it nailed.

"But that goes both ways, McBane. You were trying to save me from him. I was trying to save you from yourself. Good for the goose…good for the gander. Now get over it. Get your head in gear."

She shifted in her seat and started up the cart. "Well…gotta go…good luck today. Don't wreck my car."

She was gone as if the comment had never even happened. I'd bet my Tesla, if I ever brought it up, that I'd get decked or she'd leave tire marks on me with her Ducati.

And that was reason enough to calm my rage and put a slight, amused smile on my face.

## 23

*CJ*

The Sonoma track wasn't a course I had a problem relinquishing to Grady. Watching the man fly around the track in *my* car, truthfully, didn't feel so awful. It might be different if it were on a track where I felt I could do better. If it were Talladega or Daytona or, God forbid, my home track of Charlotte, it might be another story. I may have felt compelled to pull out my shotgun and take out the wheels of his Tesla.

But tracks at Sonoma or Watkins—if I had to give him a track, I'd give him those. Because, I had to admit, he was good. Those tracks were twists and turns, not just speed and finesse. There weren't banked turns to slingshot around, the speed was less, and the cars actually went up on two wheels if they took the turns too fast.

No, watching Grady on these tracks was more like cheering on a team member rather than being envious over watching someone else driving my car.

I closed my eyes behind my sunglasses and shook my head

slightly. When he drove at Michigan in a few weeks, I was sure I would change my tune. I had to stop feeling so compliant around him. He was supposed to be my competition, not my comrade. If he was a leech like Dermott, it would be easier. Having him try to play the white knight was unnerving. It should've annoyed me as it always did when men felt the need to rescue me.

Aunt Sadie always said, "There's nothing more dangerous to an independent woman than a white knight with good intentions." Meaning, a good man whose flaw was viewing women as damsels in need of rescuing. "God bless the white knight. His job wasn't always to save the damsel. Sometimes his job was to have her back while she slayed the dragon herself. Sometimes his job was to kiss her senseless when she's done."

Grady seemed legitimately concerned for me, even if his role was a bit confused.

Although, him defending me was a bit more exhilarating than my pride wanted to admit. It also confused me.

I wasn't a princess in an ivory tower. But I was beginning to realize that sometimes I wanted the white knight, damnit. I wanted someone in my corner to defend me. And, I wanted his damn kiss.

"He looks pretty good out there," Harper said, as she came up next to me to watch the monitor.

I gave a slight nod, not taking my eyes off the screen. But Harper's gaze was heavy on me. "What were you two talking about earlier when you dropped him off?"

"Nothing," I said, my focus on our car passing Dewey. I gave a little fist pump in silent excitement.

"Looked like something to me. Did it have something to do with him hauling Dermott out of the Prince tent earlier?"

I waved a hand of dismissal at my friend. "Yeah, Dermott was harassing me, again. Nothing new."

"Damnit, I talked to Jordan about this." Harper pulled out her phone, scrolling through her texts. "What do you want to do about it? I will try to find new sponsorship, okay? In the meantime, I will limit his contact with you and make sure you aren't alone with him.

I just hired a new assistant, and we can work her into the mix." She slipped her phone back in her bag. "I will tell Gus and the boys—"

"Don't. It's nothing I can't handle. I gave him his second warning. Just make sure I have a backup sponsor ready, because I don't think there will be any coming back from what happens to him if there is a next time."

"CJ—"

"It's fine. I told Grady the same thing. I'm used to it. No big deal."

"I saw Grady's eyes, he wanted to rearrange Dermott's face. Seemed to be a big deal to him."

"They have issues between them. Anyway, it doesn't matter, I told him I didn't need the hero…"

"That's too bad, because I got the impression, that he liked playing it," Harper said, and walked away.

That hung in the air as I continued to watch with tentative pride as our car passed another car and gracefully maneuver around the course. Grady was still challenged by running this course with the bulkier car, but I reluctantly admitted he was doing remarkably well.

My thumb nail went to my mouth, as it did when I was frustrated.

It wasn't our car—it was mine. *Mine*. Damnit.

I sat in the pit box for part of the race with Bill, but eventually got up and paced the pit area, watching the monitor and the pit stops when he came in—catching a glimpse of him while they changed tires.

"Strange seeing him in that behemoth." Cal came up beside me. I met him earlier when I ran into him and grabbed him to help me with Grady. He'd been speaking with Harper at the time.

However, I would've known who he was regardless. He wore slacks, a baseball hat with the McBane logo, and a short-sleeve shirt, but still too dressed up for the racetrack—especially the pit area. He was darker—brown hair, hazel eyes—but the breadth of his shoulders and casualness as he stood with his hands in his pockets, he definitely was Grady's brother.

I waited for the cars to fly by us before greeting him. "Mr. McBane."

He nodded. "Cal, please." He held out his hand since we weren't properly introduced earlier.

"CJ. CJ Lomax."

He crossed his hands over his chest and peered down at me out of the corner of his eye, taking advantage of his height to look down on me. "Oh, I know who you are." The barest tilt of his lip.

*What the hell?*

"What are you doing down this way?" We continued to watch the monitor and the cars racing by sporadically. Being a road course, they were farther apart and drove at slower speeds.

"Family business."

"Come to sweep little brother back into the family fold?"

"You'd like that, wouldn't you?"

I shrugged and muttered, "It would make my life easier, that's for sure."

He let out a small chuckle.

"Well, I'm afraid it won't be that easy for either of us."

After Grady flew by in our car, Cal straightened and turned to me. "I'd have to hand it to Merrick—this competition was a stroke of genius. It's got my curiosity piqued. It will definitely be an interesting season to watch." He held out his hand to shake mine. "It was a pleasure meeting you, CJ. From what I understand, my brother has his work cut out for him." He gave me a knowing smile and strode off.

---

Unable to sit, I began to pace the pit area with a headset, listening in on the conversation between Bill, Grady, and the spotter. My eyes were riveted to the screens as I watched Grady expertly maneuver the turns, increasing his speed through the straightaways and slowly gaining position throughout the course. I almost jumped over the wall when Dewey tapped him coming out of pit road in a dirty attempt to spin him out before regaining position.

He definitely was on Dewey's shit list now for sticking up for me. That would make his life more complicated if he didn't get Merrick's contract.

When he didn't get Merrick's contract. Because I wanted Merrick's contract. Then why was I cheering for him? Why did I want him to win—to succeed? Him winning this race, a race I'd struggled at, would not help achieve my goal.

Him winning would get in the way of fulfilling my dreams. But the thought of him losing dragged me down—especially if Dewey was the cause.

God, my head was a mess.

Just then, Grady's voice came through, threatening Dewey's manhood, and I smiled.

I liked the guy. Not liked-liked. Just, I was rooting for the guy. And, fine. If I was willing to admit it, he was attractive and seemed like a pretty good egg. And he had a charming smile...his lips...his kiss...

I shook the thought out of my head.

But watching Dewey pursue him as if there were a target on his back made me want to run Dewey into the wall more than I ever had before.

An image of me as a cartoon character with steam coming out of my ears flashed across my mind.

By the end of the race, my nerves and my nails were a mess, but Grady finished eighth' which was a damn good position out of forty-three cars—even sweeter was that Dewey finished at the back of the pack.

I ran to the finish, having to hold myself back from hugging him in my shared excitement. He climbed out of the car with a satisfied smile, proud of his decent finish. He was immediately flanked by media and crew members. Someone handed him a Mingle Singles hat. I caught his slight grimace before he placed it on his head and then began scanning the crowd.

I'm pretty sure it wasn't my imagination—his smile grew as soon as he found me.

I was a besotted girl with a crush.

Oh, Lord. What is happening to me? A guy sweeps in and defends my honor and suddenly I've got hearts in my eyes. What the hell?

Unsure of my role in this situation, I held back with my hands in the back pockets of my jeans, and I glanced up at him under my lashes but gave him an involuntary smile.

What the hell was that? Was I flirting?

With his target locked on he strode toward me in slow, but purposeful, long strides, parting the sea of people. When he reached me, I straightened, more than a little aware of the cameras and the attention on the two of us.

He, however, didn't even give them a glance.

The electricity increased with each inch he drew closer to me. I couldn't be imagining this.

"So, how'd I do?" he asked, his voice low enough only I could hear.

I shrugged my shoulder, going for indifference. "Not bad. But maybe try to go a little faster and win next time?"

He threw back his head and laughed, before hooking his arm around my shoulders and pulling me into his chest, yanking on my ponytail like a big brother would. The cameras and media went crazy shouting questions. He ignored all of them and walked me over to the rest of the crew.

Warm fuzzies…warm fuzzies throughout my body. What the hell? I wanted to reach up and kiss him soundly in front of God and the entire country. Instead, I wrapped my arm around his six-pack waist. The gesture caught his attention and his side-eye gaze shifted into something different—something more intimate.

And that was the money shot the media ran with the next day.

# 24

**Grady**

The day following my race in Sonoma, CJ, Harper, Cooper, Junior, a few other personnel, and I hopped a flight from Sonoma to LA for two packed days, including a photo shoot for a car ad campaign and a talk show appearance, and capping it off with CJ and me presenting together at the ESPYs that evening.

Well-timed photos and creative captions had the media scrambling what to make of us. They declared the chemistry between us was "palpable and swoon-worthy," but the competition between us was being shoveled at them as being fierce and aggressive. We were a mystery to solve.

Junior and Harper kept us apart as much as they could. Separate cars to the airport, separate arrivals at hotels, et cetera, to keep our contact in public to a minimum and control the image.

Harper was beside herself with glee—it was a PR dream, and she was filtering through requests for joint appearances. People wanted to see for themselves. Were we enemies? Were we frienemies? Were we hate-lovers? Or whatever other descriptions they could come up with.

Junior made it clear he'd rather us be enemies he could keep in separate camps, but money was money, and dollar signs made everything okay.

It was becoming too familiar, though, when it came to interviews and inquiries, it was more about my relationship and sex life than it was about my racing.

The few times the media caught CJ and me together being snarky and flirty, they went wild.

They wanted it.

They demanded it.

Was it rival banter, flirtation, or both?

However, when it came down to race experts, they pulled no punches. They were telling it like it was. They had their predictions and favorites for the upcoming races, and they didn't side with either one of us. It was still an open field.

"I'm not going to survive this trip," I confessed to myself, as we climbed in the limo from the airport.

Cooper followed me in and sat across from me. "You're wound a bit tight. Maybe we need to call up some old friends while we are in town, or we could go out after the awards and meet some new ones."

"Yeah, maybe." But the truth was, I didn't want that kind of distraction.

Junior got in and sat next to Cooper; the door closed behind him.

"Hey, man…" he said as we got situated.

"Where are the ladies?" Cooper asked.

"They're riding in a separate car," he replied, pulling out his briefcase and began going over the day's itinerary. "My sister has this stupid photo shoot for you two this afternoon. I'm not in favor, but it's for the sponsor."

"Sounds fun," I said, without much thought.

He rolled his eyes and slammed the paper down on his lap. "You know what pisses me off? If you two were men, this would be more

'Rocky Balboa', and less 'rom-com'. That's what would be interesting."

His frustration suddenly spiked, and he pointed an accusing finger at me. "If you were smart, you'd see what this was. It's a ploy to gain her more attention. Her 'cute' routine isn't helping you. It doesn't paint you as a serious driver. It paints you as a man drawn in by a pretty face and the challenge to melt the ice princess." His voice was tinged with a sneer. "First of all, she's not worth it. Second, I thought you were serious about this move? I thought this was more than just social media followers and a popularity contest to you—that you wanted this?"

He shuffled things in his briefcase as if it would shift him from his thoughts. His tone changed to a sullen child, "I should've known it would work out to CJ's advantage, though. It always does."

Cooper and I stared at each other, stunned. I knew he disliked CJ, but Junior had serious issues with her.

"Whatever." He wanted to let go of the topic. Fine by me. "One thing that would help is if you have a date for this evening?" he asked.

That never occurred to me. "What? Excuse me?"

"For the awards ceremony, do you have a date?"

I straightened. "No, I hadn't thought about it." Wait a minute. My head popped up. "Does CJ have a date?"

Junior let out a fake, amused sound. "No. CJ doesn't date."

"Really?" Cooper's eyes were as wide as saucers at this news and he searched me for more information.

Junior lost interest in the question and was rifling through his briefcase. "Not that I'm aware. She isn't exactly a social butterfly, and none of the guys around the track see her that way."

"That's a shame," Cooper said, and I glared at him. "What? She's a beautiful, intelligent, and sharp woman. She's got a big heart, and people seem drawn to her. I'd date her..." He smirked, knowing damn well I wouldn't react while Junior was here.

Junior chuckled but didn't look up from the papers he took out. "You haven't been around her enough, then. She's a cross between a ball buster and an ice queen. She's also a tomboy who never grew up, despite all the pretty clothes my sister tries to dress her in."

That got me thinking. I paused before asking. "What about Tommy? He must have loved her."

Junior sat still. He stared blankly at the papers in front of him.

"Tommy was both a fool and too good for the likes of her," Junior murmured.

Cooper's irritation was growing. Usually, he was easy-going and mild-mannered, but Cooper was loyal and a defender of women. "What's your problem with her?" He struggled not to clench his teeth. "What's all the hate for?"

Junior shifted the papers around, but even I could tell he wasn't really reading them. He was uncomfortable with our conversation but didn't want to admit it. "I don't hate her," he said softly, "But I don't like her either."

He uttered the last statement but quickly stared between the two of us. "Everyone thinks CJ is the underdog. The one who sets fire to an industry just because she's a girl." He began tapping the papers on his briefcase, trying to straighten them. "But you want to know what I think—I think it's the opposite. I think because she's a woman, she gets a lot of leeway. She gets a lot of extra chances and extra praise that she may not deserve to compensate for the fact that she's different.

"Is CJ a decent driver, yes. She can drive. But is she the second coming? Is she the next Richard Petty, Dale Earnhardt, or Jimmie Johnson? No. So, I don't understand why she is followed with so much hype when there are men, like yourself, who are just as deserving. It's like the pendulum swings too far in the opposite direction."

He shoved the papers back in the bag, giving up the pretense of working. "It just pisses me off." He gritted out.

He dropped his hands to his lap and stared outside.

"Tommy could've been great. He would've dusted her. Truly. I miss him because we grew up together and he was my friend. But if he would've lived, watching him and CJ coming up in the ranks together would've been explosive. I don't think she would've gotten as far because he was better. She knew it. He knew it—we all knew it." He stared into the distance as if Cooper and I weren't even there any longer.

"It's why Dewey hates her so much. Dewey doesn't have Tommy's talent. He can't be mad at a dead man—especially his brother. But he can direct that anger to the one who was left alive. Dewey was furious at his little brother for proposing to CJ, but I think Dewey was equally insulted when she turned Tommy down."

Junior's eyes fell to his lap and he put his hands on his knees.

"That night…" Junior shook his head, closed his eyes, "Tommy was in rough shape, and Dewey wasn't making it any better. It was too intense for me. I found a girl I liked and decided I'd rather enjoy her company than the two brothers. I regretted the girl and leaving him that night."

"Not a day goes by that I don't wonder what if I stayed…" Junior lifted a hand and without words indicated the sad, inevitable outcome. "Dewey was the last one to see his brother alive but refuses to accept culpability. He blames CJ for manipulating and pulling his heart-sick brother along. He blames her for his brother being in the car and wrapping it around the tree."

While I knew most of this, it was Cooper's first time hearing the story that changed so many lives. "What a prick," Cooper whispered.

Junior's eyebrows rose. "Yeah, well. Dewey's always been a bit like that. Doesn't help that he isn't as talented as Tommy was and is reminded of it at every race."

I was more focused on Junior. We pulled into the entrance of the hotel and began to shift around, gathering our things.

I grabbed Junior's arm to still him. "What about you? Why the tension? Why are you so against her being at Merrick?"

Junior pulled away from me, not insulted, but not happy about the question. "Because when all was said and done, my father gave her my ride. Said I was better suited for the business side of the industry."

Then the mask completely fell. He thumbed his chest. "Before all of this happened, CJ and Tommy were the golden children coming up. CJ was being approached by several teams to race for them in the Energy Blast series. Once Tommy died, it was clear she was on the outs with the Dupree family, and CJ wasn't going to get anymore offers. My sister and CJ were always tight, and my family enveloped her further.

I had been racing in the Energy Blast circuit at the time. My father decided soon after that I was needed in the office. He gave her my ride. He replaced me with a woman. A woman. Do you have any idea how hard a pill that was to swallow—how hard it was for me to show my face at the track or to see her in my car? If Tommy hadn't died, who knows where'd she'd be. But he did and she's here. For now."

Junior was punishing CJ for taking his car.

Cooper and I caught each other's expressions as Junior stormed out of the car and made his way into the hotel.

# 25

*CJ*

Harper and I drove in the back of a Town Car alone. "We'll head over to the photo shoot first and back to the hotel to rest and change. Wait until you see what I have for you to wear tonight..." she sang the last part and it set my nerves on edge.

"Harper—" I gave a frustrated sigh.

"Don't 'Harper' me. This is LA. You're a celebrity whether you want to be one or not, and you have an image to establish and uphold." She dug through her purse that reminded me of Hermione Granger's bag in the *Deathly Hallows*. She could pull anything out of that thing.

"I can't drive next week if my ankle is broken from walking in five-inch heels."

"They are three inches...and a small platform. You'll be fine." She injected confidence I didn't really believe I possessed.

She pulled out two tubes of gloss. She handed me one, opened a silver compact and precisely applied the shiny gloss to her own.

"Don't glare at me. You will look luscious and Grady will probably follow you around like a puppy dog—"

"Stop saying things like that. Grady isn't into me like that way. Why do you of all people have to keep perpetuating the belief? I thought we were supposed to be competitors. I don't know what the hell is going on and I feel ridiculous." I wanted to throw the lip gloss across the car but refrained realizing how immature I would seem.

She paused what she was doing and stared at me as if I had thrown the lip gloss.

"Why do you feel ridiculous?"

"Because there is no way someone like Grady would ever be interested in someone

like—"

She held up her hand. "Stop. Give me a break. I've never known you to be so self-deprecating. Frankly, it doesn't suit you." Her tone was begging for patience.

"Even if he showed interest in me, even if say, we gave in to a moment of weakness, it would be foolish, it would be fleeting, and it would be stupid."

"Whoa. Wait. The hell you say?" She handed me the compact, gesturing for me to put on the gloss. "Tell me what the hell is going on with you."

As I put on the lip gloss, I filled her in about the night after the Pocono race. About Grady's visit, about Gus's interference. About how it was swept under the rug, and neither of us have discussed it again.

I was hoping she would be able to tell me what it meant.

In all my years, I'd never seen Harper speechless. "Say something." I motioned at her.

"Well—" she opened her mouth, but nothing came out. She just stared at me.

"See, even you can't believe he came on to me." I threw myself back against the seat of the car.

"Slow your roll, there." She found her words and her expression clued me in to her annoyance. "You caught me off guard because that happened weeks ago and I'm just finding out about this now.

What the hell, CJ?" She slapped my arm. "Wh-Why am I just hearing about this?"

I slunk back.

"I don't want to talk about it." I defiantly crossed my arms.

We pulled up to a curb and the car came to a stop.

"Huh. Yeah. That isn't an option for you. Unfortunately, we don't have the time and I don't have the libations needed for me to break this down." She put her hand to her forehead, "Jesus, take the wheel, I should've seen this coming. Why didn't I see this coming?"

"Because you didn't think he'd—" I gathered my things and almost threw the damn pink, pearly lip gloss back at her.

"Shut the hell up with that. No, because that man looked like he wanted to devour you from the moment he met you. Men like him don't walk away from what they want."

We stepped out of the car. She spoke briefly to the driver and then paused before turning back to me. "As your agent and manager, I'm going to tell you appearances and events like the ones we have scheduled on this trip are important in establishing you as a brand and increasing your marketability. Your exposure with Grady is something to capitalize on. The media's speculation as to who you are to each other is driving their interest." She adjusted her bag on her shoulder before walking to our destination.

"As your friend, that man looks at you like forbidden fruit...and he's starving." We approached the door to the building but before we went in, she grabbed both my hands. "Now this is where the Jekyll and Hyde parts of me differ.

"Your agent is telling you to keep your clothes on around that man and maintain a safe, appropriate distance. Let the public wonder if there is something going on between the two of you—the curiosity is what will keep them interested in both of you. But don't cross the line. If you two ever did become an item, it could jeopardize the interest you have created. Plus, you don't need the distraction while you're fighting for your career.

"Now, your best friend of countless years takes one look at Grady McBane and wants you to go jump the man at the first possible opportunity. Because, well...wow. That would be hot." She smiled and opened her eyes with excitement. "I'm conflicted, so you're on your own."

Just as quickly she flipped her switch and added, "However, both sides of me agree, having him trying to undress you with his eyes in front of the cameras is yummy! So, keep doing that."

I deflated.

"Like you said, I'm forbidden fruit. I'm not something he really wants. I'm something he can't have. He's in LA. Home of super-models and actresses. Have you seen the list, and it is a long list, of women connected to him? Yeah. I won't be seeing him this trip." And not having his attention, seeing him give it to someone else, wasn't going to help my mixed emotions concerning him.

Harper squeezed my hand and opened the door. "We will see."

We walked into the warehouse studio where Grady and I were going to pose for a joint ad campaign for the car company that supplied our engines. I grumbled to Harper, "I better not be crawling on the hood of a car in a bikini."

She shook her head, smiling. "No, you're not."

We spoke briefly to the photographer about what was involved —a few poses of the two of us and then a few with the car. I went to my wardrobe room to prepare, and then came out to join the photographer when I was ready.

Given my outfit, I wasn't too concerned about the shoot. I wore painted-on, skin-tight jeans that still had a nice amount of stretch to them, and a silky indigo blue shirt with several buttons missing. My hair was teased out and my make-up was heavy and smoky. There were stilettos involved, but I figured I wouldn't be walking much, so I was safe.

I walked over to the photographer who was set up in front of the company's latest sports convertible.

What I wasn't prepared for was Grady.

Holy bejeezus.

His five o'clock shadow was in full effect, his hair was stylishly messy, and I swore it shone more than usual. However, all of that was seen out of the periphery of my locked-on, tractor-beam-like focus of his naked, gorgeous, tanned, sculpted chest.

I'd had that chest under my hands, but I never saw it. I felt cheated. I was so cheated.

His stride was between a saunter and a swagger. Yeah, he knew I was checking him out, and his smirk was indicative of him enjoying every minute of it—maybe even more than I was. How had I never seen him shirtless before?

His faded jeans hung low enough on his hips I doubted there was anything under them. Commando. Oh, my.

His feet were bare—I don't know with everything else why, or how, I noticed that, but it just made it hotter.

I made a conscious effort to close my mouth; Icrossed my arms, and cocked out one hip.

"Did they forget to give you clothes?"

His eyes perused me from my stilettos, to my hair, and then zeroed back on my chest. I'd claim it was cold, but that wasn't what had his eyes drawn to my chest. It was my body's response and he fricking knew it. His smirk turned into a three-alarm grin.

Grady strode into my space until he hovered over me. "You look hot."

"You look undressed." I stared up but didn't move back.

"It seems that's the way women want me."

The photographer ran over to us. "No, no. We don't want to waste that chemistry here. Get to your spots. I need to capture all of that on film."

I rolled my eyes with exaggeration and turned on my heel. Did I mention the photographer was a woman? Of course, that is why all this made sense.

I really shouldn't complain. I was so worried about being objectified—isn't this better?

She positioned us to stand in front of each other. The convertible sports car was strategically placed behind us.

"Act natural, even talk to each other if you want and forget I'm here. Agnes! Get the lights!" The photographer began moving around us, but Grady's eyes never left mine.

"Don't know how she expects me to act natural," I grumbled and shifted on my feet.

"Does something about me make you uneasy?" He lifted an eyebrow.

"You mean your half-nakedness?" I said and looked away.

He chuckled. "So, I do affect you. Good to know. I wasn't so sure."

"As if it would matter." What was I saying?

Both eyebrows lifted and he hooked his thumbs to his front pockets. "Why, Charlotte Jean, are you feeling neglected?"

"Shut up." I scowled and glanced down to see the photographer under us and shooting an upward angle. I sent a death glare at her. Well, that probably won't help my image.

She stopped clicking and gestured to me. "That's perfect! No, keep going."

I couldn't bear to look at either of them, so I turned around, about ready to flee. He put his hand on my shoulder and turned me back. "CJ, I'm just messing with you. Come on, I'm sorry."

His hand went under my chin and he lifted my face to his.

His damn beautiful eyes transformed me into a moth to his flame. I hated feeling so trapped by him. But he was touching me… was close to me and looking at me with warmth and familiarity….

The photographer's clicking was background noise, but she muttered, "That's great, keep going."

I almost let out a laugh when Grady gave her a side-eye glare. She caught it and backed up a bit, but the camera's clicking indicated she caught it on film, too.

"Give us a minute." His words were a command, not a request.

She backed off. God-man had spoken.

Grady's hands gently slid down both my arms and captured my hands. I didn't stare directly into his light, knowing what it did to my concentration, but I could feel the weight of his concern. "What's going on? What's wrong?"

I was discombobulated. He was making me a fool.

I shrugged him off and walked toward the back of the set to the sexy convertible that seemed to mock the person I was trying to be. I waved it off. "It's nothing—me being stupid."

He sauntered over, yes, I watched him saunter…why is it when men are shirtless, they seemed to walk differently? Slower and like a peacock.

Wait. Why was I doing that to myself? I wasn't being stupid. This shit was confusing.

"Charlotte," he whispered.

Oh, Lordy.

"What is it?" He bent his head to make eye contact.

"It's this…" Breaking the connection, I gestured between us. "You coming over to my house. Us practically attacking each other…only stopping because Gus showed up." I turned from him because even though I found the courage to be blunt about it, I wasn't confident enough to do it to his face. "It's us both pretending it didn't happen…not even mentioning it." I gestured in frustration. "And then it's this ruse they have us acting out." I glanced over my shoulder at him. He stood, legs spread, his arms folded across his chest and focused on me. But surprisingly he wasn't smiling, wasn't making light of anything, and wasn't moving to react.

"I'm not good at being coy or dancing around some type of flirtatious game." I pointed at the two of us. "This. Whatever is going on with us is very confusing to me, and I don't like that Harper wants to me to act a certain way, Merrick wants me to act a certain way, and then there's what the media thinks is going on, and whatever game you're playing with me, it's…it's…unnerving and upsetting and distracting and…I'm not good at…any of it." I moved over and leaned against the trunk of the car.

I crossed my arms, taking a brief glance at my well-defined cleavage, thanks to a bra that had to be engineered by someone from MIT for the gravity-defying abilities it had. I scanned down my legs to the damn stilettos mocking me.

It reminded me of the first time we met. "Do you remember what happened the last time you saw me in stilettos?"

His mouth hinted at a salacious half grin. His tongue darted out and licked his bottom lip, as he stared at mine. "Oh, I remember."

Heat traveled up my neck and over my cheeks. "Yeah, well, that pretty much sums up my attempt at femininity. I'm not good at flirting or playing the sexy femme fatale Harper wants me to be—

what everyone expects me to be. This confident, sexy, strong woman—"

"Wait…wait." He closed his eyes and held up his hand. "Stop." He grabbed my hand and put it on his chest. His naked chest. I stared at my hand resting over his heart. I studied the faint freckles scattered around his chest that spoke of the time he must spend in the sun, and the small, light sprinkle of blond hair, wishing I could caress his chest and discover how soft it was.

"Do you feel that?" He cupped my cheek, tilting my face slightly and pulling me into his orbit. "Do you feel how it beats?" His eyes darted back and forth between mine, searching for understanding. "I didn't just run a race. You do that. You cause my heart to beat that way. And you do it every damn time I'm around you. Whether it's your race suit, jean shorts, or mile-high stilettos. It isn't just your snark, your determination, or your beauty. It's—it's all of you."

Click-click-click…click…click… The photographer's intrusive lens was two feet from us. "Yes, that is perfect, you guys. Could you move a bit more to the right of the car emblem so we could get it in the shot? That would be perfect."

Grady's cheeks flared a bit pink as he stepped back, and our connection was broken. Before I dropped my hand from his chest, I stood on my toes, pulled him down to meet me and kissed his cheek. I didn't care if she got this on film.

"Thank you," I whispered words just for him.

The rest of the session took place and we did as we were asked. I couldn't say it was comfortable, but I would at least have the most romantic moment of my life captured on film.

Not many people can claim that.

# 26

*Grady*

This woman had me climbing up the hood of a car...is this what my life has become?

The photographer flitted around me as if this were the freaking *National Geographic* photoshoot and I was a damn mountain lion in the wild. She had CJ behind the wheel of the convertible and me "stalking my prey" —her words.

"Yes, Grady...give her the eyes, drop your shoulder, stick out your ass in the air like a tail."

You've got to be kidding me with this shit.

Meanwhile, I'm fighting hard—okay, not the right term—I'm fighting strongly against the bulge I can't get rid of in my pants. If the photographer captures that, I will absolutely pack my bags and move to Switzerland. Or maybe Morocco.

Damn.

This is humiliating. I'm all for being eye candy. In the past I thoroughly enjoyed being the object of women's affection. And, no lie…CJ was eye-fucking me and she wasn't even aware of it—it was sexy as hell.

If she didn't stop licking her lips, I was going to pull her out of that car and bite them.

When she caught herself about to drool, she'd try to cover it and smirk at me. But if that photographer told me one more time to stick my ass in the air… My annoyance was radiating even though I was going for seduction.

The light blush to her cheeks that appeared once I walked onto the set and hadn't left her face didn't go unnoticed. I don't think it was entirely from the heat of the lamps. But that only made things, besides my ego, swell more.

I kept hoping they'd turn up the fan a tad and it would blow her blouse open just a bit more. It would be fair. I knew she was wearing a bra, but I really wanted a better glimpse of her cleavage. To me it was more seductive than fully exposed breasts. It kept you wanting and wondering. Plus, the angle I was poised in hanging over her, gave me a good shot down her shirt…if the fan would blow just a tad more from the left.

This is what I've become.

I ducked my head and stared at the member of my body shooting toward the object of my attention.

CJ let out a small giggle. She giggled. It was adorable and so unlike her. I looked up from under my lashes at her. "I'm not done talking to you about the effect you have on me."

She stilled. "You have a funny way of showing it."

"Oh, trust me, sweetheart, it's quite a challenge to not show it."

Sonofabitch.

"Come on, Grady…just a bit more. Try shifting your leg. Or… actually, let's get you on your knees with a full shot of your chest as you kneel over her…."

And expose my "growing" fascination of CJ's cleavage… "Nope. I'm done."

CJ's laugh washed over me like a tidal wave. It was beautiful even if it was at me and not with me.

But the photographer wouldn't be thwarted. "Um, okay…well, how about we restage…"

Cooper, for once not buried in his phone, was still attempting to shield his amusement. I shot him a *Do-your-job-and-wrap-this-up-I-want-to-leave* look that he's come to know very well.

He took the hint, looking down at his watch, then nudged Harper, who was startled from her phone. "I'm afraid we're on a tight schedule and have to leave shortly."

Harper slipped her phone back in her pocket and added, "Maybe one more shot and we have to leave. I believe the client wanted something with low lights and the two of them in shadows, or something seductive."

I glared at Cooper and he shrugged as if to say, *I tried.*

"Alright, let's get one more thing in. Agnes, change to the other lighting and let's rotate to the side of the car."

I waited until the photographer was distracted and her camera was out of her hands.

"A moment, please. CJ and I need to speak privately." I jumped off the side of the car facing away from everyone. I reached in the car, lifted CJ, and slung her over my shoulder, caveman-style.

"Grady, what the hell…" She slapped me on the ass. Quite soundly. It was hot and only made my smile larger and the tightness in my pants more distinct.

"We have unfinished business. Give us five…" I looked at her ass and lifted my eyebrows in appreciation. "Or maybe fifteen minutes."

I took her to the back of the studio, to the dressing area I utilized earlier, and closed the door. As soon as her feet hit the floor, her hands were on her hips. "What the ever-loving hell are you doing?"

"I'm proving how much I'm not ignoring you." I growled. "How real my attraction to you is." I backed her up against the door of the dressing room. Her gaze dropped. Her hands going directly to my naked chest.

I cupped her beautiful face, tipping it up to me until she met my eyes. "You're gorgeous. I'm as hard as granite from staring at your cleavage for the last twenty minutes…"

"You're a man…a stiff breeze could do that…"

"Shut up and take a fucking compliment, Charlotte." I brushed my thumb across her cheek. Her focus darted from my eyes to my mouth. Damn.

"I didn't address that night…but ither did you. I assumed by the way you dismissed me when Gus showed up, you felt like it was a mistake. That his presence knocked some sense into you. I didn't want to make things more awkward by bringing it up. But trust me, I've wanted to kiss you again…"

I stared at her lips until I couldn't wait any longer. When her tongue darted, I took it as an invitation, a challenge, and lowered myself slowly into the kiss, giving her time to stop me.

Instead, she met me halfway.

Her arms wrapped around me, pulling me down to her. She was sweet and warm and so small in my arms, but so full of life and energy.

The breasts I'd been ogling over all day were up against me with only a thin piece of material between them—material I wanted to rip off. I cupped her ass in both hands, wanting to lift her up and push between her legs.

Her arms were roaming from my neck to my back and even back down to my chest and up to my jaw.

"Grady…" she moaned my name, and I swear it was the most seductive thing I'd ever heard. I kissed down her neck and back up behind her ear. I was trailing back down, determined to make my way to her breasts—

"Excuse me…Mr. McBane…Ms. Lomax? If you're done… um…talking…they're ready for you back on set. Your people said you have to get ready to leave and they need a few more shots."

CJ froze even as her breath was coming fast and heavy.

I hung my head, "Sonofabitch. Can no one leave us alone for more than a few minutes?"

"Damnit." She straightened and squirmed out of my arms. "Do you know what this looks like?" She wobbled on her feet, and I swung an arm around her to steady her.

I pulled her back into me and kissed her on top of her head. "You're so damn adorable."

She shoved at me. "Enough."

She was annoyed. Although I didn't understand why, and she didn't give me a chance to ask. She was out the door, leaving me to deal with the fact that I couldn't leave the dressing room with evident arousal sporting in my pants. Until I had CJ in my bed, this was a losing battle.

# 2 7

## CJ

"I'm going to kill you."

"You say that every time you put on a dress." Harper adjusted the slip of material draped over my body, disguised as clothing.

"This is barely a napkin."

"It met your requirements. It isn't flashy. It doesn't have a plunging neckline, and it covers your breasts."

I picked at the hemline—the one that barely reached mid-thigh.

The dress was a little black dress. Little being the principal word. It had a slight shimmer to it and a modest boat neckline that cut strategically across the edge of my shoulders. Things took a drastic turn in the back. I turned halfway to view the deep plunge exposing everything down to the small of my back. The two halves were held together at the shoulders with a silver chain.

Harper had the hairdresser style my hair in a twist to accentuate the neck and back. My makeup consisted of simple, but smokey eyes, and a deep red on my lips.

Harper took in a deep breath and then breathed out, "Wow."

I stared at myself. She'd dressed me before. But she dressed me the way she would dress herself. This was different, more conservative from the front and from the back, bolder than what she would wear. Even though it was still a dress—she'd listened to what I didn't want, and it was more me than her.

She brought over the simple black Loubou heels. Only three inches this time. I'd also been wearing them around the house at home to get used to them. They were going to be my "go-to" heels at home—I even bought an extra pair—so I would be used to them and not fall into the arms of any god-men any more.

"Let's get going. We're supposed to meet them downstairs." Harper handed me an unassuming black clutch with my cell and lipstick. Nothing bedazzled or glittering this time.

I tore my eyes off my own reflection to take in Harper's outfit. Her beautiful blond hair was shiny and straight. She wore a Grecian-style, one-shoulder, dark navy dress that draped to her knees, and paired it with sexy metallic sandals.

I smiled at her. "You're striking, as always." She smiled back as we left the room.

"Wait until Grady gets a load of you..." Mischief danced in Harper's eye.

"Don't start." I stepped up to the elevator.

"Come on. What was up with the hand to the chest thing? I've been waiting for you to tell me—you know, me—your best friend. I know you won't answer once we get around everyone, so spill now." We walked into the elevator and I pushed the button to take us to the lobby.

I waved her away. "Nothing to tell. We were playing to the camera."

"Don't give me that. The sexual chemistry was so combustible, we were lucky no one lit a match. Hell, I was tempted to jump him."

"You should have. It wouldn't matter to him who it was." We arrived and I walked off first.

"Bullshit." She followed, lengthening her strides to keep in step with me. Her brows were drawn, and her tone annoyed. "CJ—"

"Grady would be the first to tell you his reputation is well-earned. He loves women—all women. He's handsome and could charm a nun out of her habit—" We were in the lobby now, and I searched the area for something to distract Harper from this conversation.

"Yes, but—" I tuned Harper's argument out. I found proof and it made me want to vomit—I didn't want to be right.

I took in a deep breath.

I tried to bleach out the memory of our time in the dressing room this afternoon. The memory of his naked chest under my hands, the feel of his hair as my hands combed through it, the way he looked at me….it was cheapened by the manicured claws currently mimicking the same movements by the surgically enhanced Barbie draped over him, practically in his lap as he sat in the lobby.

I gave Harper an exaggerated, pointed look and channeled my inner Vanna White before walking up behind Grady. I cocked out my hips, struck a pose, and gave a grand flourish of my hands presenting my proof before plastering on my best plastic smile and altering my voice. "And…I rest my case."

I clapped my hands together and walked toward the bar, allowing for an extra swing in my step. I was hurt, but hell if I'd admit it. I'd rather focus on the fact that I was right.

I wasn't anything special to him.

I was CJ. He was Grady.

The woman he was smiling at—the kind of woman he was used to—was perfectly put together. Blond hair, long legs—she screamed sex.

Hell, she probably screamed during sex.

I closed my eyes. I didn't need that image. Him having sex with someone like her.

"Beer, bartender." You know what, screw it. "Actually, give me a shot of Fireball, too. It's going to be a long night." I was going to be forced to play this part and spend time with Grady. He was going to be a kid in a candy store with the women in LA, and I was going to be forced to watch.

I walked to the side of the bar and sat, so I could watch the door. The shot came first, and I downed it before the bartender even put it on the bar top.

Harper walked in behind me. Slowly. "He heard you—Grady."

The bartender gave me a cautious expression, quickly placing a draft in front of me. Now that was a man who knew what a woman needed.

"Don't know how he could with the woman breathing in his ear —you know, I don't give a crap." I took a deep swig of the beer, not caring how unladylike it was, or that my lipstick left a huge, blood-red smudge on the glass.

"CJ..." Harper sat next to me.

I held up a hand. "Don't. I'm here. I will get through tonight, but you won't push him on me anymore. If you're my friend, you will cut this shit out." I gulped down the beer as any man from my garage would. "Let the media speculate whatever they damn well please, but we will never be anything besides competitors."

This afternoon he had me pegged up against the door in the dressing room. Now he has a woman on his lap in the lobby. Fine. Maybe that's his way, but it isn't mine. I had another pull off the beer. "I've got no time for these games and I'm not someone's play-thing. I have priorities."

Besides, I have my own reputation to protect.

"However, the minute he's seen sucking face or more with another woman, you know they will spin it as something different. They will start speculating that I'm heartbroken, even if they never confirmed we were ever together." My tone raised and my arms began flailing with indignation. "Pity for the girl who lost the boy, and then it will be pity for the girl who lost her ride."

Harper ordered a wine and sat next to me. "You don't know that." Her tone wasn't convincing.

"He's Grady—the men want to be him, and the women want to be with him. When all is said and done, he will be the hero." I couldn't think of a scenario where he didn't come out on top, and I despised that my hands were beginning to shake.

Harper stayed quiet, and it was like a hole opened in my stomach. I expected her to defend me again. To tell me I was wrong. Instead, she was contemplative. Maybe I was closer to being right than I thought I was.

Crap. Not even my best friend was going to lie to me anymore.

# 28

*Grady*

My cock was going to rebel against me.

I tried to have a conversation with it in the shower that evening, and even "stroked" its ego, but it wasn't happy with me.

Close proximity to CJ all afternoon, the kiss, the groping...and then nothing.

My cock definitely was unhappy with me.

And then in walked Isabella Mossimo, an Italian actress I spent some time with last summer. She just showed up. Of course, someone with Isabella's ego didn't bother to think I may already have a date because most men would just change their plans to be with her. She also had a way of causing scenes when she felt ignored or slighted.

I ran back to Chicago last time I was in LA with her—she was a lot of drama.

I greeted Isabella and tried to explain I was waiting for a group —didn't faze her. I explained I was waiting for Harper and CJ, clearly indicating we had dates—she didn't care. I sat in the chair and said, "It was good to see you again," clearly trying to end our conversation, and she sat on the arm of the chair and draped herself over it. She pouted, even stuck her breasts in my face.

Before I could remove her, she slipped into my lap, bit my earlobe, and with her sexy voice said, "Grady, I remember last year? How hot we were? I remembered. I didn't wear panties this time."

Behind me another, more dominant, female voice kicked me in the stomach. "And I rest my case."

I stood so quickly, Isabella flew off my lap and I had to catch her before her ass hit the ground.

CJ.

Fuck.

My cock popped up and Isabella figured it was for her.

"Yes," Isabella giggled and tried to push me back in the chair. "I knew you remembered…"

Shit. "No. I mean…sorry."

I pried Isabella off me just as I saw the beautiful, very naked back of CJ as she walked to the bar. Her ass swayed like a metronome that my pulse rate synced itself to.

My cock acted as a dog on a scent and started to follow her.

Lord, help me. Isabella was yanking on my arm like a leash. Then came her whining. It was what preceded her full-scale drama, tabloid-worthy meltdown. Isabella didn't take rejection lightly.

Cooper was on his phone in a nearby group of chairs. I gave him the *Dude-help-a-brother-out* look. His response was to shrug and motion to his phone. His eyes skimmed over me and widened—he saw CJ and her dress and the swing of her hips. He pointedly looked at Isabella and my expression, chuckled, then mouthed, "You're so screwed." I was going to kill him. I gave him a very juvenile gesture involving a middle finger, and I don't regret it.

Junior walked off the elevator and caught my eye.

"Grady, aren't you happy to see me?" Isabella's voice began to rise, and I knew it was moments away from screeching. Junior walked over. Perfect.

"Isabella, actually I wanted to introduce you to my *boss*. The owner of my team." Okay, so I was blowing smoke up her ass and inflating Junior a bit, but it was for a good cause. Isabella loved money and power. If she thought Junior had either, I may get out of this unscathed. "Everett Merrick, Junior, I'd like to introduce you to Isabella Mossimo." Junior's eyes had stars in them.

"No introduction needed. I know exactly who Ms. Mossimo is, and it's an honor to meet you."

I thought the man may bend over and kiss her hand. Dial it back, man.

But Isabella always appreciated anything that inflated her ego, and she let me go.

I raced to the bar. Cooper followed at a slower pace and said, "We don't have long. The car will be here soon."

"Go make sure Junior takes Isabella in a separate car. Make sure he keeps her away from me." I practically grabbed Cooper. "Please, man. I need to fix this."

Cooper held up his hand in placation. "Alright, relax."

I surveyed the bar until I found her. She wore a beautiful, back-less, black dress that accentuated her toned body. Her breasts were completely covered. However, since she was clearly braless, the material laid perfectly over the swell of her breasts. It made my mind wander, and was sexier than any push-up, exposing, low-cut design. My hands begged to touch, to lift, and to caress.

I wove through the chairs and approached her and Harper from behind, admiring the view close-up. Her entire back was bare, and I wanted to…needed to touch it. However, I knew by her tone in the lobby, if there was ever a time CJ would kick me in the balls, it would be now.

My dick wasn't getting the warning.

No amount of rearranging was going to keep him in line. *Cold showers for days, my man. Calm the hell down.*

Cooper caught up with me, leaning forward in a low tone. "Junior is in la-la-land, literally. No problem with him taking Isabella, separately. But Allie and Star were trying to reach us and were hoping you could get them into the after-party. That might be fun—" He went silent. I hadn't removed my gaze from CJ and Harper. "Oh, wow. Grady…" He chuckled. "Nevermind."

"Shut the fuck up..." I gritted my teeth and smiled. I didn't need Cooper giving me shit. I wanted my hand on her back and I didn't want to remove it all night. I wanted all the men in that auditorium—hell, all the men throughout the country who were going to have wet dreams about her after tonight's broadcast—to see my brand on her skin.

"You're so screwed. I'll tell Allie and Star you have plans... Do I need to remind you that this is a horrible idea? You need to check yourself, my man. Checkered flag. Remember?"

I didn't answer. In the back of my mind, my libido was attempting to hog-tie my conscience and my conscience was checking out.

Harper saw me, and CJ caught her looking at me.

"Don't you gentlemen clean up nicely." Harper's accent was even stronger outside the Carolinas. "Your suit and tie will look amazing next to CJ's dress—it will be perfect."

There was a moment of awkward silence. I said nothing. CJ's stare was blank and disengaging.

"Well, you two are breathtaking." Cooper jumped in because clearly my mouth wasn't ready to join the party. Cooper rescuing me was a new occurrence; usually he was the one tongue-tied and following my lead.

My eyes were working hard, memorizing every inch of her—studying the texture of her hair, the richness of the red on her lips, and the narrowing of her eyes.

More awkward silence.

Cooper nudged me again. "Don't the women look amazing, Grady?" Then, trying to figure out a way to give me more time to join the world of intelligent conversationalists, he added, "Those dresses are beautiful—"

"But I think they forgot the back of yours." It was a very bad attempt at lightening the moment. Even to me, it sounded like an insult or a rebuke.

CJ's reaction was a derisive smirk.

She jumped off the bar stool and turned around, showing me the beautiful outline of her back. Up close it was mouthwatering.

The way the material draped the small of her back was like an arrow that led to her perfectly rounded ass. She turned her head around, looking over her shoulder and asked, "You noticed, huh? Like it?"

I nodded. Trying to figure out a way to stop being an idiot.

"Good." She grabbed her purse off the bar, and then turned halfway, taking a step toward me. "I'm glad you like the back, because it will be the only view of me you will have this evening. Just stay three steps behind me and we will both be happy."

# 29

## CJ

He hasn't left my side. It was more than just an invisible tether that held us together. When we got out of the car and walked the carpet, his hand was on my back. As we walked through the crowd, he tried to hold my hand so we didn't separate, but I pulled out of it. By the time we made it to the seats, though, I'd had enough.

I even insisted on Harper sitting between us in the audience, threatening a full-scale scene if she didn't. Harper's Southern, all-is-well smile was plastered on her face as we stood in the aisle debating seating arrangements, "CJ, honey. Let's just take a seat so the camera can see the two of you in the same shot when they turn on the audience."

"Remember Daytona two years ago…" I glared at Harper with a silent communication, reminding her of the fiasco that led to a man almost singing soprano the rest of his life, and Harper earning her paycheck in smoothing out the fallout.

From the speed in which Harper sat her ass down in between us, she remembered Daytona, and Cooper and Grady took the hint.

The rest of the evening was uneventful. I kept true to my statement and stayed a step or two ahead of Grady all night. Even making a point to be more social than I usually was, just so I didn't get stuck talking with him.

Grady and I were asked to present an award. They announced us as the "dynamite, dueling race duo." We smiled and walked out. Again, I made sure to walk a step or two in front of him to emphasize we weren't a couple. We read the scripted lines and handed out the award. Even as we walked off stage, I kept my distance until I was literally swept off my feet.

Davy Johnson, Carolina's running back and my longtime friend, came and picked me up, twirling me around. First, no one in their right mind would try that. Second, I didn't even know I had the ability to let out a girly shriek. It was quite annoying. I liked Davy, so I didn't hit him too hard.

Davy gave me season tickets every year. Plus, my, oh my, the scowl on Grady's face…the move clearly pissed Grady off. So, I gave Davy some leeway.

"Look at you, Ms. Hotness." He held my arm up in the air and twirled me around like a ballerina. I never saw Davy all dressed up and handsome. His dark mocha skin looked beautiful with his custom-made suit, and I had to admit my heart fluttered a bit at his smile of appreciation. "You clean up nicely. If they hadn't announced you on the stage, I wouldn't have known it was the little pipsqueak who never gets out of her Chucks and T-shirts. Can't wear that dress on the bike without being indecent." He smiled devilishly; the man was a tireless but harmless flirt. He was an old friend of Tommy's and would never look at me any other way.

We talked for a bit, the entire time, Grady's eyes bored a hole through me. "What's with your partner over there?" Davy asked. "I gotta know the story with you two, and not just this media hype. I can't tell if he wants to tie you to his bed or to the bumper of his car."

I smacked Davy's arm. "Shut up." I crossed my arms over my chest. "It's nothing. It's just this stupid PR contest thing."

Davy's brows went up. "So the contest isn't real?"

"Oh, it's as real as a heart attack. It's the only real thing they're printing, though. Grady and I have nothing else to do with each other besides that." *Liar, liar, pants on fire.*

I knew his touch the moment his hand skimmed my back. "CJ, come on, let's go."

Grady.

"Grady McBane." I motioned to Grady. "Meet Davy Johnson. Davy is an old friend of mine from Charlotte."

Davy held out his hand and Grady shook it, never removing his left hand from the small of my back.

Someone called Davy's name. "Alright, well, I got to go. Are you going to the after-party?"

"I think so. It depends." I didn't look at Grady, but he shifted and widened his hand on my back.

"It depends? No. It doesn't depend. What's it depend on?" He glanced briefly at Grady and his smile widened. "Hell, no. We're both in a town at the same time. You're going." He began walking away backwards, toward the side door. He held out his long arm and pointed at me to drive home his point. "Tell Harper to get your skinny white asses over there, or I will come find you both." He smiled his swoon-worthy smile, "I mean it."

Grady stepped closer, his body hovering possessively behind me, barely any space between us.

I gave him a genuine, if not flirtatious, smile back and sang, "Bye, Davy."

Davy's grin was blinding, and his gaze rolled over both Grady and me.

With each level of possession Grady demonstrated, I never stepped away—and Davy noticed.

---

Harper was quiet as we left the awards and went to the limo that would drive us to the after-party. I could tell she was stewing about something—most likely the way I'd been behaving. I walked away from Grady after we saw Davy, and we didn't really interact much afterwards.

We slide in and closed the door; the partition between us and the driver was up. I turned to my best friend and said, "Fine. Let's have it."

She pulled out her phone and ignored me. From the ambient light, I could make out the tightness of her features as she reined in her frustration with me.

"I know you're ticked at me about something, so just spill." I crossed my legs and settled in for the bitch session.

"Fine." She practically threw her precious phone into her clutch purse and whipped her head at me. "You want to know. I think you're a stubborn fool."

I stared straight ahead, my face heated. I'd asked for it. "Why?" I clenched my teeth. I knew why. "Because I won't play along with this? Because I won't swoon at his attention? Why me, Harper?"

"Why?" She watched me as I shifted, suddenly defensive and not wanting to discuss this.

I pointed at myself. "He's on billboards and has women swooning. And I'm me. This…" I gestured to my dress and shoes. "This isn't me. This is a façade…"

Harper threw down her hands down in annoyance. "You know, just knock it off. I'm so tired of the pity party already." Her face was a twisted expression I rarely saw directed at me. "You're always touting yourself as this strong, kick-ass woman who takes no prisoners on the track and behind the wheel. But put you in a pair of heels and a wonderful man tells you he's interested in you, and you act like a church mouse." Hands on her hips, she cocked her head and lifted an eyebrow at me.

"They're just men. In the car, behind the wheel, or in the bedroom. They're the same. And so are you. You're just as worthy and just as beautiful and just as strong. Who cares if you're more interested in what's under the hood of a machine than you are of the latest style trends? Do you think all women are into fashion?"

She motioned to me. "Are you really so vain that you think

you're the only woman out there who doesn't read *Cosmo* and *Vogue* but still manages to love men…and still be attracted to men?"

She pointed at me, her face flushed. "The only one standing in the way of you and Grady is yourself. Not Grady's womanizing—as far as I can tell, he hasn't been with a single woman since he's been here. It's your own damn fear and your own damn insecurity that's the problem. You have a past. So does Grady. Who cares?"

She threw her hands in the air in exasperation. "The only question that should be crossing your mind is do you want him? Do you want him, CJ? It's the only question you need to consider." She locked eyes with me; she wasn't going to let go until she got an answer.

"If you don't, fine. Let's not talk about it again. If you do want him, grow some lady-balls and do something about it. Stop pushing him away. And stop this, 'Oh, poor me…a beautiful man is flirting with me and keeps pulling me into dark corners but, hmmm. I don't think he really likes me…boo hoo hoo.' Get a grip and do something." She shoved my shoulder. Hard.

Stunned. Speechless.

My best friend had just put me in my place.

I shifted in my seat again, and, I moved a bit away from her.

"Wait. Just wait. Did you forget my very career depends on whether I beat this man? If he beats me, I'm done. No one will hire me."

Harper's voice raised in frustration. "This doesn't even have to do with Grady—this has to do with you. Opening yourself up to being with someone—not shutting down the idea or pushing it away. Grady McBane is the first man to make you look alive when you aren't behind the wheel of a race car. Yes, it's complicated, and yes, it sucks. But screw the idea that your world will end if you sex up Grady McBane."

Harper's face was flushed with anger and she threw her hands up in the air. "I'm so done with all of this—"

"For Christ's sake, Harper!" I flew from confused and perplexed to indignant. "You should be putting me on a flight back to Charlotte tonight telling me to stay the hell away from the man, not telling me to go jump him. You're screwing with my head as much as he is." I wanted to get out of the damn limo. "Goddamnit! Why don't you take some of your own damn advice and get a life, too? Listen to what you're saying to me about moving on."

She flinched. And I knew I went too far. In all our years of friendship, I'd never struck such a low blow. We both had things that held us down—held us back.

I stared out the window, cussing under my breath about god-men and best friends messing with my mind, and everyone needing to stay the hell out of my business.

"I'm sorry. I didn't mean it."

Out of the periphery, I saw her shake her head but not look at me. "It's fine. You're right. We both need to be shaken up a bit, I think."

I pulled down my hair from the updo, pulling the pins out and running my hands through it, beginning to feel more like myself.

We sat in silence, both in our own thoughts. I fought the feeling of being alone again. Harper was my friend. I knew that. But there was a divide between us.

She let out a sigh of ceasefire. "We'll figure out the career thing. Don't worry about that. We'll think of something. I'm sorry. I just want you happy in every facet of your life. Not just racing." Her eyes dropped, and with the slight shake of her head, she attempted to change our mood. We pulled up to the entrance of the club where the after-party was being held. "For now, I need a drink. Being your friend tends to drive me to drink." She said it with a teasing tone, but I think we both felt the truth behind it.

I needed to figure out what the hell I really wanted. I wanted to drive. I wanted to be a champion.

I wanted...I wanted someone in my life. I wanted someone to kiss me on pit road when I climbed in my car, and someone to celebrate with me when I was in the winner's circle.

I wanted someone to greet me when I got home. So, I guess I wanted someone.

I guess I wanted to be okay with wanting someone.

Did I want Grady McBane to be the person who had the power to take away everything I wanted? Did I trust him to have that power over me? Because honestly, it just wasn't that simple.

Now, I needed a drink, too.

# 3 0

*Grady*

Me following CJ—that was basically my evening.

Following a step behind her—all night. We split after the awards. CJ was going to the after-party. Of course, that meant I was... following her.

I was at the bar ordering another Glenlivet and scanning the crowd. Raine Smith, the Top 40 sensation, whom I wasn't even sure was twenty-one, was climbing me like a jungle gym. Damnit. Where was Cooper?

"Wow. I never realized how tall you were..." Raine cooed and hung on my bicep. She ran her hand down my chest inside my jacket. Damn, these young ones were bold. I pivoted, trying to dislodge her hand before it ran too far south. Lifting my glass to stop it from being hit, I spotted CJ at a booth.

She was laughing and relaxed and was surrounded by no fewer than four—no, five guys, including, Mr. Davy *If-He-Wants-to-Hold-a-Football-Again-He-Better-Remove-His-Arm* Johnson, who had her leaning into him.

What the hell...

Cooper was walking by and I grabbed him. "Cooper, Raine...
Raine, Cooper." And I took her hand and handed her to him. "I
have to...go...talk with someone."

I made a beeline to the booth that had all my attention. As I
drew closer, I recognized an up-and-coming country singer and a
few other drivers from the Energy Blast series.

I was stopped by another female figure. I broke my focus from
the booth long enough to recognize it was Harper. "Grady."

I nodded in greeting.

She held my forearm to gain my attention. "Let's get a drink."

I showed her my drink.

"Well, buy me one, then."

She guided me to a quieter end of the bar, but still within view
of the booth, and I grabbed the bartender for Harper to order a
drink.

CJ threw her head back, laughing with more abandon than I
ever saw from her, and fell farther into football player's arms.

What. The. Fuck.

I drank my scotch.

"He's just a friend. An old friend. CJ's known him since his
rookie days. Davy is harmless."

I thinned my lips. Not the way he was staring at her. It wasn't
harmless. It was calculating.

Harper turned toward the booth, her elbows on the bar behind
her. "You really like her."

I stayed silent, killing Carolina's top-scoring running back with
my death glare.

"I'll take the lack of an answer as an answer." Harper took a sip
of her martini. "CJ isn't like other women. CJ spends so much time
trying to convince people to forget she's a woman, that she forgets
people can view her as a *desirable* woman. You have your work cut
out for you."

"I don't think she cares what I think."

"Oh, she cares. She just doesn't know what to do with you."

I peeked at Harper out of the side of my eyes, not wanting to admit how much I wanted her to elaborate.

She leaned close and whispered, "You need to tell her what to do with you. You need to show her what you want to do with her."

"You're forgetting the point that we're supposed to be bitter enemies. One of us is going to be out of a job at the end of the season."

Harper waved that off as she took a step back and watched her best friend practically stomp out the door. "Trust me, I'm working on that." Harper flashed me a knowing smile. "You," she pointed at me. "Go work on that." She pointed at the door as her best friend left with Davy Jackson.

Oh, hell no.

## 3 1

CJ

Harper and Grady were in a dark corner talking, and it struck me how perfect they looked together. It also bothered the hell out of me. Harper's words reminding me to make a decision were echoing through my head, and I didn't realize I had zoned Davy out.

"Earth to CJ?" He was sitting next to me in the booth, turned in my direction with his hand on the back of the seat behind me. He glanced over his shoulder in the direction I was staring. "Oh, I see a little green on your cheeks…"

I snapped out of it. "I don't know what you're talking about."

"Yes, you do." He smiled a devilish smile that had made many women blush. "But it's nothing like the rage on your man's face as he stares at us. Doesn't seem to like the way I'm talking with you."

"Shut up." I jabbed at him.

Davy winked at me. "Just play along…" Davy leaned over and whispered in my ear, while his hand caressed the other side of my neck as if pulling me into an embrace.

I giggled. "What the hell are you doing?" Davy touching me this way was weird…even

if it was pretend.

"Well, I can't say my moves ever made a woman laugh before."

"That's because I'm not just any woman."

"No, doll, you aren't. But you're a woman. You're just a woman whose eyes are

already set on a certain man," he said, putting a finger under my chin the way Grady did. Except his touch felt brotherly. No warm fuzzies.

"And you can tell my moves aren't real, right?" he said with a direct stare at me.

"Of course, because you're Davy and—"

"And you don't have feelings for me."

"Well, yeah." I shrugged.

"Now, take a look over my shoulder at your man…" He gestured with his thumb.

"He's not my man…"

Davy closed his eyes and repeated slowly, "Look over at him… what is he doing?"

I swallowed. "He is listening to Harper and staring at us."

"He's pissed, isn't he?" He leaned his elbow on the table.

I shrugged. He did look angry. But it could be something Harper was saying. "Maybe."

Davy smiled his toothy, adorable grin. "Get out of here. Actually, let's make a bet. I'll walk you out of here and I'll bet you he follows. If I win, I get your Ducati for a weekend. If you win, I'll get you season opener tickets next season."

"Deal. But I want fifty-yard line."

He nodded. "I already know what I'm doing with that Ducati."

We moved out of the booth and stretched. "It isn't as if you couldn't buy a Ducati in every color."

"Yeah, but it's sweeter when it's yours, and I will know how much it will bother you."

He put his arm around my neck, pulling me into his chest. Oh, he was definitely milking this. I pushed back at him.

"Come on, doll. Let's see if Romeo falls for the bait."

# 3 2

**Grady**

This woman was going to drive me insane.

Insane.

Because right now, I was about to commit murder.

I'd never wanted to kill a man for simply putting his hands around a woman's shoulders.

I followed them through the crowded club, pushing past a few people who were trying to get my attention. My eye was on the target. I wasn't going to lose them. They were leaving. Why were they leaving?

No way in hell they were leaving together. I didn't care how platonic anyone says their friendship is.

I sped up my pace.

His hand was slipping down her back. He was touching her back—her bare back. Hell. No. I was on the verge of breaking some of the most talented hands in the NFL.

I walked out in the warm LA night air, and a few feet past the door, I pulled up short.

CJ and Davy had stopped right outside the nightclub, as if the shithead was waiting…for me. He turned around and smiled at me as if we were old, lifelong friends.

"Grady McBane. Nice to see you again."

He removed his hand from her. That was a start.

He held out his hand and grabbed mine to shake it. "Thank you."

Thank you? Thank you for what? Not breaking his hand?

He pointed at CJ. "Doll, I will be in touch about the Ducati." He winked at her and began walking backward toward the club. He spread his arms wide and his smile grew larger. "Enjoy the evening, you two."

I turned to CJ, and I'm sure my expression was caught between murderous and perplexed.

"You just cost me my Ducati for a weekend." Without further explanation, she turned on her heel and walked to the valet.

"What?" I followed—because that is what I always do. I followed her—everywhere it seemed.

"What are you doing, Grady?" she said as we reached the valet.

I stopped following her and let out a pathetic laugh. "Hell if I know."

A few taxis were scouting the place and I hailed one. "Enough of me chasing you around. I think we need to talk." I led us to one that was pulling up by the curb.

"Grady—"

Someone came up behind us just as the taxi pulled up in front of us. "Hey, isn't that CJ Lomax?"

All my normal, jovial demeanor was gone, replaced by determination, and I glared at the
newcomers.

"Hey, Grady! Come have a drink with us…" a masculine voice called out.

"Oh, Grady! I'm so glad I caught you." I peered over my shoulder.

I never regretted my past flings until this week. "Allie." She flung herself at me, even though I still held CJ's arm, and then rubbed against my non-occupied side as if she could pull me from her. "Why don't you come in and buy me a drink, Grady? We can catch up. I thought you'd call me while you were in town like you usually do."

CJ pulled away from my other arm.

Nope, not doing this again.

I pulled away from Allie. "I didn't call because I'm taken. We were just leaving." I grabbed CJ by the hand and propelled her to the open door of the taxi.

We climbed in, and I gave the taxi driver the name of our hotel.

The taxi drove half a block before CJ broke the silence. "Taken, huh? Who is the lucky woman?"

"Cut the crap." I gave up the fight and pulled her into a demanding kiss, surprising her. But within the span of a moan, she melted and joined me. Her mouth opened, her chest and shoulders relaxed, and she held onto my biceps as my hands threaded through her hair.

I dove in, claiming her mouth, her words, her very breath. My hands roamed over her bare back, feeling the softness of her skin as I drew her closer to me.

I skimmed my hands down the sides of her, feeling the outside swell of her breasts. I wanted to rip that chain off her back, pulling the entire dress down, exposing her breasts. The mere thought of them unfurled under the dress taunted me all evening.

I placed my hand over her heart and felt it beat rapidly in tandem with my own. She arched into me and moaned as I rubbed my thumb over a hardened nipple. I would need to inspect further, of course, but I suspected there was nothing beneath this dress except skin. My mouth watered, my thumb flicked. She squirmed.

We both gasped for air as we broke apart and leaned our foreheads together. Neither of us spoke, but we stared into each other's eyes; the streetlights of LA were the only illumination for the inside the cab.

While I was aware of the driver and our surroundings, I don't think either of us cared. I watched my thumb as it traced her chin and jaw. My gaze captured the outline of her swollen lips. I wondered how much she'd let me get away with in the back of this cab.

Her eyes were hooded, and she bit her bottom lip. Her eyes darted from my eyes to my lips. Her hands skimmed my chest, as if she were unsure what to do, where to put them. They roamed up and down my biceps and shoulders. Her tongue darted out to wet her lips and suddenly her uncertainty gave way to desire, and she drew me closer, as if to kiss me again.

God, I wanted to pull her over my lap, have her straddle my hips, flush against me.

No sooner was the thought in my head, it was reality. CJ straddled me, her slinky dress pulled up so high, I pulled down the back to make sure the driver didn't catch a backside view of her ass before I did.

She fitted herself to me, every part of her against me. She bent down, grabbed my face and took control of the kiss. My smile was so big it almost made it difficult to kiss her. I cupped her backside and began to slowly, subtly rock her against me.

Damn, we needed to get to the hotel. Now.

I pulled my lips away and drew in a deep breath before saying to her. "Just to be clear. This is going to happen."

She pulled back. Her eyes were still hooded and heated, her face flushed, but her expression wasn't the same. She wasn't as assertive. She wasn't climbing off, but she wasn't going farther. She kissed me and wrapped her arms around my neck—holding on to me tightly. The passion wasn't gone, it was thoughtful.

I nuzzled her neck, I caressed her and kissed her. However, before we went farther...before I took it farther, she was going to have to lead.

We got to the hotel. I wanted her to reach for me. She didn't. She kept a casual distance, surveying the lobby for someone or something. Reality hit us. It wouldn't be good for people to see us arm in arm going up to a hotel suite together.

She pushed the button to her floor. Luckily, no one else was in the elevator, but she still stood away from me, her head down, smoothing out her hair and fidgeting with her purse, in her own thoughts.

We walked quietly to her room. She never said one way or another whether I should be following, and I didn't know what she was thinking. She opened the room and walked in, not inviting me in, but not closing the door and telling me to leave. I stood at the door waiting for instruction.

I leaned against the door and crossed my arms. The room was dark with only the bright city lights giving ambiance to the room.

She walked into the room, kicked off her shoes and turned to see I hadn't entered. "What are you doing?"

"Waiting for you to freak out. Tell me to get the hell out."

She rolled her eyes at me. "Shut up. Come in and close the door."

I straightened and walked directly to her until I was inches from her. "Tell me you want me."

"Wanting you was never the issue." She fidgeted.

"Fine, then fuck everything else." I bent, kissing her, keeping it seductive but brief. Using all my willpower for the next step. "But, Charlotte, honey. You're in the driver's seat. Do you want me?"

She stood still, remaining silent.

"I…I…don't…it isn't a good idea…"

Oh my God, she was going to say no. I ran my hand through my hair. This woman was going to be the death of me.

I backed up to the door. Held up my hands in defeat. "I don't beg, and I don't force myself on anyone. Desire is a two-way street. You're right, this is already a complicated situation. And I have just as much to risk as you do. My career means just as much to me."

I stopped, slipped my hands in my pockets and tried hard to pretend this wasn't tearing me apart. "But, I know, besides driving a fast car, you're the only thing in my life that makes me smile. I know Karma is a complete bitch, telling me I'd have to choose. But I also know I can't be with you tonight, and tomorrow have you say it was a mistake. It will crush me. It would be harder than just walking away." There wasn't anything left to say. "So, that's it. You know where I am. It's up to you, CJ. Do you want to figure this out together or are we just going to go back to our respective corners and pretend the only heat we have is on the track?" With that, I walked out of the room, feeling a new hollowness I didn't realize I had.

# 33

## CJ

*Go after him! You idiot!* My hormones were screaming at me. My breasts ached. My lips ached. Everything ached.

But he just walked away. How could he just walk away? If he felt what I felt...if he wanted me as bad as I wanted him—how could he just walk away?

I replayed what he said in my head. He wanted me. I wanted him. Karma *was* a bitch. We both had so much to lose—

*Focus. Grit. Unapologetic determination.*

*Kissing. Touching. Unending orgasms.*

No. No. That's not the mantra I lived by. But my libido made up a new one that was resonating in my brain.

I threw myself on the bed and buried my face in my hands, letting out a monster groan that originated from deep within me.

It wasn't just the sexual need that was killing me. It was the touch, the intense feelings and warmth being with him promised.

As much of an independent woman as I always prided myself to be, this man made me feel…cherished—even when I fought against believing in it.

Now, he was asking me to believe in it—all of it.

And I was being a chicken-shit.

I wasn't being a take-no-prisoners, unapologetic badass. No, I was being a whiney, *I'm-not-worthy* girl who mopes and fishes for compliments.

That wasn't who I was.

What was so wrong with taking what I wanted?

He could hurt me.

He could hurt my career, my reputation…my heart.

*Yeah, well, then, I'll bury him.*

These past few months should've been some of the most stressful and full of intense pressure. Instead, they had been the most exciting. I cheered and looked for him at the finish line, whether it was him or me in the driver's seat. Imagine more of that—but with sex.

And I knew…I just knew…the sex would be—

I catapulted off the bed and, still shoeless, ran for the door before I could analyze it further.

I threw it into high gear and went for it. No point in brakes now. Slingshot through the turn and fly.

What was waiting for me when I opened the door would be forever in my memory.

Across from my room, leaning against the wall, head bowed, was my god-man, legs crossed, arms crossed, peering up with stormy, gray-blue eyes from beneath mussed-up blond hair. Hair I mussed up in the taxi. His perfect lips were relaxed, but the concern in his eyes wasn't camouflaged by his hair.

I stood still in the doorway, unsure of what to say now that he was two feet in front of me.

He straightened slowly and his gaze was locked onto mine.

I fell into his trap. He stalked toward me, like a lithe jaguar to prey. Before reaching for me he said, "What took you so long?"

I held out my hand and placed it over his heart. No other words or permission were needed.

He lifted me into his arms; I wrapped my legs around him. He cupped my ass and walked farther into the room and waited for the hotel door to close behind us. Being held a few inches above him, I cupped his beautiful face in my hands, enjoying the scruff against my fingers and tracing his bottom lip with my thumb, as he let out a moan and walked us to the bed. He sat on the edge of the bed, allowing me to straddle him on my knees. I rubbed against him and he closed his eyes, letting out his breath as I combed my hand through his hair and tugged on it.

"Just kiss me already. I'm going to lose it," he growled. He was trying to let me drive this car.

I smiled and leaned down to press my lips to his, opening almost immediately and running my tongue across his bottom lip, where my thumb once was.

It was like taking off his restraints. He pulled me so close to him; I was hiked up and against him tightly. One hand on my ass, one traveling up my back. He took over the kiss, taking it deep, and I let him shift gears.

"How much do you like this dress?" His voice was deep, gravelly, and his breathing erratic.

"I thought it was pretty, but it was a bitch to wear," I answered in all honesty.

"Okay, because I've wanted to do this all night," he said, lying back slightly, taking both shoulders of the dress and ripping it off my back. The metal chain holding the back together snapped, and tore apart. He paused, taking in my face as he lowered the two sides of the dress slowly, revealing my bare breasts.

"I knew it," he whispered. "So fucking sexy."

I pulled my arms out of the remains of the dress, letting it pool at my waist.

Grady's eyes were dilated, fixated on my breasts; his mouth was parted. His large, rough hands swallowed my small breasts, squeezing lightly and moving toward the nipple where he pinched slightly, causing me to rock forward against him. He noticed and smirked. Doing it again, garnered the same response. He pulled me down to tease one breast with his tongue, while staring up at me before sucking it into his mouth, hard. Again, I surged against his pelvis, this time he grabbed my backside and held it to him, rubbing himself against my core.

"Grady...Oh hell..."

I never knew my breasts were so sensitive.

"Oh, God, Grady. I...I..." I yanked his shirt off, unsure if I even pulled off buttons. I wanted my breasts against his naked flesh. I ran my fingers over his nipples, and I kissed his neck and nibbled on his earlobe.

He rolled us over, me on my back and him beside me. He pulled off what remained of my dress and draped a leg possessively over a thigh. He ran his hand up and down my torso—neck, breasts, stomach, between my legs and back up. When his hand brushed over my panties, I began to imagine what that mouth would feel like between my legs.

Grady teased. Through his kisses, I felt the small smile on his lips from my growing frustration. His hands would travel down my body and under my panties, beginning to part me only to dart back up my chest and play with my nipple, tempting me to grab his hand and shove it down where I wanted it. He finally brushed over my clit —hallelujah—sending me reeling. He pushed down on it, rubbing in a few circles, and I had a small, sharp, quick orgasm that had me leaving fingernail marks on Grady's arm.

"Oh, hell yes." The phrase came out in a loud, unintelligible moan. I wasn't sure if it was mine or Grady's. I threw my head back and he kissed my exposed neck. I knew I was rocking against his hand and I didn't care. It had been years since a man had touched me so intimately and it wasn't going to take long to—

"Oh, Grady...I'm—"

"Yes, Charlotte. Give in..." His hoarse whisper was all I needed to fulfill the promise his hand was making. I threw my head back and let go.

I tried to cry out his name, but air was non-existent in my body.

Time disappeared. Bliss.

He rocked his hand against me until all the aftershocks finished. He wrapped me in his arms and pulled up to the pillows, cradling me in his arms. Not speaking, but caressing and kissing me as I came down from my high.

But I wanted more.

I stroked his stomach, admiring the contours and promising myself further exploration—just not now. I didn't have the patience for it right now.

He was propped up on his elbows, his eyes hooded, his jaw slack as his gaze burned me as he watched me recover.

I sat up, unhooked his belt and slacks. I got off the bed, naked as the day I was born, and removed his shoes and clothes, leaving on his boxers. My inhibitions were gone.

The man wanted me.

His breathing was ragged as he settled his weight on me and I was caught beneath him. His heat, his body, his desire surrounded me, but instead of feeling caged, I never felt so secure.

His hair was so disheveled, I had to run my hands through it as I pulled his head down. He moaned from the contact and rewarded me with a thrust of his hips to prove he was lined up exactly where I wanted him.

He grinded against me as I wrapped my legs around his waist— every part of our body touching, meshing, electrifying. Only the thin fabric of his boxers kept us apart.

He rocked against me and I against him. "Yes, fuck yeah. That's it. God, you're perfect." I pulled his head back and stared at him, needing to see his face as he said those words. I needed the sincerity.

He released my breast and stopped the motion against our cores. He pushed up on an elbow and caught my eyes in his as he placed his palm against my cheek. "Yes, you. You're perfect. Perfect for me." He kissed my forehead, my nose, my cheek, and my mouth. The gestures so reverent and sweet—at odds with the heat the rest of our bodies were producing.

"I would trade my soul to be inside you right now, but it would break my heart to lose you tomorrow." His eyes were intense, but his words were said with such gentleness that it tore at my heart.

Who was this man and what the hell rabbit hole was I falling into?

I refused to ponder it. This was the most passionate moment of my life. I wanted to be lost in it and for time to stop.

I kissed him as a way to answer, but he pulled back.

"Say it. I need to hear you say you want me."

"I want you. I want this."

"Hell, yes."

His boxers were gone. He had a condom out and on in record time.

His hands were down my sides, cupping my ass and drawing up my legs.

I braced my hand on his shoulder, tensing slightly. "Easy, cowboy. It's been awhile since I was in a rodeo…"

He paused. Concern crossed his features. "You haven't…since…"

I shook my head.

He leaned down and kissed me softly, lowering my legs.

"Oh, no you don't." I grabbed his ass, pushing his erection against my core.

"Don't you stop now! I didn't say I was a reformed virgin…" I smiled to ease his concern and caressed his face. "I want this."

Possession darkened his eyes as he maintained eye contact. He braced himself above me, then leaned down and captured my mouth. With my hands on his lower back, he pulled back and guided himself inside me. Slowly, steady. Pulling out and then back in with a slow, rhythmic motion. By the slight shake of his lower body, the restraint was costing him. I pulled myself up to kiss his neck. When he was fully seated, he let out a groan and paused, giving me a moment.

I couldn't stand the pause. I began to buck against him, wanting him to move. His lips were against my neck and I felt his smile.

"I need…" I didn't have the words.

"I know what you need."

And then we both began to move. Slow at first, and then into an increasing movement…together we found our rhythm. I held onto him and he buried his head into me.

We didn't speak. There wasn't any space between us for words.

There were gasps and moans and maybe an occasional, "Yes" or "More" and an "Oh, God" or I may have let out an "Oh, fuck" and Grady may have let out a sinister chuckle.

When I began to climb, he got quiet, his face reddened, his pace quickened, and he reached between us, touching me, and it sent me flying. He followed moments after, releasing my name as if it were the reins that had bound him to the Earth.

# 34

## Grady

I haven't experienced anything that required more restraint or more strength than putting my woman in a thirty-three-hundred-pound machine without kissing her goodbye, knowing there were forty-two other assholes gunning for her.

My woman. CJ was my woman. Nothing was more natural than believing that.

Daytona was one of the few races where restrictor plates were put on the engines to restrict airflow to engines and keep the speed down on the cars. The course was one of the bigger ones, two-and-a-half miles with long, straight stretches where cars' speeds—without restrictor plates—would have rendered them difficult to control, and make them dangerous to the drivers and the spectators.

A byproduct of restrictor plate racing was drafting—an aerodynamic technique where cars teamed up and lined up within inches of each other to cut the drag, and therefore allowing additional gain of speed and less gas consumption. The result was driving in tight packs, often three wide.

Cars driving at high rates of speed, on long tracks, within inches of each other—well, you can imagine the danger—and the excitement—involved.

Some would argue the restrictor plate races required more talent from the drivers.

Some would argue they needed more luck to survive them.

I would agree. It took an insane amount of restraint to watch my woman climb in a car and drive for the next four-hundred miles. It went against every instinct in my body that was screaming to protect her. It never occurred to me what a burden it would be to date a driver. I knew too much. I knew all that could go wrong.

But this was who she was. This was the woman I fell for—the one who defied reason and the one who beamed with anticipation.

We promised to act normally in public, and we made a special effort to appear stand-offish. No one suspected anything except Cooper and Harper. Cooper had been fishing, making comments about the change in my mood, but I hadn't said anything. I'm sure Harper knew more, but I hadn't talked to CJ about it.

We did have rules, though. The biggest one was that no one could know anything was going on with us.

I couldn't touch her in public.

I had to give her a smirk and walk away when Bill came over to talk with her.

As she strapped herself into our car, I lowered my hat to hide my concern, stuck my sweaty palms in my jeans, and made my way to the top of the trailer to watch the race like every other member of the team. Thank God we were in Florida in July. It could explain the flush of color and the sweat rolling down my face.

I was more nervous than a long-tailed dog in a room full of rocking chairs.

I think the Carolinas were wearing off on me.

One of the crew handed me a set of headphones and gestured to a seat next to where Bill usually sat. Harper came up and stood behind me, her own set of headgear in hand. I stood to give her my seat, and she waved me off. "No, I can never sit during a race. Too much energy."

She did a double take at my expression, and a soft smile spread across her face. She leaned down and put a hand on my shoulder. "She's done this several times before, you know...isn't like you haven't seen her race."

I turned from her, not wanting my vulnerability to show. "I know." My back straightened and I picked up the pen in front of me, playing with it. "But—something about this feels different."

She squeezed my shoulder.

"These are CJ's favorite tracks."

"You don't have to tell me. She was jumping out of her skin this morning—"

Harper removed her hand. "Okay—let's stop this conversation right there. I don't think I want any more information about her or her skin in the morning. I think it may cross some sort of BFF line unless it comes from her."

The announcer declared the beginning of the race. "Drivers start your engines." And even though I wasn't the one in the car, my heart began to race.

Until my girl was back in front of me, in my arms, in one piece, my heart wasn't going to be safe.

---

I should've known. Even though Dewey wasn't directly after CJ, I knew enough to know something was going to go down.

CJ had been running a good clean race. She started at fourteenth, and had a few slow pitstops, so she wasn't where she wanted to be, but was inching up through the pack, making it to around eighth. Going into the back turn, CJ had been drafting her teammate Brian Hines, as most teams do at restrictor plate races, to gain speed and reduce drag.

Murray Roberts, Dewey's buddy, caught up to them and clearly was jockeying for position coming out of the straightaway. Murray side-swiped Brian, sending him up towards the wall out of position. Brian over-corrected and came down into CJ. It would be debatable whether it was intentional; with the cars inches apart, the only one who knew was Murray—and maybe Dewey.

The result was the same.

CJ's car resembled a bumper car as it traveled around the track.

Harper let out a startled expletive.

I tried to stand, but my knees were weak.

CJ's car began dancing with Brian's and then the other cars stepped in, wanting to partner with her. One jerked CJ from the back, another plowed into her driver's side and turned her, before a final one wanted her out of the way and threw her into the apron, and then into the retaining wall, where she finally gave up the waltz.

Each car hitting her was a punch to my body until my mind went numb unable to track what was happening. Harper shook me and I blinked rapidly.

Her front end was demolished. The hood resembled an accordion, covering the windshield. Smoke and a small fire was pouring out from some undisclosed location.

I paused a moment, waiting for the tell-tale sign—Did the window net come down?

I didn't see her.

Where was she?

Her driver's side was against the wall and I couldn't see her goddamn window. I needed to see the net was down signaling she was okay.

"CJ." There wasn't enough air for the name to be audible.

I threw down everything, knocked back the chair, and pushed at everyone as I ran.

In my shock and fear, I failed to remember the vastness of the track, and that I wasn't going to get to her quickly. I forgot what I watched on a television screen was not right in front of me, and she was probably at least a mile away.

Harper pulled up next to me in a golf cart. "Get in."

We waited for what seemed like hours. Eventually CJ came walking out, stiff and slow, and mad as a hornet.

Harper and I jumped up to her side.

"What did the doctors say?"

CJ's eyes were downcast, her lips in a thin line and barely opened when she said, "I may have a mild"—she glared at both of us to get the point across—"concussion."

I clenched my fists.

The driver in me knew this came with the territory. Hitting walls in a machine doing a hundred-and-ninety mph, it didn't matter if you were strapped in with every restraint known to man, your brain was still going to bump around.

The boyfriend—for lack of a better term—in me wanted blood.

"Who was it? I heard it was Murray?" she said. "I need to know before I walk outside."

"Murray got into Brian." I needed to kiss her. Damn this secret-relationship-shit. I needed to comfort my woman.

She nodded. "Alright." She gestured to me. "You walk out first. Maybe you can draw some of them away. Then Harper and I will walk out. It'll look weird if we all walk out together. As it is, it will start up the rumor mill with you being here."

Bill chose that moment to walk in. "Hey there, killer. You still alright in the head?"

"When have I ever been alright in the head?" She gave him a lackluster smile, and a small grimace flitted across her face. Her head was bothering her more than she was letting on.

Damnit.

"Let's get you out of here." I may not be able to publicly claim her, but I definitely was taking charge. I walked over to Bill and spoke quietly. "She has a concussion."

She pushed herself between us and glared. "I *might* have a mild one." But then she swayed before grabbing onto my forearm.

Bill and I shared a look.

With Bill here, we looked like part of a team, so I let him take the lead. "Alright, let's go."

We walked as a unit out of the infield medical center, and

toward the waiting carts to take us back to the trailers. I was forced to stand back as the media had at her. They swarmed her with questions, stoking the rivalry and asking for her thoughts of the wreck.

"CJ, what did you see?"

"Grady, does this mean you're taking over CJ's races?"

CJ shut that down quickly and didn't give anyone else a chance to answer. "Hell no, he's not."

"CJ, have you seen the replay?"

"Are you going to talk with Murray?"

She gave them a tight-lipped smile, one where I had to wonder if she was plotting someone's death. "Oh, I'll have words with Murray, don't you worry."

# 35

## *CJ*

The next few days were a rollercoaster. I was forced to recover from what was a confirmed concussion, which sidelined me from racing for at least two weeks—well, that was still up for debate. The next race at Kentucky was Grady's anyway—so it gave me time to convince them to let me race at New Hampshire without sacrificing a race to him.

It also meant I was supposed to sit still.

Sit. Still. I didn't do that well.

No running. Minimal exercise, and lots of rest. I was good with that for a few days, because even though I refused to admit it, I was sore and my head was killing me...after that, I was going stir-crazy.

Grady and I hadn't really defined what was going on with us, but he showed up almost every evening, and when I opened the door, I was greeted with his towering frame leaning against it, and butterflies went crazy inside me. I always thought that a dopey expression, yet I was becoming a cliché.

God, I sounded ridiculous.

Today he came straight from the track and was showering while I was unpacking the food he brought over.

*Ding-dong.*

I had been contemplating, or slightly freaking out at, at how damn domesticated we were acting, and I didn't check before answering the door.

"Gus?"

*Oh, crap.*

"Hey, CJ." His smile was warm and friendly. "I wanted to stop by and check on you on my way home. See how you were doing." He held up a box from my favorite Charlotte bakery. "I came by bearing gifts."

"Oh, um." I was so stunned and unsure how to react, I hadn't realized how open the front door was or that he took it as a signal to walk in.

Familiar with my house, he walked straight to the kitchen. "Aren't you climbing the walls yet? The guys and I had a running bet as to when you'd show back up. You already cost me twenty bucks. I had bet two days ago." He put the box on the kitchen counter. "Hey, since when do you eat Indian? Wow, you must be hungry…"

The shower wasn't running—good news. I wouldn't have to explain why it was on…wait. The shower was off. That meant Grady could walk out anytime.

I reached for a quick explanation and spoke loudly, hoping Grady could hear me. "Harper ordered the food; she said she may stop by later."

"Oh. Well, maybe I'll hang out and wait for her." He pulled up a chair and made himself at home. "I wanted to talk to you anyway."

I stood in the doorway between the hallway and the kitchen, continuing to look over my shoulder. "What about?"

"Why are you acting weird? Are you sure you're okay?"

I stepped farther into the kitchen. "I'm fine. Really. What did you need?"

Gus stood, linked his arms across his broad chest and braced himself. "About Grady."

"What about Grady?"

"About the way he's been around you lately."

"What do you mean?" *Oh, crap.*

"I don't like the way he's been looking at you—the way he's been acting around you?" Gus's voice became dangerously low. *Oh, crap.*

"Gus, what the hell are you talking about?"

"He clearly wants you, and the worst thing you could do right now is fall for his shit."

And of course, at that very moment, Grady McBane walked into my kitchen—in a towel.

The world halted on its axis—Gus, one of my oldest friends, on my right—and Grady, the man I'm sleeping with, the man I'm competing with, naked in a towel, on my left—and me, with a head injury and clearly screwing this up, in the middle, with absolutely no idea what to do next.

"Well, I guess I should've seen this coming," Gus said, breaking the silence. He took a step back from me. "But I didn't, because I thought you had more sense and more self-respect. But, then again, you did hit your head pretty hard."

Grady widened his stance and crossed his arms, and I feared for the sturdiness of the towel.

I had no words. I didn't feel like I owed Gus any explanation. Yet, I wasn't sure I should let him leave without one. "Gus, I...I need you to not say anything."

He let out a low guffaw. "What the hell are you thinking?"

I took a deep breath as I steadied my voice and went in. "I'm thinking this isn't any of your business."

He turned on me. "None of my business?" He exploded and threw up his hands.

"You've always had such a good head on your shoulders. And you're so close to having something you've always wanted. Who the hell are you? How could you be so self-destructive?"

He shook his head with disappointment. He waved his hand at

the two of us. "Because that is what you're doing. Involving yourself with him is self-destructive."

He dropped his head and rubbed his eyes. "I have to go."

My heart was cracking. Gus was one of my best friends. It was at that moment I realized that he was a barometer I used to measure my decisions, my conscience, and he was disappointed in me.

I dropped my head in shame.

Grady wasn't having it. He lifted my head and kissed my cheek before turning to a quickly departing Gus. "If you care about her, you won't leave her this way."

"If you cared about her…you wouldn't have started this." Then he looked at me. "Mark my words, this will end badly, darlin'."

And without any other indication of what he would do next, he left.

# 3 6

**Grady**

The next morning, Merrick called and wanted to meet. I was sure Gus had run to him and snitched, and I was bracing myself for the fallout.

In the shower, I distracted myself with all the different ways things could go down the shit hole, when the shower door opened, and small arms wrapped around me; a naked body was pressed against me.

I wasn't complaining—neither was my cock. This could only mean good things.

A smile spread as I swiveled my head as far as I could, catching her eyes as her hand drifted down to my groin.

After the accident, I'd been unsure whether to initiate sex. She literally had a headache most of the time and I felt like the biggest schmuck just thinking about it—even if I was walking around with a permanent hard-on.

I wanted to care for her and made it clear I was staying regardless.

I cooked for her, teased her, did whatever I could to entertain her, except for orgasms, and made sure she rested.

Her expression was a mixture of hunger and hesitance as she slowly wrapped her hand around my cock. I leaned my head back, closed my eyes, and let out a loud, approving groan.

I glanced down out of the corner of my eye and saw her staring up with a hint of surprise. I closed my eyes and resumed enjoying the attention. She kissed my back, and with her other hand caressed my chest and stomach.

I began rocking my hips. "Don't worry, love. I'm a sure thing."

I felt the smile creep over her face against my back.

"Aren't most men?"

"Well, if you haven't figured it out by now, I'm not most men."

She squeezed slightly. "Yes, I noticed." Her voice held mischief. "I'd like to study how different you are..." She turned me.

The sight of her...along with her hands stroking me...was almost enough to do the job. The desire in her eyes, the parting of her lips. Her breasts were wet. With water dripping off her hard nipples, I reached over and brushed my thumb over one, tweaking it, and she gasped, closing her eyes in pleasure.

"So, you have a long list of samples to compare me to?" I tweaked the other nipple, this time pinching it. I cupped her between her legs, feeling the wetness, and knowing it wasn't from the shower. Her mouth dropped open more, and I watched her as she stroked me with more intent.

She continued to rub my cock with her hand and brushed the tip with her thumb, causing me to jerk slightly before lowering herself to her knees.

"I said it had been awhile since I'd had intercourse." She licked her lips. "But I'm not a saint, I've... read and I've been studying."

I grasped her shoulder and threaded my hand through her hair. I had a vague sense of wanting to know what she'd been reading... or studying. Later.

Later.

After that beautiful kind of morning, going to see Merrick was like heading to the guillotine with a skip in my step.

"Have a seat, Grady," Merrick said after greeting me. He walked around the desk and leaned on the edge. "I wanted to have words with you about CJ and the incident at Daytona." Merrick walked around his desk, leaning against the front of it and staring down at me like a father lecturing his son. "I saw the murderous expression on your face when you saw her coming out of the infield center. I know that look. I want to make it clear—"

Thank God I had the smarts to keep my mouth closed until Merrick had a chance to give me his lecture about not seeking retribution against the Dupree crew for wrecking CJ—not the one about sleeping with his other driver. *Whew.*

Back to Dewey and his crew of minions.

"—and even if I'm surprised to see you and CJ forming a kind of loyalty toward each other, it wouldn't behoove you to get tangled up in that rivalry."

Caught up in all the many ways I wanted to ram them into the nearest wall, with or without a car, I failed to focus on my boss. "I'm sorry, sir. What do you mean?"

"The rivalry between CJ and Dewey…don't get caught up in it. It wouldn't help your career to make enemies with the Dupree family, and as much of a pinhead as that boy is, his family will back him, always. He's the only son they have left, and they will always side with him. You need to realize this."

"Yes, I caught onto that already. But, with all due respect, it's more than a rivalry, sir. The man truly hates her—" I straightened and sat on the edge of my seat. "For Christ's sake, they wrecked your car and hurt her…"

His lips tightened and he crossed his arms. He wasn't used to being talked to this way. I was questioning his actions. "I'm well aware what it cost me and CJ, son."

He was pulling out the "son." I was being condescended to. While it was pissing me off, he was in a position of power, and he was reminding me.

"I'm a bit more familiar with the shit going on around here and how it relates to her and to our organization. That being said, I'm telling you to stay the hell out of it." He took in a calming breath, and still staring at me, he appeared to be gathering patience. "Dewey unjustifiably blames her for his brother's death. But he's also a jackass and no one can get him to drop it. One of these days, either the powers that be will throw his ass out, or his family will wise up and stop throwing money at him."

I sat forward in my chair. "Sir, he could really hurt her. Look what's happened already."

Merrick waved it off as he walked and sat back behind his desk. "CJ's a big girl and she's fine. It's part of the sport. We don't know for sure she was targeted. She knows that. It wasn't even Dewey, anyway. Murray has nothing against CJ—I'm sure it was just a misjudgment. You know as well as everybody else how that could happen. On the restrictor tracks it happens more often—"

"Sir, I know. I realize that, but his association with—"

He held up his hand. "Son, it won't do any good to fan those flames. Let it go. It won't do you any good to start making enemies.

"But—" Why was I debating this with him?

"Grady, piece of advice. I know there are other teams looking for drivers next year. You don't want to start making enemies this early. There are rivalries. They're rampant. But enemies are a whole different ball of wax. Dewey and CJ are enemies. You don't want to be part of that in your precarious position."

*He's reminding me I don't have a job—not yet.*

*He's telling me I may not be with Merrick.*

*Shit. He's warning me.*

*Shit.*

"Concentrate on dazzling the field with your skill. Focus on Kentucky and the races following. If CJ isn't cleared, you'll be up the weekend after that at New Hampshire, and then Pocono and Watkins Glen. That's four consecutive tracks. It will be the longest stretch you've done and will be telling as to how you can handle a normal season."

"I doubt CJ won't be able to race New Hampshire," I said off-hand, standing and ready to leave. The driver in me was giddy at the prospect of racing four straight races. The boyfriend, or what-ever we were, in me was cringing at the idea of CJ not being cleared for that race.

She'd be fit to be tied.

Merrick stood in front of me and said, "Well, it won't be up to her. The doctor won't let her on the track if she isn't up to snuff."

I just nodded. The driver and boyfriend were fighting, and I couldn't trust them to agree on uttering words, so I left.

---

Kentucky was my first true traditional stock car event, a moderate track with moderate length, banks, speed. Instead of being consumed with excitement, I was niggled with a bit of disappointment. I was bummed because CJ wasn't there to cheer me on, to share it with me, or to give me shit.

I was so screwed.

First, I was using words like bummed and niggled. Who did that?

I needed to find my man-card.

Second, since when did I care if a woman's presence determined the intensity of my
excitement? There was going to be speed and adrenaline flowing through my veins.

Third, I should be focusing on crushing CJ's dreams, annihilating her record, and taking
this car from her. Not on what she's wearing and wondering if she's watching. Of course, she's watching—but is she hoping I'd wreck?

So. Screwed.

We never really addressed the rather large, freaking ever-growing elephant in our room, but we had to soon. It wasn't as if we worked nine-to-five and kissed each other every morning before we left for our respective jobs. She was going to start racing again next week. We needed to figure out what was going on and how we were going to handle it going forward.

Damn.

Despite the immature sneers from Dewey before the race, despite the conflicting emotions I had about CJ and her absence, despite the slight nervousness I refused to admit I was harboring, the extra practice and the films I watched helped, and I finished eleventh. I was congratulated when I finished, garnering more attention from the media than the veteran winner from the media. While it didn't seem like much to an outsider, out of a field of forty-two other drivers, for a first time on a traditional stock car track, it was respectable, and it garnered a lot of attention.

"Grady, how's it feel to finish your first true stock car race?"

"Grady, where is CJ?"

"Did she wish you luck today?"

"Did she give you any suggestions or advice before the race—"

The last one I was compelled to answer the last one. "Yeah, she told me to go fast and not

to wreck our car." It was basically what she said whenever she was around.

But it just invited more questions. "Does that mean you spoke with her this morning?"

"Is it true she's in town? Maybe in the stands?"

Cooper came over to meet me, shoving the media back and handing me a ball cap. "Let

the man breathe…"

We walked away from the crowd and toward the back of the pit, to the garage and the team's trailer, where Cooper discreetly handed me the phone. He didn't need to tell me who was on it. The way he refused to make eye contact, and how he slipped it in my hand without another word, suggested his clandestine caller was the woman herself.

I smiled upon putting the phone to my ear. "Hey, beautiful."

"Did you wreck my car?"

"Hello to you, too…"

"So, did you?"

"Don't act like you didn't watch…you obviously knew when to call me. Besides, even if I traded paint with a few people, they employ a huge staff of people whose jobs it is to make sure the car looks brand new before it's your turn next week. In fact, they will probably change the paint scheme tomorrow. And…we have like, two other backups. Relax."

She hmphed and began on her commentary. "The car was loose out of the turns and you were passing too high, too often…"

"Can we save the critique for when I get home?" As I said it, Cooper gave me a side-eye glance and I realized how domesticated I sounded.

"And when will that be?"

"Well, given that I literally just got out of the car, I'm not quite sure." I smiled. "Why? Do you miss me?"

Silence.

I loved it, because I knew she did. Otherwise, she wouldn't have called so quickly, otherwise. I imagined her picking at her nails because I cornered her into admitting it.

She abruptly changed the topic—which also confirmed that she did. "When do I get to see this new lake house you supposedly bought? I'm going mad in this house."

"I'm set to close on it tomorrow. Maybe we can drive up the day after? I need to get it set up and I don't know when I will have time—"

"You mean you don't know your schedule and if you'll be practicing for New Hampshire," she said with a new tension in her voice.

"CJ—"

"I'm doing fine. I see the doctor in a few days. I'll be ready for New Hampshire."

"Okay, listen. We can talk about it later. Let me call you when we're on the jet and I'll let you know. Actually, let me text, that way I don't have to worry about privacy."

"Okay. Fine." She was quiet for a heartbeat before adding, "Has he said anything?" She was talking about Gus.

"Nothing to me—no. At least nothing that wasn't related to the car and connected with an expletive. Since he's responsible for the team, it's hard to avoid him. The car didn't burst into flames and the brakes didn't fail, so I guess that's a good sign."

"Yeah, well, there's always the next race," she mumbled.

## 3 7

***CJ***

I got my wish and was back in the car for the New Hampshire race. I probably should have sat my ass at home.

I have no excuse for my poor performance at New Hampshire. But it sucked. Bad qualifying. Bad restarts. Bad pitstops. I finished in the thirties. I don't even quantify anything below the twenties.

After climbing out of the car, and avoiding any media brave enough to approach me, I didn't even make eye contact with Grady. The media diverted to him once I was a no-go.

Great.

As I walked away, I heard them hounding him. "Grady, what do you think of CJ's performance today?"

"What would you have done differently?"

"Do you think this helps your standings?"

I quickened my pace, determined not to hear his answers. My path was blocked when I

ran straight into Gus, who stared over my head at Grady holding court with the reporters.

Gus nodded at Grady with his hands on his hips. "See that. That's the bed you made, darlin'."

"Screw you, Gus." My voice was low, and barely held back more venomous words as I walked around him.

Bill tried to approach, and I bit his head off before making a beeline, double-time, to the trailer. Once I reached what I thought would be my sanctuary, I almost took off the door and paced the floor inside like a caged animal. The door had been left open, and I overheard Harper talking with Grady outside, warning him it wasn't the best time to talk with me.

I was being handled. That pissed me off, too.

"I can hear you. Both of you, get the hell out of here," I warned.

I stripped out of my suit, leaving it on the floor, and walked to the back of the trailer. I knew the media and everyone else would want an explanation for why I performed so poorly. I had none.

The last thing anyone wanted to do right now was speak to me.

Harper stepped in, taking one for the team. "CJ, honey."

"I don't want to talk."

"It wasn't that bad."

"Shut it."

"Everyone has bad races, CJ. You were due for one."

I stepped out in a T-shirt and underwear. I pointed at her, harnessing my anger so I didn't unleash it. Afraid of tears. They accompanied my anger more often than sadness. "Shut. It."

My eyes burned.

Damnit.

Nothing I hated more than tears. And the more my eyes burned, the more pissed off I got. I was losing control of my emotions, and nothing showed weakness more than my freaking tears.

I drew myself up and closed my eyes briefly to regain control. My BFF knew me. She stood still, not offering any comforting words or a hug, because she absolutely knew me. She knew I wanted to find my inner strength before I broke. I needed to.

"I cannot allow bad races. Harper, I cannot afford to have one bad race."

She stood still, tilted her head, and waited.

"He's doing well. He's doing better than I thought he would. He's talented. He's a natural. He's blending into the team and into the industry without any issue. People love him, I…I—" I began to stutter. "I can't afford to have a bad race." My voice hitched and the first tear fell.

Harper stepped to me and her arms came around me. I let her hug me for a brief moment, and then I stepped away because I was determined not to let my emotions go.

I didn't cry.

Because I wasn't going to be *that* girl.

I was so freaking confused. I was angry, I was scared, I was so damn frustrated.

He was going to win. He was going to walk away with everything.

Including my heart, because I didn't think our relationship—or whatever was happening between us—was going to survive this season. I wasn't sure I was going to either.

---

Grady and I avoided being seen together at the track. I wasn't up for our normal banter. I was too volatile, and he was being pursued by reporters and fans at the track. His popularity was growing.

So, I had some time to get my shit together before we saw each other back in Charlotte. He texted me several times to check on me, but my responses were the same. "I don't want to talk about it. It sucked. I fucked up. And I don't want to discuss it." And that was it.

He was a driver. He got it.

So, we didn't discuss it.

I got home, he came over, gave me a massage, and took my mind off everything in all sorts of ways.

We laid quietly in my bed that evening, me draped over his chest, him stroking one of his hands through my long hair and caressing my thigh with the other…each of us with our own thoughts. He kissed the top of my head and said, "You know we need to talk about what is happening with us…and what looms ahead. We can't just keep avoiding being seen together. We can't pretend to live two different lives."

I took in a deep breath.

"I know."

"If I weren't the man you were competing against, if I were just your boyfriend, would you have called me yesterday? Would you have been willing to talk to me about the race?"

"Honestly, no."

He pulled back a bit to see me. "Why?"

Not wanting to make eye contact, I stared at his chest and the circles I made with my fingers. "Because I was pissed at myself and I still don't want to talk about it."

He kissed my forehead. "Fair enough. But we still need to talk about us."

I burrowed closer to him. "Not now."

He tightened his grip on me, and I wished he would never let go. "Okay, not now."

---

The next race was Grady at Pocono. The build-up to the race was huge since it was where I won just a few months ago, and it would be the first time he raced there.

The competitor in me was reveling in it. I would've strutted my ass all around reminding my rival who owned that track the last time the drivers were up there. Instead, the girl-friend—or whatever I was—wanted to downplay it and support him.

Who the hell was I? I was a mess.

Grady stayed at my house the night before he left. I was still in a tank and sleep shorts, saying goodbye at the door. He pulled me close, hands on my ass, kissing my forehead. "Any last-minute advice?"

My emotions were a jumbled mess. I roped my arms around his neck, wanting to kiss him and drag him back into my room.

But I drew up short as my competitiveness reared its head and piped in, *"You're on your own, buddy…"*

I wanted to give him the lowdown on the drivers to watch on the track—the ones who

were cocky and most likely to make a mistake. But that was Gus's and the spotter's job—not mine.

Instead, I raised up on my toes, gave him a peck on his lips, and broke out of his embrace with a cocky, "Drive fast and don't wreck our car."

"Our car, huh?"

I let that one slip.

I watched the race from the pit, too nervous to even pace.

I'd underestimated him.

Truly, I did.

I used to think I was overestimating myself; but no, I underestimated him.

The bugger finished in the top five. In the scheme of things, it was unheard of. Given his experience, it was comparable to my win in some circles. Given how poorly I was doing, it spoke volumes.

The girlfriend in me was happy for him.

The competitor was seething.

Grady crossed the finish line squeezing past the number five by a tire length. The team erupted. My face fell. How was I supposed to seem unaffected?

He was doing better and I was becoming dead weight. I wrecked the car at Daytona and barely finished the last one.

I stepped down from the pit box and pushed through the crowd. I mistakenly thought the reporters and crowd would be flocking to Victory Lane, or even to Grady, for comments and reactions.

I was wrong. A reporter jumped out at me to capture my reaction as I was walking by. "CJ, fantastic running into you! Grady had an amazing showing today. Top five at a track you yourself had won just a few months ago. That kind of takes the edge off your lead with Merrick's challenge."

Asshole.

"Many may be wondering if your win was chalked up more to

Gus Quinlan's talent and the preparedness of the team since both you, and a novice like Grady McBane, had such good finishes here."

*Oh, my God. Fucking asshole.*

*Hands on hips. 1...breath in...2...breath out...3—*

Harper came up behind me, subtly grabbing both of my clenching wrists in her hand.

"He probably wants to have children someday, even though he shouldn't be allowed to procreate."

I gritted my teeth. "Grady is a talented driver. Gus Quinlan and his crew are hardworking and good at their jobs. They made a good team today and deserve where they placed. Don't minimize it for either of them."

"So, you're saying Grady is just as good as a driver as you are?" He arched a brow at me, thinking he got a printable quote.

"I think Grady is a talented driver. That's why Merrick has him up against me. I didn't say he was going to beat me." I left it at that and walked away.

Walking this tightrope was hurting my head.

---

I escaped to my RV as soon as I could without being obvious. The team was planning on rolling out in a few hours, so I changed into yoga pants and a tank top, planning on getting some sleep, when there was a knock at my door.

I stepped down the stairs and cautiously opened the door to the RV. Grady lifted me into his arms, carrying me back up the stairs, burying his face in my hair and growling, "There's my girl."

I was more focused on how quickly the door closed, cutting off any possible exposure. It was dark enough outside, but there were people milling around. The last thing we needed was anyone seeing us.

He walked farther into the RV, past the captain's chairs and toward the bedroom. I pulled back. "Grady, stop. You shouldn't be here. What if someone saw you?"

"I don't care, screw 'em." He kissed me as we were passing the kitchen.

I kissed him briefly, then pulled back, a bit irritated at his lack of concern. "Grady—"

He gave me an indulgent, boyish smile. "I wanted to see you. I am way too pumped to go to bed..." His voice dropped seductively as he kissed down my neck, "...at least alone."

As he walked into the bedroom, he whispered, "You were all I thought about." He kissed each cheek. With our gaze inches apart, we were locked on, so there was no denying his sincerity. "I was running the last ten laps, passing Johnson, passing Lucas. I heard your voice, not Gus, not Aaron. I heard you...pushing me, and of course, chastising me." He laid me on the bed and hovered over me. "Your belief in me...your determination and focus." Lowering himself, he placed both arms around my face, caging me in. I felt the evidence of his excitement against me as he centered himself between my legs.

He brushed his thumbs over my cheeks, and I was captivated. "I may not have won the damn thing, CJ. But it was because of you, and all the joy you have brought into my life that today was a fucking fantastic day for me—the best I've had in a while." He kissed me again. This one hot, consuming, and I was weakened. My hands combed through his hair. My breasts lifted up against his chest as my heart and breathing picked up the pace.

Then it was his turn to pull back. He wasn't done being sweet. "Out on the track I had you in my head. And when I was done, all I wanted was to be here with you, in your bed."

I was unable to respond with words. If my head was a mess before, my heart was mush now.

His hands traveled under my thin tank top. I blinked and it was gone. His mouth teased my nipples for the briefest moment, not nearly long enough, and I let out a sound of protest and tried to drag his head back to them. He clearly had other plans and was impatient to move on. He cupped me between my legs where I pulsed, and he smiled when I let out a pitiful moan. Getting on his knees, he pulled off my pants and descended on me, his smile changing to hunger and showing no mercy.

He was enthusiastic and relentless. I forgot we were in an RV parked close together with other RVs. Grady threw a hand over my mouth and chuckled—which, by the way, felt amazing, too.

We enjoyed each other for the next two hours. Perhaps a bit too enthusiastically. "Probably a good thing I don't plan on showing my face again before we hit the road. Maybe people will think the noise came from Gus's RV since he is parked across from me." I tried to rationalize.

Grady was propped on an elbow, caressing the side of my breast, studying my nipple as it hardened. I swiped at his hand. "Well, that may have been true. But I'm pretty sure the RV was rocking and there's no denying that. I think everyone within about forty to fifty yards will know you got lucky last night. The speculation will be with who." He wiggled his eyebrows.

Instead of embarrassment, I immediately plunged into freak-out mode.

"Oh, God. Do you think they will suspect it was you?"

Grady looked like I had smacked him. "Jesus, CJ, is the thought so disgusting? That people would think you lowered yourself to my level?" He rolled over and got up.

"Of course not." But I was still freaking out over the possibility. "I told you we have to be careful though." Grady was already getting dressed.

"I didn't say we weren't being careful," he growled, bent down, and aggressively grabbed his shirt as if it was trying to escape him.

"Grady, you don't understand what it looks like for me. For guys, it doesn't matter who they're sleeping with. It's different for me—for any woman."

Not exactly great pillow talk.

I lifted the sheet to my breasts and sat up. "Grady, come on, you know what I mean. It's about the contract. I can't...we can't—"

"Yes, I know. We can't be seen. I pour my heart out to you... come over to make love to you. You aren't worried that people hear you moaning and screaming during sex, but who they think it is giving you that mind-blowing sex. Good thing you didn't say my name…it was mostly 'Oh God'." He stopped and glared at me. "Was that intentional? Are you hoping they think it's Gus?"

"Come on, Grady—"

"I'm leaving. Maybe you can call Gus and arrange for him to spend the night over here, or maybe you can scream his name a few times, just to throw people off."

"You're a real asshole."

"Glad you figured that out." He glared at me and left.

Once back home, things didn't improve.

CJ: "Are you still pissed at me?"

No response. Which I took as his response.

I swore I wasn't going to text again, but I was getting pissed myself.

CJ: "Okay, fine, you're pissed at me. But not talking to me is ridiculous."

No response. I really was getting pissed now. I waited half an hour. It was all I could do. I paced, trying to resist the urge to call Harper to bitch to someone. She'd tell me to go talk to him. I didn't want to go talk to him, because frankly, I didn't know what I wanted to say.

Because I didn't know what I wanted from him.

I wanted to throw my phone. I put it down. I paced some more. I picked it up. I texted again.

CJ: What the hell is your problem? Fine, I'm sorry. I'm sorry I made you feel bad. Okay? Stop acting like a girl and get over it.

. . .

Just as I hit send, the doorbell rang.

Still flaming pissed and full of adrenaline, I flew to the door and opened it so fast it almost rebounded back at me.

The afternoon sun was haloing him, and once again I was reminded of the thunder god.

Damnit. His hair was disheveled, his face was grim. He was staring at his phone.

A smirk lifted one side of his face, and he stared up at me from the side.

After the initial shock of seeing him on my front doorstep, I crossed my shaking hands across my chest and popped a hip. "What are you doing here?"

He held up his phone and shook it. "I came by for my apology in person, it seems."

Not for the first time, I wished for the power of paralyzing death rays to shoot out of my eyes. Or at least ones that maimed. I settled for glares of future, unmitigated consequences. "I just sent that text, so what was your real reason for coming over here?"

"Why don't you invite me in so we don't have this discussion on the porch where everyone can see me?"

"You're an ass," I said, walking into the house, leaving it up to him to follow.

He caught the screen door and entered. "So you keep reminding me."

I walked into the family room, sitting on the sectional and pulling a pillow protectively into my lap. As if that would both protect me and comfort me from his presence.

With his hands in the pockets of his cargo shorts, he stood in front of me, assessing the situation and me. I suspected he would sit on the other side of the sofa, or in a chair, or just stand. He did neither, opting to move over some papers I had on the coffee table that sat directly in front of me, and sitting on it while turning my body to face him.

He yanked the pillow from my hands. Shifting his weight forward, he cupped his big hands around mine, and then raised them up to kiss them. "I'm sorry, too."

My eyes fell to our joined hands as he held them between us, and he caressed them with his thumb.

"I've been thinking a lot about this—about the contract, about us—we need to just get through this. We need to figure out a way to survive it. I want to be with you, CJ. I want us to find a way out of this. Okay?"

My heart squeezed.

My stomach fluttered.

"I mean it. I know we're asking a lot from the world. But I want it all." He stared at me and I didn't know what to say.

"Let's dream bigger," he whispered. "Let's have it all."

My voice broke and I felt wetness gather in my eyes, "But how?"

He shrugged. "Don't know yet. But if we don't even dare to ask for it, how do we ever expect to get it?"

He stood me up, then moved us around and sat us both on the sofa while gathering me in his arms.

"Together we will figure this out. We will play the game and race the race. Together we will think of something."

I held him tight as a tear fell down my cheek. I tried to memorize every thought, every feeling. I wasn't sure if it was the sweetness of his words, the hope he was giving me, or the naiveté I was buying into that would ultimately wreck us both.

# 38

## CJ

In the following weeks, we were cool competitors on the track, with quips and great parting shots to each other for the cameras.

Off the track, we were anything but cool. He'd whisper something when we were alone to make me blush, and then back me into a corner somewhere and ask, "How about we go peel this suit off you and see how far down that blush travels," kissing me senseless. The danger in getting caught, the make-out sessions that would leave me reeling and weak in the knees with promises of what was to come later.

While Gus hadn't spilled our secret to anyone, the tension between him and me was increasing, as was the animosity between him and Grady. We were snapping at each other on the headsets about ridiculous things, and more than once I caught the crew wincing at our interaction.

I was walking to the hauler at Richmond. It was a good track for me, and I had high hopes of turning things around. It was a D-shaped, three-quarter mile track with minimal banking, and the races were always at night, which added a bit more excitement to them.

I didn't even crack the top twenty.

I got out of the car, handed off my gear to a crew member, and head off in the direction of the hauler.t I saw Harper blocking Gus as he pointed at me. "The problem isn't the fucking car, Harper. The problem is she needs to get her head out of her ass."

Great. I picked up my pace, keeping an eye on what was happening, while also trying to slip through the crowd as quickly as possible dodging fans and reporters.

Grady came up behind Harper and joined in.

"Fuck you, McBane." Gus's face was bright red as he started to lean into Grady; Sass grabbed hold of him. "This is your fault. She was fine. The cars were fine. The team was fine until you showed up."

Wonderful. I would've closed my eyes, but I couldn't walk fast with my eyes closed. The crowd around them grew as it sounded like there were men pushing and shoving, and more cussing.

A few members of the media caught me in their snare before I could escape to the maze of haulers.

"CJ, with Grady's success, what are your plans after the season if Merrick chooses Grady over you for the number thirty-six car?"

"CJ, have you been approached with any other offers?"

"CJ, how are you holding up with the pressure of the competition? Are there any bad feelings toward Grady?"

I had nothing to give them. I didn't know what to say.

Gus walked up behind me, grabbing my elbow. "That's it for now, everyone. CJ has to get moving."

Judging by the firm grip he had on my arm, it was clear my estranged friend had decided this was a moment he wanted to have a come-to-Jesus with me.

I yanked my arm away from him. "Where is Harper?"

"Looking for you, I imagine. But we need to have a few words."

I turned on him and roared. "You know what? Fine. You want to talk, fine. But so help me God, August, if you lay your hands on me again, you will be singing soprano. We clear? I don't know who the hell you think you're talking to?'

"I thought I was talking to my friend. A woman with a head on her shoulders."

"Screw you. If you want to have this conversation, you will watch the insults, or it won't last long," I said without turning around.

He followed me into the hauler, the incandescent bulbs burned my eyes as we entered and walked down the center aisle, filled with extra car parts and machinery, to the back where there was a meeting room. I was about to slam the door to the adjacent room on him when he caught it. I was already unzipping my race suit and peeling it off, letting the top hang at my hips. With the questions from the reporters still chipping away at my ego, I tried to get in the right head space to deal with him.

Gus didn't seem to register this—or just didn't care. He walked in and closed the door behind him and leaned quietly against it, arms crossed, head down.

I stopped and threw my arms out wide. "What? What do you want to say?"

He stood silent.

Without room to pace, I just turned in circles like a caged tiger, Gus with a stick ready to poke at me.

"Are you here to tell me all the ways I fucked up tonight? Are you here to point out all the ways I'm failing?"

He shook his head slowly, still not looking up from his shoes.

"Why the hell are you here?"

"To tell you to get your head out of your ass."

"Screw you, G."

He stormed up and was in my face in the blink of an eye, pointing his finger at my chest.

"No, screw you. *This* isn't you." His eyes burned into me. Burned through me. "You've got your damn head in the clouds. He's walking around here like he's already won. You look like a rookie."

I drew back.

His voice was scathing as he gestured at me with derision that I never imagined I'd ever see coming from my friend. "You show up at the track and you can't keep your head in the damn race? Has he fucked you so thoroughly that you're walking around in oblivion?"

I threw the punch before I even knew I clenched my fist.

I didn't slap. Having been around men all my life, I knew how to throw a punch.

A good one.

I may not be able to take a man down—but I could bloody a nose.

*I will not cry. I will not cry.*

I scowled at him with fury emanating from my heart and tried not to let the pain he inflicted seep through. Gus was my friend. Tommy's friend. One of the few people whose opinion meant something to me.

He thought I was a failure and a whore. And he was ashamed of me.

To hell with him. I discreetly shook my now-sore hand. "Get. Out."

Blood oozed from his nose. He grabbed some napkins off the table and held it to his face. His unreadable gaze never wavered from mine. But he didn't respond, and he didn't move.

"Get. Out." My volume raised.

He broke eye contact, his breath also heavy.

"Get. The. Fuck. Away from me!" I closed my eyes in a last-ditch effort for control. The torrent of immeasurable emotions was banging on the barn doors, demanding escape, and I was tempted to let them loose on this man.

*Focus. Grit. Unapologetic determination.*

*Frustration. Pain. Impending defeat.*

Who was this man I called my friend? Who was this girl I'd become?

"CJ...I'm—"

"Just...just go." I turned around and wished I weren't cornered in the back of the hauler, realizing too late that most of the crew could probably could hear us.

Gus left, slamming the door behind him.

I locked the door, quickly ditched my racing suit, changing back into the shirt and jeans I had on earlier. I grabbed a water bottle, dampened a napkin, and used it to wash off my face. I focused on my breathing and trying hard to control my tears before straightening and throwing on a team hat. Taking a final, deep, ragged breath, I walked out to the back of the hauler and into the main area. Bill sat in one of the chairs. The rest of the hauler was unusually empty, but a flurry of activity outside indicated they were breaking down and packing up.

Wild Bill was kicked back, legs spread, his arm rested on a table as if it should have a beer in its hand. He studied me. "You good?"

Not trusting my voice or my temper, I nodded once.

He nodded over his shoulder. "Gus's face…you did that?"

I dug my hands in my pockets and nodded again.

"Want to tell me why?"

"No."

"I've noticed a lot of tension with him and you, and him and Grady."

I opened my mouth to speak.

He held up his hand. "I don't want to know the drama and I really don't want to know the details. If you punched him, I'm sure he deserved it. But Gus has been your biggest supporter. He's hurt you and you've hurt him. Give it some time and be done with it."

I didn't respond because I wasn't sure what would happen with Gus and me—and that was a source of sadness.

"As far as Grady…" Bill rubbed his finger across his mouth and then looked up at me. "CJ, the boy knows what he's doing. I'm not saying he doesn't have genuine feelings for you, because I believe he just might. But darlin', while he may be able to have his cake and eat it, too, I'm not sure you will have that same option. You need to run on all cylinders. I get the bad showing at New Hampshire, having come off that concussion, and maybe even the one after that. But darlin', this isn't you. This isn't your best. You need to get your shit together, or you will lose everything."

My body began to shake. I'd like to think it was the adrenaline crash—from the race…from my run in with Gus. But deep inside, I think it was the fear clawing at me. Fear of failure.

"I've taken you as far as I can. Gus, Harper, the crew—we're all in your corner. But you're the one in the seat. There isn't room in there for both of you. If Grady loses, he'll be offered another position. If you lose…with your history with the Duprees…you'll probably head back to Energy Blast…if you're lucky. I don't tell you this to scare you…"

He stood up so suddenly it startled me.

He stepped toward me. "Actually, I am going to scare you." He spoke without his laid-back manner, with more urgency and aggressiveness. "Grady McBane is a charming, talented, marketing machine. He's caught on quicker than any driver I've come across. Get your head out of the clouds, move his ass out of your bed, and get back to being the ornery driver with a chip on her shoulder—Merrick may be the only way you can get where you want to be."

Each word was like a boulder laid on me. It made my heart heavier and my resentment greater. I respected Wild Bill more than anyone. I felt his censure and I took this ass-kicking the hardest.

He let out a deep sigh.

"It's obvious to everyone you have feelings for the boy. I know it's hard—since Tommy. …I don't know, maybe just put them on the back burner until this can be cleared up. If they are real, they'll be there when it's over."

He came over and patted me on the shoulder, and I realized I was shaking. That was as close as Bill came to affection. Even in the heaviness of the moment I had to smile slightly at the uncharacteristic gesture and how uncomfortable he must be with it.

"Now, let's get the hell out of here. Get back to your RV. The crew needs to pack up and get the hauler out of here."

From outside there were muffled voices. "What the hell are you doing here?" Gus.

"Well, this is the team hauler…I'm part of the team." And Grady.

"Not this weekend you're not."

Fantastic. Just what I needed.

Bill drew in a deep breath and let it out in a whoosh, as if gathering strength for the next crisis, and walked out the door. "Here we go again."

When I followed, Gus was up in Grady's face, a few of the boys between them.

"She doesn't need you around here." Gus lunged.

"It doesn't look like she wants you around either—" Grady accentuated the barb with a smirk.

Shit.

Harper came running up to my side and grabbed me, dragging me to the waiting golf cart. "Come on. Let's get out of here. Let the boys sort these fools out. You being here will just cause them to beat their chest more and add fuel to the fire."

I let her lead me away. After all, I needed to go off and lick my wounds, build my barricades, and regroup.

# 39

## CJ

The next day, once I was home, Grady texted and said he was on his way over. I tried to talk him out of it, but he wouldn't take no for an answer.

"They finished renovating my house and moved me in. Pack a bag. We're going to the lake."

I tried everything. He wouldn't hear it.

He practically tackled me when I answered the door. His charm-o-meter was spiking. His arms around me, he picked me up, propped me against the wall, and breathed me in before kissing me. "I missed you."

Those words, being in his arms, feeling his heat and seeing the smile on his face, it was what made me so conflicted. Moments like those paralyzed my senses. I wanted the rest of the world to take a flying leap. I wanted this man. I never wanted him to stop looking at me the way he was looking at me at that moment.

He growled, put me down, and smacked by backside. "Go pack a bag, I'm stealing you away."

"Grady…I'm exhausted. The last thing I want to do is pack again."

He opened my closet and began searching for something. "Come on, Charlotte, I want to take you to my house—ravish you and lavish you."

"What are you doing?" I grabbed at him.

"Packing for you. Where's your bag?"

"What's the rush? Can we discuss this?"

"No. I'm eager to start on the ravishing portion of the weekend, and I don't want to start it here or we may never get there." He teased his eyebrows at me and gave me a once-over.

"You look beautiful, by the way." He grabbed me around the neck and drew me up to meet his mouth. He kissed me, teasing my bottom lip with his tongue, sucking on it gently, the way he knew drove me crazy and made my legs weak. Then he pulled away abruptly and stepped back.

"Pack." He pointed at the closet.

His enthusiasm was infectious—him, here like this…it was as if we led two separate lives. Our lives at the track, where I knew we needed to be different people, and the one at home, where I knew I could get used to this in my life.

For now, he had me on board with the "ravishing and lavishing" plan, and I was intrigued enough to give it a shot.

Grady's lake house wasn't far from downtown Charlotte. We drove up I-77 in his Tesla Roadster, his hand on my thigh as his thumb moved slowly back and forth. It teased me, making me aware of its lack of progress moving farther up.

I shifted in my seat, squeezing my legs together, trying to move Grady's hand with just a little of my own maneuvering. Glancing out of the corner of my eye, I saw a slight lift of his lip. He knew what I was doing.

"You okay?" Cheeky bastard.

"Yep." I put my elbow on the door and looked out the window.

He stopped moving it when it reached its new location, which was even more frustrating.

I searched for something else to talk about. Get my mind off what was and wasn't happening between my legs.

My eyes zeroed in on the removable glass roof. "Why not remove the top? It's such a beautiful day?"

His hand didn't move, but his choice of changed. Instead of his thumb, his pinky, which was dangerously closer to my core, began to move—with earnest. "Because if the roof was removed, the truckers would get a good view of me touching you, and of you enjoying it."

I realized my jean shorts were loose around my thighs, and his rogue pinky was slipping inside—excruciatingly slow, teasing the outer seam of my thigh. My hands clawed at the door and the middle console to stop myself from brushing against his hand.

"Grady...what are you doing? Don't you need your hand on the wheel?"

"I'm good. I'm a pretty talented driver, after all."

I closed my eyes and he moved closer to the seam of my panties.

"Grady..."

"Just relax...put the seat back and relax."

"Someone will see..."

"No one will see. The windows are tinted, and you're low enough. Unless you want someone to see..."

I backhanded his arm playfully, but then lowered the back of the seat and stretched my hands over my head.

He chuckled with an evil, mischievous laugh, and moved his entire hand farther into my shorts.

He rubbed his pinky across my center.

It made me want more.

"Unbutton your pants," he growled.

"Grady...you're driving..."

"We've got another fifteen minutes on the interstate. I can make you much more relaxed in less than that. Unbutton your pants."

I did as he said.

He slipped his hand down my pants, pushing them down to allow himself more room.

"God, CJ, you're enjoying this, aren't you...?"

I moved my hips—I couldn't help myself. This was the most

erotic thing I'd ever done. "Don't crash. This would be hard to explain to everyone."

"Trust me, it is hard to keep my eyes on the road and not on you. I'm going to need you to give me a recap later. I'm thinking of all the things we're going to do to christen my new place—all the rooms, all the positions."

He kept glancing at me out of the corner of his eye, and truth be told, he was spending more time watching me than the road. The morning sun was bright, and even though he assured me the windows were tinted, the fact that we were surrounded by cars full of people, put an edge to the experience.

I was going to have an orgasm surrounded by people—whether or not they knew it.

My hips moved faster. He moved faster.

"At this rate, I may pull over to the side of the road and figure out a way to get you to straddle me. Maybe if we remove the rooftop, we can stick your head out the window as you ride me."

The visual was all it took. Me riding him. In his Tesla.

I was gone. I came loud. I squeezed his hand between my thighs, and he groaned out encouragement.

Back in the real world, I played with the back of his hair and stared at his profile and his half-cocky grin. It was tender. It wasn't me, but I couldn't help myself.

We pulled into the driveway to an unassuming modern, gray-blue home, flanked by the three-car garage and textured concrete driveway, and framed by tall trees. Grady's excitement and pride were evident in his smile and his frequent glances at me for my reaction.

"Nice digs," I said, as we walked through the spacious, bright, open floorplan with warm hardwood floors, accented with a stone fireplace and dark kitchen cabinets. The large windows illuminated with sunlight were a beacon for me to walk to the back of the house.

Grady came up behind me, wrapping one arm around my waist and the other around my neck as he whispered, "What do you think?" There was a small need for approval in his voice. He tried to cover it, but I think he wanted me to love it.

I gave him a small smile over my shoulder. "You did good, big guy."

He turned and kissed me soundly. "Good. I'll give you the tour later." Then he lifted my shirt in one movement and removed my bra in the other. He was on his knees with my breast in his mouth sucking hard, his fingers flicking the other nipple, and my knees weak within a few blinks.

"Oh, God, Grady..."

He had me in my panties standing in front of his palladium windows as he stood back, staring at me.

"You're gorgeous." He removed his shirt, and my mouth was useless to form words. I climbed him, wrapping my arms around his neck until he lifted me, cupping my ass and dragging me over to his leather sectional.

"All I could think about for the last twenty minutes was how ready you are for me. I need to take you fast and hard, honey. I need you—now."

"Hell, yes," I demanded.

He pulled off my panties, his boxers somehow already gone. He grabbed me by the knees, lining me up, and plunged inside me, in one stroke—seating himself. His neck strained as he reared back, strength and power in his thrust. My fingers raked down his chest, and I restrained from running my nails down to mark him. He held my legs and began to rock against me, moaning my name.

"Charlotte."

After a few strokes I remembered the idea he teased me with and pushed him off. I made sure to give him a firm expression as I pushed him down onto the sectional and straddled him.

"Fast and hard, huh? I can do fast and hard..."

And I rode him...fast and hard. He was slack-jawed, his eyes burning into me. He kissed me, running his tongue over my neck and chest. I threw back my head, reveling in the deepness of the connection, groaning expletives, and growling his name.

I grabbed his hands and put them on my breasts, making him cup them and flick the nipples, showing him what I wanted.

He got the message.

"Fuck, yes, that's it, so hot. So…mine. Do you hear me, Charlotte? You're mine."

"Yes!" I went faster.

He leaned back and moved one hand to brace himself and began to thrust upward. He moved the other to massage my clit while watching me with dark, possessive eyes. We were caught in each other's erotic expression as we went over the edge, screaming each other's name.

After our breathing evened out, Grady observed, "Thank God we have a lot more space here than at your place. We were loud enough to wake the dead that time."

"Serves you right for riling me up on the way out here," I said as I adjusted myself. "Where's the bathroom, I need to wash up?"

"Go, head upstairs, and down the hall to the right. I'll go get the bags." He waved me off and strode into the kitchen as he began digging into the fridge. "Get changed—hopefully into an amazing bikini. I bought a boat that I'm dying to take out on its maiden voyage." He peeked out. "I'm grabbing food and some other necessities, and we will take it out."

We spent the day on the water in Grady's new boat. With the awning up, wearing our trusty aviator sunglasses and hats, and staying away from the more popular areas, we managed to remain unnoticed. I think there were a few moments when people did a double take, but then we would slip out of the area.

Being a stock car driver around Lake Norman or Charlotte, in general, was like being a celebrity in Beverly Hills. You were more likely to be recognized than anywhere else. However, having spent a lot of time on the lake with Harper's family as a child, I was able to find us a quiet cove we used to visit to have our lunch. We were relaxing in the sun, him in a chair on the deck and me lying in the sun. I was allowing myself a rare beer when Grady broached the subject.

"Want to tell me what last night was about?"

I took another long sip of the beer to gather my thoughts. "Gus had some comments on my performance over the past few races."

"Did he now…"

"And I had an opinion about his critique."

Grady arched an eyebrow. "Remind me not to offer any commentary."

I sat up and nodded my beer at him. "You've been warned. He's probably regretting helping Tommy teach me how to throw a proper punch."

Grady let out a chuckle. "Alright. But tell me what the dickhead said."

I gazed into the distance. "Nothing that wasn't true, just things I didn't want to hear."

"Like what?"

I turned back, but still didn't look at him. "That I'm screwing up. That I'm letting you distract me—"

Grady straightened "That's—" I held up my hand to stop him from arguing.

"I know that isn't your intention. He thinks it is. That's the difference." I stood and stepped away from him, looking out over the water. "But it's the only one. Being with you is distracting me and causing me to lose my focus, lose my edge."

I had to say this. I had to lay this out there because if I say it, I'd believe it, and if I believe it, I'd do something about it. I forced myself to turn and look him in the eye. "So, help me, Grady. I think being with you is going to cost me everything."

# 40

## Grady

I'm going to kill that cocksucker.

I'm going to kill that jealous, vindictive cocksucker. I don't care if he's the crew chief.

He's going to cost me CJ. He's going to cost me my Charlotte.

"We just have to get through the season. Whoever doesn't get this car will get a contract with another team—you heard Merrick—"

"I'm screwing up. I'm not running the way I should. And if I don't get Merrick, my chances of getting another team will be slim."

"That's not true. You'll win. You know you're a better driver—"

"Let's not get into this again. Odds are in your favor. Odds are in your favor no matter the angle you look at them—"

I pulled her to sit next to me, cradled her face in my hands, and tried to convey how precious she was to me, how important her dreams—her success—was to me. "I'll quit. I'll go to Merrick tomorrow and back out."

Her eyes glistened. She held onto my hands as she gently pulled them down from her face. "You can't. There are contracts and sponsors and millions of dollars at stake. The contracts we signed give Merrick the control to choose…we have to finish the season."

I pulled her hands to my mouth and kissed one and then the other. "Then let's finish the season."

*Just give us a chance. Just give me a chance.*

She stared at my eyes. "I'm losing myself in you and it needs to stop. I can't afford to do that. Do you understand? I need to be CJ. I can't be Grady McBane's girlfriend."

"Can't you be both?"

"I'm not sure I know how."

That night, in my bed, I made love to her, slow and sweet, cherishing her and never breaking eye contact with her.

I know she felt it. I know she felt something.

A tear fell from her eye.

One solitary tear.

She closed her eyes and I kissed each one before I made love to her mouth and whispered her name, "Charlotte…" right there I almost said the words.

I swear to Christ, I almost said *the* three words.

But I knew if I did—right then, I would lose her for good. She'd run from me faster than any car we've ever driven.

I just said, "Look at me as I make love to you, sweetheart." The connection was there and that was the closest I came to giving her the words.

Later, while we were lying in bed, with her wrapped in my arms, she tried to roll off my chest. She was pulling away. She was fast asleep, and already she was trying to distance herself. I let her roll off me. I gave her a moment to snuggle into the pillow and then pulled her back against me, spooning her and anchoring her to me with a strong arm around her waist. I breathed in her scent and whispered into her dreams, "I'm not letting you go that easy."

## 41

---

# *CJ*

*Ding-dong*

"Come in!" I yelled, as I threw together my travel bag. Harper was picking me up to drive down to Darlington. Being only two hours away, we chose to drive down ourselves, rather than with the team.

The front door opened and closed, but there wasn't the pitter-patter of her heels.

I slung my bag on my shoulder and walked down the hall. "Harper?"

A sheepish Gus stood in my doorway, head down, arms crossed over his chest.

"Harper, you look like shit." I was going to kill her. I didn't need round two. I walked into my kitchen to make sure everything was turned off and to give myself a moment to gather my thoughts.

"Please don't tell me you're my ride."

He walked into the kitchen. "Yep. We needed some bonding time."

"By the look of your face, I'd say we don't bond well these days."

He took a step closer.

I went to the fridge for some water and to get some more space to breathe.

"Well, we have to work on it since we have to work together." He leaned against the counter. "I can start by apologizing for being a jackass."

I opened the fridge and grabbed two bottles of water. I stayed quiet.

I wasn't going to apologize for the punch. He deserved it.

"I also regret showing you how to throw a punch," he added.

I straightened. "Tommy taught me that."

"Yeah, well, who'd you think taught Tommy?"

I walked over and put the water in my duffle.

A sad smile graced his face. "You know he'd laugh his ass off if he saw you lay me out."

"He would've joined me if he heard what you said to me."

Gus's head dropped. "Yeah, I know. I had no right. I...I just hate what's going on. Some of that's my need to protect you—for Tommy."

He stood and rubbed both his hands over his face. "Anyway, ugh. I didn't want to get all deep the morning of your race. I only wanted to apologize." He put his hands on his hips and looked up, as if searching for direction to this conversation.

He looked over at me. "I'm sorry. I'm sorry for the hurtful things I said. I deserved this." He motioned to his face. "I didn't handle the idea of you being with Grady well. You haven't been with anyone since Tommy, and I think maybe that was weird for me, too. I think you knocked some sense into me. You're my friend, first and fore-most, and I want nothing more in this world than to see you succeed. Can you accept my apology?"

I looked at my old friend. The friend who stood by me and held me after Tommy's death. He stood up for a girl half his size, against an industry that, for the most part, didn't think she deserved to be there. He gave me encouragement and kept me in check. He was part of my makeshift family.

"I can't do this without you. But, Gus, you can't talk to me that way again. I won't tolerate it. Not from you. Not from anyone. I appreciate what you were trying to say about maintaining focus, and maybe in some way you had a point. But who I sleep with, who I have a relationship with—that isn't your business any more than it's Harper's or Merrick's or anyone else's. Can you accept that?"

He nodded. "I don't have to like it, but I can accept it."

I opened my arms and walked toward him. He leaned down and drew me up into a bear hug.

I broke the hug and said, "Now, let's get going so I can kick some Darlington ass." I grabbed my bag and walked to the door. "Are you my chauffeur? How did the crew chief become a chauffeur?"

"Because I'm the boss, and because now I've got two hours to get your head on straight."

I glared at him and held up my earbuds and phone. "This is how I plan to spend my two hours."

"Speaking of getting your head on straight. Where is your biggest distraction?"

I ignored him.

"CJ, where is your Casanova?"

"I don't know. Today, I'm trying to focus on me."

# 42

*Grady*

I was a caged tiger.

Life didn't make sense to me. Fine—it made sense, but I fucking hated it.

I backed off. She asked me to back off. Well, she didn't ask me. She basically told me *she* was backing off and I didn't really have a choice.

Like it's my fault she had a few shitty races. Everyone has a few shitty races. It's part of racing.

Doesn't mean it's my fault.

Yes, I was pouting.

I was pouting and practically kicking the dirt with my feet as I walked through the infield at Darlington, ordered not to approach her trailer or the hauler since it was her weekend to race, and she needed to focus.

I might as well be in the stands. I've practically been banned.

It's like she didn't want to admit I was even alive.

What the ever-loving hell?

"Stop pouting…" Cooper came walking up behind me.

"I'm not pouting."

I was. My hands buried in my jean pockets, my baseball cap slung low on my brow, and my shoulders slumped, I was definitely pouting.

Cooper disagreed with a dramatic roll of the eyes. "Come on, Romeo. She asked you to give her space. You know what she suggests makes sense. If what you two have going on is real, it will hold until this complication is over. She's making more sense than you at the moment. Let's go enjoy the race."

I sneered at him.

I already did a bit of press, I put on my smile and talked with the media. Told them I was there to support the entire Merrick team. I didn't single out CJ one way or the other. Regardless of how hard they tried to get me to, I stayed completely neutral. Even when I saw her across the room, no matter how hard I wanted to go wrap my arms around her, I kept my distance.

"Grady, she's doing this for both of you—"

"I know—it doesn't mean I want to sit back and wait. I can't stand not having a way out of this."

"You do and you know it. You just don't like your solution."

I turned on him. "You know that isn't a solution."

Cooper's voice was wary. "Cal has called and put out the olive branch in the form of multiple proposals—"

"He just can't stand the thought of me succeeding on my own."

Cooper sighed. "You realize what a stubborn shit you sound like, right? He'd work with getting the suspension lifted, he'd talk with your father about the team…you could have your career, and CJ could have hers. Did you even tell her about that possibility?"

I turned on Cooper and my agitation flew into full-blown indignation. "How are we even talking about this? It's all on his terms. It's not respect he's offering. He doesn't think I can cut it, and he wants to swoop in and save the day." My bitterness, and maybe misplaced pain, ramped up. Again. "Besides the fact that with the two separate racing schedules, we'd never see each other.

Something else dawned on me. "No, forget all of that. The

simple fact is I don't want to go back. I don't want to go back to open-wheel, Indy, or McBane. I like it here. I like the cars, the people, the new experiences. It's not just CJ. It's the new direction."

I exorcised the specter of my brother and walked to the pit box. My plan was to stand behind it and watch on the monitor as my woman raced. I would stay out of sight.

Like a secret.

Like a secret shame.

Like an embarrassment.

I wanted out of the shadows. The end of the season couldn't come soon enough.

I needed to do something to make this right. I looked around at all the pit boxes lined up and down pit row. In my head, I rattled off the teams and what I've learned about them, making a mental list of possibilities.

"Grady, man…what are you thinking?"

CJ didn't want me to quit, but I'd been getting a few other teams sniffing around. It was time to flirt with some other teams and see what other possibilities were out there. I didn't have to fall on the sword in front of her, but maybe if another team "lured" me away, that would work?

I started to walk off down the row.

"Grady…where are you going?" Cooper trailed behind me, a note of caution in his tone.

I had to do something besides sit around, waiting for fate.

"To take control of my life."

# 43

## CJ

Darlington was a turning point for me. It was the kick in the ass, the veritable shot in the arm I needed. It got my blood pumping.

Crossing the finish line with Muñoz on my ass, I was proud to have beaten him and finally broken the top ten. We'd been battling the entire day, and it cost both of us positioning, even costing me the lead in lap one-hundred-twenty.

When it came down to it, though, it drew out my fighter. It brought back my moxie. I liked Muñoz well enough, but I was cussing his name up and down throughout the race. But by the time we crossed the finish line, it felt good.

It felt better since he was behind me.

I'll admit to jumping out of the car with a little more spring, a small smile on my face, my chest was a little more puffed out. Someone handed me my sponsor's hat and a sponsor drink to hold while I was interviewed and photographed. I was a little more cheerful speaking with the press post-race, although they weren't as sweet to me as they had been in the past.

"So, tell me, CJ, how does it feel to finally be back on track?"

"CJ, are you concerned about Grady's universal marketing appeal?

"CJ, what did you do differently to center yourself this week? Did Grady help you or give you some tips on how he is able to focus?" Yeah, that one I wanted to make into a eunuch.

Harper, noticing the change in my smile from cheerful to possibly murderous, intervened and pulled me forward, cutting off the interviews before I cut someone's "something" off.

"You were on fire today. If not for Muñoz, you would've owned that track. Don't let an asshole distract you from that," she whispered.

I searched around for Grady before heading to the trailer to change. I found him in the back, but he wasn't looking for me.

No. He was in a dark corner standing close to Nadina Towers, an executive at DTS Shipping—the sponsor for Perry Peterman Motorsports. Too close. Her hand was resting on his forearm. She was touching him.

What the hell? Was this what he did while I was racing?

The sweetness of the evening—of the success I was riding on— turned sour in my stomach. What was he doing?

As if he heard me call his name, his head turned and he spotted me. The sea of people between us faded and his smile widened, his face lit up.

He gave Nadina a few more words, kissing her cheek goodbye. My gaze was fixed on Nadina, whose gaze was fixed on Grady's ass as it walked toward me.

He surveyed the people between us the closer he got and dimmed his smile, then slowed his walk.

I crossed my arms and narrowed my eyes as he approached. "What's up with middle-age Barbie over there?"

He looked over his shoulder briefly. "Oh, Nadina and I know each other from my Indy days; we were just catching up."

The predatory, "knowing" way she raked her gaze over him hinted at intimate knowledge of him naked.

With Grady's approach, new fascination in the two of us

produced a crowd, and the cameras turned back on. I forced a casual smirk as I walked by him before he reached me, "McBane." With a slight tilt of my head, I indicated the cameras pointed at us.

He pulled up short. A sad smile on his face. "Hey, good job out there."

Unable to come up with a sarcastic jab or witty one-liner, I nodded once and walked off toward the hauler.

"Grady, what do you think of CJ's performance today?"

"Grady, do you think she has a chance to come back? Are you concerned about your chances?"

"Boy, she's being kind of a cold bitch..." someone from the crowd commented. I wasn't sure if it was a reporter or just a bystander.

I stopped and turned on a dime, crossing my arms and seeing if he was going to answer them.

He hadn't planned on it, but with my attention now on them, he was a deer in the headlights. "Of course, I think CJ did well. Of course, I've always considered CJ a concern."

The sincerity barely registered. I rolled my eyes and continued to the trailer.

---

Even though Indianapolis Motor Speedway was a home to both stock car and open-wheel races, it still felt like it was Grady's turf. People flocked to him like he was the prodigal child returned.

My little-redheaded-stepchild complex, and my inability to be with him, added to my insecurity. I watched as well-endowed women rubbed against him, female reporters batted their eyes while asking about his dating status—one even slipped something in his hand when she left. The good man threw the paper away, but I'd bet it was a room key or phone number.

The little-redheaded-stepchild was turning green.

And because of my own decree, I had to stay away.

I would remain focused.

But my heart—that organ I never thought would be an issue when it came to my career—told me to brand him as mine.

The two parts of me—the competitor and the girlfriend—were at war with each other. I had no idea who wanted it more.

I stomped around the infield. Gus was busy with the crew readying the car. I had no idea where Harper was but didn't want to roam the infield to look for her and have to be nice to people. So, I sat in the pit box, with my aviators and my baseball hat hung low, trying not to be recognized.

Being small sometimes worked to my advantage. In the car, it meant there was almost one-hundred pounds less for the car to drag around the track. It also meant I could be less conspicuous when I wanted to be. When I was slouched down in the pit box, with the crew beneath me, no one knew I could overhear what was being discussed below. Not even Grady.

"Grady, oh, good. I'm glad I caught you." Nadina's practiced, cultured voice was nails on a chalkboard.

"Nadina, what are you doing over here?" Grady's voice wavered, as he came closer and seemed to be drawing her closer in.

"Can't an old friend come to wish you good luck?" She was being coy. Oh, Lord, save me from coy women from Grady's past.

An engine started nearby, drowning out my eavesdropping capabilities. I debated what to do next, but I imagined her touching his forearm again, and rubbing against him in his racing suit—not many warm-blooded women could resist him in his racing suit.

Before I realized it, I was marching down the stairs from the top of the pit box and rounding the back, determined to interrupt whatever this little reunion—good-luck rendezvous— was.

Even if what we had was secret and maybe even questionable, she shouldn't be in our pit area minutes before a race. She had to go.

I turned the corner to see her rubbing against him like a cat in heat. "Well, I am very excited about working together again and… renewing things…"

"Eh…hem." I wanted to cut off her claws with wire cutters, but I struggled for nonchalance. "Grady, enough with the groupies, it's time to do your job. Unless you want me to do it for you." I thumbed over my shoulder to the cars lined up.

Alright, so I wasn't good with nonchalance, or subtlety, or…well, women hitting on Grady.

That got me a glare from Nadina. "I can see why you went looking for me, darling." She stood on her toes and attempted to turn Grady's face to hers for a kiss.

He turned his head just in time, so the kiss landed on his cheek. Good thing, or I wouldn't be the only stock car driver at the track without a set of balls.

"Come on, darling, I'll put you in your car," she purred.

Hell, no.

I stepped in front of her. "Um, no. Sorry, you aren't authorized."

"Don't be ridiculous. Do you know who I am? Grady can let whomever he wants into the pit area."

I spread my stance and crossed my arms. Channeling Gandalf's, *"You-shall-not-pass."* "Not past me—not on this team, he can't."

"We'll see how long that lasts." She glared at me, then turned all sweet as honey glancing at Grady. "I'll call you later, darling, and we'll talk further without any interruption."

He just nodded. The man hadn't uttered a word. Not sure if it was self-preservation or pure stupidity. Maybe both, since his silence spoke volumes.

She sashayed her tight ass in designer pants and halter top back to where she belonged.

I whirled on Grady. My mouth was opened to let out a torrent of words. "What-the-ever-loving—"

He held up a hand. "I'm talking to her about sponsorship."

"What was she doing over here, Grady? And why were you letting her rub all over you as if she were marking her territory?"

Gus came over. "Would one of you like to take a moment and come race this beautiful car I have ready and waiting?"

"Yeah, I'm coming." Grady leaned over as if to kiss me and then stepped back, his eyes darting around, remembering where we were. His face fell, as did his gaze.

He settled for touching my bicep and said, "We'll talk later, okay?"

No, it was not okay. No, I wasn't anywhere near okay with this. I was half-tempted to hunt Nadina down and find out what the hell was going on, because I knew she'd be happy to tell me the gory details.

Now I was being ridiculous, becoming was exactly what I dreaded.

Unfocused.

Distracted.

Unreasonably resentful.

Ugh.

"Go, have a good race." I waved him off. He gave me his adorable half smile and turned to leave. When he was a few steps from walking out of sight, I shouted, "But not too good!"

That earned me an adorable wink and a full-blown smile.

God, he slayed me.

But the distracted me, the unfocused me—the unreasonable, resentful me kept asking… What was he really doing talking with Nadina?

# 44

*Grady*

I walked over to our car. One of the crewmen handed me my gloves and balaclava, and I slipped it over my head. CJ had her arms crossed, leaning that gorgeous hip against the barrier. Her aviators were on and a baseball hat rode low on her face, but I felt her eyes on me.

Trying to strike a deal with Nadina was playing with fire. I knew that. But there wasn't another way to approach Perry Peterman Motorsports without her. Nadina was an attractive woman. We had a history, brief as it was. I'll have to talk with CJ—Nadina could be a way for both CJ and me to have rides next year and put an end to this farce.

"Aw, is there trouble in paradise?" A slithering voice came out of nowhere. Dewey.

"Lover's spat?"

CJ and I stared at each other.

"Keep walking, Moist, your car is several spots back." CJ threw in a smirk.

Dewey stiffened, but kept his back to us as if to leave. I foolishly thought it was over until he turned enough to throw back over his shoulder, "Be careful, McBane. Men who fight with her before driving…" He skewered her with his glare before turning back to me. "It doesn't end well for them."

My eyes were on CJ. She wasn't just shocked, she was struck.

Without any further thought, I threw down my equipment and slammed him against the barrier wall and into our crew, who grabbed him. A few guys held me back before I could do more and get suspended from the race.

Gus came from behind the car, picked him up by his racing suit, and growled, "You must have a death wish." Sass grabbed him and escorted him past several teams, back to where his car was waiting. No one else—no other team on pit row—intervened.

All eyes turned to me and then CJ. I threw my hands up and said, "I'm fine."

My eyes were on CJ as I gave a quick scan. She met my survey with her own piercing stare. God, I wanted to grab her and kiss her as all the other drivers did with their girlfriends and wives. I wanted to claim her right there on pit road for all the world to see. She gave me a curt nod.

*I see you. I'm fine.*

She stepped up to me, stone-faced and serious. "You don't have time for this shit. Focus." She said it with strength; it left no room for me to do anything else but what she commanded from me. "And get in the damn car."

My adrenaline was flowing dangerously, and I was distracted as a crewmember helped me finish strapping into the car, slipping on my helmet and attaching the steering wheel. I gave a thumbs up, acknowledging that I could hear the spotter and Gus on the comms. They finished attaching the window net just as I heard CJ come on the comms.

"If you let that fool distract you from your job, from anything but running a good, clean race." I looked over and she had Gus's headset. "So help me God, if you wreck this car, I will personally kick your ass. Do you hear me?" She pulled off the headset and shoved it at Gus in one angry motion, glaring at me, daring me not to follow her instruction.

That's my woman.

"Are we cool?" Gus asked.

"Yep. I'm good." I smiled like a love-sick fool. "But I'm still going to wipe the floor with that asshole."

"Agreed. The line is a long one, but we will push you to the front. For now, let's show him how it's done." At least Gus and I agree on something.

I gazed out at the organized chaos that was pit road. CJ stood as if she were the center of the storm, staring at me through those aviators, leaving me unable to gauge her thoughts.

I nodded back. We were fine.

"Drivers, start your engines."

The roar of forty engines coming to life was enough to drown out anyone's thoughts.

Time to get to work.

Indianapolis was supposed to be one of my easier tracks. I could run it with an open-wheel car with my eyes closed, and even though a stock car was like riding a rhino when you were used to being on the back of a jaguar, it was still something instinctual.

However, no matter how well I knew that track, and how well I could do at it, there were thirty-nine other variables I couldn't control.

The hot shot in the number sixty-seven car tangled with the veteran leader, trying to "nudge" him out of the way—which he will deny—and it started a chain reaction that ultimately caught me. I was able to recover, even though I lost position and was now back of the pack. I'd hoped to pit, get some new tires, straighten out some damage, and make up some time.

Until good ol' Dewey thought it would be a good time to teach me a lesson by tapping my back panel. At two-hundred mph, a tap may as well be a wrecking ball. It spun me, taking out three more unfortunate guys before sending me into the grass and eventually kissing the infield barrier.

Sonofabitch. I was done.

Dewey Dickhead Dupree.

---

Off to the infield hospital to make sure my eggs weren't scrambled.

I was fine. Just pissed off.

"It's racing," Junior said to me and Cooper as we walked out. "Get over it." He wasn't happy about the outcome, obviously. Not just because of the expense of the car, but because it put me a race down, supposedly. What he didn't want me to do is go find Dewey, and do to him what he did to my car.

Cooper rolled his eyes at me. "Nice bedside manner, huh. Are you okay?"

"Yeah, I'm fine. Just sore." The race had finished. Crowds were still milling around, as were the media.

"Hey, Grady, how are you feeling?" One of the reporters, Lenny Miller, slid up next to me. "Everything good?"

"Yeah, I'm fine."

"So, CJ won't be circling around you to swoop in to take your next race?" He chuckled.

I glared at him. "It's not like that, man."

A fan stopped, holding out an autograph book, "Mr. McBane, would you mind—" I didn't listen further. I took the book and pen and signed it. Smiled as her friend took our photo and moved along, just as Cooper intervened.

Lenny wasn't giving up. "Then what's it like with the Ice Princess? I think people are dying to know what she's really like behind the scenes."

I pulled up short. I was exhausted. I just got knocked around in a real life-sized pinball machine, and I'd been the ball...and I didn't like where this was going.

"What are you getting at, Miller?" My hands on my hips, my head cocked, I studied the man and his sleazy smirk.

"Come on. Your reputation's legendary in Indy. Yet you come here and there's nothing connecting you to anything with tits and ass. There's only you and CJ, the girl who wants to be a race car

279

driver. All of a sudden, she's flirty and batting her eyelashes at you, and we watch her melt within days of you showing up. No more tight ass. No more bitchy. With her it's all smiles and laughter…and one-liners."

My ears were ringing. "Are you serious?"

Cooper was in front of me, trying to move me along, "Don't, man. He's trying to bait you."

"She's been driving like shit. For her to lose her self-proclaimed legendary focus, you must have been screwing the hell out of—"

The blow landed before I even realized it was flying, and Lenny was on the ground. I was on top of him, pulling back to land another. Cooper grabbed my arm and wrapped his other around my chest.

Lenny stayed down. Smart, motherfucker.

His mouth was bloody. I wasn't sure if it was from his nose or his lip. Didn't care. His eyes were still pristine, and I wanted to rectify that. I pulled against Cooper and growled from deep inside.

"No, man. Not worth it." Cooper was struggling to hold me. "Look around you. Phones are out…" There was a crowd surrounding us.

Lenny sat up. "Dewey told me you were probably banging her. Guess it makes sense now." He slowly stood. "You'll be hearing from my lawyers." He wiped at his mouth and walked off as if his mission had been accomplished, and another man with a camera followed him.

Wonderful.

CJ was going to have my head.

---

We got back to the RV, and Cooper took off to find me an ice pack for my hand. I walked up the stairs and began shedding my race suit. All I wanted was to change and get a stiff drink. I flicked on the lights to the RV, and found CJ sitting in one of the captain's chairs, legs crossed, beer bottle in hand, glaring at me.

"Hey," I said, my immediate happy surprise transformed to wariness at her expression.

She took a pull off her beer, studying me. "You okay?"

I flexed the hand, showing the redness on the knuckles. "Yeah, I'll be fine."

Her brows were drawn down and she sat up straighter, "Is that from the crash?"

I shook my head, "Oh, no. I wasn't hurt from that. Just tossed around and sore." I walked farther in toward the back and started stripping off the race suit.

"Then what's wrong with your hand?"

I grabbed some shorts out of my duffle and slipped them on. "It's nothing. Just had some words with Lenny Miller." I walked back out and went to the fridge to grab a beer.

"Words? What about?"

"He had words. I didn't like them." I took a pull off the beer, and I shook my head as I swallowed. "What's up with you? I thought you were trying to avoid being seen with me?" It sounded more bitter than I intended, but I was in a shitty mood. Lenny, the comments he made…the race…the way she was looking at me—like I'd done something wrong.

She stood up and slammed down her bottle. "I'm sorry. I was worried and wanted to see if you were okay. Am I impeding your plans this evening?"

"What?"

"Your plans? Is Nadina due over here? Am I in the way?"

"Oh, for fuck's sake. Are you kidding me?" I fell onto the sofa lining the side of the RV and laid my head against the back.

Out of my periphery, I saw her standing by the door like she was going to bolt. "What the hell is going on, Grady?"

Cooper broke the tension by opening the RV door and was up the stairs before realizing what he walked himself into. "Uh, sorry. Grady, here's your ice." He tossed it my way. "Sorry. Also, CJ, Harper is looking for you, and, Grady, you have a visitor who also would like a minute."

"Tell her I'll be there in a minute," CJ said.

And I said, "Fuck the visitor. I'm busy," simultaneously.

"O…kay." Cooper slunk back out of the RV. CJ and I glared at each other as he left.

"Well, I guess I better go so Nadina can have her time with you. I'm sure you have important business to discuss."

"Just stop. There is nothing with Nadina." I put my hand on her shoulder to turn her, and she shrugged me off.

"Don't touch me, reassure me, and then go off with another woman. When I said we should give each other some space, this wasn't what I meant. I didn't realize I needed to be so specific."

"It isn't like that—" Not my best opening.

She spun on me as if a light bulb turned on. "Are you sleeping with her? She pushed past me.

"Good God, no!" I reached for her.

"Don't," she scowled. "Why is she around so much? Why is she even here? If she isn't getting something out of it—if she isn't being promised something? If—"

"Because I asked her to come. I'm trying to get her to work with PPM to drop Kenny and hire me."

"And was sleeping with her part of the contract you were looking to sign?"

"Don't be ridiculous." Did she not hear what I said? "I'm trying to find a solution to this

shit contest. I'm trying to find a team, so we can end this dumbass competition."

She crossed her arms over her chest, seemingly letting this sink in. "So, you've never slept with her?"

Shit. I ran my hand over my face. I was exhausted.

"Years ago."

She threw her arms in the air and rolled her eyes. "Of course. And now she's back for seconds."

"I haven't given her any indication there would be anything physical between us."

Her voice raised to a dangerous level. "She's climbing you like a tree." CJ put up her hand. "I can't stand this conversation or how it's making me feel. I hate sounding like a jealous woman. I hate that you're making me this way, that you're putting me in this position, and that you're justifying your behavior." She began walking past me.

Then she stopped and turned. "Why go after PPM? What if they signed you? What are you going to do? Tell Merrick you quit? You'll probably win the damn contest anyway. Junior probably knows you're courting Nadina, doesn't he? Which means Merrick does. They will think you're trying to steal the sponsorship. Another feather in your cap, huh? Another reason to give the contract to you. Wow."

She rubbed her hand through her hair. "You come out smelling like a rose no matter how this falls. All you have to do now is convince me."

"I was trying to do this for us. So we could get through this. If I got a contract with

another team, we both could have a team—"

"Wait. Wait…" Her hand went up and her face morphed from processing to incredulity.

"You don't think I'm going to win. You think I'm going to lose and be left without a team. You're bowing out before it happens…" She stepped farther away from me, and with each step, hurt replaced incredulity. "You did this because you think I'm going to fail…and blame you."

"No!"

Her eyes got huge and she glanced above my head, as if looking for another answer.

"Oh, wow," she whispered, "I think the pity hurts worse." She grabbed onto the nearest chair as if to steady herself from the blow.

I tried to step closer, but she was a wounded animal. "CJ, one of us has to lose. It didn't matter who it was going to be. I was just trying to solve the problem before it came between us."

Her face hardened, and I knew that was the wrong thing to say before I even finished speaking.

What I should've said was what I was thinking. I honestly didn't know who would win, I just knew I didn't want to lose her and was desperate for a solution.

She walked to the door. "Yes, one of us is going to lose. And now, I know I just need to focus on it not being me."

"CJ, wait!" I tried to follow her as she ran out of the RV and was greeted by an audience. Harper, her Aunt Sadie, Cooper, and… great…my big brother arrived. Just the thing to make my evening super special. Cal.

I threw up my hands up in the air, "Goddamnit!"

I walked back into the RV and threw the beer in the trashcan before reaching above the refrigerator and grabbing the Glenlivet and sitting at the kitchenette, facing away from the front of the bus.

# 45

## Grady

Instinctively, I knew my big brother wasn't going to leave without having his say. I didn't have it in me to fight with him. He wasn't even on my radar tonight. Let him come, let him slay me with whatever guilt he had to cut me with, and then he could leave.

Sure enough, the door to the RV opened, footsteps came up the stairs and made their way to the kitchen. A door to the cabinet opened, and glasses clinked before a shadow hovered over me and slid into the banquette on the other side.

I held my head in my hands. "I just asked myself, 'Could the night get any worse?' and then the night brought me you. What can I do for you, big brother? Or better question, what do you want now?"

Cal unscrewed the top on the scotch and poured two fingers into each lowball glass. He pushed one toward me. "Just came to check on you."

"You flew to Indianapolis to check on me?"

"And to watch you race," he said, taking a sip of the scotch.

"…watch me race…" I said to myself, as if I needed to hear the words repeated.

He shrugged. "Alright, fine. Would it make you feel better if I said I was also looking into a business opportunity? After all, I am trying to dump a race car team."

I was indifferent to the comment of him selling the McBane team—my former team.

I drank the scotch.

"Couldn't help but overhear the discussion with CJ—"

"Wouldn't call it a discussion."

"So, you two are together?"

"Don't know what we are, but I do know it isn't anyone's business—especially yours."

Cal's glass hit the table so hard I thought it would break. The suddenness made me flinch. "Grady, cut the shit." He gripped the side of the table and growled to the heavens. "I'm so fed up with this 'poor me' crap."

"I seem to have a revolving door of people who want a piece of me tonight…" I leaned my head back and attempted to ignore what would be another lecture of what a fuck-up I was.

My brother stood up abruptly and began pacing. I peeked and saw that his indifference and cool demeanor was gone as he rubbed his hand over his forehead and down his face. Cal didn't lose his cool—not even at me. With me, it was more cold frustration or, at most, exasperation. He turned his back to me, trying to shield some of the emotion.

"What is it?" This was something more than him just coming to chew me out.

My brother wasn't angry. He was upset.

"I…Grady…this isn't Mom sending me down here to bring you home." He slowly turned but didn't meet my eyes. "This is me. I'm down here asking you to cut the shit. Dad…isn't himself." He took a deep breath, moved his hands to his hips, but not before I saw the slighted tremble in one of them.

"What is going on? Cal?"

He walked over and took the bottle, pouring more liquid into it.

"I don't know." He sat back down. "Uncle Mitch is coming out of retirement, declaring he didn't care for golfing and travel anymore. Dad is passing over more responsibilities my way. Leaving work early, some days not showing up. I don't know what is going on." He threw back the scotch. "Then there was the blowup with you."

"Something is going on at home, brother. I understand you're trying to build something here. I'm not happy with how it started, but I respect what you're doing, and I won't stop you." He absently played with the glass, studying it. "This is our family and I need you to end this feud. I need you to find a way to fix this with Dad and with me. Because we're both going to need to handle this—for Mom and Dad."

I leaned back and studied my brother, trying to read something from his face or his body language.

I'd never heard so much defeat from him. He finished the rest of his scotch. We sat there and stared at our empty glasses in silence.

"Alright. You have my attention. We're done. I'm not going back to McBane. Whatever happened to get me here, I like where I am and the autonomy it gives me for now. I think it's best for both of us, and for Dad, that I stay where I am professionally. However, I will take your word that things are going south at home. Dad certainly wasn't himself when I was there. He was thin, withdrawn, and aged. Mom kept reassuring me he just 'wasn't himself.'"

"Mom's tight-lipped, either because she's in denial over something, or because he's sworn her to secrecy. But that's another reason we need to be a united front, because it's tearing her up."

I picked up the bottle and poured us another two fingers in each glass.

I held it up to him and waited for him to look at me.

I nodded. "Okay."

He held his up to me. "Okay."

We both drank, and just like that...it was over. We looked at our glasses and set them down.

"We'll deal with that starting tomorrow." Then, my brother narrowed his eyes at me and said, "Now onto a more immediate problem—what they hell did you do to screw things up with CJ?"

---

*CJ*

The team was in Las Vegas the next weekend, and Harper drove me to the pit for my practice session.

Gus came over with his headset already on. "He isn't here. Don't let him get to you. Just focus on today. I'll take care of him and keep him away from you."

"Don't worry. Grady won't be around," I said without looking up.

In the periphery, Gus and Harper exchanged a look.

"Guys, I sent him away because I'm trying to focus, so can we please not have the *Dr. Phil* hour now. G, go see what your crew is up to and get my baby ready. Harper, let's go over the schedule for today."

All business. The moment I step out at the track—all business.

*Focus.*

*Grit.*

*Unapologetic deter—heartache.* Damnit.

My practice sucked.

I yelled at Gus over the comms. I chewed out Bill when he approached me after I got out of the car. I practically threw my helmet at the crew member trying to help me out of the car.

"What the fuck? I can get out of my own damn car."

Yeah. Rare form. My times sucked. My attitude sucked. My concentration sucked. And then Bill came lumbering over to me, and I knew I was going to get chewed out like a student in the principal's office.

We walked to a corner of the pit garage, and with a glance he scared the rest of the crew out of the area. His thick eyebrows formed into one and his mustache twitched. "Alright. What crawled up your ass this morning?"

With my bottom lip jutting out, and my eyes downcast, I had the petulant child look complete. I had my hand on my hip, shifted my weight, and then crossed my arms over my chest. Unable to stand still, I shifted my stance again with anxious energy coursing through me. It wasn't adrenaline. It was emotion. Bottled-up emotion.

It wasn't good.

It wasn't safe. Adrenaline was something I could channel. Bottled-up emotion. It was combustible and unpredictable.

I knew what was coming. But the castigation coming from Bill, my mentor, still hit me with the same effect. "Get your head out of your ass. What the hell is wrong with you?"

Silence from me. If I opened my mouth, I was afraid what shit would spew forth. Probably tears—the bane of my existence.

"Get it out now. Either to me or to Harper or to someone, but you sure as hell aren't getting back in that race car without your head screwed on straight. You're too fucking emotional right now."

Emotional. *Emotional?* I tipped over the edge.

"Why? Because I'm a girl?"

Bill's eyes squinted. Scary-squinted. He lowered them, getting in my face, and

Growled, "No. Emotional as in you're a powder keg, and I'm

not letting you detonate in one of my million-dollar cars, taking half the track out with you. You want to make this about being a girl—you're the one being a drama queen."

I stared at him. Letting what he was saying sink in.

"You know, you're always saying how you don't want people treating you differently because you're a woman. Then stop reminding them. Fuck this shit with Grady and Merrick. Go back to being you. Stop letting them mess with your head. Now get the hell out of here. Go do what you need to do in order to become sane again."

He walked away without looking back at me. I won't lie—I was a bit concerned he went to see if Grady was around, because I didn't doubt that if I didn't get my shit together, he'd pull me. It was the reason we were both at the tracks each weekend. In case one of us couldn't race—we were each other's backups. I think it was also Merrick's way of reminding us—and the public—this was still a contest.

My head was spinning, my heart was racing—and not in a good way. I wasn't even sure where to start, I was such a mess.

I made a beeline for my trailer.

I didn't even put down my gloves or unzip my suit. I practically ran.

I knew what I needed to do. I knew and I hated it. I hated it so much it was making me more unstable.

I needed to cry.

Such a sissy thing to do. But I needed a good, old-fashioned sob. I needed all the emotions swirling around inside me to get out. I needed to purge them so I could let them go and focus again. Bottling them up wasn't leaving me any room in my head to process much else.

"CJ—I—" I ran past Harper, who was steps from my trailer.

I ran into my trailer and had enough thought to lock the door. I had enough energy to climb the stairs. Tears began to trickle out as I took off the shoes and stripped off the race suit, walking to the back where the bedroom was. I stopped in the doorway of the bedroom wearing only a tank top, bra, and boy-shorts.

Grady sat on the bed. Elbows on his knees, hair disheveled as if he'd been running his hands through it.

The last person I wanted to see. The one person I needed. My lip was trembling. My resolve was fracturing.

He looked up at me from beneath his lashes. His eyes were more blue, less gray...so piercing. The sight of them was the straw that broke my resolve. His mouth dropped open as concern swept his face, a sob escaped from me, and he jumped up immediately, taking me into his arms.

"Sweetheart..." He surrounded me. His embrace so tight, it was the sensory overload I needed to keep from falling apart completely. All the pressure, all the uncertainty, the insecurity, the confusion, frustration...all the emotion poured out of me as he held me together. I hated the weakness I was showing, but surprisingly, I was thankful I wasn't alone.

"Sh...sh...it's okay. What happened?" He rubbed my back and hushed me as I sobbed, never remembering being so lost. His head cupped the back of my head as I buried my face in his neck, breathing in his scent as it helped to ground me. He walked us back to the bed and pulled me onto his lap.

I'd never been more aware of the difference in our size, and reveled in how safe it made me feel. At any other time it would chafe, but now I just buried myself farther into his arms, and as I did, he'd squeeze tighter, kissing the top of my head.

"Charlotte, honey. Please tell me what's wrong. Please, honey." He pulled back and cupped my face with one of his large hands, sweeping away a tear with one of his thumbs as he tilted my face up to his. Our eyes connected, and the torrent of emotions began to ebb, bringing rational thought back with the embarrassment mixed with a tad of shame along as an accessory.

I sat up straight in his lap, wiped my eyes, thankful I wasn't wearing mascara, but wishing for a tissue. Seeming to read my mind, Grady leaned over to the nightstand and grabbed one for me. His hands still around me, I stared up at him. "I'm so sorry." My breath hitched as my body tried to get used to breathing normal again.

"Honey, it's okay—"

"I'm sorry for this…" I gestured to me sitting on his lap. I began to stand. He tried to hold me to him. I gently removed his hands. "I'm sorry for everything that is going on with us. It's such a mess. It's making me a mess."

His expression was sad, resigned. He reached for me. This time I let him grab my hand. Our fingers linked.

"Me, too. I couldn't sleep last night." He pulled me close, and I stood between his spread legs, he rested his hands on my hips and his forehead on my chest. "I don't want to hurt you. I want…" He glanced up beneath his eyelashes and into my soul. "I want…I want you." The intimacy locked me in. I was frozen in the moment. He touched his lips to mine. Softly, reverently.

I snapped awake and took a step back. He held onto me but lightened his tone. "What happened today to cause this?"

I shrugged. "I had a shitty practice. Bill chewed me out. I've been an emotional drama queen. I'm such a girl." Even I heard the defeat in my voice.

He chuckled. "Sweetheart, you *are* a girl—why do you always sound like it's a bad thing? You're a bad ass, beautiful, amazing, talented, take-no-prisoners, sexy woman. And thank God for it." He kissed me lightly again on the lips. Not sexual—just affectionate and with a sweet smile.

I dipped my head, the shame of my weakness beginning to overtake me as my emotions receded.

"We all have our bad days." He put a finger under my chin, lifting it. "Hey, crying is better than punching a wall or someone's face. It's also better not to hide. Don't be ashamed of it."

I stepped back, this time stepping out of his hold—fidgeting and reaching for more tissues—done with this vulnerability.

"And…up go the walls. Damn." He turned his head from me.

I took in a deep breath and pasted on a smile. "Moment of weakness. Like you said, we

all have them." I blew my nose. "So, what are you doing here, anyway."

He stood. Within the small confines of the room, him standing made it almost impossible for me to move around him.

"I wanted to apologize. I didn't feel right about how we left things. I will respect your need for space right now. We only have a few more months of racing, then the season will be over." We both glanced down at his hands and I was surprised he was wringing them. Was he nervous?

"I care about you—a lot. I know that isn't the most eloquent declaration, but…well, there it is. I want more. I want to spend time with you, at the lake house, traveling, on the back of your Ducati— I'll be your bitch, I don't care."

I smiled at the thought of this man on the back of my little Ducati. He took both of my hands in his and kissed them.

"Let's just get through the next few months." I sat next to him on the bed. I put a leg under me, pivoting to face him. I stared at our clasped hands. "All my life, all I've ever wanted was a contract with a Cup team. After Tommy's death, the feud with Dewey—this goal is what has centered me and gotten me through it."

I couldn't look at him. If I looked into his eyes just for a moment, I would give in and kiss him. If I kissed him, I would use the bed behind us. "I—I want you, too. I do. But—I…"

"You want this more." He finished, pulling back.

"No!" I grabbed his hands. "I'm just so close. If I don't make it, I don't want to look back and think it was because I lost focus. I do want you. Just give me some time. Okay?" I put my hand to his cheek, rubbing against the stubble, wishing he would rub it against my bare skin.

I pulled him to me and kissed him.

He drove his hand into my hair, pulling out the ponytail. I was filthy, remnants of sweat from the practice run, but he was breathing me in, groaning as he pulled me to him and aligned our bodies. He whispered to me, "I'll wait for you."

"CJ! Bill wants you at the garage ASAP." It was one of the crew members.

I was in Grady's arms—a wonderful place to be, but not while knowing what awaited me.

"I'll be there in a minute." My eyes locked to Grady's gorgeous, but disappointed, blue ones.

"I was told to stay here until you get your ass in gear," my escort explained.

Grady showered me with little kisses over my face.

"Fine. Give me a moment to clean up."

Grady moved the kisses down my neck.

The voice from outside permeated the moment. "If you're the reason for Bill's rosy mood, you better move it."

I let out a huge sigh and pushed Grady off me gently without reproach. "I mentioned that Bill was pissed at me. Bill never gets pissed at me. He gets pissed at everyone else, but not at me. So, I really need to go."

Grady rolled to his side and studied my face—my eyes, my rat's nest of hair, and finally my lips. "Alright."

I studied his, wishing I could spend more time on them. "I—I'll miss you." That was as much of a declaration as I could give.

"I'm not going anywhere."

I stood and walked out to the hallway to gather my suit.

"Hey, CJ..."

"Yeah?"

He opened his mouth to say something but stopped. He looked past me. And then regrouped, standing up.

"Take care of our car."

## 47

***Grady***

A few weeks later, I had just returned from an early morning run when Junior called. "How fast can you make it to the office?"

I took a pull off my water bottle before asking, "Why?"

Junior's voice sounded like he was about ready to burst with the most exciting news, and it made my stomach drop. "I need you in here as soon as possible—it's about Talladega."

I just about dropped my water bottle. "Wait. Why?" That was one of CJ's favorite tracks. After the drama at Vegas, she rallied, but had a lackluster finish. Her other races showed a steady incline, but she was holding out for Talladega. All season she'd talked it. "The plan was CJ races Talladega, and I race the Charlottle road course."

Satisfaction filled Junior's tone. "Change of plans. You haven't had a chance to show your abilities at a traditional track much—"

"But CJ is going to be—"

"Livid. Yes, I know. Too bad. So sad."

"Harper—"

"My father will handle Harper. Don't worry about it. Be here by nine.

He hung up.

CJ was going to kill someone—namely me. I was so screwed.

---

I brought Cooper with me as back up—because yes, someone was going to have to stop me from strangling Junior and protect me from CJ.

Junior's smug face greeted me outside Merrick's office, and I started in on him. "What the hell's going on?"

"I spoke to my father and he agreed that you needed more of a chance to show yourself on a big track. You got swept up in CJ's drama with Dewey at the other tracks that you didn't need to be part of—"

"I didn't ask for you to—" I raised my voice.

"Doesn't matter—" he tried to wave it off.

"The hell it doesn't—" He raised his voice with frustration, and then dropped it while

glancing at his father's office. "I have too much invested in this. It isn't just about you, McBane. CJ has become hostile and unstable."

"Unstable? What the hell—"

Cooper cut in, "Are you for real?" Junior turned as if just realizing Cooper was there. "What the hell are you talking about?"

Junior straightened and adjusted his tie, taking on an air of false authority. "Daytona? Vegas? She's been driving erratically. She's been losing it on the crew. We're beginning to wonder if she can even handle the pressure."

I looked him straight in the eye, my anger burning, and shook my head. "You're really going to stoop that low?" I walked around him. "Man, I feel sorry for you, Junior. I really do. It must be so hard to be that insecure."

He stiffened, his arrogance faltered, and his face reddened. "What the hell, McBane?"

"That's the best you got, huh?" I leaned into his face. "Are we that close to losing? Is that what this is about? You're on a last-ditch smear campaign? You've got the garage buzzing about her being difficult?"

I set my sights on Merrick's office door. "That's it. I'm done." I took two long strides in that direction. "If this is what it's become, I don't want anything to do with it."

"I wouldn't do that." Junior's tone was laced with fury, but he rallied, as he said, "You quit now, you and CJ will both go down. Not only will *you* not race in stock car again, neither will she. There is plenty of fodder out there for the press to feast on. She'll be the woman you screwed and got screwed."

I dropped my head.

Cooper grabbed Junior. "You'd really do that to her?"

"For this company, yes."

I laced my arms across my chest, planted my feet, and prepared for the ultimatum that was coming, I shot daggers at Junior. He flinched, and there wasn't any satisfaction in it.

"Race Talladega. Just drive as if your career depended on it. If after this you still lose the contract, I'll drop everything with CJ. She'll have the support of this team."

I didn't break the stare.

"But so help me, Grady. I brought you in as a champion, so if you try any white-knight-on-the-horse shit and make me look like a fool—"

"—you're a dumbass," Cooper offered, then lowered his voice. "A dead one once this is over."

Junior took in a deep breath as if garnering courage. "If you make me look like a fool," he repeated, "I will ruin you both."

Cooper and I walked over to the double winding staircase at the top of the open, two-story lobby. We surveyed the scene below, taking in the souvenir shop to the left and the car display to the right.

The lobby was humming with visitors when the front doors opened. I realized I should've brought a jock strap and a cup— because all hell broke loose, and her name was CJ Lomax.

"This is bullshit. Utter bullshit." Her eyes were ablaze, and she was a woman on a mission to destroy someone or something.

Cooper was staring at his phone and seemingly deaf and unfazed by the yelling that echoed through the halls. "Any word from CJ? Has she heard the news?" Smartass.

I deadpanned, "I would say 'yes'. I'm about to get my balls handed to me."

He registered what was happening. "Oh, um, you may want to run."

"Yeah." I wasn't an idiot. I seriously considered turning for the elevator, but thought being trapped in a box was probably a bad idea.

She started up the stairs. I turned and went down the other side.

"Hey, asshole."

Damn, she saw me.

I froze when I realized I was actually running from her. Her feet made soft pitter-patter sounds coming down the stairs as she rounded on me. "Did you know about this?"

"No, of course not. Not until just now. I told—"

"Then how the hell did they give you 'Dega? How could you let them do this? The last time we talked, it was all charm and compassion—"

People were milling out of the souvenir shop from over her shoulder. "Let's not do this here." I guided her down the remaining stairs and tried to turn her to the other side of the lobby, as she yanked away from me as if I burned her. I made the mistake of trying to handle her.

Her hand was on her hip, her hip kicked out. She tilted her head to the side. "No, let's do this here. I want to know how I just got screwed with my pants still on. Hell, I didn't even have an orgasm this time."

Harper walked up next to her, her eyebrows raised, a plastic smile plastered on, and through her teeth she muttered, "CJ, I don't think the people in Raleigh heard you, you may want to raise your voice a bit more."

"You need to keep your voice down, or this will be the highlight on Race Center tonight," I added, also under my breath. I gestured to the growing crowd, a few pulling out their phones.

She scanned the area and took them in, her lips forming a thin line.

We left Harper smiling at the crowd, her Southern hospitality kicking in, asking them how they were enjoying their visit. I coerced CJ down the corridor to an empty office.

Once inside, CJ defiantly stood against the door, her face flushed.

I held up my hands. "It was Junior's idea and he went to Merrick without me knowing. He seriously just called me an hour ago."

"Isn't it convenient—" she scoffed.

"You can't be serious. You can't seriously think I did this on purpose." Jesus, who did she think I was?

She looked away. "All I know is it was mine, and now it's yours. What message does that send—about Merrick's confidence in me—about my future here."

I tried to hold out a hand to her. "I told them I didn't want it. I told them not to do it. They threatened—"

"Then why would they even think of it?"

"Junior said they'd give me another chance because of your feud with Dewey—" I was

fumbling this.

She stopped dead in her tracks. "What?"

"Junior told Merrick your behavior was erratic and your feud with Dewey cost me

Indianapolis. Having me drive Talladega was only fair since your feud with Dewey spilled over onto me. I don't agree and I told him that—"

She stared at me, speechless—which should have been a warning.

"I didn't cause those problems." Her tone and volume amped up. "You stuck your nose in where I told you not to. You got your-self tied up with him. I told you to leave it alone." She was seething. "I told you to leave me alone." She was shaking.

"CJ—"

"Did you tell them that? Did you, Grady? Did you tell them that I told you to stay out of it?"

"CJ—there isn't anything I can do. Junior is threatening to ruin both of us if I don't run Talladega. I already tried to drop out. I tried to walk into Merrick's office. It has nothing to do with me anymore; this is about Junior and his desire to win at all costs. It's not about you and me, it's —"

Wrong words…

"*Not about you and me?* There is no you and me. This was inevitable. I *knew* this was going to happen. So, you race 'Dega, you come out on top. Junior wins. Dewey wins. You win. And I'm out."

She was lumping me together with them. That crossed a line. "Damnit, CJ."

Her eyes slayed me. "I knew you were going to break my heart." Her breath hitched. "But for a little while I actually believed you."

She stormed out. I tried to follow. Harper stopped me. "Let her be."

Harper stopped me by putting her hand on my bicep to get my attention.

"*Fuck!*" I wanted to hit something. I'd reached my threshold. "Harper—"

"I know. I know this has Junior's slimy paws all over it. Give her time to calm down.

She's pissed, but she's also hurt. My brother aside, my father keeps disappointing her, and although she won't admit it, that hurts worse." She glanced away from me and out the door. "He's disappointing all of us. And if he doesn't watch it, he'll be the one disappointed with the outcome of his little game."

And with that cryptic remark, Harper set off after CJ.

# 48

*CJ*

If this wasn't the writing on the wall.

Already the commentators were having a field day. The updated schedule had already been released. When it was updated to show Grady racing at Talladega instead of me, the pity glances and the not-so-kind comments started. There was also a lot of "I told you this would happen."

I couldn't speak to Grady. Deep down, I knew I was being unfair. I didn't think he was conspiring against me. But Talladega would've been a feather in my cap—something I earned and was worthy of—and they gave it to him.

Grady, who never had to struggle like I have. Grady McBane, Indy Champion, Mr. Prince Charming—the man everyone loved. The man I lo—no, I can't.

I gritted my teeth as his image flashed across the television screen. Grady with his million-dollar, panty-melting smile in his racing suit on in front of *our* car. The screen split to show a very uncomplimentary photo of me scowling.

*"Is this the end of the road?"* was all the graphic said. I didn't need to know who they were suggesting it was the end of the road for.

The phone rang—again. It was either Grady, Harper, or Gus.

Bill gave up calling—he knew I was in "a snit," as he would put it, and wouldn't be willing to talk about it. No one else was brave enough.

I paced my house because I couldn't figure out what else to do, and I wasn't fit to go out in public—it was frowned upon to throat-punch people.

I grabbed my running shoes. If I was smart, I'd go to yoga, but I was too amped up to try to find my Zen today. If I stopped…if I tried to relax, I knew I would cry. Damn tears.

My doorbell rang, followed by a knock at my door.

I flung open the door, and Harper stood there, over-dramatically holding up her hands in front of her, ready to fend off any fists that may fly.

"I come in peace."

"I don't want to talk." I gritted my teeth, and was surprised words managed to make it past the scowl on my face.

Her brows lifted. "I know, and you don't have to talk. I'm going to talk. Let me come in."

I stepped back and allowed her entry. "Are you going to tell me that Junior came down with a horrible case of leprosy and his scrawny dick fell off? Anything else would be a disappointment."

"Um, since he's my brother and I really don't think about his dick, no." She came in, set her bag on the bar stool in the kitchen, and grabbed a water bottle from the fridge.

"Sit." She motioned to my counter as if it were her own home.

I sat down with my arms crossed.

My phone was on the counter in front of us and began to ring again.

Harper glanced down at the display. "Are you going to answer it?"

"No." I stared at her, wanting her to get out why she was here. "What do you want?"

"Oh, so now I get the bitch-treatment, too?"

I glanced away, thinning my lips. "I just don't want to talk."

She leaned in over the counter and zeroed in on me. "First off, cut the shit. I know you're pissed, but you've had your time to throw a tantrum. Everyone knows you're pissed. Now pull on your big-girl panties and let's figure out what you're going to do about it."

"Second, since when did you take things lying down?" She leaned back, mimicking my stance. "When did you decide to sit here and take what my father and Junior are shoveling?"

I jumped out of my chair. "What the hell else am I supposed to do?

"Well, you should be shopping for a back-up plan. Maybe trying to pave a path to another team. Let gossip get back to my dad that you aren't a sure thing, and you aren't going to sit around wringing your hands. What the hell do you think Grady's been doing?"

Thoughts of Nadina and her pawing him made my level of anger climb to new heights.

Harper leaned forward, her elbows on the counter.

"Your loyalty to my father and MMS is more than commendable. But you're better than second string to anyone. Let it be known. Strut around. Make contacts with other teams…"

I fidgeted in my chair. It was so obvious. But honestly, I never considered it.

"But," I swallowed, my major insecurity being brought to light. "I'm not exactly a well-liked person."

"The Duprees have had a lot of influence. However, Dewey's lost a lot of respect on and off the track. People listen to him because they don't hear from you. You've earned a lot of notoriety with this season. Your popularity has grown, and with that comes some clout. Let's put it to use."

She folded her hands together and straightened. She studied her clasped hands. "Anyway, um, there was something else I need to tell you about. But it can't go any further than this room. I wasn't going to tell you about it until it came further along. But to get you out of this funk, I thought I'd let you know what I was working on."

Her head was down but her eyes cast upwards to meet mine, a

slight, soft smile spread over her face. Slowly, her eyes began to brighten with restrained excitement.

"But, Charlotte Jean Lomax, you have to swear on a stack of Bibles and on your very career that you will keep this secret and not utter a word. You can't act differently, and you can't have pillow talk with Grady about it—especially Grady." She emphasized the last part.

"Harper, we aren't even talking. He's been nowhere near my pillow." Another ribbon of pain laced through me.

She reached out and grabbed my hand, squeezing it tightly as the emotions on her face unleashed, and extreme enthusiasm took its place. "If I can pull this off, if we can pull this off…it will be the answers to our prayers. It will set everyone on the whole circuit on their backsides." She reined in her tough love with a glint of mischief, and I really wanted to know what she had up her sleeve. "Do you want to hear about it or not?"

I nodded with more enthusiasm than I'd shown in days, and my curiosity surprisingly drop-kicked rage and frustration to the curb. She had my full attention.

Harper picked up her phone and pushed a button. "Come on in, she's ready to talk."

## 49

*Grady*

I'm so fucked.

I'm fucked if I win. I'm fucked if I lose. I'm fucked if I try to leave altogether. So, it's safe to say it's a clusterfuck. And if my mother heard me say that many fucks, I'd be fucked.

F-u-c-k.

I stormed around my lake house that I both loved and hated, because it was all about CJ. Every room, every view, everything.

There were only a few races left in the season until I could put this bullshit to rest. I just needed to find a home team for me and one for CJ, and then we could try to figure out if what we have is salvageable.

She still wasn't taking my calls. This back and forth, hot and cold, was killing me. I didn't know if I was coming or going. Frankly, I was starting to question my sanity.

Harper told me to give her some space and that she would talk to her.

But damnit. I was supposed to mean something to her still, wasn't I?

And why the hell was she taking this out on me? Of course, she's hurt and angry, and I get that some of that would be directed at me. But she's putting me at the same level as someone she hates as much as Dewey and Junior? Really?

Her saying that was like spinning out on the track—knowing there were massive projectiles coming at you, being blind to when they were going to hit, and unable to avoid them. I never saw it coming. I didn't know she could hate me over this. And honestly, it kind of pissed me off because she should know I would never do this intentionally.

Fuck it. There was only one man who could fix this so-called contest that has ruined my life for the second time, and possibly taken the one thing that means more than racing to me.

I grabbed my keys. I'm going to talk to Merrick. Fuck Junior.

My phone ringing takes me out of the focus of my mission.

*CJ Calling*

Thank God.

"Hello? CJ?" I unapologetically picked it up immediately and yes, my voice cracked. "Eh, hey." Yeah. Smooth.

"Hey. Yeah, it's me." Her voice was quiet. Calm.

Silence.

"Hi." Well, this conversation was off to a great start.

"Listen, I called to apologize for…well, for being an ass. I'm pissed. But I'm not pissed at you. I'm pissed at the situation, and I'm angry at Merrick, and I'm praying Junior gets a bout of leprosy and his dick falls off at the moment."

I smiled. Because she was back.

"But I'm not pissed at you and I was wrong to go off on you like that."

"CJ. You've got to know—"

"I don't want to rehash it. Harper and I talked, and I know you were blindsided, too. It's fine. I'll deal."

I sat on the edge of the ottoman in my living room and held my head in my hand. "I don't know what to do."

"Nothing to do. You need to drive the car. We need to play this out."

"What about us?" I couldn't stop the next words from leaving my mouth, "CJ, I miss you."

Silence. Utter silence. I never thought silence could hurt.

"Grady, I just don't think there can be an us."

She slammed me head-first into a barrier wall.

Her name came out as a gasp, "CJ…"

"Please—don't. We just shouldn't talk anymore." Her voice was soft, vulnerable. "I can't…I have to do this."

"That's it? You're giving up. That's it?" For fuck's sake, it wasn't as if I didn't have my own career to worry about. She wanted to put herself first. Fine. Then I would work on doing the same.

"Let me know when you come up with the manual on how to win your heart—if there is even a way—because obviously I don't know what the hell I'm doing. In the meantime, if you want to focus on our careers, then I will do the same. See you on the track, sweetheart."

# 50

## CJ

Mr. Merrick called me Wednesday evening, just a few days after my fallout with Grady.

The fallout, each argument, each disagreement, seemed like a nail in the coffin of our relationship, but I was having such a hard time figuring out how things were going to pan out, and was so confused. It really was better if we didn't spend time together, regardless.

"CJ, darlin', I just got a call from Brian's wife that he's laid up with the flu. Doctor's been to see him and gave him some medicine, but he's out for this weekend. Need you to pack a bag and get down there by Thursday evening."

"Okay." No arguing, no commenting, no telling him to take his substitute position and shove it. I just agreed.

I'd spoken with Harper after Grady left. I was tired of everyone else directing my life and gave her the green light on her plan for after the season ended.

Since my conversation with Harper, and the basic dissolution of my relationship with Grady, I had a new outlook on my future. I'd been reminding myself all season that my relationship with Grady had an expiration date, but that fight seemed like a self-fulfilling prophecy.

For now, I'd take it one race at a time. Each time I was in a car, I would focus just on that race.

*Focus.*

There was silence as Merrick seemed to wait for a different response.

"This means you and Grady will both be racing the same race."

"Got it."

"Okay, then. See you there. Harper knows the details." His voice was hesitant, still waiting for something else from me.

*Grit.*

"Thank you, sir." That was all the reaction I was going to give. I was done being this man's puppet. I smiled to myself because I knew with a wonderful satisfaction that my lack of response, or emotion, just thoroughly perplexed the man.

I went and packed my bag, wondering how bad a shit show this was going to turn out to be.

Harper's plan was going to be a detonation. But screw it, I was seizing control of my own life.

*Unapologetic determination.*

---

The media coverage was insane. I was barely able to leave my trailer, so at least running into Grady wasn't going to happen.

Gus said when Grady heard I was driving Brian's car, he was less than thrilled. He muttered a slew of expletives and stormed off to his trailer.

I wasn't sure what to do with the emotions that information stirred. So, I did what now did with emotions concerning Grady—I tucked them away.

My practice runs went fantastic. The car was sharp. Talladega was a favorite of mine, which was why I was so upset about losing the chance to race here. I'd won here before with Energy Blast, and even with a new team and a different car, I had high expectations.

Harper walked me to qualifying, going over the next day's itinerary, which would include dreaded appearances with Grady. There was no avoiding it. Merrick was going to milk the fact that both his drivers would be racing in the same race for the first time all season.

This gave his contest fresh life—a new twist.

I passed Grady on his way to his car for the qualifying runs. We locked eyes, and he gave me a head nod, just as if I were one of the other drivers. Well, after all, it was what I wanted.

But the hurt and anger left in his eyes still pricked my heart.

"Earth to CJ…" Harper crooned.

"Yeah, I'm here." I stepped over to my new bright blue number thirty-one car. A team member handed me the balaclava for me to slip over my head. Harper stilled me with her hand.

"Listen. You got this. You're CJ Lomax." She winked at me. "I'd hug you, but that would kill the bad-ass image, so I'll chuck you on the shoulder. I'll meet you after you make those boys cry."

I smiled as I climbed in the car. Helmet and gloves on, firing up the engine—I entered my zone where I ruled—adrenaline, free my mind…and released my heart.

Hell yeah.

Adrenaline was my God.

It flowed through my heart—protecting it, telling all the other emotions to sit the hell down—it was ruling the day.

---

I took the pole.

It meant I would start in the first position in the race tomorrow.

Not even my car. Not even my crew. And I took the motherfucking pole. Out of forty-two cars, mine ran with the fastest time today at qualifying—it was unheard of.

I floated on remnants of adrenaline, until I crashed later that evening in my trailer. As I laid in bed, a text from Grady came through.

*"Congratulations on your time."*

The same as if he were any another driver.

Actually, I take that back. If it were Brian or another driver, there wouldn't have been a text. I held my cell in my hand. I was unsure how to respond.

If I was honest, it would be, "Thank you for thinking of me. I'm sorry for the cruel things I said." But whatever. I set these terms. I had to live by them.

I typed back, *"Thank you, I appreciate it."* And hit send before I had time to ponder it any longer.

He responded, *"See you tomorrow."*

I left it at that. What else was there to say?

---

The media was crazy the next day. Grady and I had our own schedules but couldn't avoid dual appearances with sponsors. The crowd was so loud when we stood next to each other at the driver introductions, you couldn't hear the other drivers who were introduced after us. One person who seemed especially put-out by our notoriety was my good buddy, Dewey Dupree.

I made a personal promise to myself not to tangle with him. I didn't want negativity. It was all about the *focus.*

After hearing about Harper's plan—I had a new goal. I had a new mission, and it required time.

I walked down from the back of pit road, watching drivers kiss wives, girlfriends, special someones before loading up in their cars. Driver after driver—like dominos they kissed and hugged and whispered sweet words to their loved ones. I thought back to the beginning of the season and how much I both resented it and coveted it. Then, just a few months ago, hoping someday I could outwardly have that with Grady—

Grady...Grady was three cars ahead...leaning against *our* car. Smiling his charming half-smile with his devilish cocked head... smiling at Nadina as if she were his special someone. I pulled up short. My stomach plummeted to my feet, so fast I swayed. Here I

311

was walking to the front of the line, reveling in my current victory, passing by all the naysayers with a spring in my step, knowing I had a renewed purpose when my heart was aching, and he's flirting with another woman. Another woman who came to tuck him into *our* car.

Fuck it.

It's his car today. He can have the damn car.

I kept walking forward.

Making my day even more fantastic…"Well, well, well…looks like the writing is on the wall for Ms. Dixie Cup. Merrick must be coming to his senses about giving the car to a real driver. Sorry to hear about Brian being ill. Good timing to help humor you and his daughter, though, while he slowly eases you back to where you belong."

Dewey.

"What's up, Moist?" I didn't bat an eye, just kept walking.

He stepped in front of me, causing me to stop. He plastered a smile on his face, seething through clinched teeth. "Your time in the spotlight is almost up. Take your bow, bitch."

I cocked my head to the side, glanced up at him unaffected, stepped aside, and continued walking.

Dewey followed. We passed Grady, and I didn't spare him a glance with shithead trailing after me.

Gah! Men! Assholes—all of them. Why am I surrounded by assholes?

"CJ?" Grady arrived like the cavalry I didn't need or want. If I couldn't handle a

schmuck like Dewey, I'd be scared of my own shadow.

And now both of them were trailing me as I made my way to the front of the pack.

"What's going on here?" Grady said.

"Grady, Dewey was just being a gentleman and escorting me to my car," I deadpanned. "It seems he has some career advice to give me before the race."

I was done with both of them and stopped. "Don't you boys have somewhere you both have to be?" I didn't need to survey the area to know the three of us together was garnering some attention.

A gaggle of people stood behind the wall—fans, media, crew members from other teams, all gawking at the three of us. Over my shoulder I said loud enough for them to hear, "I need to get going. I have a race to run." I gestured with my thumb over my shoulder to the front of the pack of cars. I turned to the crowd and played to them.

"I was just catching up with Dewey. I never get to see him anymore. He seems to have trouble finishing races, for some reason." I tilted my head in question. "Today he's got so far to walk to the back of the pack, I thought I'd wish him luck now so he could get going." I mimicked Harper's "well-bless-his-heart" tone she used when she really wants to say, "Fuck him."

The crowd behind the wall chuckled, and camera phones caught me gesturing at Dewey, and then at the back of the line of cars. Dewey's face was seven shades of red.

The media began shouting questions at Dewey, who couldn't respond to me the way he wanted to without them overhearing.

Grady stepped up and leaned down to whisper to me, "Do you really think it's a good idea to be goading him right now?"

Condescending ass.

"Save your lectures and your so-called expert advice." I glared behind my sunglasses. "You run your race—and I'll run mine," I said through gritted teeth. "Get back and kiss your sugar-mama before the collagen-injection pout she's giving you causes her to trip over her own inflated lips."

"CJ, I told you, it isn't like that. CJ—"

I turned to the growing crowd, flirted with my eyes to the cameras, and threw so much sweetness into my tone, there wasn't any room for sincerity.

"Have a good race, boys." I adjusted my mirrored aviator sunglasses. With the flick of my ponytail, and the sashay of my hips, I reminded him I was a woman in a racing suit, walking with confidence to a starting position in front of theirs. "See ya'll in my rearview mirror, boys."

## 51

*Grady*

Great. Just great.

Not only is CJ running a faster car than me today—she's also running it with an attitude.

Driving angry can help hone your focus, or it could make you reckless. I'm one to talk. I'd been known to drive on the edge, take the risks, run on the cusp of wrecking for the extra inch—but this was CJ. The last thing you wanted the woman you care about doing was driving at two-hundred mph when she was pissed off. The other thing you didn't want was to be driving behind her while she had a target on her back, and not be able to do anything but watch what unfolds.

I'd been running back and forth in the teens most of the race and had just started inching up to around tenth. CJ was battling in the top five.

Aaron, my spotter, could probably use a drink after this race, because I was truly trying his patience. His job was to spot for me— tell me where I was in relation to other drivers, tell me when to go high, low, when to pass. Not give me updates about what she was doing. Gus was going to wring my neck if he had to tell me once again to keep my head on the car I was driving—but I knew, deep down, he was keeping an eye on her, too. He knew she was driving on the edge—as if she was out to prove something.

But my God, she was flying.

As her on-again-off-again-don't-know-what-we-are-boyfriend, I was both terrified and extremely amazed at what she was doing in that car. Not just the speed, but the instinct and finesse she pulled around others. The thought and strategy she used to stay ahead of the pack.

As her competitor for the car I was currently racing in, her effort, talent, and ambition warned me once again what I was up against.

Gus came on the headset. "Dewey's in his pit with his thumb up his ass. Byron is waving his hand for him to go. Don't know what the idiot's doing."

"Dewey is coming off pit road a lap down, behind the front of the pack." Aaron's voice came through my headset just as I saw Dewey merge in front of me.

With twenty-three laps to go, things were going to get aggressive. This was always when things got exciting. It wasn't just the win that was on the line. Track position and points were earned also. With the top drivers in the run for the Cup championship, points were earned depending on how they ended each race. While CJ and I didn't qualify for the Cup championship this season, we were in our own personal competition, and our position counted just as much to the two of us in our own private war.

"Shit," I muttered to myself. I knew exactly what he was up to. "He's waiting for her. He's dropping down a lap to wait for her."

Gus and Aaron didn't respond. Dewey couldn't catch CJ during the race, so he was going to take a lap down—go to the back of the pack, in order to catch up behind her, since she was front of the pack. It would put him right next to her.

He was sacrificing the rest of the race—just to be in position.

Fuck.

"Gus—" I growled into my headset.

Dewey was gunning on fresh tires up through the cars in fifth and sixth place. Those not realizing his intention would think he was trying to get in front of the pack to get back on the lead lap.

But Dewey didn't care anymore. He was after CJ.

He was sacrificing himself to stop her from winning.

CJ, meanwhile, was battling for second with the champion from last season. It was a contentious position, and both she and her team would be focused on that positioning—not realizing what was approaching her from behind.

"Gus—" I yelled.

"Yeah. I know—I see him. The little chickenshit. Aaron—tell Paulie. Dewey is gunning for our girl," Gus said over the mic to Aaron, our spotter in the booth—all the teams had spotters above the press box in the stands and could communicate with each other.

Dewey was one of the only cars on the track with fresh tires. It meant he had better grip, and therefore better control. He positioned himself behind the number eighty-four car that was directly behind CJ and ran up his rear before backing off. He ran up the back of the car again, tapping it, causing the car to run up the outside before it spun down the track to regain control. The length between CJ and the eighty-four car was great enough that they didn't make contact. It was subtle, but the tactic managed to nudge the car out of the way. It didn't, however, get into CJ's car as Dewey probably wished.

Bill's gravelly voice was booming in the background. "I don't care what they're claiming. You tell him I don't care who his daddy is; if he doesn't leave CJ alone, I will personally make sure he is black-flagged for the rest of the season. You hear me—next season, too. Hell, if he hurts her, Merrick will sue the entire damn company —" Bill wasn't even bothering to mute his headset. He was yelling at someone, and he didn't care who the hell heard it.

"Is someone talking to CJ? Tell her to pull back—" I added. "It isn't worth it."

Aaron chuckled. "Do you even know CJ? If anything, she's

pissed and more determined to win the race. A million Deweys couldn't stop her now."

"Patch me through to her," I demanded.

Gus was firm. "No, man. I can't have her distracted. You can't be distracted. You both need to focus. Don't make matters worse. His crew is getting an earful right now. He'd be an idiot to wreck millions of dollars' worth of machinery."

I wasn't convinced, and I doubt Gus was buying it either.

# 52

## *CJ*

I was having an awesome, fantastic, incredible day. I should've known the universe was about to knock it out from under me. I'd been running better than ever. In a car that wasn't even mine, with a team I'd never raced with, and against a man with whom I had an incredibly complicated relationship. I didn't know if I was going to have a job after today, but today, right now, I was having one of the best races of my life.

So, of course, something had to go wrong.

"The eighty-four is out," Paulie reported.

"Dewey's lost his fucking mind." Stu's voice was different than Gus's good ol' boy.

"What?" I glanced in my rearview mirror, and sure enough, the eighty-four had been trailing me, but it had disappeared.

Stu wasn't talking to me. He left his mic on and was talking to someone else. "Find out what the hell he's thinking? Tell Grady... no. Gus, get your boy in check and keep him in his sandbox. We don't need him in there making things worse." Stu's volume was raised.

"Stu, what the hell is going on?" They weren't going to ruin this for me.

I spotted Dewey's silver seventy-three, and he wasn't where I thought he would be. "Paulie, how did Dewey get behind me?" I asked. I saw him drop back behind the leaders, essentially becoming a lap down. But now he was behind me—and slowly gaining.

Silence.

Stu was the one who answered, "We aren't sure. He's gone off the reservation. He isn't answering his crew chief."

I was battling within the top three positions, but instead of concentrating on holding my own with two of the best drivers in the circuit, it was the seventy-three dropping back to the inside that had my focus.

Dewey's car engaged. He came up high, and I had to swerve to avoid him.

"What the hell is he doing?" I yelled into the comms.

"Showing his hand," Stu growled. "Paulie, tell Aaron to get Grady to focus on his own damn race. We don't need him tangling in this. We have our hands full at the moment."

"What the hell is Grady doing?" Were these assholes losing their minds?

"Don't worry. Just get the hell away from Dewey. Take the high-line and focus ahead. Hopefully, you have more car than Dewey and you can outrace him."

Paulie, my spotter, came back on the comm. "He has fresh tires, so be careful." He had more traction than I did, and it gave him an advantage, even if I did have a faster car.

I did as my spotter advised and took the outside of the track. Dewey dropped back and followed me. The two leaders stayed low, and were busy battling each other, trading paint as they came out of a turn and down the straightaway before cutting in front of me. I dropped to the inside. We had two laps left, and I wasn't going to tangle with them while Dewey was—

*Bam!* I held tight. Maintaining control of the car.

"You're okay, You're okay," Paulie reassured me.

"Sonofabitch, that little cocksucker..." Stu's anger reverberated in my headset. "CJ..."

In my rearview mirror was the asshole himself, plowing into my rear and causing my car to lurch forward, destabilize, and swerve.

"I'm okay..."

I briefly lost control, but regained it long enough to fly by the leaders, as they lost momentum while tangling with each other. Dewey, unfortunately, was still on my ass.

"Good save...you got this," Stu calmed.

"CJ, he's coming back up again..." Paulie attempted calm, but there was an edge of urgency.

"Hang in there, you're on the last lap, just focus ahead. You can do it..." Stu said.

"Go low," Paulie instructed. I came out of the turn and back to the straightaway.

I spared a glance to prepare for the next impact. There was a brief glimpse of silver, followed by a flash of red, and both cars disappeared as streaks. Red?

The Mingle Singles car was red.

Grady.

"H—oly Sh—it." The normally stoic Paulie yelled into my headset.

"What happened?" Panic laced my voice. My unfocused gaze was ahead, but my heart and mind were behind.

"Drive," Stu commanded. "Just fucking drive!"

I took the last turn and drove through the finish line, taking the checkered flag.

---

I crossed the finish line with the deafening roar of the stands. Instead of slowing down and doing the celebratory lap and burn out, I immediately wanted answers.

"Grady? Stu, Paulie—where's Grady?"

No one responded to me over the comm.

But the noise outside the car was thunderous. "Stu? Paulie?"

"I'm here, CJ. Grady wrecked. He's back in turn four."

At any track, wrecking was a risk. At this track, where speed was higher than at other tracks and cars could go airborne, wrecking... and having people not answering their comms...

I was already halfway around my victory lap and threw the car into gear, as if I were still in the race. I came out of turn three and already saw the clusterfuck that instinct told me Grady was under.

'Dega was known for "The Big One"—the one wreck that defined each race day. Grady, the certifiable idiot, was in the middle of the The Big One in spectacular fashion. But Dewey the Douche was the cause of it.

"Is his net down?" I asked, begging anyone to answer.

No one answered. "Is his net down?" I yelled but didn't wait for a reply.

Emergency vehicles were already moving to the scene as I pulled up and spun my car to a stop in the infield, trying to stay out of the way of the field of car parts, disconnecting my helmet, straps, and steering wheel, before climbing out in a swift motion. I dropped the gloves and balaclava as I began to run.

In what resembled a bomb blast of metal and car parts, I could identify at least eight cars that were involved. Four were safely down, spread out on the inside of the track. They were damaged, but the drivers were out walking around their cars— apparently aggravated, but unharmed. Two were entangled in the middle of the track, one driver still climbing out, the other had his window mesh down, indicating he was okay. None of those drivers were Grady. My eyes shifted to the two remaining cars. Dewey's silver had a car wedged against the wall. The wedged car was Grady's red Mingle Singles car, and it was on its roof. Upside down.

Which meant it rolled.

And then Dewey pegged it against the wall.

Dewey was climbing out of his car, and I was running at him on instinct. He made the mistake of removing his helmet before turning around, and I took full advantage and swung before I even stopped charging at him.

We both went flying onto the asphalt, as I took down a man almost a foot taller than me. I saw red. I was rage. I was fury.

I don't know what I hit, or how many times I hit him. I threw punches at anything that could connect. I shoved my knees into his abdomen as he laid on the asphalt and tried to cover his head and simultaneously shove me off. I wouldn't be deterred.

All the anger, all the resentment, all the hurt that man had inflicted—first Tommy, and now Grady. His selfishness, his cruelty...I wasn't going to let him take Grady from me also. His unwillingness to accept me was partially responsible for Tommy's unhappiness, maybe even his accident. His desire to destroy me could've killed Grady.

Two sets of arms pulled me off the vermin. My legs continued to flail, and I screamed like a banshee as I kicked and clawed to get back at him. They transferred me to another set of arms that pulled me to a chest reverberating with soothing words. "CJ, honey. I got this. It's okay."

Gus. His strong arms offered the pressure I needed to get myself back together. I couldn't draw in enough air. I was rage. I wasn't even conscious of my surroundings.

"Grady's okay. He's okay," Gus yelled into my ear. "Don't worry about that douchebag. We'll take care of him. You did enough damage, slugger." He squeezed me tighter, and I began to relax at the pressure. "Shhh... Please, calm down, sweetheart. Grady's looking for you. He wants to see you and he's giving the emergency people a hell of a time."

My eyes met my friend's. "Is...is he okay?" Hating the fear I heard...the weakness.

"He's definitely in better shape than old Dewey over there..." Gus smirked and gestured with a nod. "Damn, girl. I don't know what kind of fighting technique you call that...that was a mixture of streetfighter, WWE fighting, and cat-fight-girl-style."

"Shut up..."

He lifted his eyebrows, and then waggled them. "It was hot. If I wasn't concerned about you getting arrested for battery, I'd have let you have at it for a bit longer. I'm sure it will be replayed on Sports-Center for years to come—don't you worry. Dewey getting the shit beat out of him by a little hellion half his size will be a bigger blow to his masculinity than anything you landed."

I pushed off him and wiped my face. "What happened?" Gus filled me in as we walked over to where emergency personnel were helping Grady. "Grady caught wind of what Dewey was up to. And, well…he wasn't happy about it. He threw his race. He dropped back to protect you, darlin'. He came up behind Dewey, and as soon as Dewey became aggressive and we confirmed his intention with Dewey's team, he—well, not to sound overly dramatic—but he took him out." Gus lifted one side of his mouth in a respectful smile.

The emergency workers helped a shaky Grady out of the car, his helmet and gloves off. The crowd exploded in applause when it was clear he was going to walk to the ambulance on his own. Grady took two steps before straightening and looking around. His eyes locked on mine and the world could've stopped on its axis. At that moment, from thirty feet away, I saw all the sincerity was there in his face.

I ran at him and jumped into his arms, unfazed by the possibility that it may knock both of us over, and the fact that his car just rolled an unknown amount of times, or that he probably had a concussion.

He stumbled, still a bit dazed still, but I felt his chest as he laughed, and he still had enough strength in his arms to hold me tight and to nuzzle his face into my neck. I didn't care about the race, or the competition, or the media, or anything. This man. This man came to my rescue and sacrificed his own race…his own career, to see me succeed.

I got it now.

He put me down, and immediately cupped and scanned my face. "Are you okay? Did you win?"

I nodded earnestly to answer both, not trusting my voice.

"Good." He kissed my forehead, relief visibly washing over him.

Without a word, I grabbed him by the collar of his race suit and pulled him down to my level, wrapping my arms around his neck and kissed him with everything I had—right there, on the fourth turn at Talladega's track, in front of eighty-thousand race fans, and countless others watching at home.

I, Charlotte Jean Lomax, realized I was in love with Grady McBane, and I just didn't care who knew it.

# EPILOGUE

## *CJ*

I rolled over in bed, luxuriating in the warm body next to me, the beautiful fall foliage outside the picture window, and thought about the monumental day ahead of me—a day that didn't include being at a track. I slapped Grady's adorable backside while whispering, "I need to get up, birthday boy, and go to Merrick's office."

He grabbed me, pulling me back into his body, spooning me. There was nowhere in the world I wanted to be more than in bed being spooned by Grady McBane. Nonetheless, this was a pivotal day, and I needed to move. "Grady, I have to meet Harper at Merrick's. Today's the day." It was the day the ridiculous competition came to an end. I rolled over and cupped his face, kissing him lightly on the nose.

His sleepy eyes opened, and I was momentarily mesmerized by them—he was mine. I threaded my hands through his disheveled hair. It was one of my favorite pastimes. He moaned, "It's my birthday, I want my present," and his hands began to roam. I gently pulled away and he moaned again. I kissed him sweetly; deeply would've gotten me in trouble.

"You can have your present later. For now, help me get ready. I'm nervous."

He reached for my hand, entwining our fingers. "Nothing to be nervous about. Besides, you said you didn't want me to go with you."

"I know. This is between Harper, Mr. Merrick, and me. No sense in dragging you in to it—not now, at least." I stared at our hands. "Look at you, Mr. Cool—not a care in the world. It's just my whole career at stake."

He shrugged and raised my hand to his lips, kissing it. Then put his other hand behind his head, leaning back against the headboard, showing off his amazing bare chest and abs. A cheeky smile delivered, "I know my woman has it under control."

I side-eyed him as I dodged his attempts to keep me in bed and he playfully smacked my ass. "You are lucky you are so damn cute."

"—and good in bed."

I rolled my eyes. I walked to the bathroom, naked as the day I was born. "I'm going to take a nice hot shower," I said and closed the door. I heard quick shuffling from the bed and his feet hit the floor.

I locked the door and announced loudly, "Alone."

He growled, "That wasn't nice."

"Got you out of bed, didn't it? Go make me breakfast." I smiled to myself; I did that often.

"But it's myyy birthday…" He emphasized.

God, he was adorable.

―――――――――――

As I kissed my guy goodbye on the front porch, a black Audi R8 convertible pulled into the driveway. Cal McBane was an imposing figure emerging from the sleek sports car. Although different in coloring from his brother, he was a strikingly good-looking man.

"Well, looks like you'll have company while I'm gone," I said, pretending to be surprised.

"Why is he here? I didn't even know he was in town." He stared at his brother as he walked up the pathway. Grady looked down at me and gathered me in his arms, not ready to let me go. "Maybe I should go with you."

"Spend time with your brother." I lifted to my toes and gave him a peck. "I'll be back soon." I broke away as Cal approached. The brothers also had things to discuss.

"Have fun, boys."

---

Harper and I sat outside her father's office.

"Are you ready?" I stared at my friend with concern. She was putting up a good front, but because I was her soul sister, I knew her tells. She subtly smoothed down her clothes and repeatedly checked her phone, as if it would get her out of the task ahead.

"Yep." She glanced at me as she removed visages of the daughter and tried to force on the all-business persona. "He pushed us to this point," she said quietly, but with conviction.

I wasn't going to argue, so I moved on to our next concern, the absence of the third member of our cadre. "Where is she?"

"Oh, she's coming. You know her and dramatic entrances," Harper deadpanned.

Junior walked out of Merrick's office—annoyance covering his face, but he refused to make eye contact with us.

"Harper. CJ. Please, come in," Merrick boomed from inside.

"Here we go," Harper said, head held high, back straight.

After pleasantries were exchanged and we were seated, Harper dropped the bomb.

"CJ won't be signing with you for next season."

Merrick tilted his head like an antenna trying to get better reception. "Excuse me?"

Harper shifted. Trying desperately not to look like the little girl disappointing her father. "CJ and I are both taking positions with another team. Actually, CJ is taking a new position, I'm just resigning. I mean, I'm resigning and hiring CJ—"

Merrick held up his hand. "Whoa. Wait. I just struck a deal to have Brian signed with another team so both CJ and Grady could be with Merrick next season. I have a car for each of them—I worked this out, so everyone was happy. I don't understand..."

Harper and I stared at each other. We hadn't seen that coming.

I stood and stepped behind Harper's chair. "Mr. Merrick, you really should've discussed this with us beforehand."

"I didn't think I had to. I was going to surprise you both."

"It was a little presumptuous to think—" Harper's voice started to rise, and she slowly stood.

"Presumptuous!" Merrick straightened to his full height. "What the hell is going on?" He focused on me. "CJ, what the hell are you doing? Are you leaving the circuit?"

I opened my mouth to speak, but Harper held up a hand to me to stay quiet.

She put the other hand to her forehead and began to pace. "So, let me get this straight. You sent them through this hell all season just to move your chess pieces around so now, at the last minute, you can sign them both?" She stared up at her father. "You couldn't do this at any other time?"

His tone turned into Papa Bear. "Harper, don't you talk to me that way."

Harper ignored the condescension and continued to pace as she shook her head.

I leaned my body against a chair—this just took a bad turn, and all I could do was bear witness. This wasn't between two business associates anymore; with that tone and that condescending comment, it was also between father and daughter.

"What the hell is going on?" Merrick turned on me again. "CJ, I gave you and Grady what you wanted. I have cars for both of you."

"It's too—" I started.

"It's too late." Harper was sharp as she finished. "It's too late, Dad. CJ is going to drive for me."

"*You?*" His eyes bugged out of his head, and his body stiffened as if electrocuted. "Don't be ridiculous."

Harper turned, crossed her arms, and cocked a hip. "Yes, me. I am the co-owner of a new team Butler sold to me and my investors, and CJ was just signed as a principal Cup driver for next season."

"*What the hell?*" Merrick roared. "Where did you get the money to buy a team? Who would partner with a girl your age?"

The door opened, and with a dramatic flourish only she could accomplish, Aunt Sadie flew in. "She's partnering with me, Everett, and you'd be smart to realize who you were referring to as 'girl'."

Sadie walked right up to her brother and got in his space. He took a slight step back, surprised by her appearance. She smirked. "It's always been your Achille's heel, brother. You love women, you cater to them, but you underestimate and underappreciate them. Your daughter played the game and eventually out-maneuvered you boys. She deserves more respect than to be referred to as 'girl'. I, too, was someone you loved and took care of, but again you under-appreciated my value all these years, tapping me on the head, throwing me a charity cause or marrying me off. But, brother, I, too, was a better driver, and a better businessperson than you. Difference was, I couldn't do anything about it back then." Sadie walked over and joined Harper and me. "I can now."

"Everett, I know you are a good man, and we love you, but you never listened, and we are done trying to get through to you." Sadie turned around, and once she got between Harper and me, a trinity had been formed. "Now, Harper and I are going to walk out of here with another woman you underappreciated. What it comes down to is that Harper and I bought ourselves a team and—with CJ—we are going to go race cars."

Merrick was poleaxed. He grabbed the nearest chair and sat; his hand situated over his mouth that didn't seem to know how to move.

Sadie studied him intensely before walking over, combing her hand affectionately through his white hair, and patting him on the shoulder. "It will be okay."

As if that was over, she turned to us, clapped her hands together and said, "Who's up for drinks?"

We convinced Sadie to make reservations for a dinner celebration. I still had other things to see to this afternoon.

I texted Grady that I was on my way home, and he didn't indicate anything was amiss—hopefully, that was a good sign.

The boat was still tied to the dock. I didn't see any blood, and there wasn't any yelling coming from the back of the house.

Grady already knew about our plans to start the new team. In fact, he was excited about it. He wanted to join, too, but we told him now it would be just me as the principal.

There was some moping.

"We need to be in our own lanes," I told him. "Competitors on the track was like working in the same industry, but teammates was like being in the same office."

"But I'm still stuck with Junior," he whined.

I walked around the entrance to the patio and he was there— hair a beautiful, sun-kissed, rumpled mess, and his face unreadable, but not unwelcoming. "Hey, how did it go?"

"About as well as you'd think. Harper and Merrick did most of the talking. I just stood there as witness, and Sadie swooped in with the dramatic ending. We can give you the play-by- play tonight at dinner."

I searched around Grady, subtly trying to look for Cal.

"He went in to get some beer." Grady stood tall and peered down his nose at me.

"How were things here?" I walked toward the patio furniture and sat on a cushioned chair. "Did you go out on the boat?"

"Yes." My beautiful god-man pulled up an ottoman and sat so close I had to spread my legs open to accommodate him. "My brother is a rather intelligent strategist—"

"Why, that is probably the nicest thing you could say about me." Cal came out carrying three beers.

"You didn't let me finish. Intelligent strategist asshole…who took me out in the middle of the lake and asked me for a chance to drive. When I had a moment of weakness and let him take the wheel, he took the boat key, shoved it down his pants, and then proceeded to tell me the reason he stranded us in the middle of Lake Norman."

He leaned back and pointed at his brother. "Don't think that will work next time, because I will go after that damn key. I was just curious enough to know what the hell you were up to this time."

I put my hand on Grady's knee. "Grady, focus."

He turned back, hands going to his knees. "I'm mad at you for not telling me Cal was involved in this venture."

"It wasn't my idea—" I started to explain, reaching out for him.

Cal stepped in, and this is usually where things went bad. "I told you, she had nothing to do with it. It was settled by the time she was told about it. The deal was struck between Harper, Sadie, Butler, and me from the beginning. Harper doesn't want anyone to know I'm involved."

"But why are you anywhere near this?"

"Because I was there. They were discussing it. I had money to invest and I thought it

would be a good idea."

"So, it had nothing to do with me?" Grady gave him a skeptical eye.

"Of course, it had to do with you, asshat." Cal flipped his hand up at Grady. "You're in love with this woman." Cal all but yelled at us. "You are happier than I think I've ever seen you. You're more settled and more focused than I've ever seen you." He spoke to us like we needed this broken down. "You two practically brought racing to its knees this year. I analyzed ways to make this work, and when Harper approached me with this idea, it was a good solution. You have a team; CJ has a team. Why am I the bad guy again?" He threw his arms out, as if asking the heavens for an explanation.

Grady shook his head and dropped it into his hands.

Cal stepped closer; his patience was gone. "What? Don't give me that bullshit about me interfering with your life again. I'm your big brother, damnit. I can't get you to come home, so I may as well see that you are at least happy and don't lose your girl."

Grady's back rose and fell with his deep, weary breath. "I'm not shaking my head because of that." He ran both hands through his hair and clapped the back of his neck. I was at a loss at what to do, so I put my hand on his back to comfort him.

"Then what is it this time?"

Grady stared daggers up at his brother and threw his arm out at him to make a point. "Because, asshole, you just told my girlfriend I loved her before I had a chance! Way to blow it for me."

Cal's shoulders dropped, along with his face and all of his posturing. He looked at me and then at Grady and then back at me. For the first time since I met him, Cal was contrite. It didn't seem to be an emotion that sat well with him. "Um, oh. Well..." He walked over and took a pull off his beer in silence.

"Yeah." Annoyance—but not anger—dripped from Grady's tone. "Now can you go in the fucking house so I can salvage this?"

Cal became sheepish, more amused at his brother's situation. "Well, consider this a small push..." he gave me a smirk and walked inside. He raised his beer and his eyebrows to us and said over his shoulder, "Happy birthday, little brother." I had to hold onto Grady as Cal picked up his pace into the house.

Grady pointed his beer bottle at me. "Just because Cal declared my love for you doesn't mean I'm not annoyed about you keeping this from me."

"I didn't want to get in between it." I threw my hands up and said, "I'm just a driver in all this—"

A loud, rumbling came from the front of the house, and it reverberated through my stomach. "Oh, good!" I jumped up, stepped out of the cage he had me in, and started to make a dash for the driveway.

"Now what?" Grady began to follow me. "CJ, wait. You can't get away from me that easily." I couldn't, his legs were like twice as long as mine, but still, I always tried.

"Come on, birthday boy," I mocked him and took full advantage of my head start, clearing the side of the house just as Davy climbed off a beautiful motorcycle, and I jumped up to hug him as soon as he removed his helmet.

"Thank God you're here. Just in time!" I whispered into his ear, but my smile was so large, it was almost hard to speak.

"It's all good, baby girl," Davy said. "But let me put you down before your man ruins my professional football career." He set me aside, "Hey, Grady. Happy birthday, man."

Grady sauntered up, both hands in his pockets, but he slowly held out his hand to shake Davy's. "Thanks. One hell of a bike you got there."

Grady walked around, staring at the red Ducati 1199 Panigale. It was sleek, powerful, and, parked next to my baby, actually seemed a bit flashier.

Davy's smirk spread across his face. "She's not bad. Had a blast driving her over here."

Cal walked out of the house. "Hey, Davy, how's it going?"

"Not bad, you?" He held out his hand to Cal, and they shook like old friends, even if they met only a few weeks ago.

"You ready to go?" Cal walked toward his car, and Davy nodded, leaning over and kissing me on the cheek. "We will see you this evening. Sadie left me some message about cocktails and Long Island Iced Teas?"

"Oh, good Lord, I hope she hasn't already started," I cringed, and Davy gave me a shrug as he opened Cal's car door.

"Wait, wait." Grady said, "What about your bike?"

Davy threw me the keys and winked, then climbed in. "See you later," I called out as we watched them pull out and leave.

"I feel like I'm two steps behind everyone today..." Grady followed me over to the bikes.

I walked backwards, smiling at him.

He sauntered toward me, reconsidering. "Actually, let me rephrase that. I've felt that way since you stumbled into my arms." He caught me, gathering me in his arms. "I've been playing catch-up ever since."

"Oh, you know you caught me." I leaned in, kissed him hard and thoroughly, grabbed his hand, without breaking eye contact, and placed the keys in it. I whispered, "I love you, too, you know." I kissed his nose, "Happy birthday."

I broke his hold, grabbed the jackets I left on my bike, and threw his at him before smacking his ass. "Now, grab your gear, and try that baby out."

He held me from behind, his strong arms roped around me, holding me close, his face buried in my hair.

It reminded me of when we met, how he caught me from falling to my knees.

Little did I know how much he would lift me up.

He whispered in my ear, and it still sent shivers down my body. "Thank you."

I pulled back and lightly tapped his face, "Now, let's just see if you can keep up."

### *The End*

# AFTERWORD

While I tried to stay as close to the sport as possible, and give readers a true experience, I intentionally didn't delve too deeply into technical aspects of stock car to keep the story from becoming dated if the industry adjusted their format or made other changes. I also adjusted the order of races at times for creative reasons.

The inspiration for CJ Lomax is a combination of women, not one particular person. Throughout my research and her development, I was influenced by several women in and out of racing based off their passion, gumption, and how they tackle life.

From CJ, I hope to carry forth her mantra—*focus, grit, unapologetic determination*. I think, as women, no matter what role, career, or path we choose, should be reminded to use those words in our vocabulary.

I hope you enjoyed getting to know CJ. Stay tuned and see what is next for her and her crew.

The ride isn't over...

*Laralyn*

# ACKNOWLEDGMENTS

They say it takes a village to raise a child. Well, it took one to raise me as an author and for this book to become reality. It goes without saying that my husband, children, parents and in-laws were the pillars of support. But extended family, friends and neighbors also shuffled kids and lent a hand in so many ways to help me see this dream through.

Thank you to my high school crew for their unending encouragement and the ladies who joined me on a tour of Charlotte Motor Speedway during our girls' weekend. My for AZD sisters for believing in me and cheering me on.

I would never have had the courage to even put a foot on this path without my fellow romance authors who are the epitome of women lifting up other women. I've never experienced that kind of acceptance before. Meredith Bond introduced me to Washington Romance Writers. Christine Gunderson was the first to tell me a romance about a female NASCAR driver wasn't crazy.

My Damned Mob critique group—J.L. Lora, Cate Tayler and Shadow Leitner and Audrey Columbos, you offered me more than I could ever list on paper—valuable opinions, laughs, friendship, several swift kicks to the backside, and occasional sarcastic wit—to name a few.

J.L. Lora, I cannot express how much you held me together through all of this. Thank you for your encouragement, technical expertise, calming vibes and even your "side-eyes".

Brenda Chin, Holly Ingraham and Elaine York who all helped hone my skill, corrected my errors, and kept CJ on track.

Jessie Harper who held hands with me the past year as we both waded through the waters of sending our first-born children off to college and self-publishing our debuts within the same month. I don't know how we are still sane.

Shelly Alexander, mentor extraordinaire, but also my cheerleader. Thank you LERA for awarding me The Writer Award for 2019, but most of all for introducing me to Shelly.

Deranged Doctors Design—thank you for this beautiful cover and capturing the series!

Thank you, Kim Costa, with Caffeinated PR, for helping me to launch this baby.

I told you it took a village—well, maybe more like a well-populated suburban town.

But, I did it.

# ABOUT THE AUTHOR

Laralyn is a proud special needs mom, and an autism and dyslexia awareness advocate. She lives in Maryland with her husband, three children and three dogs. She is a member of Romance Writers of America, Central Pennsylvania Romance Writers, Washington Romance Writers, and other affiliate chapters.

She loves to write about witty, strong women then throw sexy, charming men in their path and see the chaos it causes. It's a great distraction from everyday life and is usually done with lazy dogs at her feet, a chai latte or Diet Coke in hand, and the promise of a glass of pinot at the end the day if the writing is worthy. She is often distracted by chatting on social media—so come join her!

Sign-up for her newsletter and learn what she's up to next by hearing about new releases, freebies, events, and more at www.laralyndoran.com